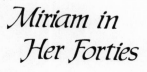

*Miriam in
Her Forties*

Books by Alan Lelchuk

American Mischief
Miriam at Thirty-four
Shrinking
Miriam in Her Forties

Miriam in Her Forties

Alan Lelchuk

Houghton Mifflin Company/Boston 1985

A Richard Todd Book

Copyright © 1985 by Alan Lelchuk

All rights reserved. No part of this work may be reproduced
or transmitted in any form or by any means, electronic or
mechanical, including photocopying and recording, or by
any information storage or retrieval system, except as
may be expressly permitted by the 1976 Copyright Act or
in writing from the publisher. Requests for permission should
be addressed in writing to Houghton Mifflin Company,
2 Park Street, Boston, Massachusetts 02108.

Library of Congress Cataloging in Publication Data

Lelchuk, Alan.
  Miriam in her forties.

  I. Title.
PS3562.E464M5 1985   813'.54   85-10774
ISBN 0-395-36979-7

Printed in the United States of America

P 10 9 8 7 6 5 4 3 2 1

To friends:
  Flora Natapoff
  Sonya and David Sofield

I wish to acknowledge the generous help given me during the writing of this book by the John Simon Guggenheim Memorial Foundation. I would also like to thank the Jerusalem Foundation for my fruitful stay at Mishkenot Sha'Ananim in Jerusalem.

Part One

1

ON the flight home she sat across the aisle from an Israeli couple and their four-year-old son, coming to the States for a year. She enjoyed the boy, delighting that he wasn't hers to worry over. She was transported back to her time of carrying Jon, his early kicks and baby-soft knee jerks, amniotic waves in her womb. Oh, a delicious time, that time: Jon in her belly-sac growing and signaling, while Stan paid hardly any attention. Mothering began then, in sensual turnings. Now, after the plane leveled off, the gentleman next to her asked if she minded his smoking, and she shook her head. Across the sky the sun had risen above the thin blue line of cloud formations, giving an illusion of horizon, and memory began to chase her round and round.

When the airline attendant had explained the procedure for getting oxygen in case of need, demonstrating with a yellow mask, she had recalled her father's gas mask from World War II: funny-looking, rubbery, its elephant trunk hanging down. Now she reclined in her seat, plugged in her earphones and got lucky with *Water Music,* and let memory flood her.

She was Dad's favorite. Her father, away weekdays in Canton or Mansfield selling appliances some years, aluminum siding other years, was home weekends. "But Papa," she asked at age seven, "why not just stay in your study and draw maps? You don't *have* to go traveling around, do you?" The gaunt man with the bushy mustache and meditative deep-set eyes — more Castilian than Siberian — always lit up when he was alone with her. "Cheery," he replied, pinching her cheek affectionately, "I have to earn a living so you kids can mess up. Drawing maps and showing you places is between us, for *fun*." She chided him with her forefinger, saying, "Like baseball, ya mean. Are we going tomorrow?" Feigning surprise, he searched his pockets — "Hmm . . . I wonder if I forgot those tickets" — whereupon she reached inside his jacket and flushed out the magical tickets.

Baseball was their private retreat, like camp-outs, when brother Aaron was off in his own dazed world, far away. Her favorites were the boy-wonder shortstop Boudreau and the shrewd catcher Jim Hegan and his battery mates, Lemon and Wynn, and of course the rookie Gene Bearden, who beat the Red Sox 8–3 in the 1948 playoff game, which Dad sneaked away from work on Monday to watch with her on the old Dumont twelve-inch set. Though he had never gotten used to forsaking his beloved Dodgers when he had moved away, Dad took consolation in the Indians pitching staff. He got seats behind home plate, when possible, so he could point out Wynn's slider, Lemon's rising fast ball, Garcia's "heavy" fast ball. (And what about the year of Herb Score, when his fast ball zigzagged this way and that, blinding everyone with its unpredictable moves?) Even now, crossing the blue-green Mediterranean, she could smell hot-dog-and-mustard from Municipal Stadium, taste the vanilla ice cream sandwich (the chocolate wafer soggy), feel the stiff crunch of Crackerjacks. By the time she was twelve she could distinguish rather regularly between a pop fly hit off the handle and a line drive smacked from the meaty part of the bat. Yes, it had helped that Aaron was more interested in motors and engines and staying by himself, which allowed her to become Dad's baseball buddy. ("You're turning that girl into a boy for sure!" Sylvia would always remark as they left for a Saturday game, and Miriam would replay that remark as she pounded her fielder's mitt, sitting in her seat, thinking that that was great with her.) "If Mitchell only had Furillo's arm," Dad would compare, and "What this club needs is a Robinson to get 'em moving!" To that emerald-green diamond and Louisville Slugger *crack!* she swore her earliest and strongest allegiance — beyond country, beyond religion.

A Brandenburg concerto came on, and she shifted positions. Bach, Handel, Billie Holiday, even country music made good company for her nowadays. Glad she had worn this beige cotton suit and chiffon scarf for the travel; it made her feel grown-up. She recalled a favorite grim photograph, a close-up of herself at age ten — ponytail, small dark face with the desperate look, brown eyes staring straight ahead, small nose, no smile. Stepmom forcing her to sit there while the horrible red-haired man dove beneath his black cape and tried to cajole her to "Look at the birdie," as if she were a little moron, and her growing afraid as Sylvia got angry when she continued to sit stonily. (Rafi loved that picture, mistaking her fear for determination. Was he right?) Sylvia had forced the family to that seedy downtown studio, MacNulty's Foto Parlor, with the artificial stage and the brocade backdrop of angels and trumpets and the vases of fake bouquets and the silly stool you had to sit on, which reminded her of forced piano lessons. Dad awkward and out of place, and Sylvia joining Mr. MacNulty in mocking him, and going on to flirt outrageously with that bow-tied buffoon. Finally they got Aaron to sit — it was the one photograph she had kept of him, from before he vanished from photographs and vanished from the name of Scheinman, taking up "Thomas Aarons" later on: his wavy hair in a high pompadour, the checkered sports jacket with the absurd shoulder padding; he was handsome at thirteen and already looking lost, remote, annihilated too. (Was he still outside Spokane or Portland somewhere, repairing diesel engines and living in a trailer with Cathy O'Donnell, his Catholic doll-wife, and three kids? At Sylvia's death, a decade or so ago, they had had to see each other briefly, and he had barely been able to look over at Miriam, his flesh and blood.) Sylvia was of course the busy beaver, hair done in a fresh bouffant colored robin orange; she was still donning her mink stole in late March (a fur costing how many vacations and fights?), teasing Mr. MacNulty to "kidnap" her "into his cave" and giggling inside like a forty-seven-year-old ingenue; busily arranging everyone in that room just as she tried to arrange everyone in her life. Oh, maybe she hadn't been too bad, she had just married the wrong man; instead of a failed salesman and furtive cartographer, whom she needled and nagged into perpetual gloom, she should have had a hot-shot furniture-store mogul who could have surprised her periodically with a new knickknack for the bathroom or hutch. Oh, poor brother, poor poor Daddy — yes, poor Sylvia too. Family riches.

A break in the music; the little boy woke and cried briefly, across from her. The sun had climbed higher and was now spraying a golden tint on the shimmering silver wing of the airplane. The fellow next to her was reading, bless him.

In her workroom in Cambridge, and Jon, her little Yani, walking uncertainly, carrying his plastic hammer, toppling now and then while she labored over contact sheets. The way he understood her tone of voice, could tell admonition from praise, smiled or frowned accordingly. Sturdy body, face alive with curiosity, hair blond (to change later), mouth and eyes alert to coffee percolating, dog barking. He loved to play there with her in the room, fumbling with building blocks, investigating forbidden corners of the closet and emerging with a galosh over his head or submerged in a fallen dress, sure of his mischief. Understanding his name, her "No," just as, a year later, he learned the power of his "No." The baby-fragrant skin and silky hair and soft muscles were one thing, but the growing coordination of feet and hands, the forming of words and whole sentences, then the elevation into teasing and irony — these were spirals of evolution not to be missed. (Of course, poor Stanley had missed them. Did all fathers? Poor men, then.) And unlike Rosie, who turned out to be a more distant baby and child, Jon loved to touch and cuddle, not to mention suck. He took as much milk as she had, and she had a terrible time weaning him; the little bastard knew the difference between nipple and nipple only too well. In the workroom he'd simply crawl to her when tired, climb up her leg and be hoisted onto her lap in a lift of joy, and in one minute flat be fast asleep, thumb in mouth, and even, she thought, fingers over eyelids. (Or was that reading back into the years, from his later habit?) Hours alone of inviolate purity, hours of pure intimacy, hours and days unsullied by the world of adults, akin in beauty to these blue and pink bands on the morning horizon.

A shift from Bach jolted her mental reel, and an older Jon turned on her now with those reproachful eyes, once she had started seeing men again after her year off, "away" (his term for her year of breakdown and bereavement). Even with Rafi, whom he truly liked; he bristled, changing mood involuntarily, when spotting Rafi's pajamas, Dop-kit, hairbrush. Still. One of the truest pleasures of being away summers — admit it — was the release from subjugation to son. A fact. Hard for her to escape the guilt, no matter how often Dr. Levanda had warned about it. So, hooray for verdigris sea and peach orchard and kibbutz routine, despite the occasional summer guilt-dream.

"Was this your first visit?" the passenger next to her asked.

The words broke her reverie, and she gradually switched gears to the here-and-now ordinary. "No, I've been there before," she responded at last.

"Are you Jewish?" The man was fiftyish, with a pale prominent face and a fine head of silvery hair.

"Yes," she said, slightly complimented. "What did you think?"

"Oh, maybe Italian, or even Greek."

Unwittingly she felt her short curly hair, stroked her nose. "All the same tribe, I suppose."

He laughed and nodded and explained an abstruse theory about the lost tribe, but she had already settled back into memory-down . . . Jon in her bedroom at night, with Rosie asleep, to rehearse his part in the upcoming school play. Wearing a black cape and lavender turban, plus makeup, he swirls into the room, a daring Peter Pan. Leaping with entrechats in this special performance for her, he jumps from bureau to bed, crying out his lines in half-serious, half-mocking derring-do! Oh, sweetest, sweetest Yani. At thirteen already an insomniac of sorts; he wanted those hours alone with her again, no Rosie or Rafi or society, just like the old baby days, and she'd allowed it, wanted it, charmed and seduced by his Peter Pan or Spiderman or Freddy Lynn on the run — her thick-haired actor, magician, son, boy. In play of course he would seduce her back into full adoration. And when he wasn't performing, he'd have a heart-to-heart, just the two of them, discussing and dissecting all possible subjects — boy and girl friends, school and teachers, Rafi, Stan, Harry, acting, writing, basketball, sister, cancer, body building, and lately Judaism. With his long hair done up like a pirate, his face rouged and painted, his voice in the stage of breaking and changing, he'd let out his special cries and puns, playing with Pan wherever possible. (Did he want to be an actor? "Nah, I'd rather be . . . an ironist!" His face lit up, after he thought he'd understood the meaning of the word, at thirteen.) Meanwhile, most-loyal-fan Mom lay in her bed, a propped spectator, witnessing this ridiculous, irresistible creation of her blood and genes. Genes from Stan in his height and mop of hair and ease with science and math. And from Miriam? Extra energy, volatile moods, delight in his own company, excessive sensitivity/vulnerability, a feel for literature. An interesting combination maybe, she'd daydream — except for the culture; America the Beautiful would seduce those frail innocent genes. Then what? She'd concentrate instead on the boyish face turning into manliness, the body slim but now filling out in the chest, the ectomorphic shape. "Cheesus, Mom, you're supposed to give me my *cue*, will ya!"

The airplane lurched upward suddenly and she grabbed instinctively for Rafi, and got the stranger's arm and held on for dear life.

At last: "Sorry."

"It's all right," he returned easily.

"God moving his furniture," she repeated from childhood.

He laughed. "I haven't heard that in a while."

The sudden ease of native understanding. The jet righted itself, and the sky dipped back to normal.

The man introduced himself as Wallace Scott Beaumont — "Friends call me Scotty" — and described his two weeks in Israel on a medical tour. He was a cardiovascular surgeon at Boston's Mass. General, he modestly asserted, and was surprised to discover that Miriam hailed from Cambridge. Israeli medicine was truly impressive, he assessed, and he went on to talk about the hospitals he had visited: Tel Hashomer, Shaare Tzedek, the two Hadassahs ("Scopus is the better place to get ill at"). She listened to the fine pitch of his voice and observed the broad, good face and smoothly shaved skin. Something else perhaps. The touch of formality. Yes, even here, in this TWA chat, he was carefully polite, somewhat formal. She found herself appreciating this slight distance, this personal boundary, after the ubiquitous informality of the Israelis.

Somewhere between the British and Israeli extremes, the American way was poised, casually formal, refreshing.

"Look at me going on this way. And you — have you been visiting friends or family? On a group tour, or . . . ?" The cordiality in the blue eyes; the dry tenor voice.

"I come rather regularly," she explained, and said something about her peculiar situation, how she lived part-time with her kibbutznik professor, while noting how downright handsome this man was. In an especially Gentile way, she realized, having been inundated by Jews these past few months. Oh, she had missed her Christians, her Americans! How simple, silly, basic.

Restraining herself, she inquired like a mature adult about his surgery, after warding off his modesty ("You'll be pretty bored, I think"), she listened to the odd terms, *blood flow* and *prolene, intermittent sutures* and *respirator, porcine valve, terdek, coronary* . . . How many worlds were out there that she had no idea of?

"You don't have a Boston accent," she interceded. "Where are you from?"

"I'd better not." He smiled, showing a row of fine teeth. "From the West. Montana. A country boy, actually," he threw off at the end, for amusement.

"From where in Montana?"

"Where?" He looked at her. "Outside Missoula, a tiny place — you probably never heard of Missoula."

Scolding now: *"Where?"*

He gave in. "Flathead Lake. All right?" He removed his horn-rim reading glasses, and she saw the slate blue of the eyes. A fleck of white in the black iris too. A character mark? she wondered. He rubbed the bridge of his nose, irritated by the nosepiece. Immediately she liked the way he did that: a plain gesture, free of ego.

"I like to hear the name, though I've never been out that way," she acknowledged, and he smiled.

"Why should you have been?"

His white skin reminded her of the pale moon overlooking the Negev at night, and she developed an instant theory, namely that the moon was the Christian sign, pale, remote, cool, in contrast to the intense yellow sun of the Sinai, sign of the Jews. One heated, the other calmed; too much of one burned, while the other, in excess, bored. She needed both, she decided. (But Mir, isn't your Jew, your quiet Israeli, a little of both?)

"This is my second trip," he was saying, "and I'm still marveling at how advanced the Israelis are. In technique and technology they're right up there with us. And at the better hospitals the equipment is sophisticated in areas like nuclear medicine. Would you know of Elscint Company, in Haifa? Impressive."

So are you, she thought, admiring his unpretentiousness, the white shirt open at the neck. "I don't think I've ever seen an American doctor without a tie on," she offered.

He looked down and noticed it himself. Laughed. "I'm afraid I'm one of those creatures who're naturally adaptable. Put me in the Caribbean and . . . Don't worry, at home I'll turn back again, like the pumpkin. Though I must add, the informality is very attractive. I'm a country boy, remember? And the climate; that makes ties rather impractical, too."

Was he a shy closet rebel? She smiled privately, her theory punctured already. She liked the old-fashioned white shirt, free of pens or pencils in the breast pocket like some accountant. And when he excused himself to go to the bathroom a few minutes later, she found her eyes measuring him. Lanky. A six-footer. A body of loose angles, slender waist; legs slightly bowed. A cowpoke perhaps, rather than this serious doctor. The broad shoulders and squarish good looks contrasted nicely with the delicate gestures and trained courtesy. A frontiersman with manners? Involuntarily she found herself imagining that long body up close, the narrow hips, the long bony fingers. Imagined for an unlicensed moment that easy length upon her . . . Immersed in the sweet fantasy, she almost reached out for him when he returned and sat back down! Blushing, embarrassed, she looked away and studied the simple blue sky with the lines of pink above and the white clouds floating below. Told herself, in self-defense, that she was merely studying him for her series of male nudes. Well, why not? . . . Her imagination excited and confused her. Fidelity permitted fantasy, didn't it? She was moving away from illicit desire, toward warm guilt. Would she ever be tamed fully? Who and where were the cool women of the world, whose proper upbringing and perhaps passive faculties created a natural damper for unwanted desire? *Are you talking about one Miriam Scheinman of a decade ago?*

In payment, as it were, she let the stranger — or "Scotty," as she tried out — return to his *New England Journal of Medicine,* and she shifted her thoughts back to Rafi. *Click,* switch men and feeling like lenses . . . She tried, concentrated. Lit a cigarette, the first of the trip, and inhaled deeply. It pleased her to think of him — her trim, stable friend, with his secret tenacity, Israeli habits, Nabatean dreams. Things came easily between them. Responsibility and obligation were words that arose only after nouns signaling good times. Did you have to become a Gulliver in love, tied and bound by the loved one and the pieties of the culture? She hoped that wasn't what she had learned from her own education. After signing on for conjugal pleasure and watching it turn slowly into obligation, obligation into subtle coerciveness and that into repressed pain and fury, you forgot all about the original motive — *if* the motive was pleasure in the first place. No, caring had to include its high proportion of attraction and play and measured freedom, as much as anything grave and serious. Oh, it was difficult indeed breaking through the locked gates of Christian Duty and Jewish Responsibility and American Puritanism, but once you were through and out there roaming free in the wide open spaces, the new unbounded territory, you'd never go back. Never again.

"Your ash," Dr. Beaumont advised.

"Oh." She noticed, smiling at him. Was this why she was having such sweet, sly thoughts about freedom now? Were they a carryover from the earlier fantasy, transferred now to the right man? Would the brain ever stop working overtime? Brain, or awakened urges?

She lowered her ash, her libido. "Thanks. But why'd you choose the smoking section?"

"Do you think doctors are all virtue? Or common sense? Well, not this one, on occasion." He took a small flat wooden box from his briefcase and opened it, revealing a handful of slender cigars, and cautioned some secrecy. "Cuban, when I can get them."

"Where'd you . . . ?"

"Havana. Before Israel."

"You get around."

He half smiled, not with pleasure. "The rewards of age. Once-a-year sojourns."

Age and what else — prestige, excellence? "Are you famous?"

This time he laughed easily. "Hardly. I'm not De Bakey or Barnard, if that's what you're getting at. I'm known in my profession somewhat, but nothing more. Do you know the Lown group in Brookline? No, why should you. Here, try one?"

"Sure. Thank you."

He held out a light for her — a gesture from another era, another place.

With Dr. Beaumont nodding, she puffed and puffed. "No need to inhale, right?"

"No need," he repeated. "But get the taste, that's the point."

Slowly she sucked on the cigar, cajoling the tobacco and exhaling.

"What's that you're reading, if I may ask?"

She held up her Colette novel.

He shook his head, ignorant. "Is that what you do — literary studies?"

She coughed a little and smiled. "No, nothing literary. I'm a photographer. But I like reading. Sometimes even good books."

"I wish I had more time for it. But that's the worst thing about being a doctor — no time for anything but medicine. 'A good doctor is a narrow man,' my old Stanford professor once told us, but I never believed he was being honest. Now I do. I keep threatening myself and my family that I'll take a year off soon to do other things. But soon never seems to be now."

"It *is* lovely." She held up the cigar. "Next time you're in Havana, pick me up some."

He handed her the shallow wooden box and told her to keep them.

She wouldn't have it, though. "I've waited this long, I can wait another year or so. Tell me about the family, why don't you?"

He tried the cigar box once more, then relented and narrated. He had a wife and two children, both away at school. Daughter in med school, Cornell; son, Greg, a senior at Williams — "interested in the arts, thank God." A home in Concord. Thoughts of moving to a condo on Beacon Hill in the near future, at his wife's wish. Then he modified that. "Well, maybe it is time to taste a city again."

"Why?"

"To keep from getting old, maybe." He shrugged, putting away his Havanas. "Suburbs are fine for raising children, but if you can't live in the real countryside, then I prefer the city. *If* I can take it. We'll see. Though Boston isn't half bad, I imagine."

She asked why not the country, and he explained that his wife found the prospect too remote and isolating. "She's right too, for her, I'm sure. Probably for both of us," he allowed.

A gentleman, this fellow. Without jargon, too. Civilized, thoughtful, decent; too much so? At a cost somewhere?

"How old are you?"

He looked at her with narrow blue eyes. "Fifty-five."

He didn't ask back, of course, but she thought to even it out. "Forty-two."

"Hello, forty-two." He put out his hand.

She took it. "Hello, fifty-five."

And returned to her reading. Back to Colette and her unique heroine, Léa, so easy with hedonism and wise with aging. (As read by this more common heroine, uncertain with pleasure and confused about aging.) Would Boeing become the Widener Library of the space age, the one safe place from the distraction of telephone, children, friends, loved one? Holding her paperback and calmed by jet-hum, she realized that this was the stylish way to continue the Great Reading Tradition . . . Or, she wondered, was all this rhetoric a fanciful way of avoiding the appeal of this fellow?

Actually, she had come to look forward to these long traverses of ozone and time zones, from day to night and country to country, useful interludes between feelings and cultures. Like Montana here, a charming interlude. (But useful too?) Back now to the world of gray skies, of responsibility and loot, of needles and darts from the outside world (bitchy locals, competitive photographers). In a curious way she was a marked woman in the tight Cambridge world. First for her bold failures, later for modest successes. Especially for winding up on her feet after a long fall. The ideal was the timid life, filled with conformity and complacency, brimming with administrative banality and boasting of dinner parties. If you didn't fit a familiar category — the contented wife, the fashionable ideologue, the malleable malcontent, to cite three "friends" — you didn't fit. Ugh.

She was still tucked into her safety belt; she unhooked it now. "Feeling safer?"

Good question. "Yes, I always feel safer with a man if I'm on a plane, for some reason."

"Especially a married man," he joked. "Safer than parachutes."

She smiled, stared at her Colette. A married man. Who wasn't, that she knew? Well, Harry, of course. Once upon a time she had had her own, of course; but as a lover? Well, Colin. But with his wife ill that way, the situation had not been quite normal. No, she had veered away from that course; too traitorous, she had felt. Schoolgirl rule or moral principle? Take your pick. For a brief moment her own married man, Husband, returned like a specter, reminding her, curiously, of her hospital ward several years later. Pain by association. A century ago, those twin hells. Flying seemed to make dark memory safer.

She reached forward and lifted out a magazine, to lose herself in perfume and liquor advertisements. She was inundated instead by ads for vibrators, the gadgets coated with ladies-magazine euphemisms. Why not advertise dildos and make it plain?

An article caught her attention — "How Rape Made Me Stronger" — and she read it through, comparing it with her own case. Looking for insight or resonant detail, Miriam got neither. The writer, assaulted in her suburban Baltimore home, claimed that the rape had led to divorce, antimale feelings, and a triumphant turn toward the lesbian life. There was little description of the assaulter or act (except for vague generalization), or of whether the gay turning had older, deeper roots. Miriam put down the *Redbook* and remembered her own long night of eight years ago, her attack on the Cambridge Common. Recalled her inclination, if not downright intention, for self-destruction that night. Later, in her sessions of healing with Dr. L, she had come to understand the context and motive clearly, even had had to be cleared of excessive guilt by the doctor. "Why not? The *good* citizens had just destroyed your photographs over in the city hall museum, so you would use the *bad* citizens to do damage to your body, yes?" Frank words, short-cut logic. And the truth hurt: that she had gone to the park wanting to do herself damage, even though when it came, she naturally fought it. But the whole act, with its subtle stages and shadowy moments, was filled with such ambiguities! Such specifics! Even here, in the high, rarefied air, she could recapture in startling clarity the smell of lilac mingling with the black fellow's after-shave lotion, the panicky fear in the white boy's eyes and her sense that he might get violent if she didn't help get him erect, the wild confusing battle within — her own body mocking her as much as the high-yellow dude (who had demonstrated more pleasure than meanness, so that she had actually half wished to repeat the act in ordinary life).

The plane jerked for a moment, and then steadied itself.

The consequences had cut deeper, longer — yes. Immediate humiliation in Brigham's, the police escorting her out, her skirtless thighs shocking her while she sat in the police cruiser, the sirens wailing . . . a night in Cambridge City, then the Boston hospital, until finally the rescue by Dr. Levanda, who took her home with her and ministered, mothered, and shrank her through that long, lonely year. Having to learn to *want* again (talking, caring), to allow slow forgiveness of the self, to have the children visit, with Yani becoming guardian and cheerleader at age seven. She treasured her hideout that year: the flowered wallpaper, the small aquarium, the gabled ceiling. As an Ann Arbor undergrad she had yearned for a Paris atelier, and at thirty-four she had wound up in a Belmont attic. But survival was survival. And the self-destructiveness, she saw, was the other side of her troublemaking, dating back to her efforts to gain revenge against Sylvia and the other respectables for their attempts to keep her away from Dad and to squash her assertive will. Oh, that fear of darkness had cast its shadow, and she could still feel it cross her every so often. And yet, having come through it, she felt herself surer, more solid. So much so, in fact, that she had developed a kind of intimacy with that black stranger — a fantasy intimacy to be sure, but a relationship nevertheless; who was he, why did he do it, what did he think? For he had been not brutal with her, not sadistic, but determined, interested. She half smiled at her own innocent, perverse investigation, and knew that the man had also become a metaphor of sorts, a terrifying nightmare that would always haunt and pursue her, especially when she felt most secure, most at ease. Yes —

"By the way, have you spent any time at Beth Israel?" the doctor inquired.

She was taken aback by his direction. Where'd he . . . ? "Uh, no, not really." I don't think so, she wanted to say. How did he *know*, this stranger? Did everyone know secretly about the unlocked Number Two East Ward where she had stayed nearly a month? Uncanny. Or was he knowledgeable? "Why do you ask?" — before paranoia set in.

"Sorry, it is an odd question. But I heard it's gone downhill, and wondered about it. I'm due to be on a panel of overseers looking in on it soon." He put his finger to his lips, securing secrecy. "Why me, God knows. But hospitals are getting to be like prisons — institutions unsure of themselves. Which is to the good, probably. They're like people — aging makes us all creak, and maybe croak. But I'm sorry about the question."

His unease was unnecessary, she felt. "Yes, I know what you mean. But you don't look like you're beginning to croak."

"Thanks. But you should see me."

Yes, perhaps. "Hey, this taste is exquisite. Three cheers for Havana." On her second cigar.

"For its tobacco, yes."

Ah, conservative; good. A good adversary for her liberal instincts, liberal friends. The Havanas recalled her father's Dutch Masters cigar boxes, with the circle of Rembrandt-looking fellows staring solemnly at her and the golden cellophane wrappers to make her rings . . . She readjusted her earphones, pleased that Dr. Beaumont was not a chatterer and delighted to hear the *Dumky Trio* playing. Her year of depression had led to music listening rather than human listening, starting with the old Emerson radio in Dr. Levanda's attic room and moving to the small stereo she had finally managed on her own. Native cheer by Fats Waller and Bessie Smith, melody by Mozart and energy by Beethoven, intricacies by Bach and comedies by Beatles. Though she had occasionally smoked some grass and once even snorted a line of cocaine while listening, she mostly tuned in under the influence of her feelings alone. That was intense enough. If there is a Platonic Good up there, she thought, down here it has translated into music. Now Dvořák lifted her with his repetitions and variations, a pleasure at a different level from earlier gratifications. Blue and pink bands arced across the morning sky, and she cupped her eyes momentarily with her hands, a Levanda trick, hearing more distant harmonies.

She put her head back and stretched and rolled her neck, a habit from the orchards, where she had picked peaches and plums six mornings a week. Smiled inwardly at the slender frizzy-haired woman, an agricultural double dressed in khaki shorts, halter and blue shirt, and army fatigue cap; a Cambridge woman disguised as a kibbutznik. In that green rectangle amid gray-white desert she had performed her dull morning duty while reflecting on her recent, middle years. Years of recovery after her frenzy of surplus freedom in her thirties; a long convalescence of ordinariness punctuated by interludes of adventuring. Shadowy Andrei from Budapest via MIT linguistics, who gave her a modest education in East European obsessiveness (how political revolt tunneled into the sexual). The Thorndikes of Belmont, those well-heeled Babbitts of the sixties who had returned to her life to pay her exorbitantly for a weekend of photographing their homespun horseplay, called middle-class orgy. A brief affair with Eric from Oxford, a budding photojournalist of aristocratic blood who looked upon her as a "great creative Jewess" (oh well, British English allowed for many nuances, anti-Semitism included). Okay, she had acknowledged that risk-taking and curiosity were in her blood as well as her profession. But she knew too, nowadays, that there were limits, boundaries. Sanity and lucidity were the aims of these grown-up years, weren't they? Though she herself was still in the making, still surging with questions and doubts, rather than settling for certitudes and posturings.

The glossy magazine in her lap featured a television goddess in her forties and the story of how she had swept through husbands and troubles like a wind through leaves, herself untouched, unsullied. Well, Miriam felt touched, if not sullied.

The airline hostess asked if she wished a drink, and she took a Bloody Mary.

Oaths to remember, she recited. Park Place and Boardwalk were

more American than any ideology or movement. Boudreau of
Cleveland and childhood was as much a part of her as Atget of
Paris. Yani, dearest Yani, needed her discipline as much as love,
despite her debilitating guilt over her year away. And whatever
grand idea or issue came along — women's rights, the aesthetic
life, tribal feeling — it was a frail thing alongside life itself, if you
gave it a chance. If you *lived* and didn't back off because of (or
into?) middle-age fear, sly cowardice, or subtle complacency (masked
as prudence, of course, and shaped with wit). Despite stages of
completion, say, she was still very much a Miriam in the making,
refining her feelings, finding her deepest wantings. Not closing
down now, but opening out, no matter what past wounds or
personal betrayal. A woman realistic enough to live in the crude
here and now, while at the same time trying to make space for
clean reflectiveness and useful memory. And spiritual excitement?
Here and there, in bits and pieces. (Lines from Dickinson and
Donne, scenes from early Fellini and middle Bellow, Vermeers and
Matisses.) A Virgo seeking new bouts with experience, new contingency plans for survival and philosophy. Attachments: to her
two hostages of fortune, her Leica and photographs, her man in
the desert. Oh yes, to herself too. (This must be acknowledged,
after years of taking that item for granted.) Another loyalty would
be nice, but to what, whom? Were irony and skepticism good
enough as ends as well as means?

"I think she looks like you quite a bit, though the hair is straighter.
Don't you think?"

The doctor was showing her Jean Seberg in a magazine, on the
streets of Paris in her youth. Resemblance? Well . . .

"You mean the look of defeat?"

"No." He shook his head. "I mean the *good* looks."

"That's better," she half chided. "She committed suicide, didn't
she?"

"I'm just reading about it. A sad story with the FBI and drug
addiction. Did you ever see her act?"

"She was perfect in *Breathless*."

"Oh? I'm afraid I never saw it. Just the good looks, I meant."

"I know. Thanks. Excuse me a minute." She stood up, stretched,
and walked up the aisle to the bathroom in midplane. Yes Jean,

I did in fact like you, though who could go wrong with Belmondo as her partner?

She peed, washed her face, faced that face in the small mirror. Really Sebergish? Maybe. But her nose was more pert or pug, wasn't it? And did Jean have these furtive lines crisscrossing by the corners of the eyes? Not on your life. At least, not on Hollywood's life. The lips and mouth here were her mother's, expressive and yielding; the eyes were Dad's hazel color, with alertness and mirth and maybe mischief-making revealed up close. Yes, the doctor was right, the look here was not that of defeat (oh, he should have seen me a decade ago!) but rather one of determination, tenacity . . . vulnerability. Well, why not? As for the body below — the body-siege of middle-aging had begun. Still, despite the sags and loosenings, the hips projected fine and firm, the breasts had (fortunately) always been small, and the legs were decent if a little thick in the thighs. (Oh, thighs, would that you had heard my adolescent prayers to shed an inch or two! But then there was Rafi, who seemed to swoon over them. Men, men, and their hallucinatory turn-ons.) Anyway, she'd have to look through her self-portraits in black and white to measure the full damage done by the subtle artist Time. She rouged her face lightly (why?), smoothed her skirt and jacket, and left the curious confessional.

She settled back into her seat, smiled at her companion, and closed her eyes, seeing the jagged mountains of the Negev, the improvised soccer field for the kids, and Coach Rafi, carrying the soccer ball, approaching her. Narrow-waisted, in shorts and T-shirt, wearing his brimmed hat and embarrassed smile of satisfaction . . . her private wildebeest, good enough to nibble at and eat up. She hooked his arm and arranged his Windbreaker over his shoulders, and as he chatted about the club's progress — "These working-class British kids may give us a real team, different from the Long Island Jews" — she secreted his scent, a trail of perspiration and vanilla, a heady aroma.

Later, in their apartment, he played Bjorling on the tape.

They made love. At first touching sensitive necks, earlobes, underarms; brushing nipples. Early on in their courtship, in a seedy Cambridge apartment, a Maine fishing village, a Negev room, she had noted his clumsy passion and occasional impotence and spec-

ulated upon their sources. Marriage breakup and subsequent guilt,
insecurity. Conjugal duty rather than potent pleasure. The life of
monogamy for twenty-five years. The pressures of being an Israeli
male. Whatever, cunningly she had labored to revitalize him, re-
plenish full confidence, full potency. Accustom him to the ways
of the body — his, hers, theirs together. He was a good pupil, too,
a kind of eager schoolboy looking forward to his private lessons.
An ironic reversal of roles for her, who a brief decade ago had
been the pupil. She came to know the run of his lean back, the
crook of his neck, the muscular thighs and strong calves, the velvety
member hiding out in its curly nest. Intimate surfaces: her dominion.

They made love. Needs spiritual and emotional fulfilled in acts
carnal. Who would have thought it? Not she. Moved above him
surely, tantalizingly. Long, long ago she had been a Serious Girl,
a Good Girl, hollow in experience, naive with ideas, shallow about
pleasure. Hadn't believed in the sensual world. (Fishes in her childhood aquarium swam *sensuously*, yes.) Desire itself had slowly
atrophied, unbeknownst to her. At age thirty-three she might have
been fifty-three: drained, dry, semimenopausal. There. He moaned
slightly. She liked the slow control up on top. Knew well her
darling's years of privation, his thralldom to monogamy. Knew it
from her own life too, too well. Oh dear, this is a subtle sport, in
the middle years. Curled up in their pleasure cone amid flowering
scents in this small summer bedroom. Her photos of his tels above
the bed: mounds of dirt camouflaging old secrets, ancient societies. Gradually he had learned how to please her, to surprise himself; each learned how to hold out slowly, familiarly, for the
other. Intimacy shaped so very differently with each man — Stan
and Jamie, Adrien and Harry, Colin and Andrei, now this
Rafi . . . Months of establishing trust and ease, and then slipping
off that float and swimming out to hidden coves and sudden inlets.
(Aquarium adult?) Silently, with swims and caresses and knowledgeable touches, he had organized competence, developed imagination. Each period of absence between them seemed to drive
passion deeper the next time around. And for the first time in years
she felt this opening of herself, this wanting a man in her emotions,
while she informed him of what an excellent lover he had become,

the words corresponding to surfaces, which he mocked appropriately by saying she wanted him for his body only. Not *only*, she had kidded back, moving ever so finely now, edges playing. And oh yes, the prick was a perfect pupil, stretching hard for its lesson in her soft wet opening of instruction.

They were fucking now, his vanilla aroma perfuming the room and her senses. After he had learned trust, she had slowly led him to censor his politeness and shift ahead to greed, seeking ample desire. Applied to him the lessons of her thirties, using the other for the self's wants, allowing the self to be used for the same sweet purposes, to begin to drive toward down-and-out lust, as foreign as fear or terror. Into that lovely paradox of supreme selfishness and willing servitude, an education as much moral as physical. For pleasure had become something of an adult commandment — "The heart asks pleasure first," she recalled — like reading books and looking at pictures in youth. How peculiar! Breathing deeply now, yoga breaths. Out of chance and instinct, not reason, she had stumbled into this knowledge, and this natural resource had made her stronger, surer. Coming now, this was the man she would love now, she proclaimed to herself, coming, the man she would care for and attend to, give her time to and herself to, spend herself with and exchange with, for after spending so much time with that self (hers), it was releasing, oh so wildly neatly releasing, to entrust it to someone else now, and the two zones intersected and caught here, longitude of memory and latitude of flesh, in this slow splash of pleasure.

She held onto her armrests and peeked about, flushed and embarrassed. Paused, replayed more.

Afterward they lay in silence, intertwined, indivisible, indistinguishable. Slowly the walls and shutters returned, birds chattered outside, the self gained gravity and realized satisfaction. She sneaked glances at his face in repose: the small straight nose, long eyelashes and light eyebrows, curly hair and slender neck. Her man. She played with the sound of *her man,* like a chord of music. Man, friend, comrade (in arms?). Because of that unblemished smooth skin and taut figure he looked younger than forty-nine, or was it simply that forty-nine looked splendid? His skin went more pink and red than brown with sun; her private redskin. This quiet was part of the ritual, a serene close, and she lingered within, filling the silence with feeling. For a moment other rooms, other moments passed through her, like a ray of sun through a glass of sherry, refracting the light amber. A glittering prism, this Miriam . . .

Hours later, they were making their descent into Logan.

"It always surprises me how good it feels to set foot on home ground again," the doctor said as the plane approached lower over the ocean. "Sentimentalist. Or chauvinist."

"We're not there yet," she superstitiously corrected.

"Don't worry, we will be momentarily."

Big jet descending slowly, the ocean rising to meet them; she anticipated the dejection of the first days of settling back in. The shock of seeing the apartment after the summer evacuation. The dullish life without Rafi for six months or so, and adjusting to the new rhythm. (Would her new pictures of him nude suffice?) Single, and on her own again. And now the creeping fear of not landing on the tarmac but falling short, into the soup.

Somehow the doctor was holding her hand when the huge bird set down with a light bump on the runway, safe and sound. She was not even perspiring — a triumph.

He smiled his big-sky smile and told her she had done fine — how did he know? — and she realized she liked that praise from him. Curious. And his real grip?

On the portable stairway leading to the ground she was hit by the hot September air.

"Don't stumble now," he advised at her elbow as she nearly tripped.

A small pleasure, to know that this kindly man was looking after her. Was the pleasure from the courtesy, or the man?

The humid Boston heat contrasted with the dry air of the desert, of Rafi's kibbutz.

Through acres of pastel corridors they walked, passing formally dressed passengers and inundated by what Jon called "cornflake music." So spiffy and up-to-date these natives looked alongside the bedraggled Israelis. In their pin-striped seersucker suits, purple pantaloons, peplum tops, and satiny blousons, bearing loads of tennis and golfing gear, they were hunters of distraction, Lord &

Taylor Romans, she thought. And this too hit you immediately, here in the airport.

Presently she and the doctor were waiting for their luggage at the horseshoe carousel, behind the first line of eager passengers. A large crowd waited, worn and warm, but polite, civil. She found pleasure in her Americans, with their harmless addictions and pastel temperaments.

"Look." He motioned toward a group of young giants waiting at an adjacent carousel. "Must be a basketball team."

"Hmmm," she mused. "If I'm not mistaken, those are the Celtics."

"Really? In all my years in Boston, I've never seen them play. I've been a Bruins fan — maybe for too long."

"Shame on you." She couldn't resist. "They're the best thing about Boston. You should go."

He turned his head slightly, a vulnerable gesture. "Maybe. Someday."

"That means never," she said, and seeing him confirm it with a smile, she added impulsively, "I'll take you one day."

"You're a fan?" he asked, his brows raised. "You're a woman of parts, I'm beginning to see."

"One or two, yes." A date with Dr. Wallace Scott Beaumont struck her as being like a high school prom invitation.

He paused, trying to say something. "Uh, someone's probably going to meet me . . . Would you like a lift?"

The stumbling dissuaded her. Wife, son? Why didn't he . . . ? "No, I think it'll be easier to grab a cab. You go on, why don't you?"

First he helped her with her two bags and carried them to the customs counter. There, waiting, he took her phone number — wetting the pencil point — and gave her his, at the hospital. "Should I call you in a few weeks, and we can make those game plans over lunch?"

"It's a deal," she said, signing her customs card and answering the perfunctory questions.

"Good operating," she said, by way of good-bye.

He smiled. "Good photographing."

Before departing he found a porter to take her bags out to the taxi line. And as she followed the porter she tried to find him in the crowd. Why? She succeeded — and what she was looking for, almost idly, had fine legs and short blond hair and . . . his daughter, you fool, not his wife.

Warm sulfurous air. Ramps and garages. Low, leaden light. In the taxi at last, her thoughts swirled. What had she done with this Dr. Beaumont? Why? Was it time to return to old friend Journal in order to discover the meaning of her acts? . . . Superego heating up over a pleasant airplane meeting. Like the furnace air. Crazy. Actually she felt all right, pretty good. Feelings roamed, landed on her Rafi . . . wished she was returning now to his sturdy chest and strong hands and lovely crook . . . Tried to focus on the present. On tunnel traffic, Storrow Drive, the hurly-burly of city survival. Raise the defense levels, sister, here comes Cambridge! How do you confront all this girdered practicality and concrete necessity and struggle for the green stuff without the aid of fantasy, illusion, sensuality? (And now, more and more, memory.) Those sweeteners of life, after your children. So, privately she'd live with her sweeteners, her adult Boardwalks and Park Places, while outwardly she'd feign interest in cracked vinyl, dirty streets, this old driver here with his gabardine cap. Play native, she told herself, loud and lewd and frenzied; but inwardly play yourself, vulnerable, reflective, adventurous. Keep a low profile and sneak back into the culture via the back door, slowly, quietly . . . Overtired. She dozed.

The heavyset taxi driver turned out to be crude but kind hearted, and after waking her in Cambridge, insisted on carrying her bags up the stairs.

"Israel?" he asked, bushy eyelids lifting as he noted the baggage tags. "No good. My family, me, there. No nice life. Worse for Russia." A broad smile creased his stocky face. "America okay."

She would have liked to talk with him maybe, but not now. "Your name?"

"Rabi-*no*vitch."

"Whole name?"

"What? Rabi-*novitch*." Instructing a child.

"Thanks, Mr. Rabinowitz?" She shook his hand and tipped him.

Nodding, he lingered, looking around with a kind of familial curiosity that reminded her of an ancient Jewish aunt from Florida. "You live *alone* here? Too big space for *one*. You should a man have here. I'm Leo, for Leonid, yeah?" He wrote down his address, using a broken-off pencil, and handed it to her. "Should you need *epos* something."

She gave him a little wave, wanted to peck his cheek like she pecked Aunt Fanny's. An odd breed, on the point of vanishing.

Kept her fingers crossed as she went to the kitchen in search of her hiding place. All right! A half-bottle of Ballantine's was intact. Now if . . . she lucked out again, finding ice cubes in the tray. Shook loose a few for her drink, and took her glass into the living room, where she floated down onto her couch. No looking around now, or unpacking. Sipped her scotch, and felt like a groundhog who had gotten lucky and didn't have to go back down for six more weeks. Got up, put on the first Mozart she came to on the record shelf, and returned to the couch. Oh, the world wasn't half bad when you could fly halfway across it, land in one piece, return home safely to sip scotch and listen to clarinets, and soon enough have your darlings back! A purple martin returning to its northern nest every spring. Kicking off her low pumps, she reached way out and removed the telephone receiver. Hungry for deep sleep, she saw an envelope that Rabi-*no*vitch had brought in and set on her valises.

Don't read it, she told herself, opening it. The landlord telling her to scram, after what those kids she'd sublet to had done?

> Welcome back, kid. Hope you're not yet turned Orthodox. Call me when you're up and around — I'll buy you dinner. I can fill you in on all the exciting happenings — actually, very little. A long boring summer, the baseball a bummer. But the clams and shrimp are jumping, in the red tide of course — and guess what? There's another good Szechuan restaurant in town. No. 1051. I've waited to try it with you. H.

Dearest Harry. If there was any friend she had missed, it was this one.

Warmed by the note, she settled back down, turning on her side. Grateful that Mozart would turn off by himself on the old phonograph. Very soon, this serene confusion of men would dissolve itself in dreams, and when she awoke, at some absurd early-morning hour, it would be the perfect time to put away things without distraction. Then, tomorrow, Yani, Rosie. (Tucked away with Stan still.) Hostages to fortune maybe, but also partial rewards for imperfect mortals. She felt the thin ridges of corduroy on her pillow cover, remembered Rafi's sports jacket and Dr. Levanda's couch, and was glad she had gotten to Dr. L's grave at Revivim. The dead had their secure place in her life nowadays, she knew as she slipped into sleep.

2

THE next day, before retrieving the kids after school, she took a promenade along the streets of Cambridge, to get acquainted again. Humid, hot, bleak, packed with pedestrians; a contrast to white desert, pastel Dimona. A winding sheet of battleship gray seemed to enshroud the town and its citizens, a result of old climate and new commercialism. Cambridge was no longer the small town of student gaiety and sixties anarchy, of book-loving professors and backpacking youngsters. On Mass. Ave. by Widener she stopped and eyed two women administrators with attaché cases, a couple of junior execs lounging by a red Audi 5000, a group of three-piece pin-striped lawyers carrying legal briefs. A change. What had happened to the surging spirit of rebellion, the exotic charades of liberty and idealism? Instead of seedy secondhand bookstores and greasy-spoon cafeterias and cozy open-air cafés, brassy chainstores proliferated, huckstering everything from drugs to books to burgers. The new Money Class — Harvard Business School portfolio consultants, condo-converting entrepreneurs, hit-and-run therapists — had put down roots into the old intellectual soil. The hustlers were edging out the eggheads. Oh, she preferred her eggs! She missed the romantic music of the Square — comic street improvisations, polymorphous radicalism, day care for dropouts in front of Harvard Trust and the Coop. Yes, it had been excessive, the theater folly, the chicks and piglets and foals running the Harvard Square farm. But wouldn't Matthiesson, Le Corbusier, Mumford, have preferred that sort of kid-stuff illusion to this grown-up utilitarianism?

In the Square she tried to escape the slamming and pounding of the new subway project by trying on a pair of leather boots "on sale" for $85. Walking about the shop, which also sold Indian jewelry from the Southwest, she saw a poster: "Nix the Nukes Before They Nuke You." Would the nukes crash any louder than this banging? She imagined the missiles in Utah and Nevada, poised to go, while here the unseen formula read Buy and Forget. Enjoy and Forget. If the whole thing went up, you'd hardly know what hit you. Oh, Serious, Obvious. (Self-consciousness; thou art our true modern cowardice.) She asked the clerk, "Do you think I can run fast in these clogs?" He glanced sideways at her, not appreciating the point: "Do you want running shoes or dressy boots?" Just joshing, fella. Should she buy Nikes instead? She paid for the boots with her MasterCard, thinking of her MIT paycheck at the end of the month, and fled into the churning streets. A contemporary hell, this MBTA jackhammering and gouging, a prison sentence of five to seven. God. Down Church Street she meandered, observing new shops of videocassettes, VCRs, computers. Would Klee use a Kaypro? Buy and Forget. Okay, she'd play along, go native for a while.

The reunion with the kids was lovely, but swift; their hectic social schedules immediately took them away. (Rosie accepted her Bedouin blouse with a wondering look; how would friends like it? Yani, however, loved his hooded navy-blue Hebrew U. sweatshirt.) An hour of affection and distraction.

Miriam's rhythm in these first days was all screwed up, because of jet lag and resettlement. Daytime strolling, nighttime hibernating, early morning unpacking, chores and bills. Getting used to sleeping alone again, insomnia. Just after dinner, during those first evenings, she'd slide into a deep sleep, and awaken about 2:00 or 3:00 A.M. to take care of chores. The time-zone change made her feel like she was working graveyard shift in the factory, and passing the kids on the evening shift. She didn't worry too much; they'd get their time in. But it would take a few weeks to put the apartment together again. The surface looked tidy enough, but things had been misplaced, changed around, lost maybe. And her temporary darkroom had been converted into a storage area. Her fault, for not locking it up.

In Somerville she checked out her studio, a large, partitioned rectangle at the top of a container factory. Everything was in order there — the lenses and tripods, developing trays and chemicals, the enlarger and the files of photos. The painter who shared it had taken care of it fine. This was her home away from home, leased after her Radcliffe Institute year. Breaking it up into two spaces, one for rental, enabled her to pay about $40 a month for the whole. Not bad. Good old Somerville — rough, tough living, superb Portuguese markets, good values (and space) for your money. And with Harry around to check it out twice a summer, the situation was ideal. Did anyone else perceive crude Somerville as lending itself to the Ideal?

Not ideal was having to pay bills, wash clothes, answer the telephone, and make arrangements again, after months during which Mother Kibbutz provided all for you. Here the anxiety about money was felt. Her savings and checking accounts didn't console her much. She smiled, thinking of friends who occasionally would sigh, "Do you realize I had to dip into capital last month?" Her only capital was in her name. Teaching at MIT part-time for $12,500 a year barely paid the bills, and she was down to the last $3000 of her family inheritance. (Seventy-five hundred each went to her and her brother.) Stan helped with child support, but she hadn't wanted any alimony; Rafi was able to pull his own weight, nothing more. Poor as church mice, she and he. In chic Cambridge, where most families had two salaries, a trust fund here and there, a new Volvo wagon to bop about in, she felt her near-poverty as a lonely virtue. Should she take in washing, babysit kids, or (as the new movies suggested) hustle the streets for change? Closing her checkbook after paying more bills, she thought how MIT kept her dangling as a part-timer, subject to the whims and envies of tenured colleagues. Tenure, for so many, meant a free ride — to complacency, pomposity, power. Yet other colleagues were alive, alert, caring. Oh well, not tonight. Teaching was another matter — uncorrupting, educational, intense. The three or four best kids were able and serious, and interesting to teach, to tend, to watch grow. She picked up *Photography Annual* and skimmed the pages, looking for one or two shots that revealed talent. Noticing a photo of two sunbathers, she gazed at her own body and realized that three months in the sun had done a browning job on her.

To celebrate her homecoming in that first week, she decided to get a styled haircut. So, for almost two hours, she sat in one of the new high-powered Cambridge boutiques and had her hair shampooed, cut, shaped, blow-dried, fussed over, while she looked through the magazines of the native ladies: *Cosmopolitan, Glamour, Vogue.* The amenities of home scraped at her nervous system — the "analytical" talk by a movie star of forty about clitoral orgasm, the ads for moisture-free underpants and vaginal sprays, the cannibalistic confessions about divorces turned into feasts of celebration. And the array of nonfaces — faces without character, faces without pain or anxiety, unease or guilt, faces that denied womanhood. Only the prices had changed; the sky was the limit for dresses, pants, skirts, camisoles, shoes, sweaters. Stick to Filene's Basement, kid. She turned to another magazine, *Playgirl,* and after five minutes of that sophistication she had had enough. One pornography for another. Oh well. Finally she had a look at the women's-movement magazine and read two pieces. One concerned new role models for young women and was filled with adjectives that applied to successful businessmen. The other was about two new female movie directors, and praised them lavishly; unfortunately, Miriam had seen their movies. Intermittently, while reading, she gazed at the women in the boutique and counted an even half-dozen who had been packaged precisely according to the magazine ads, from belts with insignia to the latest designer jeans to Indian turquoise jewelry. Poor Miriam, she chided herself, where have you been for the past twenty years? Why are you stuck in the price-and-taste zone of the nineteen-fifties and -sixties?

When the young hairdresser at last presented her image in the mirror to her, Miriam looked with curiosity — who was that? Not an uninteresting face, surrounded by all that dark hair, but a different one. She didn't look too bad, not at all, Miriam secretly felt.

"Well, how do you like it, dear?" crowed the fey young fellow, from Newton via Malibu-fantasy.

"I think you did a fine job, Louis. Thank you."

The slender cockatoo nodded at her and at himself in the mirror.

Outside she felt that girlish illusion of a new face showing to the world, as though the hairdo were performing, and she brimmed with a child's excitement. Surely, as she walked down Brattle toward the Square, here and there she passed by some friend or acquaintance who just didn't recognize her in her new disguise as a semiperson in the warm, hazy day. Disguises, masks, costumes, the daily theater. She thought of some of the creamy clichés — flatten your tummy, bolster your bust, freshen your smell. Felt lucky that somehow she had escaped those common traps. She stopped at the Harvard Square Cinema, which had been turned into a rerun theater, and noted that one of the Vietnam movies of the past few years was returning. She'd see it, and a few others, she decided.

Back home, Jon voiced serious skepticism about the new hairdo: "Cheesus, Mom, what'd you go and do *that* for?" Disliking, as usual, any change in her whatsoever. Rosie was more open: "Excellent, Mom. You look . . . just kinda different. Weird in a way, but okay."

That evening, after a dinner of chicken and rice and broccoli — "I won't eat meat or fowl anymore; it's disgusting," Jon said, heaping rice with broccoli and gulping milk — she wrote a letter to Rafi, called her friend Mary Ann and made a lunch date, and went to her makeshift darkroom for the first time. From eight to eleven she immersed herself in chemicals and acids, water and film, darkness and UV light. Slow, meticulous labor. She took her contact sheets to the dining room and held up her magnifying glass to inspect them, a doctor with X-rays, marking the best ones with red *x*'s for printing.

Jon appeared in his pajamas, saying he was "starving bad." She wanted to tell him to eat his dinner next time, but held off. He brought a peanut-butter-and-jelly sandwich and a carton of milk into the dining room and sat down. "How'd it go, Mom?"

"Mom" was always the signal for more warmth, more affectionate talk. Usually she got the punishing distance of "Miry" or "Miriam" these past years. This was no school performance, now, just private talk.

She waited while he wolfed his sandwich, his high cheekbones reflecting her father's.

Jon stopped to say, "How come I was never bar mitzvahed?"

Without looking away from her sheets, containing her amazement, she said, "You didn't seem very interested, I guess, when your father suggested it."

"But what'd *you* think?"

She tried to concentrate; on sheets or this stunning talk? "I guess it didn't mean that much to me either."

"That's just what I thought," he said.

She stared at him now, surprised to see hurt and maybe anger on his thin, intense face.

"Yani, what are you talking about? When did you get interested in . . . in all this? And why not *then?*"

"Because. And I am now. At least I should have had a *choice*, don't ya think?"

She was perplexed. "But you did — a clear choice. No one ever said you couldn't or shouldn't. On the contrary, your father suggested a bar mitzvah to you for three or four straight months, and you stopped talking to him because he was bugging you, don't you remember?"

"Yeah. But what about *you?*"

"Me? What do you mean?"

"Why didn't *you* take a position?"

She looked around for a smoke, wondering how to answer. Of course, if she had insisted then, he would have resented her deeply, both for siding with Stan against him and for not letting him choose for himself. She found her pack of cigarettes and lit one up.

"Twenty-five thousand women died in America of lung cancer last year," he observed, "from doing that."

"One more won't change that statistic much, then."

"Don't be dumb, yeah. And don't change the subject. You didn't *want* me bar mitzvahed, did you?"

"To me, it didn't make that much difference. What made a difference was to know clearly how you felt about it, and to act accordingly."

"Well, cheesus." He shifted awkwardly in his chair, twisting one leg under the other and lifting the carton of milk to his mouth.

She had to allow him his ill manners just now, she knew.

"Tell me, what's brought on all this sudden interest?"

" 'Cause. Bruce Horowitz was bar mitzvahed this summer, and

I went to it and it was kinda neat. And then I'm taking this religion course at Commonwealth, and being Jewish is kinda interesting. But *you* don't care about that, do you?"

She forced a small smile. "Not the religious part, no." She had a vision of Jon with sidecurls and black coat, swaying back and forth in Mea Shearim. That's just what she needed.

"See? That's just what I mean!"

"What?"

"That you don't care about it — and therefore you don't want me to care about it. Boy, you're really something — you go date an Israeli and yet you don't have me bar mitzvahed. What did Rafi think about it? I bet you never told him, did you?" He leaned forward, his dark, intense face a mirror of hers.

Oh God, what a mixture of comedy, accusation, intimacy. But how did you separate one from the other two? "Yes, actually, we discussed it." A small lie; Rafi knew her too well to get mixed up in that sort of family matter.

"And what did he think?"

The truth, partially, now. "Well, he thought . . . it was not a great idea to skip it. But it wasn't his business."

His face brightened with victory. "And you did anyway. *Why?*"

Foolish to try to be logical with him when he was this way. "Look," she said, "it's water under the bridge. Would you like to be bar mitzvahed now?"

"I'm gonna be *fifteen,* or have you forgotten?" He glowered. "Who's gonna do it now? Or want it?"

"Well, I can look into it," she offered, not knowing what she was talking about.

He eyed her skeptically. "Hmmm. You mean you think it's still possible? You think a rabbi would do it now?"

"Sure," she gambled, having no idea. "Why not?"

"Hmmm." He stood up and downed the rest of his quart, then suddenly yawned wide and stretched.

In five minutes he'd be fast asleep, she saw.

Seriously now, for his own information, he asked her, "You don't feel very Jewish, do you?"

Did she? "Yes, I do, actually, but not in a religious way."

"Well, I don't quite get the distinction, ya know. Not at all."

"I'll explain it to you sometime, but not now. Why don't you go to sleep, and we'll talk about it soon, okay?"

"Yeah. But remember, *soon*."

"I'll clean that food up. Hey, can I have a goodnight hug and kiss?"

Since he had scored a triumph, he permitted the affection. He came to her side of the table and buried his face in her neck, and she kissed his thick hair and even rubbed his back. For two whole minutes, pure rubbing bliss, transporting her to his baby days.

He almost fell asleep right there, arched awkwardly in her arms.

"Hey, better get to bed. You're too heavy to carry these days."

He nodded sleepily, raised himself with effort, and walked off, almost tripping over his slumping pajama bottoms.

Fix that drawstring, she noted, still basking in the goodnight affection. Oh, let him win all those academic word battles if I can get those hugs and squeezes!

Later, in her bed, she wondered indeed how Jewish she was, and what that meant. Anything she should know about?

She smoked, pensive in the semidarkness. How mistaken outsiders were concerning Israelis. In fact they were very much like Americans — a casual, secular, informal people. Throw in irony and humor for the Jewish–Yiddish side. The religion, especially as personified in the religious leaders who imposed their rules and laws upon the state, was anathema; look how Rafi's kids, teenagers, already hated the religious with a passion. In other words, her own hostility to all things religious, here in America, was mirrored by the Jews there. Well, *her* Jews there. Under no circumstances would she permit the indoctrination of one of her kids by a rabbi. Especially on behalf of a God who had permitted some two million children to die recently. Oh, if one of the kids wanted to learn Hebrew or seriously study certain traditions, that was fine. But no clerics, please. No Sunday-school brainwashing in order to make the kids aware of their "Jewish tradition." And no schmaltz either. She was, and would remain, firmly anticlerical, antireligionist.

She put on the bedside light and put out her cigarette. She eyed a picture of herself in the eighth grade, dressed in her basketball duds, a sometime substitute on a local boys' team. On one knee, holding a ball; she had been small and very fast, nicknamed "Gnat," a decent dribbler and ball handler. An outsider then, she remained one now in her Jewishness, her temperament. Yes, she felt a certain strangeness out there in Christian America, but it was a strangeness she rather liked, perhaps cultivated. Being Jewish meant being strange, just as being Miriam meant being different — an oblique angle for viewing things, society. But how then do you feel the Jewishness? What I read, how I talk and think, what I admire and loathe, in the way of being rather than in the way of ritual. Intensity and self-irony were crucial to the temperament. A polemical will. A sense of moral justice ahead of economic self-interest, a willingness to stick your neck out for the underdog, brown, red. A fighting identification with Jews when they were maligned or persecuted. A historical sense about the old and recent fate of the Jews, evolving from European anti-Semitism to the Nazi Holocaust. (Because I remember that fate and history, I admire America all the more; no such tradition exists here, of institutionalized anti-Semitism. Americans on the whole don't much like bullies or pogroms, and will, if pushed, stand up and fight both. Which was why she loved her Gentiles here, and looked forward to inundating herself with them and their polite, genteel, lonely ways.) So, in part, she was an enlightened and paradoxical soul, beyond ancient myths and medieval prejudices, Jewish and assimilated at the same time. A paradox? Sure. But why not? . . . And what about The Fate of the Jewish People? Mostly a red herring, a rhetorical formula. Who in the world would want such a burden except Moses, some self-righteous rabbi, or a shrewd con man? Let "the people" take care of themselves, and she would take care of herself. Wasn't that a big enough job? Looking closely at her dog-eared photo, she thought how much easier it was to dribble and ball-handle than to perform the current tasks — mothering, photographing, befriending, or playing Jewish. She yawned, doused the light, and headed for sleep, an imperfect Jewess for sure.

Two days later, on Thursday, she had decided upon seeing one of the Vietnam movies around when she received a surprise phone call.

The gravelly tenor cheered her immediately. "Doctor Beaumont — why, I thought you'd never call," she drawled in her best slow Scarlett O'Hara before switching back to fast Miriam Scheinman. "Actually, perfect timing. Look, what hour are you finished operating today?"

"Today? I don't operate — just paperwork and then rounds to make, and . . ."

"Must be fate. Why not join me for a four o'clock movie in downtown Boston?"

"Did I hear you right?"

Did *she?* "Sure."

"My, you can move fast."

Not with everyone, she realized. "Come on, you can always finish up paperwork. Use a shredder if you have to. And after the movie we can make our basketball plans."

"So you haven't forgotten? You weren't kidding after all?"

"Cheri One Cinema, by the Sheraton. Outside at ten to four, say."

"Are you always so full of, uh, vinegar?"

"You've left out the piss, Doctor. The timing is too good for us to pass it up. Besides, I want to hear your opinion about this movie. I tend to be too critical."

"Well, I don't see that many, to tell you the truth." A pause. "Okay, I'll be there. Ten to." And he hung up.

She held the receiver in her hand, rushed by a swift fantasy of being in the arms of that tall Montana renegade as he bent to kiss her. A high school crush come alive. She smiled, putting down the magical telephone and vaguely questioning what she was up to. Following your impulses, that's all, she answered. But why did they have to rush ahead of reason, purpose?

She put the matter out of mind until she saw him by the Cheri, tall and lanky as she remembered. It was no airplane fantasy, and he had already bought the tickets. His blue eyes had a touch of sapphire, she perceived in the overcast light.

"You've changed your hairdo, haven't you?" he remarked, taking her arm courteously. "Gives you a different air." He escorted her into the nearly empty, elaborate theater.

"Forlorn without people, isn't it?"

He looked around. "Never thought about it that way." He held out a pack of sugarless lemon drops, and she took one.

"Were you in any war?"

"Not exactly," he said. "I was in the Navy at the end of World War II but saw no real combat, if that's what you mean."

"Where were you stationed?"

"South Pacific, mostly. On a carrier, near the end of the war. Spent time in all sorts of exotic places — New Guinea, Luzon, Australia. But it was mop-up time by then."

The theater darkened, the curtain drew open slowly, and she calculated she now had one friend who had been in the North African campaign and another in the South Pacific — on the desert and on the sea. Now, she teased herself, should she get a soldier from the Battle of the Bulge? Up on the screen the old MGM lion, looking as young and vigorous as ever, roared. Cheers for old lions!

The film was overlong, extraloud, and overloaded. There were lots of helicopters and ketchupy limbs and overkill scenes, jazzed up by blaring rock music; this camouflage of high decibels and bloated violence did little to cover up the movie's pretentious and confused story. If she felt bored by the first part, then the last hour or so, in which the great Conrad novella about moral deterioration was used as a guiding model, was vulgar, offensive, and unbearably slow. And the once-superb American actor was now an indecipherable hulk, mumbling and embarrassing, evincing a bovine shape and sense of drama.

She felt betrayed by what her beloved Hollywood had turned into, by these dumb new directors. Later, at a Boylston Street restaurant, she and the doctor had a cup of coffee.

"Poor Brando," she sympathized, "they've done a number on him out there. Turned a great actor into a poor cow. He should have hired Olivier to be his protector. And to get him a theater piece a year."

"I did have a hard time catching his words."

"And poor me, too — they've ruined an old movie fan's fun." She accepted pastry and asked what he thought about the rest of the film.

The doctor's face looked quizzical. "Powerful at times, I thought. Though too heavy with violence. The music was a bit loud, too," he added.

Was he being modest or just contained in his critique? Or was it that she was too critical, as usual — about her movies, books, people? Why not take it all in and accept easily what they dished out? All that shoot-'em-up pabulum and Technicolor melodrama served with rock-and-roll pop, called culture?

"And you?" His blue eyes stared, innocent and inquiring.

"I don't know where to start — maybe I shouldn't."

"No, please do."

" 'Gidget Goes to Literature.' Joseph Conrad interpreted by Sandra Dee." She saw he was not following, so she backtracked. "A godawful movie. A confused argument, to begin with. For example, if Colonel Kurtz went off the far end *because* of the Vietnam War, then that point should have been emphasized and developed. As it stands, Vietnam and Kurtz are two separate, unrelated stories."

He considered that. "Go on."

"That whole last hour was insufferably long, and why? So *Heart of Darkness* could be brought into the movie. Embarrassing. The whole narrative line of Marlowe, which in the Conrad story is filled with moral dilemma, is vulgarized beyond belief. As for the hysterical beginning —"

"Hold on, I haven't read Conrad since college." He took her hands down from midair. "And I had no idea you took your movies so *seriously,* or at least watched them so much more analytically than I. Didn't you think many of the war scenes rather . . . realistic?" He shrugged. "Am I wrong?"

Was her "male intelligence" rearing its assertive head? "Do you think Technicolor and rock music and fancy camera angles add to the realistic or to the fake? Look, I bet for thirty-five million bucks, you and I could manage some realistic scenes, don't you think?"

He drained his coffee, eyebrows raising.

God, he'd look good in a Stetson, she daydreamed.

"Is that what it cost?" he said finally. "Hmmm. We've just begun fund raising for a new cancer wing at the hospital. A three-year program, and we're looking for the outrageous sum of twelve point five million dollars." He smiled. "I see what you mean; that's a hell of a lot for . . . for . . ."

"For ketchup and blanks and helicopters, yes." She ate her

danish and realized she hadn't been with a man who wore a tie in years. Especially to the movies!

"What are you smiling at?" he asked, embarrassed now.

"Just noticing that you dress more formally here than in Israel."

He gazed down at himself as if conscious of his costume for the first time. "I warned you, didn't I?"

Not Harry's denims or Rafi's khakis and sandals, but a knit tie, white button-down shirt, Madras sports jacket.

"Am I hired?"

"Yes. *If* you can take shorthand."

"Okay." He smiled. "Now let's talk about the Celtics; when do they begin?"

They made a date for late October, and he hailed a taxi and set her into it. As he lowered his head, she saw that he verged on kissing her on the cheek but hesitated. So she aided him, taking him by the back of his neck and persuading his lips down to her face. They were harder than she had imagined. He blushed and remained pink as the cab drove off.

In the early twilight the Charles glinted with whitecaps, ribboning its way around the Boston skyline, narrowing and sneaking its way up to the countryside. The dark blue river wavered in the wind, reflecting points of light from the low hard sun. Should I come back as a river near a city one day and run for a few thousand years? The memory of his voice and tall, slender body ran through her now, making her waver too. If I were a river, could Dr. Beaumont be my green banks?

At home she fed the kids, and, it being a Friday, she let Rose go off to a friend's house for the night and Jon to a rock concert at the high school. Alone, she exulted in the cozy solitude, setting out Siskind, Bourke-White, and *Camera Arts,* rereading her dearest Rafi's letter, on the sly watching her new emotion for that Western gentleman grow, like a baby plant. No, she informed herself, you're not going to have serious split affections, I won't permit it. Oh, she did miss those Gentile ways, and boys, when in Israel! The easy formality of the American, the graceful tone of Montana tolerance . . .

She sat in her living room, listening to the jazz on the radio and browsing through the autobiography of Margaret Bourke-White, that dynamo who had started out in Miriam's hometown in the 1920s, and gone on, through *Fortune* and *Life,* to become an American star. (Miriam still admired her factory interiors from Cleveland in the twenties.) With gusto and breezy bravado the renowned photographer described her flamboyant adventures, while this quieter photographer, curled in her chair, realized how lucky she was to have had her own small adventure. Not wild treks through the Caucasus but small walks along Boylston Street, in the company of a married surgeon, not a Tartar chieftain. Which was scarier? she wondered.

But later, in sleep, she had an intense dream in which her real mother was fixing dinner for Miriam and her brother in the small kitchen. That nest-feeling of familiarity, with Miriam reading, as usual, while Aaron fixed a locomotive engine. Only, when Mom turned to put the food down, the place settings had not yet been prepared: Miriam's job. Her mother took her by the shoulders and spoke to her in that soft voice, and her face grew beautifully, painfully vivid: the light brown hair, brown eyes, expressive mouth, high forehead. Her look now was fairly stern, and disappointed, and Miriam felt terrible. Yet when she started to cry, her mother immediately changed tone and held her, and with easy caring told her not to take it so hard. Just then Miriam awoke, startled at the vividness of her mother's presence (down to the old apron), and sat up in bed, in the darkness. Oh Mama, Mama, why did you leave me so young? Why? And ever since, for these past thirty-five years, Mom, it's hurt and hurt and hurt. Not fair, Mother!

Slowly she grew accustomed to the shadows, the moment, the ghostly presence, the loss. She got up wearily and went to her own kitchen, where she put on a saucepan with milk and was soon sipping the warm liquid at the table. Half praying that she'd be able to vanish the painful visitor for the night, and half hoping that the vividness of that warm, loving woman who was taken from her when she was ten, and who she went on missing for the next three decades, would never diminish and fade. That was a long, long time to be missing someone, wasn't it? Here and now she had a son and a daughter in the next rooms to worry over, to take care of, to mother, and yet she was still being besieged regularly by the loss of her own mother. No, no, no, not fair! Too confusing!

Back in bed she tried to calm her senses by reading a chapter of Hardy, to escape the haunting presence and to return via a different entry to sleep. Hours went by, however, in grieving ambiguity, before she found it.

3

AFTER a week in blue jeans or fatigues, she was glad to dress up and feel grown-up again: a pair of velvet cords, a pea-green Italian sweater (with bra), low pumps. A cap, for flair? Maybe. Applying lipstick, she thought what a curious sort of "blind date" — her first "open healing session," owing to the kindness of Vera, worldly soul. There was always this dilemma, she realized, staring in the mirror, of what to wear, how to present oneself. Let the wrinkles show for maturity, or clean them up for sparkle, youth? Easier to be a Chinese Maoist in dress than a native of democratic pluralism. Two blind dates from high school came back to her. Little Judah Bergman had picked her up in his Impala convertible and taken her to a Young Judea *latke* party, where he tried to mingle Zionism with petting in a Shaker Heights bedroom. No dice for Miss Clean. Mario Scalesi was a different sort, a big *bulvan* of a fellow, an all-state football end, black-haired and handsome, who proved to be so shy and intimidated by her that *she* took *his* hand in the movies. And on a later date he actually cooked her a wonderful lasagna and opened up, gabbing endlessly about his beloved Cleveland Browns and his dream of replacing Dante Lavelli one day. Oh dear Mario, do you remember how I told you about the other Dante, with tutorial seriousness?

She went out early to take a spin on Mem. Drive, lulled by the lovely autumnal twilight, by the looping river, by her solitary reverie. Was there an evolution in all these small acts, odd doings, perambulations among decisions, judgments, values, men — the sort of Education she had imagined in her literary youth? Where you discovered errors in yourself and *zappo!* you made change and progress? She inhaled and blew smoke out her nostrils. The realer motion appeared to be sideways, in circles maybe, filled with concealed, surprising repetitions. How determined a creature were you, bound by genes and early environment, strapped like Gulliver by infancy, childhood? Well, she didn't feel so bound. You took your stand against unnecessary guilt, aggravated personal wounds, masochistic tendencies, and at the same time looked to test yourself against your vulnerability, prejudices. But supposing you were tested and found wanting? Did you accept that imperfect self as your fate? Or try to fight back? The stripes of rose and mauve on the horizon seemed to filter her questions: How did you separate dangerous act from acceptable, even advisable adventure? How much intimacy did you need, or could you take, in your forties? And adult love — did it really only exist when it focused on your children, where ego was less invested in power competitions? All the rest, hard ambition? All the rest, vanity and passion?

She drove west on the maze of highways past Soldiers Field, past the modern-sculpture site where, years ago, she had come upon a couple locked in abandon and she had snapped her camera, like some African hunter facing a wild rhino, before being chased. With her Leica in her hands, in those days she had been like that, reckless and dangerous (to herself as well as prey). A large digital clock above a motel flashed the weather and time in dotted sequence. Her self-propositions had arrived some eight years ago, during her year up from her breakdown, and she had been working on them ever since. Only without her wise doctor from Ljubljana, Dr. Levanda, it was harder to distinguish and understand, let alone act. We need guides in our lives, intimate, wise guides — like Dad's fisherman friend who had taken along an Inuit guide when he went to virgin salmon rivers in Alaska. Where were they when your mother died, your one and only shrink departed, your son was disturbed (by you), new attractions appeared? *Sympathy, great sympathy at the right moments, could be crucial for sanity.* Martignetti's was just ahead, stop for scotch? She pulled into the parking lot and headed back.

Cruising along the meandering river, she felt transported for some reason to the dusty town of Dimona in the Negev, to the pastel colors and odd odors, and that curious black man. Any age from forty to sixty, he was a Falasha Jew; he wore a tattered white robe and beaded yarmulke, and spoke to her in Hebrew, laughing when he realized she knew very little. Then, in halting, broken English, he managed to ask her for help with the Israeli authorities, to try and get his family out of Addis Ababa. The name had stirred her child's imagination when her father had shown her Djerba, Izmir, Aden on his maps, and in the hot Israeli sun she was mesmerized by the Falasha's long face, a beveled topography of black mahogany and strange lighter patches (sun spots?): an ancient atlas in itself. She had promised vaguely to do what she could for him; he had tried to give her his old Bible, then he had finished his hot tea and nodded to her, saying "Mishpucha" before rising and walking off. She had been astounded, no less, to discover that they were of the same people, and had felt an odd fear, along with kinship, slide through her in that midday sun. Why the memory now?

As she circled back into Cambridge, her new friend drifted into her mind. His tall frame, Scandinavian bones, firm grip, easy ways. Names circled too: "Fogarty catheters" and "DeBakey forceps" and "Dacron graft." New mysteries. Was she leaving monogamy again? She had had twelve years of marital life, in which she had played the faithful wife and known one man only. A state of innocence where you could not even *imagine* other bodies in your consciousness, let alone in bed. Where you could not think seriously of knowing men intimately. Oh, she knew now that monogamy imposed its own spiritual, as well as physical, limitations. A full knowing of another included the full geography and ways of the body too, didn't it? . . . Did confinement make for rich commitment, with rewards more special? Yes, and no.

Trowbridge Street ended her musing, and she had to maneuver to get onto snaking Irving. Presently she double-parked her Valiant jalopy alongside the fancy Peugeot of her friend and honked her horn twice.

In a moment Vera appeared: a strawberry blond with a high-strung pace in her walk and a frenetic gaze in her gray eyes. Gasping as she got in, she kissed Miriam on the lips and said, "Well, don't keep me in suspense, tell me all about those heroic sabras of yours, or whatever you call those *mad Jews* over there!" Whereupon she launched into a monologue about her own bouts with Orthodox Judaism, including a stay, years ago, in Hasidic Williamsburg in Brooklyn. Miriam listened and drove, smiling privately, unable to get a word in edgewise. The fiftyish wife of an eminent sociologist at Harvard, this sturdy European survivor was a powerful little dynamo who strode into new areas of conquest — activist politics, Sufism, ecology, radical psychotherapy, Orthodox Judaism — the way one swept into different rooms. Frequently she was on the road with her husband, traveling around the globe to Third World countries and, it seemed, fourth-dimension consciousness. Now, as she waved her hands and fixed her hair and chattered on endlessly, Miriam disregarded the show and returned to earlier times, when Vera had been around to help her, had not ducked out. Just as in recent years, when she hadn't tried to punish Miriam for her healthy calm, her man. So Miriam didn't mind putting up with the characteristic ego number of this emotional Polish Jewbird, and laughed at her caustic comments about the religious wives in the Hasidic community and their sexual self-abasements. "And as for their leader — why, the Ayatollah has nothing on the Brooklyn Lubavitcher!"

They approached a huge clapboard house tucked behind Mt. Auburn Cemetery. "You see what you're reduced to," said Vera, "when you leave your family of five in Wellesley Hills and take up with a young patient." The estate was surrounded by large lawns and high hedges, and had an especially lovely tree near the entrance.

"What is that?"

"Japanese maple, I think," advised Vera. "Imported by the doctor. On top of everything else, he's a Jap-freak. Park there."

Miriam parked beside the hedgerow and they headed for the long house, which had as many wings as a medieval fortress.

"You wouldn't know that it was one of the original Puritan dwellings." Vera smiled knowingly. "What's the date there — 1720? Yes. It's said that Cotton Mather lived here for a time."

"When it was a bit smaller," surmised Miriam, gazing at the

elephantine structure and trying to discern the original Colonial.

"This wing was built just for Group," Vera announced with pride. "Dr. Hardie lives and swears by it, though he still keeps a few private patients." The grounds were heady with aroma, and the thick maple leaves shimmered golden in the October evening. Each group met twice a week, she explained, and on Friday nights visitors were welcome. The doctor maintained four such groups, in addition to his hospital advising and private patients. "Oh yes, he also runs some superb halfway houses which you *must* see sometime. He's a *macher* as well as an amazing soul."

More *macher* than soul, Miriam imagined, observing the black Mercedes convertible and silver Italian sports car in the private driveway.

"Not exactly the ascetic type, is he?"

Vera stared, broke into a laugh, and shook her head. "Stylish, aren't they? I never trust those monastery boys playing at shrink, anyway."

Miriam considered that. "Should we enter?"

"Wait a sec. Let's take a peek at the patients' cars." Vera tugged Miriam's arm. "See if you can match the car with the client. It's a *fun* game — René's colleague taught it to me. Come."

She escorted Miriam around the other side of the compound, where, along the opposite hedgerow, at least a dozen cars were parked, half on the bank. "Okay, we'll begin right here — this station wagon is a Buick, and the simulated wood panels may be an attempt to recapture the past. I guess a suburban, middle-aged, family person, maybe from Lexington. Too neat, that dash, for a man. So we have a housewife-matron, right? A start. Now, look here — a real live Cadillac DeVille, in Cambridge! What do you think?"

Laughing, Miriam remembered a store owner on Mass. Ave. who had tried to put the make on her. "Owns a small electrical light-fixture firm. Middle-aged male. Aggressive."

"*Nice.* Hey, try this, a new one on me. A Saab sports car. Sonett? Christ. You go."

Miriam shook her head. "No idea. A . . . connoisseur of sorts. Will stick out."

"You're cooking." Vera nodded. "Okay — flashy red Pontiac Firebird. Uh, flashy thirty-five-year-old, into computers?"

"Or a mama's boy let loose from MIT?"

Vera tapped her arm. "Here, a Volks Rabbit. A slender young lady, or laddie, uptight as hell — a well-organized bitch of some gender. Call this one: full Volvo sedan, with all the trimmings, sparkling clean."

Miriam moseyed about, observing the recent wax job and the entirely shiny silver buckles on all the seat straps. Raising her finger with mock portentousness, she declared, "Overworried about safety, this one. A young man, in his thirties, going on sixty. Aging prematurely, and a*fraid*."

"Nice! Afraid to fuck too, right?"

Miriam raised her eyebrows and tipped her head skeptically.

"Aha, who do we have here? Brand new Mercedes sedan. E-a-s-y: a shrink visiting for the occasion. Only a shrink could afford this; only a shrink would go for this security, and this conservative model. *Black!* Ugh — a diehard Freudian."

Miriam shushed her. "And that Honda?"

"We'd better scat — come. Hondas are followers who think they're trend-setters. Some daffy rich girl from the Philly mainline who's ashamed to tool around in the new BMW she'd secretly love. Only a guess."

"Oh, you mean unlike the other confident assessments."

They walked back toward the entrance.

Vera said, "Well, you just keep the models in mind, okay? How are you going to tell the players without the scorecard? And in this case, the only scorecards are these mo-biles."

"It'd be easier, I assure you, if we had spotted a Green Hornet or a Batmobile."

"Huh?"

"Didn't you ever listen to radio or read the comics?"

"Not in Warsaw, please."

The blond housekeeper who let them in had a European accent, and asked whether they wished coffee or tea. She led them through a carpeted vestibule to a long rectangular area the size of a small basketball court, with a raised platform in the center. In the darkened audience area around it, several pumpkin-colored leather loveseats and assorted chairs were arranged. In corners, set like sentries, were huge potted plants: rubber and cactus, and intimidating. The two women found an empty two-seat sofa and sat down, adjusting their eyes to the indirect light. It was something like a theater before the curtain went up.

On the platform, six or eight figures were milling about or sitting on straight-backed cane chairs. A stout middle-aged man wearing a silk suit was chatting with a thin, sallow-faced, mustached young fellow who kept looking around, to see who might be watching. A pretty, bespectacled woman of thirty who wore her brown hair swept back sat impassively smoking, while alongside her an older lady tried, in vain it seemed, to engage her in conversation. An academic-looking man in a corduroy jacket and sweater sat reading a paperback as if he were in a library. Among them all floated a large blond lady wearing high black boots and a flowered skirt and colorful shawl; back and forth she ambled, smoking, sipping liquor, impervious to colleagues and setting. The entire platform was lit by modern track lighting from the ceiling; thin beams of light shot down at sharp angles onto the participants.

"*Our Town?*" Miriam asked, captivated.

At first Vera stared, baffled, then she broke into a smile. "Yes, it's one of Doctor's underlying ideas about Group. Dramatic tension, dynamic cast."

"This place costs a pretty penny," Miriam couldn't help saying.

"Concentrate on the healing," Vera advised, drinking the coffee brought by the housekeeper. "Watch the clients. Did you pick out the Sonett yet?"

Miriam smiled. "Yup. Our *big* friend. How does she get in and out of it?"

Vera laughed. "We're agreed. She likes things difficult."

On stage, the older woman seemed the only truly nervous one, glancing regularly at the audience while being spurned by the younger woman next to her.

"Are they used to being on view? Most of them seem very at ease up there."

A smile of benevolence that highlighted her youthful freckles appeared on Vera's face. "Give them time. And give them Doctor."

A man on the next couch leaned over and asked Miriam for a light, and she handed her lighter to him. She noticed a scattering of maybe a dozen guests, the faces obscure, in the darkened area.

A sudden hush came over the room: a concert audience sighting the arrival of the conductor.

Dr. Hardie was about fifty, on the short side, and wore a white turtleneck with a black blouson draped over his shoulders, directorlike. His face was slightly moon-shaped, with wisps of hair winging his ears. Someone took his hand as he approached, but the doctor quickly instructed him to take a seat. The doctor carried a small black medical bag and had a brisk, short step full of resoluteness. The two men talking on stage stopped, and the older lady ceased pursuing her companion and took out a bag of knitting. The other clients also immediately responded to the doctor's presence, coming to quiet attention — except for the tall blond, who continued her languorous parade, seemingly unaffected and uncaring.

"Ladies and gentlemen, perhaps we can begin." The voice was crisp and clear, the accent a bit difficult to make out. He set his bag down, fidgeted with it a moment, and took a seat.

The participants sat down. The tall dreamer took her sweet time, however, before eventually getting seated, drink in hand. As she walked by the young fellow with the mustache, he took special care to move his legs aside.

When she finally sat down, the doctor abruptly got up, walked over to her, took the glass from her hand, and sniffed it. Curtly he declared, "If you do this again, I'll send you home before the session."

The woman bolted up, stung; almost a full head taller than the stocky doctor, she walked haughtily toward the exit staircase.

The doctor deposited the glass on a small side table and turned back to his chair on the platform. Cordially he asked, "Mrs. Mullins, would you care to begin?"

"Aha, station wagon," slipped in Vera.

Knitting rapidly, the neatly dressed matron began to stammer. "N-nothing r-really happened. That is . . . there was n-nothing of interest." She looked up from her Peter Pan collar and gave a nervous little smile.

The big blond lady now retraced her steps across the stage and sat back down, crossing her legs.

Everyone studiously avoided paying any attention.

"Oh come on, Mrs. Mullins, please," said the thin fellow with the mustache and a somewhat squeaky voice. "Let's not waste precious time this hour." He made a sucking sound of irritation.

Pushed, she relented. "Well . . . one thing d-did occur. On Sunday — I mean, I did try . . . on Sunday night I, uh, made this special dinner. That is, Henry had to see it was special; I cooked for two hours, and . . ." Her mouth and face drooped. "We just ate it. Said . . . nothing." She sort of whimpered.

"Oh come on, Kate. Come on."

Kate Mullins blew her nose, glanced around quickly like a squirrel gathering nuts. "I know it sounds . . . so silly. So darned silly! Forgive me."

"It's all right, Mrs. Mullins," offered the girl alongside, who was sitting very straight and did not look over. "Really, it's quite all right."

Mrs. Mullins suddenly stared at the girl for a long moment, with surprising force, before looking back down at her work.

The stout man now began to say something, but was interrupted by the doctor, who queried, "Kate, why did you look at her like that just now — at Melissa?"

"Oh no," protested Mrs. Mullins, "I didn't look —"

"Kaate." The voice was a dagger pinning her.

Near tears, she burst forth. "Well, she's so . . . so darned *cold* to me always. Just before the session, for example. But now, when you're all here, watching, she's . . . *this* way. Looking concerned!"

The young woman didn't change expression; she continued staring straight ahead, smoking deliberately. Everyone waited, watched. Melissa sat upright, not flinching or turning.

"Now, Kate," the doctor said, shifting emphasis. "Henry and you ate dinner but said nothing, is that right?"

Mrs. Mullins began knitting rapidly again. "Yes — I mean, he made small talk here and there. Perfectly polite. As always. Not awkward. He even complimented me on the food" — she smiled here — "said it was the fanciest pork chop meal he had ever had." She paused. "But . . . but you see, he knew it was special, something very special, but he asked nothing." Her crying was sudden and steady, like a light drizzle.

The pudgy gentleman now leaned forward and said in a low, husky, New York voice, "Why didn't you confront him, Kate? You promised us you would, remember?"

Mr. Cadillac, thought Miriam.

Mrs. Mullins's face drooped. She shook her head. "I, uh, tried. I did. *Really* I did."

Melissa spoke. "This is the third week, Mrs. Mullins, that you've given us this same promise."

"You bitch!" the tall blond suddenly charged in a Scandinavian accent. "You ice-cold maiden bitch!"

Without breaking stride, Melissa observed, "I'm only telling the truth, stating the facts. And you all know it."

"The fact is you're compassionate as ice," said the blond.

"And that Kate is having a *very* hard time," offered the middle-aged man.

"And could use some sympathy from us, her best friends. Which you're incapable of."

The girl tried to look at her accusers but found it difficult. Her posture remained boarding-school upright, and her cheeks were white and cool.

"Sorry, Mrs. Mullins," advised the fellow with the squeaky voice, Robert. "Please continue, won't you?"

The older woman had regained her composure slightly. She spoke softly at first, and plaintively. "Honest, I did try. But it's so hard. So darned difficult when you've been married for as long as we have. And when do you do it? In the morning before he goes off to work? At night when — when we're going to bed, when . . . I can't, not then. And in the early evening when we're having cocktails — why, that's the most pleasant, kindly time of day, with Henry telling me about the office, reading the *Globe*. I . . . hate to break it up so horribly. Who knows, maybe he's not even . . ." She was near tears.

"Kate." The doctor called her to attention. "Do you mind that your husband is sleeping with this girl?"

She looked away. He called her name again, and when she looked at him this time, two big tears rolled down her cheeks and she slowly nodded.

Salting the wound, the doctor pursued by asking, "Are you *sure* it disturbs you?"

"Oh God, Doctor." Her face fell into complete disarray. "Oh God!"

The stout man practically leaped the several steps to the woman and gave her his handkerchief. "It's going to be all right, Mrs. Mullins. We're with you in this now, and later, when you confront him."

She looked up at him imploringly, a lost little girl seeking help. She managed "Thank you, Sam," and he took her hand. Simultaneously, Robert came up and took her other hand, and it was like playing ring-around-the-rosie, with everyone beaming.

After a minute or two of togetherness, however, an awkward silence set in, and the men left off holding Mrs. Mullins's hands, looked around sheepishly, and returned to their chairs.

"Kate, are you afraid to speak to him? Why?"

She shook her head, unable to speak.

"Why?" the doctor repeated.

"Because I'm afraid . . . he'll leave . . . and I, I . . ." She teetered and pushed her loose hair back in vain. "I couldn't take that!"

"But why not, Kate?" intervened Robert, unbuttoning his cardigan like a prosecutor about to cross-examine. "Why not? You know how he —"

"Kate," the doctor interrupted, "do you want to talk to him about his infidelity?"

She nodded, crying again.

The doctor stood and walked to her. "Do you recall when you told us how your father had disappointed you on your birthday? And how, by the lake, you weren't able to tell him of your disappointment? Do you remember, Kate?"

She nodded.

"Now, how old were you then?"

She picked up her knitting, but the doctor took it from her hand and squatted in front of her.

She shook her head in misery.

"Kate."

She mumbled something.

"We can't hear you, Kate."

"Fourteen."

"Kate, do you want to be fourteen still?"

She looked up at him; shook her head ever so slowly.

"Then you must talk to him," he said very deliberately. "Do you understand? Now tell us *why* you must talk to him."

"Because I'm so unhappy!"

The doctor nodded at the correct answer and said, "How old are you now, Kate?"

She mumbled again, and he said they couldn't hear.

"Fifty-two."

"Good. Do you want to be fifty-two or fourteen, Kate?"

Her face in anguish, she shook her head. "Fifty-two." She added softly, "An adult."

The doctor smiled thinly and relented. "*Good.* Now, you will carry it through this week, won't you? So that we can all be proud of you, Kate. All of us here."

She looked at him, trying hard for definiteness. She nodded, her face swollen, her hair falling again from its bun.

He stayed right in front of her. "You'll confront him this week. When, specifically? What day? Kate? Tell us."

Slowly she nodded again. "Tomorrow."

"When tomorrow?"

"Uh . . . at drinks."

"Tomorrow, then, at six o'clock."

"Six-thirty," she corrected, pausing to admit, "He likes his news."

The doctor pounced. "Kate, tell him at six o'clock. *Interrupt* his news."

She looked up at him, in pain from her guilty confession. "I'll try. Hard."

"Can I have your hand on that, Kate?"

Kate nodded and put out her hand onto Dr. Hardie's arm. In a curious ritual, he held it locked there and stared at her for a long minute.

When the doctor moved away and the spell was broken, Vera leaned over and whispered to Miriam, "Exciting, isn't it?"

"Sad," she retorted. "Depressing." Hearing for the first time the sound of running water, she asked Vera what it was. "A Japanese waterfall on the other side of this room which, maybe, we'll see later."

Back at center stage, the doctor turned to the young man who hadn't uttered a single word, had read throughout the session. In a calm voice he asked, "Leon, would you like to tell us anything?"

The fellow responded indifferently, with a faraway look. "Oh well, not much has happened this week." Glasses, sharp nose, curly hair. In his thirties.

"Your Volvo safety-boy?" Vera asked.

Miriam was beginning to feel uneasy with Vera's derisiveness.

"It's been two weeks since you've contributed," the big blond informed the young man courteously.

"Well . . ." His head tilted to one side; his face wore a slightly helpless look.

Somewhat sternly, Dr. Hardie said, "Leon, I feel you're not *giving* anything. Just *taking*. All the time, my friend, *taking*."

Sam assented, and Melissa nodded coolly.

Leon half smiled, pulled at his lip, seemed to shrug. He kept his place in his paperback.

The doctor took a half-dozen quick little steps, stood in front of the young man, and encouraged him with his hands. "Give, Leon. Let it come. *Give*. Stop holding it in. *Help* yourself."

Leon's face creased with anxiety. He removed his eyeglasses and began wiping them meticulously. The doctor reached down and took the glasses away, and Leon quickly reached for them.

"Good, good." The doctor applauded the response, handing them back. "That's a beginning." He returned to his own chair.

Adjusting one stem at a time, Leon returned the rimless glasses to his eyes. Then, annoyed at his involuntary action, he retreated into himself.

"Are you still seeing Erin?" squeaky Robert asked.

With reluctance, Leon nodded.

"Why?"

"I guess I love her."

"But you don't *make* love to her," injected Melissa efficiently.

"I'd rather not . . . tonight, if you don't mind," Leon said to no one.

"Why are you *stuck* this way? Why? Can't you read your actions?"

Resigned, he nodded, shifting his position awkwardly.

"Leon, you've been with us for almost six weeks now," Melissa explained methodically, "and you're *giving* us very little."

He nodded, depressed.

"Tell us about the visit to your mother," offered the Scandinavian woman. "Did you make it?"

He breathed deeply. "Not much to tell."

"Is she well?"

He nodded. "She's all right."

"How does she like Erin? Ever met her?"

He shrugged. "She thinks she doesn't know how to dress too well." He smiled, a puny smile. "Erin wore sandals to a dinner party."

"When?"

"Oh, a few months ago."

"How's your mother's arthritis, by the way?" put in Mrs. Mullins, knitting away cheerfully now, out of the limelight.

Leon leaned forward with interest. "It's difficult for her to straighten up sometimes. Let alone walk easily."

"Didn't you say," the doctor asked, "that she took a trip last year to Israel to see your sister?"

"Yeah."

"Didn't she have to walk quite a lot on that trip?"

"I suppose so."

"Maybe she's not as ill when you're not around."

Leon's face drained of color. "I don't think so."

"Why do you go down there every two weeks?" pressed Robert.

"What do you mean? She's my mother, and she's *old*. And I'm the only one she has . . . besides my sister."

"Sam," the doctor said to the stout man, who had opened his collar and loosened his tie, "you look like you'd like to get into this. Do you have something to say?"

Sam's face grew animated, as if he were about to eat a large meal. "Yeah, sure. Look, kid, I've watched you pussyfoot around and be handled with kid gloves now for a goddamned month. Don't you get it? If you don't cut the string to your mother once and for all, she's going to make you queer as a three-dollar bill! And you're going to keep whacking off. Believe me, kid, I know."

Leon looked at him, stunned, as if he were talking about flying saucers. "What?"

"You heard me. Look, we're here because we're *with* you. We want you to pull out of this nose dive you're in. Straighten out and fly right, okay? But the way you're going, pickin' up no hints whatsoever —"

"You fat schmuck, what the hell are you talking about!"

Sam, radiating with combat, answered, "I'm talking about your life, kid — why you're frightened to death of women, why you can't leave your pecker alone. Yeah, yeah, don't protest; I know your type. Face the truth, Leon, the fucking-A truth!"

Mrs. Mullins looked about nervously; the large blond tried to intercede, as did squeaky Robert, but Dr. Hardie held up his hand in order to keep the pot simmering.

"You're going to be *queer*, kid, if you keep this up. Turn to boys and fag bars. Get it?"

"You fat schmuck, you're just dumb!"

Sam got up and waddled to the seated young man. "Look, kid, if you don't get your mother's tits out of your mouth, you're going to go after little swishy asses!" He twitched his broad hips in front of Leon.

Exasperated, desperate, Leon rose up, revealing his small size. Then he took a roundhouse swing at the larger, heavier man.

Sam easily blocked it, and Leon swung again. Sam took hold of him and sat him down. Helpless, Leon curled into himself and began shaking like a beaten dog.

Immediately the entire group, save for Melissa, gathered around him, holding, touching, stroking him, encouraging his crying as a "step forward." Dr. Hardie stood behind the phalanx, a quarterback behind his line, surveying the field.

"You're one of us now," comforted Kate Mullins. "It's all right, dear, we've all been through this. It's a *breakthrough point*," she announced triumphantly.

"Yeah, kid, yeah. Look, Leon, I'm sorry —"

"Sam!"

The fat man was curbed by the doctor's command and suppressed his apology.

At the doctor's signal the clients began returning to their chairs, and as they did Leon began mumbling some sort of confession. "She always has this cat around . . . Every time it seems I want to make a serious pass at her, there's Nero in her arms. Just at the wrong moments . . . And I always wind up sitting on the sofa alone . . ."

Curiously, no one was listening now, and finally Melissa said, as though by rote, "*Feel* your pain now, Leon. Don't try to ver- balize it away. Acknowledge it inside."

The tumult had died down. Leon's voice trailed off; the room seemed larger and quieter with the drama — that drama — re- solved.

"So, Leana, how have you been?" asked the doctor cordially. "Eating well?"

The big blond cast a venomous look at her questioner. "Yes," she answered. "Yes."

"Why do you think you came here with that drink when you know it's prohibited?"

Her gray eyes narrowed at the question, and she brushed blond strands from her forehead. "I *despise* these sessions. I should start coming. I mean stop."

Smiles and meaningful glances passed among the group mem- bers.

"But why don't you?" responded the doctor. "You keep threat- ening us."

"That's a good question," Robert peeped gently. "Why did you bring that drink?"

She twisted in her chair, too big for it. "To spite the bastard. The little shaman over there." Her eyes lit up, excited. "The *fake* shaman."

The doctor lit a small cigar, puffed vigorously, and crossed his legs.

"Must we go through this same thing *again?*" asked Melissa wearily. "We know these hang-ups. Can't we move forward, Lena?"

"Le-*ana*." She stood up, looking like some blond buffalo ready to charge. "Shut up, you."

"Dear, don't you want to avoid your temper?" Kate Mul- lins offered maternally. "Wasn't that one of the things to work out?"

Leana stood frozen between action and reflection. Finally she eased her hands down from her hips and sat herself down.

Miriam thought how handsome she looked in anger and must look in passion. The impassiveness in her face had shifted into color and expression.

"Oh, dear, that's really so much better," Mrs. Mullins observed.

"Why don't you tell us how you've been — and about your daughter."

The large woman suddenly sagged in her chair, the wind taken from her sails. "I, uh, left her with her father for a while . . . too many things happening now."

"Like what, Leana?" asked Robert.

She gazed at him. The electricity was charging again. "Like *men,* Bobby."

Robert flushed and looked about.

"Another one *after* — what's his name?" queried Sam.

"Alex," recalled Melissa accurately.

"Alex was an age ago," Leana pointed out. "What a flake he turned out to be."

"Flake?" Leon repeated the word, casually picking his nose. "How?"

She shook her head, motioned with her forefinger. "Wanted to get married. Or at least have a commitment. Hah! *I don't give com-mit-ments,* I informed him." She sang with cheer.

"What do you give, Leana?" Melissa inquired.

Leana considered, then answered the girl across the circle directly. "At least I don't have a high school lock on my box, if that's what you mean."

Blushing, Melissa continued. "Why do you torture these men?"

"I never looked at it that way," observed Robert, pondering.

Leana exhaled. "For fun," she decided. "After all, they've tortured me."

"Haven't you contributed to it?" the doctor asked.

"It takes two to tango," Sam said, smiling.

She half glanced at him. "With you, it takes one, it seems."

His face registered the words immediately. "You bitch," he uttered. "It's a wonder anyone is ever able to make love to you — the scenes you pull!"

"Oh Sam, please," Leana tossed off. "I don't hold it against you."

"Hold it against me? You — you —"

"Really, Leana, this is going too far," interceded Kate Mullins, growing excited. "You really are not supposed to involve people in Group in private relations. You know the rules. Really!"

"Ask Sam who involved who."

"Sam?"

Sam took off his tie and rolled it in a ball, saying, "Well, I . . . had a cup of coffee, and . . ."

"Oh, Leana, come off it," Melissa interrupted, her pale cheeks glistening now. "There isn't a creature that wears pants whom you don't take to bed. And then do a number on. Fred, Arthur, Alex, Sam, whoever. When are you going to face the plain, disturbing facts and go on from there?"

"Yes, dear, it does look as if —"

Leana's fierce tone was trimmed by resignation. "Do you all think it's easy, being me? Looking like me? Having had a father who loved me the way he did and then suddenly abandoned me?" She was near tears.

"Died, Leana. Died," corrected the doctor. "It's not quite the same thing."

"What's the difference?" She bit her lip and fingered the edge of her shawl. "Please . . . you don't know what it's like. He was the only worthwhile thing in my life."

"But it's been almost eleven years, Leana. *Eleven.*"

"So what? So goddamned what? He didn't care that I was big and awkward. Or had big breasts at age fourteen. Or — He loved me, that's what counted. And *forgave* me when I did something wrong." She looked up now, hurt. "Not like you characters. Always on top of me. Always on my back. For any little fucking thing. Always making me feel . . . ashamed. Awkward. Hugely awkward."

"But Leana, we're *with* you in this!"

"Yes, of course, dear. We're all in the same boat."

She looked up at them, at the doctor. "And you?"

"What do *you* think?"

"I . . . I think that deep down, you dislike me."

"Why?"

"Because . . . 'cause . . ." She shrugged.

"Because I wouldn't sleep with you?"

She rolled her neck. "Oh, I don't know. I don't know why."

"I *don't* dislike you, Leana. On the contrary, the more I know you, the more respect I have for your full potential."

She looked up at the doctor, her eyes widening. "Really?"

"Really."

"If only I could believe that, Dr. Hardie."

"Do you think Doctor lies?" asked Robert.

She turned quickly, changing in mood too. "Everybody lies, dodo. Even me to you."

Shaken, Robert retreated.

Leon spoke up. "In other words, your *perception* is that everyone lies."

"Even Doctor here, with his lousy, phony omnipotence. If he's from the Midwest, why does he try to sound as if he's from the English Midlands?"

Dr. Hardie, holding two fingers in the air like candles in the darkness, interjected, "Leana, do we really need a defensive posture for every inquiry or remark? You're stronger than that, I believe."

"Doctor is right, Leana. You really are awfully defensive, you know. If —"

"Oh, Bobby, leave it alone." She patted his thigh nonchalantly, without looking at him.

"And you can't insult me anymore," Robert cried, grabbing her hand. "I won't permit it!"

"Good for you, Robert," Melissa said admiringly.

"Yes," echoed Mrs. Mullins. "Stand up to her."

Leana looked at the furious yet fearful young man, now rising from his seat. "Yes, stand up to me, Bobby." She smiled fully, and seductively ran one finger down his thigh. "I want that, too."

Getting half-erect, Robert turned away in shame and began shaking.

"Scream, Bobby — go ahead, do it," encouraged Melissa, rising from her chair in excitement. "Scream for all of us, Bobby. Go ahead." She was now standing in the middle, eager. "*Do it.*"

And Robert, in painful turmoil, began whimpering. Slowly he allowed himself to groan, and finally he got down on his knees and began to yell. It was not a scream but a yell for help, the cry of an animal in trouble calling for aid, a controlled, long howl.

Melissa approached closer, leaned toward Robert, and said, softly but clearly, "Go deeper. Get hard; show her the insult; show us how to do it, how much it hurts, Bobby. *Go ahead.*" Passionate.

His yell reached somewhere else, new not so much in decibels
as in direction, in source, and as Robert soared out into this loud,
wild territory, Mrs. Mullins came over and tapped Melissa. The
girl came out of her rapt excitement and looked around, embarrassed. By this time Robert was curled into a fetal position and
wound deeply into his scream of lament, pain, confusion, a shriek
of torture too, and as the sound echoed around the room, the
piercing squeaky distortion seemed to invade everyone's pores.
Miriam wanted to shut the young man up, put him out of his
misery, but the doctor, standing with the others, puffed on his
cigar and let the screaming go on, and on, and on. Vera grabbed
Miriam's wrist in excitement. Miriam couldn't take it any longer,
but she was held in her seat by Vera.

Finally, after three or four minutes (which seemed like four
hours), the doctor softly uttered an order and the clients went to
Robert and held him and hugged him, and kissed him too. Melissa
sat on the floor looking straight ahead, her face flushed.

In the crepuscular light, the group looked like characters in a
dream play . . . And gradually a scene of her own returned to
Miriam: *Andrei's Cambridge apartment, which was a copy of his
flat in Budapest, he had explained with his pleasureless smile. Old
gilt-framed pictures hung on the walls; thick damask covered the
tables; an embroidered velvet garment with wide sleeves ("a Roman
Catholic dalmatic, my dear, worn by one of our bishops") hung
over his bed; family photos stood on a highboy. He had a 1920s
davenport covered with cheap brocade, eliminated all natural light
with thick drapes, and had placed a huge wall mirror behind a
ballet bar. The place was a bizarre combination of rococo stuffiness
and European decadence. He lectured her on the innocence of
Americans: "What you don't know and won't face about the world
will destroy the world, not you, and that is your evil genius. Here,
sitting in the lap of luxury, how can you believe or understand
tales of fingernails ripped out, testes sliced open, eyes soldered
closed, daughters made to despise you and betray you? These are
fables for you — modern fairy tales from Grimm, you understand?
Personally, I adore your country — and despise it, secretly, because of your supreme, vulgar innocence. Now come and do as I
ask, and stop being the silly schoolgirl, please." And Miriam, mes-*

merized by the oppressive surroundings, the Liszt rhapsodies, the wild talk, the whisky, the candlelight, the eccentric power of the man, had given in. Dressed in the mannish suit he had handed her, complete with brimmed hat, she had tied him up to a chair — thinking of a children's game she had played at age eleven — and lowered herself to him, baring her breast for him to suck, which he did greedily; and after an eternity of teasing gratification, she had loosened the ropes so that he could kneel across her (at his direction) and be spanked properly, first on his black briefs and then on naked buttocks, until he moved her on to applying the short cat-o'-nine-tails methodically, surely. A Let's Pretend, a charade, she consoled herself; nothing more. Slowly, yes, she had become his impresario of power and magic, enveloped in her own erotic haze, tremendously excited and frightened too. And when he had begun to moan aloud, it had taken her a few minutes to realize she had better turn up the phonograph, to protect them from nervous neighbors in the fashionable old house. Oh yes: his sexual groaning, like some animal in heat, had been a siren to her, like a coyote's call, bewildering her further, exciting her; and it had been no surprise when he asked permission to put his head beneath her skirt and continue his slavish worship there. Yes yes yes she had gone ahead with it, allowed it, pleasured in it, while he had pursued her front and then back with a dog's zeal, turning her around and turning her imagination and senses around, spinning the scene into something deeply strange and dangerously adventurous and darkly memorable, like some childhood trauma . . . Afterward, in Brigham's in Central Square, she had ordered a dish of ice cream and studied a photo from Walker Evans's collection, "Cary Ross's Bedroom, New York 1937," trying to come down into the light and space. She reveled in the normalcy of the photo's single iron beds, tightly made, with puffy pillows, separated by a night table and a gooseneck lamp; there were two Cubist pictures on the walls. She had studied that photo, looking up every now and then to make sure no one was staring at her, knowing, until she had finally heard the waitress or someone asking if she didn't want to stand up.

"He's asking if you would like to come up." Vera nudged her.

She jumped, stunned. Darling Vera, his provocateur.

Heart trembling, she shook her head. Why was it so damn dark down here?

The little man called to her, and she shook her head.

But he came down and took her hand, and she felt caught, and powerless, and she could hardly believe she was being drawn up onto the stage. Was this real or imagined, projected?

Stunned, she saw herself sitting stiffly on a straight-backed chair. Quietly frightened, with this fellow kneeling in front of her. Why were men kneeling before her these days?

"Come now, tell us a little about your life. Who are you, Miriam? A photographer, I understand. In other words" — he smiled, a few beads of perspiration on his narrow forehead — "*a professional voyeur*. How do you cope with this problem? Tell us. And why are your hands so cold?"

The fraud was amazing, wasn't he? He had *read* her somehow, had penetrated her consciousness! But she dared not speak!

"Come now, surely you've let the camera down at times, and entered into real life. Tell us about a recent incident, dear lady. Let it *flow* from you. *Give us* something, why don't you? It'll relax you, I assure you."

She sat transfixed, caught between feverish memory and fierce father-confessor, Budapest set and Cambridge stage, disturbed Hungarian and cunning Midwesterner. Oh yes, she did want to talk about the dark affair, her tight fears, but not with him, not in any public —

"Leave her alone, you runt." Blond Leana intervened, placing a hand on Miriam's shoulder. "Pick on one of your own soldiers, General Nappy."

Dr. Hardie raised himself and took Leana's arm with force.

And Miriam was released from the hypnotic spell, from the fantastic transitions and transpositions of site and feeling, and she breathed deeply, seeking fresh air. Quietly she sneaked from the stage at the side, in the shifting darkness. Oh, she had been taken somewhere, she sensed — first by memory, then by theater; and she knew the folly of her earlier arrogance, and something of the power of this contemporary palace of dreams, night confessions, weird cures. Especially when people were vulnerable, wanting, haunted.

Vera asked if she was okay, and Miriam gave out a breezy yes, admiring her own ventriloquist power. She begged off staying around for the socializing, and made her way out of the theater and down a long hallway to the nearest exit. On the walls were framed pictures of exotic birds with huge beaks and vivid plumage — a tropical aviary that accompanied you all the way out.

Outside, the trees, lawns, and slight wind all consoled her, and she headed for her car like a quarterhorse cooling down after a race. Thought what a native line of descent this was, from Cotton Mather to Dr. Hardie.

"Hey, you really *move* when you get a mind to," Vera was saying, catching up. "You never got a chance to see Doctor's Japanese waterfalls — his hydrotherapy room."

In the car Vera prattled on, and Miriam tried to recover, understand. Would she always be traveling back to private corridors of dalliance? Or just at appropriate moments, when self-chastisement seemed like absolution? And was it that bad out there — were *so many* filled with confusion and pain?

"Did he really have you going? Or did you have yourself going?"

Miriam looked over at her mercurial friend, smoking, brushing hair from her forehead. She asked, "Why'd you have him pick on me?"

Vera smiled strangely. "He has *powers,* doesn't he?" Meaning, I wanted you to see him up close?

"Maybe so," Miriam granted, humbled by her own demons. The risky life of being out there on her own, deep-sea fishing in the choppy waters of modern life, hit home. Haunted her. Oh, it was safer by far to stay put on the shores of regular life, ordered by domestic boundaries and made solid by normal rituals and rewards. So what if passion died, love grew enervated and subtly changed, the immediacy of life faded? A grisaille of peace, exchanged for Pollack splashes of energy and impulse . . . She caught herself, not really enamored of that life anymore either. Chastened again. Now, she pursued her own dividing line more carefully than she had before. And what was the big deal, after all — she had been involved in some sort of dark parable of Budapest shadows folded within a Cambridge bazaar. But here she was, out free, flying; right? To be chastened now and then was a small price to pay for those harrowing memories, Byzantine moments, she thought, wishing for more pep in her car! And who knows, maybe her intense imagination had overheated the situation anyway?

"His healing powers are *fan*-tastic," marveled Vera, lighting up again, off to herself, but also signaling to Miriam.

Was Vera also saying that the doctor had powers elsewhere too — like in bed? Did she now want to be asked about that? Miriam thought so, and asked.

Vera replied with a sidelong glance and a sly smile. She exhaled slowly, exuded secret victory.

We love ourselves every chance we get, Miriam knew. And oh, we've learned so well in these times how to squeeze the last ounce of self-love out of every sentence, every situation! It is our greatest art, perhaps. She let Vera's victory and mystery ride, and concentrated on the road, the river, thinking how she'd like to look at the stars tonight, maybe, and see whether she could sight a new constellation. Or maybe look again at those eerie photographs of Andrei and herself, which she had hidden away during these past months of kibbutz peace and orderly pleasures.

"By the way," Miriam put in, recalling their high school game, "how do you read me in this battered Valiant?"

"In disguise," Vera chirped scientifically. "In total disguise."

4

WHERE and when does an affair start, she wondered, wandering in the brisk November winds with her camera, starting out on the streets by the river in Cambridgeport. Was it to be dated from the actual meeting of bodies, or from earlier stirrings of feeling? Was it to be traced back yet further, to the point of near-invisibility, in which attractions come from some deep gene affinity? Can the flavor of a man be like the taste of a madeleine, serving to spur moments of specialness that slowly accumulate into a time of transcendence? Was it truthful, then, or childishly fictitious, to cite that day or this room in the assessment of beginnings? Furthermore, was the abstract question relevant unless she considered the angle of sensibility revealed in this hour of her life? Hardly. For what signified an affair at forty-two may not have constituted one five years ago. Surely, with the new blocks of experience that made up her continuing bridge of reality (between illusion and projection) situations too deserved new nouns, new names, new interpretations. So the present affair was quite another matter from romances of a younger age.

The peripatetic student snapped a dozen photographs in black and white of dilapidated buildings set alongside new townhouses on Western Avenue. How telling, this contrast, she thought; and how telling, too, her rarefied reflections about a very earthy reality.

Quite another matter too, this present affair with Dr. Wallace Scott Beaumont, from the ongoing romance with her dear Rafi.

For Dr. Beaumont had an altogether different feel and tone, evoked a different emotion and situation, from her Israeli man. This Christian gentleman was indeed both a Christian and a gentleman, a courtly fellow. Dr. B. held doors and chairs, lit cigarettes, dressed formally, accompanied single damsels at night; he was a sort of Green Knight with a scalpel for a sword, a white Seville for a horse. Though a surgeon for some twenty-five years, he remained more concerned with ethical decency than capital gains, cared more for patients than tax shelters. Not partisan in politics, his vote went to any civilized Democrat or Republican who supported land and animal conservation, clean water and clean air. He was a Sierra Club member, an avid Appalachian hiker, but an unsentimental creature about humans — "So you think I'm a cowboy, eh? You should meet a few of the real ones. As a rule, they're about the lowest breed around. At least, they were when I was growing up." Loyalty to friends, including fidelity in marriage, was a cardinal value. Until Miriam came along "to disturb that value and me," he confided, disconcerted.

The Western knight fitted into her life just as he fitted into her body: easily, just like that, without either of them expecting or particularly wanting it. Precisely because they were both committed seriously to others and therefore believed that, if anything, their affair was a simple, passing thing, an attraction lasting as long as the lighting of a match, they did not think about — let alone guard against — deeper emotions. Too bad. For very soon they had grown attached, without quite knowing or acknowledging it. Stealthily blunt passion became subtle caring, like summer moving into autumn, splendid autumn. By mid-November they were meeting regularly, furtively, for dinner or a movie, or yes, a basketball game, and then frequently they took a hotel room, and later returned to their separate lives without the strain of trying to fit the other in. He was officially married, of course, and Miriam was seriously involved, unofficially married; and certainly she did not wish to bring the doctor into her apartment, for the kids' sake and hers. Consequently, the hotel room, or on occasion the country inn — a lovely one in Sudbury, another in Manchester-by-the-Sea — became their rendezvous point, a turf that disturbed them much less than any home territory might have. Each seemed relieved to know that there was not the slightest chance of his or her breaking away from a settled, routine life; in other words, each's permanent home and attachment was not threatened but remained intact and safe; they firmly believed this.

He had been faithful, the doctor claimed, and this transgression, his first in thirty years of marriage, frightened him as much as it flattered her. "My father was a womanizer," he explained, sipping espresso in a small, anonymous restaurant on the South Shore, "and when I kept my mother company late into the night, I swore that above all else, I wouldn't follow in his footsteps." His long pale face and long strong hands were already memories of beauty to her as she sat there; was that embossed wallpaper the kind they used in brothels? she wondered. "And I didn't," he continued. "Until now, I suppose."

"Oh, I wouldn't call this womanizing exactly." She half laughed. "Miriamizing, maybe."

Reluctantly, then, against his will and obliquely, as it were, he was drawn to her, grew closer to her. And his ambivalence or reluctance seemed to resolve itself, she felt, in the sensual act, where the gentlemanly doctor, her "parfit knight," traded in that cool, courtly being for a hungrier self who occasionally hurt her with his unleashed urges.

"I get carried away sometimes — stop me when I'm hurting you," he offered.

"You mean stop you when it stops being pleasurable; I will."

He played back the sentence to make sure he understood, focusing her with those slate-blue eyes which, in passion, seemed to change to sapphire.

For her, it was interesting how pure their lovemaking was despite its illicitness and despite its eccentric turns and idiosyncratic impulses. Unlike the early, problematic stages with Rafi, these scenes were immediately right in their lust, in mutual desire, in the ease of kneeling and the abandon of turning about, in the natural waiting for the other to come before coming oneself. Yet this activity of the body seemed in the service of something else; a fine vehicle, perhaps, pursuing a finer condition, whatever its name. Though Miriam knew, and the doctor came to know too, that the body was fine enough, was condition and vehicle enough.

"I don't know if it's you or if it's . . . doing this for the first time, but it's just more exciting, and beyond what I knew about or imagined," he confessed one night, holding her in his arms. And she, who long ago had given up on the ability of spoken words to convey the deep feelings, retorted, "It's the Celtics. You're simply becoming hooked. A fan."

Another thing she noticed during those warming months of early winter, when November brought this early music to her spirit, was the foreign element at work — a paradoxical element that made her soul leap with new feeling and her body speed with sensuality. She began to see that it was his native quality, his pure Americanness, that intrigued her. So much of him was truly foreign to her: the Lutheran background, the Montana prairie upbringing, the coming of age at "awesome" Harvard (on a hockey scholarship), the suburban marriage, the straightforward personality (Stan's had been Bronx Dostoievskian). All this made her feel her strangeness and her Jewishness, as well as (paradoxically) her American grain, more. She sensed, because of this native, how much she liked the natives, and at the same time how much she loved her Jews. Early winter in Cambridge with Dr. Beaumont was emphasizing, then, by way of contrast, another attraction of kibbutz summers — which she had thought were attractive because of Rafi alone. Wrong. Her attachment went beyond the man, to the Jews and the country they had created. The affair with the Gentile doctor was making explicit her fondness for her own quirky tribe.

Rafi wrote her about once a week, and she read his letters with fondness and yearning and . . . something like guilt? Her new situation did not fundamentally interfere with her feelings for Rafi. Yes, it provided unease, a measure of guilt. But she was not married now, she emphasized to herself, and neither Rafi nor Miriam asked the other what went on in their absences. Each trusted the other to his or her discretion, privacy, what-have-you, encouraging independence, even dignity. Not that she assumed or even thought that Rafi had other women; it was rather that she sought to put no pressure on him whatsoever, subtle or obvious. Pressure, obligation, guilt — these were not the sorts of ropes to hold them together, she had promised. For such ropes, such bondage, had sapped energy and damaged emotion in her married life. So how he acted when he was away from her was his, and only his, business. Respect seemed cleaner that way. If it turned out that he had a mistress in, say, Beersheba, she hoped only her vanity would be pricked, not her ego injured. Whereas if he worked for the Israeli secret service and kept *that* secret from her, she'd feel deep resentment.

His letters were written in small, clear English and filled with cool, ironic touches about this major mishap at the site or that comic incident at the kibbutz. There was always a dig or two at the "little Polish terrorist" who was ruining the country and Zionism with his lunatic legalisms and "Biblical politics": "I'm getting the feeling like I'm in an occupied country with these new fanatics around." In fact, in the last few months Rafi had taken part in several Peace Now demonstrations in Kiryat Arba, the Gush Emunim settlement outside Hebron — something he had never done before. At the end of each letter was a countdown to their March meeting, when she'd have to "go straight again," and "give up her lovers." Humorous, until recently.

March and Rafi. What then, adventurous friend? she asked herself one evening, getting ready to see the rejuvenated Celtics with Dr. Beaumont.

Nowadays, she understood, her relationships sustained her in a manner wholly different from what she had managed in her thirties. During those days of frenzied release from the lengthy prison sentence of her marriage, with fellows like Jamie, Adrien Cuthbert III, Harry, she had been something like a little girl brought into a candy store after four years in the Gulag. Days and nights of trying out this man, that passion, this technique. And, why shouldn't she have been attracted and attached to each and every new sweet? Those men had uplifted her, restored her body as well as her confidence, created a mirror for her well-being. If others had looked upon her then as wild or whorish, so be it; it was difficult enough figuring oneself out, acting with wisdom in the midst of crisis, without having to stop to think of her image to others. And if it were true that she had been vulgar and even immoral then, so what? After thirty-four years of playing the Good Girl, with all of her careful rules, she had deserved a year's furlough, surely. If good Catholics sinned, so a good secular Jewess could sin too. Besides, sin was not without its intrinsic interest and revelation — something that perhaps could not be said of saintliness. Now in her life, however, she was poised at the start of a different stage, poised between the frenzy of those liberated years and the slow motion of old age. On a high plateau, say, where energy formed its own value if not morality. For now she felt, along with her sanity, energy (not frenzy) flowing through her, and she felt this flow as a force against the creeping inertia of aging and dying (masked perhaps as complacency).

Walking, photographing, and reflecting suited her during these windy days of November; the teaching at MIT she did by instinct and repetition. (The kids didn't get interesting until later in the year, after they had mastered some basic technique.) When you were going good, she reasoned, the changeableness of New England weather in early winter was more delight than burden.

Not that she enjoyed the idea of seeing a married man. On the contrary, this bothered her, when she thought about it that way. So she tried not to think about it, and mostly succeeded. A cop-out from moral choice? Perhaps. But moral choice was not the same as moral purity, which in adulthood frequently exacted too high a price. Truth was, she had never before "seen" a married man and didn't quite know what to make of it. God, how one almost forgot one's own life! What about her ruddy-faced English friend of eight years ago, whom she met at the fiction section in a Brattle Street bookstore? She was in such dire need then, and Colin too, that his ill wife was almost an excuse for intimacy. Now: was it her responsibility or the doctor's? But who could consider such principles or problems in the peachy air of his company? "My Doctor J.," she playfully called her Doctor B. when his height and stride would dissolve all things Serious and Heavy.

This delicious air had never been more apparent than in their third or fourth meeting, after they had become a couple. He managed to take the afternoon off and they spent it in the countryside, walking by the Sudbury River and enjoying trout for lunch at a local inn before going up to their wallpapered dormer room. There he said to her, "You look exhausted. Why don't I draw you a warm bath?" Miriam, dazed by the suggestion, assented. Slowly she got undressed, feeling most odd, little-girlish, as she entered the old claw-footed porcelain bathtub, with this strange man in attendance. The water was hot and splendid as she lay there. Then he proceeded to help her bathe — like a Japanese attendant, she imagined. He rolled up his sleeves and began with her legs, using a washcloth and soap, going up and down the inside and then the outside of each leg, slowly and surely, climaxing with a full massage of her feet. This last laid her completely at ease, in his hands, and she was only half-conscious for the rest. He washed her back gradually, up and down, side to side, making it feel broad and wide and toned. Next he did her chest, washing her breasts in a motion that made her feel too gorgeous and excited, which he sensed; he eased up and moved on to her sides and belly, washed in circles, and finally her pubic area, which he cleaned firmly, wonderfully. By the time he was done she hardly knew where or what she was; the white bathroom had become a blurry piece of heaven, and she an angel anointed.

The experience went on. Letting the water run out, he lifted her up and out and began to dry her thoroughly while she stood on the bathmat amid swirls of steam and heat. He proceeded to towel her down with the same care and slowness with which he had washed her. Using the thick bath towel with a brisk tenderness, he covered each slope and curve, bone and breast, like a skier discovering and exploring a terrain. Was it there, in the drying, or earlier, in the bath itself, she wondered later, that the memory from childhood rose, of how her father had lifted her out of her bath and dried her down — she a little bit of a thing, maybe four or five years old — in a ritual of love adored by each? He too had had long hands and a firm grip, and while he dried her they had talked baseball or planned trips. This habit was later aborted by her stepmother, who, in one of her perennial fits of jealousy accused Miriam's father of being obscene with his daughter, said it was "going to ruin her," and demanded that he cease. The loss of that bath ritual a few times a week had torn at Miriam, made her hate that woman; she lay on her pillow later and swore vengeance. And though she didn't know the word *obscene,* she'd always remembered it and later learned it well; it was the first "big" word she learned, after *dirigible.*

The adult experience now in the country bathroom brought

back an indescribable sweetness, a feeling of fatherly love so vivid and exquisite that she would retain its flavor and touch forever. Oh, how secure and perfect she had felt then, as Dad's "little sweet pea pod," feeling indeed like some carefully tended plant under his green thumb, smelling of soapy cleanliness; and that childhood sweetness combined with the present tenderness, crossing the girlish paternity with the adult caring, mingled with and compounded the pleasure, so that standing there, she was not standing there, she was little and green and pea-poddish, a shoot in bloom rubbed and scented by this new guardian of her health.

This was The Bath.

Afterward, lying in bed and observing the slant of late-afternoon light through the narrow window, she stayed still and quiet, and the doctor, with perfectly tuned instinct, said nothing himself but read in a big wing chair, not breaking her reverie with sensual touch or intruding with talk. And she lay there with her father's smell and Dr. B.'s smell joining that of Johnson's Baby Shampoo, and she felt hooked by the heroin of childhood memory.

Wasn't this small infidelity, she wondered, worth that large fidelity? The Bath would stay with her, would linger and caress, and whatever doubts or inhibitions she may have had, she shed because of its wonders. A different sort of healing, perhaps, from what that other doctor had prescribed.

So the winter proceeded, cold and windy on the outside but a cunning camouflage for the summery feelings flowing within, feelings rich with memory and green with surprise.

Besides her doctor she had her teaching and her pictures. At MIT she worked three days a week at her workshop and history of photography classes. In the latter she had a fine time showing the work of her favorite photographers — Atget, Kertész, Bravo, Evans, Lange, Steichen, the Westons, Cartier-Bresson, Man Ray, White, Siskind — and talking about composition, exposure, selection, montage, shutter speed, subject matter. Some of her students also took the workshop, where the talent varied greatly; four or five showed promise. She found herself teaching to these talented few, giving assignments that were fit for the best — simple assignments, and therefore the most difficult to execute well: shooting their homes and neighborhoods, family and friends, a loved and familiar landscape. Over and over again they would shoot these same subjects, she explained, until they had achieved a vision of their own of familiar objects. She knew from experience that by term's end, certainly year's end, three or four students would be taking the work seriously, and even seriously approaching accomplishment. And she would feel accomplished too.

For her own work she had her recent summer photographs, contact sheets of desert landscapes and limestone formations, assorted fruits and vegetables. Equally important was the new series of nude portraits of Rafi, for her private collection. Might she supplement that series? she wondered. She pondered that question, and one night when Dr. Beaumont was watching the Celtics leap from the perfect parquet floor to the basket and above, she asked him whether he would pose for her one day. "In the nude," she added casually.

He stared, skeptical and amused, and retorted, "Are you in the pornography business?"

She ran a finger down his long pale cheek and said, "In the photography business. Often that includes bodies. Not unlike what doctors work with, I understand. So, will you pose one day?"

He wagged a forefinger at her. "Mother warned me about your kind. One day, perhaps. Let me get used to the idea, now that I see you're half serious. Though it may take forty years or so."

Oh my straight and good knight, she thought, taking his hand to her lap, you don't know how quickly forty years can fly by, if you're in the right frame of mind. And she drifted to other frames, other rooms, soon to be gotten, she felt. A seduction with the lens which promised challenge, opened vistas — democratic vistas, she played — calling out to Cornbread to make more inside moves!

Meanwhile, other work presented itself, by chance as it were. One evening, rummaging through a cluttered closet, she came across an ancient family album that she had somehow retained. Leafing through it, she discovered a series of old pictures, tinted for effect, that she hadn't seen in years and hardly recalled. Photographs of great-grandparents in East Europe, at the turn of the century and before. Those on her mother's side were a family of shtetl merchants, mercenary in the smile, she thought; no wonder

Mother was a saint! Hard lives, hard people. But on Dad's side, something quite different: study and learning. Great-grandfather Scheinowtsky was a rabbi, with full sidecurls and a long beard, and his stern gaze, photographed in Warsaw in the late 1880s, was still alarming today. In the sunken eyes and high cheekbones she saw her own father, his grandson. Was that why Papa had become such a devoted cynic and agnostic, to escape that heritage and gaze? Why Sir Richard Burton and Lewis and Clark meant more to him than Hasidic rabbis? And *Sporting News* more than Torah? The rabbi and his brood of nine looked as if they had just stepped out of the Old Testament, let alone the Old World. No wonder Papa had become strongly assimilated. Yet the gene for scholarship had stayed, she perceived; Jewish learning had been translated into cartography, map collecting, travel history. What you did to escape your shape and origin, Papa, and how you never did, after all; just modified things a bit. Darwin and Mendel were smarter than Moses — and you, Daddy.

Was *she* still trying to escape somehow? (Escaping and returning; sure.) And what about Jon's petition for his bar mitzvah — should she remind him of it? She found out he could, after all, go through with the ceremony at any time, but since he had left off asking, she kept still. Smart? Or stupid? Well, one.

But the album had inspired her, and the next afternoon, a gray Wednesday in December, she headed toward Inman Square by way of Broadway. At Tremont Street she turned and checked the address. A narrow side street with peeling two- and three-deckers, leaning, shabby, and abject. In the middle of the street she almost passed by what she was looking for. Behind an old black iron gate stood a large, beat-up building like a rotting battleship, the brick fading and chipping, graffiti scrawled everywhere; there were two barely rubbed out swastikas. Foolish kids, dabbling with the gravest symbols. The name Beth Shalom Synagogue was half effaced; the Star of David was missing two points. What did she want? She went through the open gate, tried the wooden front door, and to her surprise found it open. Walked in, feeling most strange. The last "synagogue" she had been in was the handsome all-purpose chapel at Harvard University; this was different. If anything the interior was in worse repair than the outside: wooden pews broken, walls mildewed, ceiling cracked and smoke-stained, two windows boarded up. The disrepair shocked her, and she instinctively took out her camera and recorded it with a half-dozen snaps.

A noise from up beyond the stage frightened her, and she immediately put away her Leica. Waited. Heard a glass tinkling. She walked up the aisle (its carpet torn) still not knowing what exactly she was pursuing.

A short stubby man wearing an old black fedora and a scarf tucked inside his blue serge suit was cleaning up at a long table. Looking up, squinting, he said, *"Nu?"*

Uncertain, glad she had hidden her camera, she told him her name.

With his forefinger he tipped up his brim. "What can I do for you?" He had a thick European–Yiddish accent, and a two-day-old stubble on his round cheeks.

Noting the cups and saucers on the table, she said, "A cup of tea?"

He laughed, with little pleasure, revealing yellow teeth. "Will some schnapps do?"

She smiled. "Sure."

He opened a half-filled bottle of brandy and poured two shot glasses, then gave her one. His fingernails were long and dirty. *"L'chaim!"*

"L'chaim." She repeated the toast, sipping.

The man drank his down in one gulp and let it settle, his pallid face coloring just the slightest bit. *"Nu?* You have a son maybe you want bar mitzvahed, lady?"

Well, yes, she did in a way; well, not really. But it was beside the point. She wondered aloud, "Where are you from?"

"From?" He stared at her as if she were asking him the mystery of the universe. *"From?"* This time, as if it were the most trivial question in the world. He shrugged his shoulders, hidden within the oversized secondhand suit. He made a face and began to clean the glasses with a dish towel, saying, "You don't mind, Missus, while we talk?" When she shook her head, he repeated, "From?" When from? Now, you mean, or then?"

"No, originally, I mean."

"O-rig-i-nally," he said in sing-song, making another face. What was this woman up to, talking to a lowly shammes? He shrugged again, scratched his ear, wiped his drinking glasses. Looked at her, to check . . . yes, she was still interested. Then, as if narrating a trip to the supermarket where he had had some difficulties at the checkout counter, he told his story — a story of hiding out in Russia, in holes in the ground, during the early years of World War II; of being turned in by peasants and sent to a concentration camp; of a crazy, unreal escape and of wandering and hiding for a year or more in Yugoslavia; of finally achieving refugee status in Trieste after the war; of a marriage there and of waiting in a refugee camp for a year; of eventually sneaking into America as an illegal immigrant. Here he had raised three children, and thanks to the rebbe they had all gotten an education. He held up two fingers, like showing gold: "Two through college."

Strangely, in the middle of his talk she snapped his picture, then took another as he finished. These were photos for herself; she wanted to have his face, recorded during the telling. And it didn't frighten him at all, only made him laugh sheepishly and point at her for some reason. This strange lady. Ridiculous. And she, who didn't quite know what she was doing either, believed the same thing.

Because of this shammes, this Viktor Shlonsky, she pushed her impulse into a working idea and grew quietly excited. Should she write the kibbutz now and tell them that yes, she would have a show for them next fall?

She asked Viktor when the rabbi would be in, she had a question for him, and he told her to come Friday morning early — or she could call him at home maybe? Miriam took the number.

Raising his eyebrows, the burly man asked, "So what magazine are you filming me for? *Hadassah?*"

She smiled warmly. "Which one do you read?"

He almost laughed for real now, pushing the fedora back on his balding pate. "Read? Who has time for reading? Now and then someone gives me a *Hadassah* or maybe *Time,* and I fall asleep with it."

"Come, show me the synagogue," she said, and he replied, "If you want, why not? Until I close up."

She moseyed about the shabby place, unswept, dingy, unrepaired. On the platform, the wooden tabernacle was chipping, and there was no Torah within.

"We lock it away in the cellar. *Pisher* vandals. Take it out for services only." He shrugged.

She moved over a few steps and asked, "How old is this?"

"What, the menorah?" He walked over and lifted it, turning it about. "*Ver veist?* Ask the rebbe; he'll know."

Nodding, she set it down on the misshapen wooden table and took several close-ups of it.

"You think it's important?"

She shrugged. "Probably not. Just — a reminder?"

He removed his hat, combed the sides of his hair with a long, half-toothless comb, then replaced the fedora.

Moved by this man, she said, "Nice meeting you, and thank you."

"For nothing," he returned.

"Maybe I'll see you again."

"Why not? I'm always here, God willing."

She turned to go.

"You want to leave a card, maybe? For the rebbe?"

Yes, she should have cards printed up, like all the formal pip-squeaks of the world. "I'll come back," she said and waved.

She left the broken-down synagogue brimming with feeling for Shlonsky and for her project. She couldn't wait to get home and take notes on her new, surprising direction. Looking back, she saw the synagogue as a Negev ruin of sorts, a relic in the middle of modern Cambridge.

That night after dinner, when Rosie was asleep and Jon was doing homework, she jotted down notes in her small spiral note-book to accompany her photos of Viktor, the synagogue, the men-orah. From nude males to discarded Jews; no wonder you're difficult to keep up with.

While she was putting on water for tea, the telephone rang.

"Just checking in," said the doctor's familiar mellow voice, "to see if you're well."

"Just dandy, actually. Alive with a new project."

"What is it?"

"I'll tell you when I see you. Or not."

"I didn't know adults got excited by their work."

"They don't. I do."

"I see. I'm slightly envious."

"Good."

"Next Thursday at the Public Garden, about four-thirty. Is that okay?"

She checked it mentally. "Sounds fine. Even super."

"You're high — don't lose the excitement by then."

"I'll try not to. Who knows, maybe I'll even show you some photos. A test run."

A pause.

"I missed you today. Terribly. Just before operating."

She didn't know what to say. "Did the patient live?"

"Yes."

"Then you didn't miss me enough. See you next week, Montana."

He laughed, a laugh so different from the hollow, pleasureless laugh of Viktor Shlonsky. "Looking forward to it. Goodnight."

"Goodnight, friend. Thanks."

She hung up, still feeling excited. That voice, which always cheered her, now slid her into momentary fantasy . . . The screaming kettle took her back to her tea, and she brought a pot and mug back to the dining-room table and her work. Where was it all heading? Was the realism too disturbing? She tried to define what she meant by that —

The telephone rang again.

She got up. Dr. B.? Or Rafi, long distance from the kibbutz? She picked it up, excited by her intuition. "Hi!" she called out loudly, then said her few words of Hebrew greeting: "*Manashe mah?*"

"Hi yourself, baby. But why so loud?"

She sucked in her breath. The voice was male, unfamiliar, nearby. She fought to find her natural voice. "Who is this?"

"Oh, you know, baby."

She tried to recall the husky voice. "No, who?"

"Aw, come on. You saw me just the other day."

A joke? A bad one? Her heart beat rapidly.

"Who —"

"Sssh. I'm hot for you, honey. Really hot. And I'm gonna get you, *Miss* Miriam."

The name made her dizzy, made her almost fall over. With a slow, deliberate motion, she laid the receiver back on the hook and sat down on a chair, stunned. She hugged herself, pulling her sweater close.

The telephone rang again. Once, twice, three times.

Without quite knowing what she was doing, she lifted it up and said, controlling her voice, "Look, why don't you cut this out? Do I have to go through the motions of calling the police, having the number changed, the whole route?"

"Ssshh, cool your engines. I'm in this for keeps, darlin'. I keep an eye on you, I mean I *look* at you, sister, and I *want* you. Get it? Change your number, change your address — no sweat; I'm right there with you. You're a *fine* fox, and I'm gonna feel your fur. So you just stay cool, ya hear? And wait . . . I'll be in touch."

Click.

She held the receiver until it began to buzz. Perspiration formed on her forehead. She sat there, tears coming to her yes, her heart thumping. Slowly she dropped the receiver, but left it off the hook.

At home, safe, working . . . and hunted down! Not fair!

For three or four minutes she sat that way, in a state of shock. The room, so solid and private a minute ago, was now a liquid glass box, wavering and transparent.

Did men ever go through this? she wondered, smoking.

Finally she moved: stood up, put on a light in her bedroom, checked Rosie, fast asleep, and then Jon, reading in bed. "You all right?" she asked, putting on her calmest face. Annoyed, he answered, "Huh? What's with you?" She nodded and left. Next, checked the locks downstairs and at the front door. Decided to install a new warning system downstairs; maybe the police could advise? Seventy-five bucks is cheap for security, right? Security, hah. Felt safer over there where the PLO used Katyushas. She closed the burlap curtains in the living room for the first time in five years. Returned to her tea, found it cold, decided to reheat it in a saucepan. The dirty bastard.

She wished she could call Scotty Beaumont; but she couldn't, not at home.

Harry?

The police first. Silly, but necessary. Even with her old record as a crazy person.

She dialed the emergency number, and the policeman on duty said it would probably be better to report the call in person the next day at the station, but he'd take the information anyway. She gave it as well as she could. "Negro or Caucasian, could you tell?" Could she? She thought it was a black man's voice, was almost sure; but either you were sure or you weren't. She explained her ambivalence, and Sergeant Holmes said okay, if the guy called again tonight, let them know. Sure, she understood. What could they do? "Tell you what, we'll send a cruiser by once every hour or so for the next few hours. Just in case. How's that, Miss, huh?" She thanked the sergeant and said that would be helpful.

Afraid, in her own living room. Should she call Rafi, seven hours ahead in time? Even if he was there, she'd never reach him at the kibbutz.

Harry?

Yes.

Alone with the kids in her apartment and terrorized this way. Wild, unreal. She was a civilian tossed into the front line of battle without arms or training. She scratched like a cat at the cracked leather of her chair, afraid like a little girl. Maybe buy a gun and learn to shoot, to protect the kids at least?

She poured a glass of sherry and put on the radio and turned to an all-night talk show. Outside, the world buzzed on. The topics ranged from food carcinogens to the Russian menace, and she listened to the human voices prattling on like a lifesaver of normality. Should she dial WBZ for help?

After ten minutes of this game, she telephoned Harry.

As usual, he was practical and comforting. Yes, she had her name in the telephone book under "M. Scheinman." Yes, it was possible for someone to see her address. "But how did he get the 'Miriam' if he's a stranger? And I know I didn't recognize the voice." Suppressing her tears as she went into the details.

"Slow down," he said, calming her. "Look, it would be easy enough to get your first name if he knew your address. From MIT maybe, or a show somewhere. Another thing — with a handkerchief over his mouth, he could disguise his voice easily. And you wouldn't recognize it. I'll try it on you sometime."

"Warn me first, okay?"

"That's better. Look, do you want me to come over, stay there tonight? It's easy."

Yes, she wanted that badly, badly! "Oh, it's . . . unnecessary. Thanks. I mean, I'll make do. But it's . . . good to hear you, and if anything else happens, can I call you? I mean, even if it's quite late?"

"Just ring, and I'll be there in a few minutes. Don't hesitate, okay?"

"Okay." She waited, had no more to say. "Thanks."

"No problem. Remember, I'm here, and in a few minutes I can be there."

She hung up, loving him. Took the phone off the hook. Drank her tea. Tried to read about the family of Sassoons. How would Flora have handled this? She'd have had her two servants take charge, that's how. Next Miriam leafed through photos of Jerusalem, starting with the Ottoman Empire and the British Mandate. A series of cozy neighborhoods, upon which the modern city was built in the last fifty years, alive with flowers, trees, tasteful stone houses. She longed to be there now, in German Colony say, or in her kibbutz room, reading quietly. Bored to death was preferable to stabbed to death.

Near midnight she tried sleeping, but during the first half hour she rose up at the slightest noise — a rattling window, a slamming door, mysterious sounds. She had left two lights on, and also the radio, a childhood habit. Nerves tossed and turned her. The hours passed like long days, and it was only when the first cracks of dawn appeared that she drifted off to sleep. Soon enough, however, the alarm clock beeped her awake to feed the kids and get them off to school. But the real alarm was over, temporarily at least. Exhausted, she was nevertheless grateful.

At ten the police indeed showed up — police salaries at issue recently with the City Council — a black Mutt and a white Jeff, and routinely they jotted down the information. In the midst of the interview, Jeff wondered whether Miriam had cuticle scissors he could use on a bad hangnail. She fixed him with a look and asked what the chances were of discovering the fellow. Mutt told her not to expect too much in the way of results. "But," he re-assured her almost eagerly, "if any action starts, that's another matter." Wasn't that a bit late, she wondered privately, and what kind of "action" did they mean? Their useless visit shook her. However, she had to rush to make an eleven o'clock class, and took off.

Racing through the huge, cavernous corridors of Building 1074, she glanced over her shoulder to see if she could spot anyone suspicious. Or following her. The halls were busy, and nearly everyone looked suspicious. She made it to class out of breath, five minutes late, and was thankful that the projector was there. She had brought the slides. As she gave her opening remarks, she gazed around at the twenty or so faces; did she have a secret enemy there? The one black student, Stephen Liston, had become a good friend, she thought; should she hire him to figure it out? She turned off the lights and began showing the O'Keefe series of photographs by the young Steiglitz. She half listened to her own fear as she spoke about the virtues of realism and the challenges of the nude, trying to efface it by means of that subtle series of black-and-white portraits of the painter-model. When a student asked about the problems involved in composing a series of photos, a subject that interested her, she could think of nothing to say.

Later, out in the windy, sunny December afternoon, she care-fully glanced around at the bus stop. She felt herself a native now, on the lookout for someone tailing her, either for real or in par-anoid fantasy. On the bus ride home she kept looking about, always with apparent casualness, and she discovered how many people were actually looking at her, wanting to attract her atten-tion. An oval-faced man with spectacles, across the aisle, every now and then lowered his *Globe* to check her out. A Spanish-speaking teenager with a black hat and a hawkish nose stared at her relentlessly while chatting with a friend, and periodically grinned at her. A woman in her thirties, chewing gum and reading a pa-perback novel, eyed her fiercely every time she turned the page. Or so it seemed. Faces of hunger, curiosity, loneliness, desperation; wanting eye contact, wanting a fight, wanting a fuck, wanting what else? Was this *why* they rode the bus — to get a piece of the action they kept hearing about?

And so it went for the next few weeks, wherever she went —

to the Broadway Super Market, to Shea's Cleaners, to the Parthenon Restaurant: on the lookout. One afternoon, for example, leaving the college library, she was sure she had spotted the caller: a husky man in his mid-forties, eyeing her, smoking. And when she looked around suddenly, there he was, staring, under the guise of reading. Furious, afraid, she walked directly to him and asked if he had a light. He gave her one, with a silver lighter, as if he expected this. Smiling and bowing slightly, he said with an accent, "Emil Lustig, iv you pleaze. Vrom Warsaw, vizitor vor a year." Leaning forward conspiratorially, he added, "In A.I. lab." He had a craggy weather-beaten face, now that she saw him up close. "You American woman are zomezing. How *bold* you are. Permit me; are you at freedom for dinner?" Politely she declined; the situation was too crazy for her. "Bad timing, Emil," she said, walking off. Was she on some weird East European kinky list?

At the apartment she brought in a Mr. Garrity, locksmith, who for $172 and change put two special devices on the door. The first was an iron brace that you set against the door and slipped into the lock; the second was an attached siren system. Garrity's array of locks glistened like a jeweler's drawer, and he spoke about them with a jeweler's addiction. ("These Chapmans are the Cadillacs of the business, Marion, they don't come finer!") When she closed the door and locked it for the evening, however, she felt as though she were locking herself *in* for the evening — a prisoner's apartment — as much as locking someone out. When Jon saw it, his face furrowed gravely. "Mom, what's happening? Are you having those old troubles again?" That reference to her breakdown stung! She explained briefly about the "nutty" phone call, and said that this was just temporary protection. To her amazement, this excited him tremendously. "No kiddin'! That's just happened on *Baretta* two weeks ago! Mom, should we call in a private eye, d'ya think?" His face glowed with the news, and he warmed toward his mother, a potential character in a TV series.

Her native innocence showed itself again when she told a few friends about the phone call, and learned that such abuse was almost taken for granted. "Don't worry," consoled Vera with easy wisdom, "if they're serious, they don't bother to call first. It was just a phone freak." Oh. There seemed to be so many different kinds of freaks to live with these days, she reflected; how did you keep tabs on them? And what about those who did not call first?

In the end, what saved her nervous system from overload in these weeks of anxiety — besides the steady companionship of Scott Beaumont — was her work. With her idea alive, she began to sniff around, keeping her mental focus within the lenses of Leica and Rollei and Polaroid. She tried to concentrate on composition, subject matter, printing, steadily on the alert for someone who was staring unnaturally, something that was obstructing her. Lots of false starts and stops — this peculiar smiling clerk; that slim, impassive house painter; a loping, half-dazed hippie — premonitions and figures about which she had never before thought twice. But nothing concrete turned up. She got no more phone calls during these weeks; it was a month of shadows, of work-searching, of worrying about someone peeking in on her privacy. Yet she felt rich too, with pictures, idea, new man. (Oh yes, nothing like the adventure of a new liaison.) Odd congruence; odd month out.

In the background hovered a larger question: What happened when Rafi arrived sometime in early spring? But feeling her energy surge in several different circuits of wanting, she felt solid and secure about any upcoming decision or dilemma. Felt solid within the core of herself; no meltdown here, now. Though perhaps the nerves rang alarms at certain moments, sounding warnings, cautions. She listened.

And it helped that she managed at last — or so soon? — a session of photographing her fine-boned, lanky doctor, as pale and perfect as any long-stemmed white chrysanthemum; he had reluctantly, shyly, surprisingly, accepted her invitation.

The photographic immaculate conception was effected this way. They were lying in bed in a small Newburyport motel, and she had just brought on a delicious fucking by means of stroking his testicles and pressing his anus with her finger, and he said, after recovering, "You know, I think I'm ready to do anything for you, stopping short of the illegal, that you'd ask."

"Be careful," she replied, caressing his smooth-shaven face, "or I might take you up on that."

His blue eyes sparkled. "What good is love if it's not tested?"

She smiled. "Love, or pleasure?"

"Are the two so different?"

"Only too often."

"Love *and* pleasure, then."

She felt the firm chin and wide, bony shoulders. "That sounds lovely. Just like your bold offer. I'll think on it."

"Naturally, no holdups or family breakups or —"

"Oh Beaumont, you're a fine Christian, and I won't betray that, I assure you." His arm was around her waist and her hand was upon his face; she felt their naked bodies as one entwined nude, and immediately joined her ongoing project to his proposition, making those two into one also.

And so later, over coffee and rolls, she made her proposal, in earnest, and he held his coffee cup aloft, flabbergasted. Said: "Are you really serious? Is this usual fare for your friends?" Paused, sipped, said: "I didn't think you'd take me up so swiftly, or make it so difficult." Smiling, his face giving off a pale blush. "I'm much too intimidated, shy, puritanical, whatever, even to think seriously about that. Me, a model? What would my colleagues say?"

She nibbled at her croissant and retorted, " 'My, Scotty, we didn't know you had such a fine torso hiding under your clothes.' Something like that. Don't worry, they'll never see the photos. Think about it, and I promise I won't hold you to any promises."

Exactly a week later, while driving, he said, "All right, I'll give it a try."

"Huh?"

"Forsaking my good sense and inhibitions for your eccentric vocation and lenses. Or should I say pornography? Anyway, why not? Is it any more dangerous or improbable than this entire romance?"

"Dangerous, huh? Interesting adjective to describe us. Here, take the McGrath for Somerville; thank you." And she took his arm as if he had just agreed to marry her. Or asked her.

In the studio, while she set up the strobe lighting and her tripod, he undressed behind a screen and got into a white terrycloth robe. And presently she was directing him into various poses, sitting and standing.

Observing his tall, angular frame, smallish buttocks, long, slender legs, she saw how clothes dissembled. How female his physiognomy was in many aspects! He was handsome in his vulnerability, becoming in body-reticence. Through her cross-hatch and close-up lens, she sighted surprising planes and revealing convexities, an anatomy of pale subtlety. He was more a Cranach figure than a Western cowboy. As she arranged him against the white wall or on the worn green sofa, she saw clearly for the first time what she had felt periodically without naming: the feminine side of her friend. Just as he was in manner and understanding, he was in gesture, skin, figure almost as much female as male; this intrigued her. A delicacy of soul, a depth of ambiguity, this man had, and these were made manifest now by means of old Rollei 3x4.

Transforming him into her model, she turned into Photographer, pure and hard. Yet alongside her aesthetic curiosity lurked a sense of ownership, of permanence. He'd be not only a memory of hers, when and if they ever separated (for good), but an objective entity, a hard, unblurred fact. Like a mushroom, a head of lettuce, a Yosemite sky, or a Parisian scene, Dr. Beaumont was being transfused, by light and lens and composition, with new meaning and value. And Miriam too was being transfused by means of this labor; she was immersed in caring as though she were rocking a baby in need. For Miriam this was the music sounding above daily noises and adult doings, and she listened, labored, listened. Made arrangements: a Man Ray question mark against the white backdrop; a Manuel Bravo odalisque lounging on the floor mat; a Weston figure reading a book with crossed legs. Gradually she felt growing between them a convection of intimacy, new and unspoken, different for each. She knew too that another satisfaction would emerge later, amid chemicals and darkness and solitude, when she proceeded with the process of selecting and developing prints. Then art would add a double scoop of pleasure to the hour, the act. Or was that double trouble? she mocked privately.

"I'm tired," he said finally, after nearly two hours. "Can we call it a day?"

"Sure. Just hold this one pose." She clicked twice and finished up, tossing him his robe and adding, "You were swell, and probably won't recognize yourself. *If* I show them to you."

"I'm not sure I'll be able to face actual photos, to tell you the truth. You hold onto them, till I get my nerve up. And keep them to yourself, it goes without saying."

"Gotcha. If the *Globe* calls, I'll tell them to contact the model directly."

"Yes, do that." He smiled for the first time, drinking fruit juice after his performance.

She rolled her neck and stretched herself languidly, feeling the tension of shooting intensely.

Modest, he went behind the screen to dress himself.

She sat on the sofa and sipped sherry and thought about how dear America fucked up its young men. If gentlemen, they had no passion. If passionate, they were brutish. If ambivalent or unsure, they became too neurotic. But the few who slipped through, like the doctor here, and kept their several sides intact along with their male ways and assertiveness, were the lucky ones. So that was one of his secrets. Where did he get the genes from, the mother?

"My mother?" he asked in great surprise. "How'd she get into this? Believe me, if she could see her son today, she'd do a double take. Though she was quite a lady — took an awful lot in, without blinking too much. I think she would have enjoyed you, to your dismay. She seemed to go for outsiders."

"Hmm . . . even pornographers?"

He raised a toast to her. "If they were friends of her son's."

5

On the turnpike west they cruised through rising hills and long straightaways, Mary Lou Watson scattering autobiographical bits like ashes. She smoked, laughed, and dressed like a teenager, though she was on the far side of forty-five. She had grown up in Minneapolis, then gone to Smith College and RISD, met John in Cambridge, married early, and had kids "when I was a kid myself, an adolescent in my twenties!" A short, raucous laugh. Her shoulder-length hair bounced on her blue parka, and Miriam had to touch her arm to brake her speed. Her father, "a three-martini-lunch banker," at first had railed against John and his "architecture notions," but had accepted him when he designed a fine bank in Chelmsford. "Dad was sure the big bad East would spoil and corrupt me, while he was soaking up the Beefeater like a sponge and ruining his liver and life from it, poor devil! Mom lived alone in that mausoleum of a house for twenty years, on memory and pride, breathing despair — aaiii!" She threw up her hands like a banshee, and Miriam grabbed the wheel, just in case. "Why is everyone west of the Mississippi — no, the Susquehanna — so paranoid about the East? Envy, stupidity? Christ, oh dear Christ. Speaking of whom, don't grow up Lutheran if you can help it, especially with Minnesota winters." She leaned closer to Miriam. "At least in Sweden you can root for Bergman — all we have is Bud Grant."

On and on she rapped and ranted, and Miriam absorbed it all

during the gray Friday afternoon, feeling sympathy, curiosity, amusement. She looked with warmth at her friend's animated face with its prominent nose; the quarter Indian blood showed in the ruddy coloring, and perhaps the spirit of rebellion against all that Lutheran childhood and, maybe, husbands-as-fathers. She admired Mary Lou's freedom from piety and awareness of prejudice, but wondered where "full steam ahead," her motto, would lead her.

Northampton, when they landed in less than two hours, was not grim for an old mill town. It had a good-sized main street lined by churches and banks, low commercial buildings of brick, and store windows spruced up with showy colors and striped canopies. "You didn't see this sort of thing in my day," Mary Lou said with a laugh. "Cambridge has infiltrated!"

She drove them up a hill for a brief tour of the women's college: red brick buildings, churchy spires, spacious lawns and old trees. "This was a 'proper' school in my day," she informed Miriam, "despite the occasional scandal. Altogether about as daring as Sunday School!"

They doubled back and parked on a side street, in a municipal lot that faced a long mural painted on the stucco side of a commercial building. The mural depicted women, with each other or with children but without men — women welding, nursing, mothering, at work in the fields, and on the march — idyllic scenes, actually, painted with large-scale realism in splashy yellows, bright blues, pristine greens. "Women in Northampton, 1740–1960" read the printed title.

"What do you think?" asked Mary Lou.

"Feminist realism? Rose has a coloring book with scenes like this. Have you seen the Orozco mural up at Dartmouth?"

Crossing the narrow street, Mary Lou shook her head. "Should I have?"

"Oh, it's pretty good in its way," Miriam said, and she proceeded to describe that impressive, stylized mural representing the history of the Mexican Revolution. "*Now* it's a splendid feather in the school's cap, but in the 1930s it came close to being whitewashed, literally, because the town found out Orozco was a Commie."

"Okay, I'll go see it. But now get ready for the best hamburgers in town."

Up front Packard's was a noisy bar with booths, but in back was a quiet oval dining room, with no rock-hammer noise. As they entered it, a willowy blond stood and came forward to hug and kiss Mary Lou, who embraced her back. After a staring, awkward moment, the woman introduced the friend she had been sitting with, Deb, to Miriam and Mary Lou. When they were all seated around the red checked tablecloth, the friend corrected Miriam's pronunciation, spelling out "D-e-b-r-a, no *orah*," and smiled happily. For response, Miriam looked at her.

"We've ordered four specials — I hope that's cool," Connie said. "Hey, we want to get decent seats for that first lecture." Dressed nattily in an engineer's cap and matching overalls with a denim shirt, Connie had a small, pretty face, short, dirty, strawberry blond hair, and an efficient manner.

"Who's speaking tonight?" asked Mary Lou.

"Claire Duchamps. From Yale." Debra beamed. "One of the *really* fine minds around," she added, nodding to verify the statement.

"Gosh, it's good to see you!" Mary Lou took her friend's long hand and squeezed it.

Debra, a Hebrew *chai* dangling over her turtleneck, turned to look for the waitress.

Over her thick hamburger, Miriam listened to talk about the weekend's activities — the kickoff lecture tonight, the Saturday workshops and feature movie, the closing seminar on Sunday morning. "If any of us can manage to wake before noon," chimed in Debra. "We *are* going to have some fun, ya know!"

While Connie, Mary Lou, and Debra talked, Connie nodded every so often at Miriam, including her. At some point she announced she had heard a lot about Miriam, adding, "I know shit about kibbutzes, but I'm keen to learn about the roles of women there. How badly do they get shafted as compared to the rest of society?"

"For sure — I mean, hearing about you," agreed Debra. "I've been an admirer of yours since your Fogg show, when I was still at the Cliffe. And of course *everyone* around those parts has heard about the famous Boston City Hall show in the seventies."

"Thank you," Miriam said, flattered. Though a dozen photos in the Fogg did not constitute a show, to be sure. As for Connie's question, Miriam doubted whether she could accurately explain the experience of kibbutz life; it would be better to describe Israel's burgeoning women's movement, which included kibbutz women. But what the hell did Miriam know about any of that — or care? Zilch. Should she confess the unvarnished truth: that she used the kibbutz for her own R and R (Rafi and relaxation)?

In one car they went to the lecture, Connie deftly settling Debra in back with Miriam while Mary Lou sat up front. Chess, with one's old and new lovers.

The lecture room in Seelye Hall was soon overcrowded, so the audience adjourned down the corridor to a small amphitheater. Mostly female, the crowd wore boots, jeans, and sweaters, nary a skirt or dress, and most people seemed to know one another, clustering in cliques of three and four. Dates, times, and places were signaled to each other before the talk. ("It's something like a church social." Mary Lou giggled, and Connie punched her on the arm — an intimate playfulness, thought Miriam.)

A slender professor of philosophy, wearing high suede boots and a severe haircut, performed the introductions. First she recited the weekend agenda; then she went on to announce the speaker, calling Professor Duchamps one of the "leading Marxist-feminist theorists" of the era and citing several of her works. Lazily, Miriam wished she were at home reading her Colette, attending to that singular feminine voice, rather than this collective one.

The speaker was an auburn-haired woman in her late thirties, and her subject was Freud and recent feminist criticism. Before the talk began she handed out mimeographed sheets containing a few pieces of Freud's writing (including a description of a dream) and several pages of feminist criticism of them. Dressed casually in a simple cardigan, blouse, and skirt, she lectured from notes in a slow, low-keyed manner. Essentially, she defended Freud from excessive and simple-minded feminist critiques, though the premise suffusing the talk was that of course Freud had been a male writing about women in the Victorian era. To Miriam she had an appealing European manner, with few star-frills or ego-flashes. But she used a lingo that Miriam felt fuzzied rather than clarified issues: "sexual hierarchization," "the signifier" (woman) and "the signified" (man), "the feminine discourse," and (part of a sentence that Miriam scribbled down) "the hierarchical model of male domination which conventionally structures the relationship of man and woman." Why not use simpler English? Miriam wondered, futilely trying to wade through that thick marsh. Am I stupid? Must this stuff be so specialized? Does consciousness raising have to mean abstract or Latinate words and impenetrable phrasing? She began to concentrate on the fine, measured voice and the curious accent, which seemed something other than French — Moroccan, Israeli? Was she a refugee of some sort? If so, Miriam wouldn't mind hearing about her various voyages, transformations. One refugee to another.

During the question period, Miriam was interested to see the audience immediately jump on the speaker for her moderate attitude toward Dr. Freud.

"You seem to imply that there is something, after all, to be *learned* from him," advanced the philosophy professor, with open disdain. "Well, you can't be serious about that, can you, from a feminist perspective?"

"Quite serious. And I did not imply it, I said it directly."

A chap sporting an odd earring in one ear and a huge-brimmed hat chafed noticeably. "Aren't you going overboard in knocking all those serious critiques made of Freud in the last five years? Take the piece by Chodorow in the special issue of *Diacritics,* which I'm afraid you oversimplified, and which —"

"Do you have a question?"

A hefty woman at his side tugged at his arm, but the young man, red-faced, stammered and proceeded into his explication, although he was finally stopped altogether by his companion. Frieda and a baby Lawrence? Miriam pondered.

"Don't you think that Nietzsche exerted a great influence on Freud's thinking?" asked an older lady. "And therefore that to claim, as you do, that Freud was the first thinker really to call attention to 'the question of woman' is somewhat, or greatly, hyperbolic?"

"No, I'm not sure that Nietzsche exerted any real influence at all," Professor Duchamps replied. "Certainly not in any discernible way so far as psychoanalytical theory is concerned."

When the woman continued to push Nietzsche, the professor

quietly put the discussion to a close by saying, "I'm afraid you do not understand the psychoanalytic process, or theory, at all. This is not the place to learn it, either." She turned to another questioner.

Slowly, surely, Miriam came to feel that the atmosphere was not merely church-social but, more important perhaps, Vatican-orthodox. Serious freedom of speech, or maybe independence of mind, seemed far-fetched, out of the question. These were born-again believers, of a different mode. Oh, they could use a Dr. Levanda here, or old friend Kelley — a reassuring European or a streetsmart cowgirl to shake things up a bit. This doctrinaire atmosphere killed real questioning or real feeling. Too bad.

Afterward Connie observed, "Quite stunning, don't you think?"

"That's o-n-e f-i-n-e m-i-n-d," cooed Debra.

Miriam felt she should answer their questioning looks. "Something to think about."

They made the short drive to the Iron Horse Tavern, for drinks. A young guitarist with a Southern accent entertained with witty folk songs, while the full house of females chattered, drank, stopped at tables, coupled off.

Was the entire town like this? Was Miry indeed "lesbophobic," as Mary Lou had kidded? Could be.

"Well, yeah, kinda — we're trying," Connie explained. "We like to think we're creating a sort of matriarchal hegemony around these parts. It may even be that we represent the cutting edge of the whole gay feminist movement. And not merely in theory, but in practice too."

"Praxis over theory." Debra smiled.

Over several pitchers of draft beer during the next hour and a half, Miriam observed women holding hands and caressing one another's hair and necks. At her table, Connie was rather masterful at keeping both Debra and Mary Lou attentive. Periodically she'd take Mary Lou's hand and squeeze it, or run her fingers through Debra's long hair, reassuring her.

Discussing the work of Atwood, Piercy, Rich, this cool Constance was a shrewd customer, Miriam decided. An emigré from Chicopee, Irish parents, Catholic high school, and a Springfield area convent. She had gotten a few degrees from U. Mass. and made herself into a successful therapist, after starting out a school-teacher. Stylish too, with that cute cap meticulously perched on her head all through the evening, despite a half-dozen beers at least. A working-class cap: Fonda parody or plain old vanity?

At some point she winked at Miriam and asked, "How's it going?"

Miriam nodded. "Just fine."

"You're not a drinker, are you?"

Miriam confessed, "Well, no, but not because of principle."

The vigorous woman leaned forward and advised, "You can turn loose around these parts. There's no man to fast-load you into the sack once you're tipsy." She threw in a yellow smile. "So stay cool."

Advice, Miriam thought, still nursing her second beer. Be quiet in company, and they sought you out, tried to socialize you and make you theirs.

Later, at Debra and Connie's place, Miriam was given a room to herself, and she appreciated the touches of Judaica around the apartment — a small menorah on a bureau, a photo of a wedding couple beneath a huppah, a set of Graetz's *History of the Jews.* Nice. Were there a crucifix, rosary, and New Testament among Connie's memorabilia? "Who's that?" she inquired, to and of the tattered photograph stuck in the beveled mirror, and Connie answered, "Dad, still in his railroad garb. Thirty-five years on the B & M. Trains saw more of him than I did."

The next day, a cold hazy morning with the sun trying its best to squeak through, the local women took the visitors to the legendary bookstore in town. Located on a curving side street with a certain brackish charm, Womanfyre Books was devoted to female and feminist items only and had specialized areas for literary studies, lesbian works, women writers, and books about women. It had a rack for little magazines and quarterlies such as *Feminist Review, Moving Out, Earth's Daughters,* and a record rack for groups like Joy of Cooking, Purple Night Shades, the Go-Gos, the Wrong Stuff, Coyotes. Sections of and on Emma Goldman, Simone de Beauvoir, Susan Anthony, Virginia Woolf, Margaret Fuller, Elizabeth Cady Stanton; a shelf of Plath, Chopin, Rich, Lessing, Sexton; histories of the women's movement by psychoanalysts, historians, Marxists. Posters and T-shirts of mothers and daughters, lesbian lovers, female rock groups, women writers. (Where was a set of George Eliot, Jane Austen? Miriam wondered idly.)

As Miriam browsed, she felt more and more like she was being immersed in a foreign element, where the air was composed differently, the particles were new. Underwater at Sinai? Not quite. For here the difference was in the new species and the new way of looking at things — or seeing through everything to catch its *true* meaning.

A woman accidentally brushed her arm and apologized. "Do I happen to know you from somewhere?"

Miriam shook her head. "Not that I know of."

The woman smiled cordially. "Angela Jacques, pronounced Jakes." Put her hand out. "I live in Williamsburg. And you?"

Somewhat surprised, Miriam had to recover for a moment before revealing her name and Cambridge affiliation.

Cat's gray-green eyes; smallish face with a touch of eyeshadow; Mexican cardigan over dark turtleneck. The voice raspy. "Do you browse here often?"

Miriam shook her head and had started to turn away when Angela said, "I'm not trying to pick you up. Just being friendly. Forgive me."

Miriam felt guilty, silly. Smiled awkwardly, and then, to ease the moment and the woman's feelings, offered, "I'm just visiting for the weekend. For the conference. I'm with them." And she indicated Connie and Mary Lou in the next aisle.

"Do you happen to be a May Sarton fan?"

Miriam paused. "No, actually. Though I suppose I've never really given her work a chance." A small lie.

"Do you have time for a quick coffee, or a beer at the Horse?" Adjusting her shoulder bag, Angela flashed an oblong turquoise ring alongside a silver pinky ring. On her other wrist a black and silver bracelet jangled.

"Can't just now, thanks. But maybe we'll run into each other again." Was she scared, nervous? Trying to overcompensate? If this Angela were an Angelo, for example, would she agree to a coffee now?

"Another time then," Angela promptly agreed, smiling narrowly. Before turning away, she asked, "Are you an artist of some sort?"

"No," Miriam answered, "just a schoolteacher."

The more she walked around the town afterward, the more she came to see that Mary Lou's warning had been correct. Northampton was not your ordinary town, college or otherwise. It was a whole new social ballgame, one where the players who counted were female. Yes, indeed, strolling amid Thorne's snappy shops, maybe she was lesbophobic. A gain or a loss, this state?

In the late afternoon, after attending one of the workshops (on male violence), she went to the movies with her hosts. The Academy Theater was a gracious turn-of-the-century brick building, used in the past for opera and vaudeville. The seats were velvety and deep; the private boxes, stacked four tiers high, were gilt-edged; the silver and glass chandeliers hung from the high, scalloped ceiling with European elegance.

"Quite a joint," Miriam noted.

"And that's quite a way to put it." Connie laughed, touching Miriam's arm.

"They still have an occasional light opera or ballet here, you know," Debra informed them.

The movie was not in such a grand tradition, however. Made by a young male director, *JoAnna* was the tale of a disgruntled housewife who, because of dissatisfaction with her academic, sexist husband, turned to her female night-school teacher for physical and emotional comfort. Her evolution to lesbian ways was accompanied by one-night stands with an army officer (a believable lonely female) plus a steady stream of foolish or abusive men. JoAnna herself was a remarkably uninteresting woman, so far as Miriam was concerned; she showed little mind, was quirky at best, and had hardly any erotic appeal. The complete straw woman, Miriam decided halfway through the tendentious and amateurish picture. "You're squirming," Mary Lou said, laughing at one point. Miriam replied, "It shows, huh? Sorry." Could any woman director have made such a poor and inauthentic film? Whenever she could, she caught sight of the subtle refinements of the theater, from curved hardwoods to thick, Vermeer-like stage curtain. Why

not have some William Powell and Myrna Loy for two hours here?
Or some Hepburn wit?

The largely female crowd, however, enjoyed the film and actually applauded at the end. "He shows real empathy for our
situation," one woman said.

"Not too bad, considering a male wrote and directed it. JoAnna
could have been a tad headier, maybe."

And Connie observed, "A bit crude in spots, but overall rather
realistic, and strong, hey? Courageous for a male to make — what
say you, Miry?"

Inching along the jammed aisle, Miriam began: "I didn't really
feel much — the radical change didn't seem to provide much *affect*,
to her or to the audience. For me, that is." She tried to keep her
voice and seditiousness low. "I thought it was inauthentic, at every
important moment."

"Yeah, there was a certain amount of cerebralizing," confirmed
Debra, nodding. "I see what you mean."

Not at all what I mean, pal. "Actually, I think he was pandering
to gay females."

Connie shot her a sideways look. "Oh?"

Miriam stared back at her, and watched the angry look dissolve.

"Maybe the director is saying that for intellectuals, or semi-
intellectuals," Connie said, "*feeling* gay is problematic."

"You don't really take JoAnna to be an intellectual, of any
sort?" Miriam retorted, trying to restrain her fury — at the insipid
picture, or the party-line defense. Oh, Dr. B. should see me now,
playing movie critic again! "She can hardly talk, thinks reading is
a bore, and doesn't seem to have any interests. I'd rate her at a
slug's level."

Mary Lou laughed and took Connie's arm. "I told you she can
be harsh!"

"Yeah — a *male* intelligence!" joked Debra.

Out in the lobby Connie changed tactics. "Well, you have a
certain point, though I think you're evaluating the film from a
literary point of view, not a cinematic one. The look and shape
of an intellectual changes when you're dealing with characters on
the screen, you know. Brrr! Well, folks, button up, here comes
winter!"

Indeed, the wind had risen while they were inside, and snowflakes were flying about madly.

"Walk or drive to the party?"

"Are you joshing? This may be a nor'easter. Let's make a run for the car!"

Giggling like a schoolgirl, Debra challenged Connie to a race, and they dashed down the street, arms pumping, exhilarated. The spurt of innocence suddenly afforded Miriam a picture of them as high school kids, and she felt more kindly immediately.

"Watch out." Miriam took Mary Lou's arm, and they walked out onto the slippery street.

"No race?" asked Mary Lou with a laugh.

"Not tonight," Miriam responded. "Though they did look like they were having fun."

"What do you make out of that relationship?" Mary Lou inquired. "Think opposites like that can stay . . . attracted for more than a few months?"

Miriam shook her head. "I have no idea about such matters. Relationships. Who stays, who goes, who splits, why. One of the great mysteries of the universe — maybe more mysterious than the original big bang."

"C'mon, you gays," cried out Debra, holding open the Datsun door, "let's make it!"

"Gays" or "guys"? Miriam wondered, sliding in the back seat.

After ten minutes of slow driving, they got out of the car, and Miriam asked Debra what she had said. Yes, "gays."

Miriam set her hand on the chunky shoulder. "I'm not gay, Debra."

Snowflakes fluttered onto the young woman's rosy cheeks, and she stammered, "Oh . . . I thought you and Mary Lou . . . Sorry."

Miriam started them walking again, and asked where they were heading.

"Oh gosh, you've never been to The Club Room before? Well, it's a select place, I'll tell you that. *People* mag asked three times to do a piece on it, but 'thank you, no thank you' is what they got. It's a high, a major high!"

"Actually," cautioned Connie before entering, "this group is, uh, a bit hyperbolic. A fringe end of the whole cloth. So take it in stride."

The room itself was low, actually, a low-ceilinged, rectangular basement located beneath a plain two-family house. It was a playful parody of an old-fashioned boys' club room, with posters of women athletes and two male pinups, lining the walls, along with several humorous, obscene photos of heterosexual lovers. Subdued lights and streamers of old-style crepe paper running in diagonals across the ceiling gave the place a feeling of vivid, permanent festivity. Smells of licorice and patchouli mingled with those of grass and smoke in the air.

The names and faces came fast and furious, and frequently in pairs: Clara and Emily, Weezie and Cindy, Clem and Muffi, Julie and Tyler, Sonia and Lisa, Ray and Brooke. Drinks were served at a corner bar by a young male bartender; food was brought around on trays periodically by another male, older, and maybe gay himself. The dress was big-city stylish, ranging from beige jumpsuits to stovepipe overalls, from slinky crepe dresses to shiny ski outfits, from jeans, shirts, and hockey and football jerseys to mannish suits. Talk and smoke drifted, glasses tinkled, glances were given, hands were held. "Have a Fun Party" read a hand-lettered sign.

An outsider, Miriam stayed off in a corner, propped in a wing chair. She was pleased by an old familiar blowup of Florence Chadwick, slicked in oil, just after her English Channel swim. Someone had a memory here. Her *Junior Scholastic News* arose in her vision, and she sipped her wine, gazing at the kaleidoscopic room.

A young woman with a colorful headband, an upturned nose, and one long pigtail asked if she minded, sat down on her armrest, and pouted. In Leningrad, she'd be a Degas ballerina.

"It's a bore, all this debating and struggling, if you ask me. Shit. Why don't we all split to Oregon and join the Rajneesh movement and love each other — including men? Yeah." She seemed to see Miriam now for the first time; her baby blues were glassy. "What d'ya think?"

"Are you okay?"

"Oh, you sense it, huh? Just broke up with my partner and feel crash-down blues out. A zombie — know what I mean?"

She smiled broadly, drank from her glass, and started to lay a hand on Miriam's shoulder. Just then another woman came along and admonished her. "Come on, Livvy, enough's enough. Let's get you some fresh air, friend."

Livvy twisted away, but the older woman, wearing a tie and suit, held onto her arm firmly and lifted her up, apologizing to Miriam. "Sorry, really. Just one of those nights."

Miriam nodded. She felt something for the jilted young woman, and remembered "Just One of Those Things" by . . . Sinatra? Always the prisoner of her era.

"Which do you prefer, early or late Sontag?" The rapid nasal voice belonged to a slender, prematurely gray woman of maybe thirty-five, who sat down and spoke as though Miriam were an old friend.

Miriam had an impulse to say, "I prefer early Greer Garson," but she acknowledged, "I liked Sontag's book on photography. Are you a great fan?"

Dangling a cigarette from the corner of her mouth, the woman spoke in rapid-fire New Yorkese: "Who else is there since de Beauvoir quit? Oh yeah, Morgan and Brownmiller, et cetera, do their jobs, but, well, Sontag is Sontag. Though I wish the hell she'd take on the really gut issues. Can you see Sontag moving on gay intellectuals still in the closet? Or vaginal versus clitoral orgasm? She'd up the ante *and* the energy level, I bet. I'm Harriet by the way, Harriet Druckerman. What are you into?"

Figuring out how to take all this. "Miriam Scheinman, schoolteacher. Would you excuse me a minute? I've got to get a refill."

At the bar she had her goblet replenished by the blond Adonis, then journeyed to the far side of the long basement. Several couples were dancing to the low rock music, and while Miriam observed the meaningful smiles and small touches she suddenly had a whiff of Jerusalem during chamsin, when the hot Sahara wind blew dust and mystery into your soul, along with sultry unpredictability.

"Hi."

"Huh?"

"Me. Remember? The witless Sarton admirer."

In wool slacks and white blouse, wearing a handsome silver pendant on her chest, the woman looked fit, adult, stylish.

"It's Angela, right?"

"*Excellent* memory." She raised her glass. "Cheers."

Miriam toasted with her.

"Are you a dancer?" Angela held out her arms.

"No, not really. But I enjoy watching."

"Didn't think so. Too bad, I love it. Bodies in motion. When I was married, I thought I hated it. Just shows what husbands can do for your favorite tastes." Cheerful smile. "Have you had one yourself?"

"Who hasn't?" That was the wrong remark in this crowd, she realized.

"Did you get the whole package — kids too?"

Miriam drank. "Yes. But those I still have. Thankfully."

"Oh. Are you into the mothering scene?"

"You mean am I into the living and breathing scene?"

"Mine are with Jay. For a few years anyway. I used to feel this guilt trip in the first months, but the freedom punched that out pretty quick."

Miriam noted a poster of Bacall that had graffiti scribbled across it. Nothing was sacred anymore. Was that really freedom, haloed in guilt, grief? Freedom, or slow torture? Self-projecting again; call if off.

"Have you seen the map yet?"

"What? No, I guess I haven't."

"Come, let me introduce you to the neatest item in The Club Room. Only members are allowed." Angela took Miriam's hand and they weaved their way through the dancers, talkers, loungers. Once through the intricate crowd, Miriam released her hand.

They arrived at a partitioned-off room in the back of the basement proper, where a large map of Northampton was tacked on a portable blackboard. Fixing her vision Miriam saw that red, blue, black, and yellow flags were pinned up, like on a military map.

"What do you think?"

She gave a dumb smile and guessed. "Secret missile sites?"

"Well, sort of. Gay sites, secret and unsecret. Places inhabited by, taken over by, strongly leaning toward — or away from — gays and the gay life."

It took a full minute for the peculiar strategy to sink in. Was

Angela serious, or joking? Like a dazed schoolgirl, Miriam walked closer to the board and saw, in small, clear print, a battle-zone grid laid out for the whole city, covering shops, schools, apartment houses, community buildings, even churches and banks. Amazed, she said, "I don't believe it . . . All right, enlighten me — blacks, reds?"

Angela smoked, her eyes glinting with triumph. "Blacks are strongholds of sexism, which remain to be seriously infiltrated. Yellows, borderline innocents and closet cowards, still hanging on the fence. Reds are ours, in firm control. And blues are *leaning,* under the influence of."

A pause. In the eerie atmosphere, Miriam shook her head dumbly. "If this is for real, this army is serious."

"Yes, I guess we are." Then Angela laughed. "About some things, anyway."

"No tanks or howitzers yet?"

"Those are their methods. Males make the wars and do the killing. 'Violence is Patriarchy' — remember the workshop? We're trying to do things a little differently." She sat on a steel desk.

"But it's a war, right?"

"For sure. A war against sexism, basically, but against the other evils too."

"Heterosexuality?"

Angela smiled, bemused. "A matter of taste, personal opinion. So far as I'm concerned, no. Not really. But for some others . . ." She shrugged broad shoulders. "Nothing wrong with a radical minority from that direction, though. A counterbalance to the mob that puts down gays daily and deliberately — you know. Anyway, you've seen the map. I'm going to get me another Johnny Walker; can I —"

Regaining her composure, Miriam said, "Now come on, hold it, you can't really be serious. I mean, you can't *know* the facts of your case for that map. Look, here at the college, for example, you have these different flags. Now how the hell —"

Angela took her arm and led her to a corner of the room, where she flicked on a fluorescent light. "Here's the baby; isn't he cute? He does all our major figuring." An L-shaped desk held a computer with a screen, a printer, a file cabinet, assorted software, pamphlets. "Apple to the rescue. We put all the data from the Smithies right here, into our friendly floppy disks, and keep it updated constantly. When a specific department — for example, art history — turns a majority gay, we put it straightaway into red flags. But not a moment before. Male robots" — she stroked the computer with careful emphasis — "do you play with them?"

Miriam recalled the shack in the orchard of her kibbutz in the Negev desert, with the IBM computer that controlled watering; Rachel referred to it in the male gender too. Oh, the world is turning, Miry, faster than you know about! "How do you find out when a department has turned into a majority gay?"

"Oh, that's not so difficult to assess, around these parts."

Angela ran her hand through her short straight hair, pulling it forward toward her forehead. "Refill?"

"Sure." Though Miriam had had two drinks, her usual quotient. But she had more to digest now, here.

By herself, she stood around, still slightly agog, disoriented, bemused by the flagged map. Like Dad's maps of World War II, showing the fascist armies in defeat as reflected in the *Times*'s black arrows and dotted black lines. Christ, what was she doing here, in this surreal den? She meandered out of the room and encountered smells of cologne in a darkened storage area . . . Where was her camera for all of this? Oh Harry or Dr. Levanda, I wish you were with me now, wandering in this hallucinatory territory.

A sign for the john; she turned the corner to enter. Voices stopped her. Close by. What the hell? Whispers, moans. Cues of the erotic. She turned away, but was pulled up short by a familiar, hoarse little laugh. She couldn't resist peeking through piles of curtains and cartons: crepuscular outline of two familiar bodies working on each other, the cunning willowy therapist locked into and caressed by Mary Lou on that convenient couch. Odd, to see women, grown women, sneaking this way. Shades of teenage! Her faculties grew fuzzy.

Deeply embarrassed, she moved off quietly and escaped to the bathroom, where she tossed cold water on her face and neck and looked in the mirror. Saw herself. Still there. Surviving, learning, in this peculiar classroom. She remembered some sentimental scenes: Mary Lou standing up vigorously to a bad Shady Hill teacher, jousting with husband John at the Lexington dinner table, brandishing her M.A. in child development at age forty-five . . . What did all these present shenanigans mean then? Who knew? It was screwy. She dried her face and emerged.

In the map room she found Angela already back, with a smile and a goblet.

"Oh, you found John. Good."

"Yes."

"You okay?"

"Fine. Thanks." Still uncomfortable with the scene she had witnessed. "Too much wine, probably."

"Want to change to something else? There's some nice coke that goes well with wine."

Miriam was about to say yes, then realized again her innocence. Their coke was not her Coke. "Can I get a Perrier?"

Angela laughed, a good throaty laugh now. "Sure. Come along."

Miriam brightened and followed.

Standing at the bar, Angela said, "How about a quick rundown of the players? Why not, so you know Who's Who in Smithieland. Number 40 is Carly J. — ex-prof of American history at Mt. Holyoke. Part owner of a local restaurant now, and she's working on a biography of the woman behind Francis Parkman. The American Standard Beauty over there, that's Pam Palmerston — used to labor on *Ryan's Hope* before switching soaps to NBC. From North Dakota, where they make 'em sincere, neurotic, raw-boned. A weekender. The character who resembles Amelia in that parachute outfit is one Felicity Adams, from the original Adams family if you don't mind; splits her time between Cambridge and here; a nutritionist. Believes that bisexuality is a product of what you eat; lots of brewer's yeast and tiger's milk and vitamin D and your sexual life will be open and generous and 'long-lived.' " She accepted their drinks, and they moved off. "The tall, strong black chick in the nightgown dress is Althea White, a part-time golfing pro who came to live hereabouts two years ago, because of that size-six blond, a Smith poet who knows every line of Sylvia's by heart. Over there, our resident bluestocking: Naomi Goldberger. Introspective, haunted; our gay Kafka. And then there's Audrey, Audrey Blythe Towers, one of the wealthiest and daffiest psyches in these fifty states; resides in Carmel, California, but hangs out in Northampton for most of the year. Flies in and out in her own little Lear. Has excellent taste in art, however, so I can only praise her. Want some J.W. in your Schweppes? Hey, let's grab that two-seater. And this corner creature, one Ms. Shafer Tosco, all pearly teeth and long legs, a refugee from the New York City Center Ballet. She's rumored to have been Balanchine's favorite, while being one of us all the way through. Quite a dancer, but also quite a daisyhead. To be watched but avoided." Sitting down, Angela added, "Forgive the cuteness of these thumbnail portraits, but these folks are pretty cute numbers. Fighters too. Every one a rebel, a gutsy guerrilla." She drank. "Don't worry, the rest of Northampton town is more toned-down, low-key."

Miriam, half exhausted, drank too. "To normalcy."

Angela laughed. "So have you been playing it tame since you split from your domestic nest?" she asked, one arm languid on the Chippendale frame.

"Tame." Miriam repeated the word, finding new angles and undertones in the way this woman pronounced the word. "Yes, I suppose so. From a certain viewpoint, yes."

Angela had taken to sucking an ice cube. Steadily she eyed Miriam, eyes glimmering red, like some Persian cat measuring an unknown foe. Slowly, carefully, she reached across the narrow space between them — a space that seemed to Miriam like a desert cavern — and ran the back of her hand down Miriam's arm, starting at the shoulder and finishing at her hand. The gesture took no more than five seconds, yet to Miriam it was an eternity. The touch was not cute, not sly, and not unpleasant. But it was most strange in effect.

"I don't pretend to know what you're thinking," Angela spoke up immediately, quietly, "but not everything is to be *thought through*. I mean, some things just happen, and we should let them just happen. Like a poem, or a picture, say. Or am I way off, in your estimation?"

Miriam could have moved away; it would have been easy enough. She knew that a pass of sorts had been made — of sorts? — and that soon another was coming, probably. But she deliberately stayed put, stayed on the cramped velvet couch asserting to herself somewhere that if this were a strange man, she would not necessarily get up and leave just yet. For he was not being obnoxious or rude or downright foolish, but rather . . . ?

"What do you do, Angela? Do you work for a living?"

She laughed, a good laugh. "I'm not exactly a Martian, you know. Sculpture — wood and metal, mostly. You know, it took me half a lifetime to discover that what I like best to do was what I liked to do as a child — work with my hands and *feel* different materials. Can you believe that for ten years, while I was married, I never knew that simple truth? Pretty foggy, huh?" She smiled, relaxed. "Marriage — it numbs you to yourself."

"What'd your husband do?"

A slender brunette leaned down and whispered to Angela, who shook her head.

"Sorry . . . English professor. Ever meet the species?"

"Now and then."

"A Victorian specialist. Author of *Clough's Poetry: The Middle Road.* You know it, I'm sure. In later years he thought of himself as something of a modern critic. For Jay, the change was like going down the Amazon in a kayak. It took lots of balls, he'd tell you every day." Her face shifted; her tone too. "Sorry, I'm sounding snotty. He was okay, really. Just limited — in scope, ambitions. The Modern Language Association was the sun that his earth, his work, revolved around. And the worst of it was that I got used to him, thoroughly used to him and his ways, like a worm in dirt — I didn't even know it was dirt anymore. Ohhh fuck, the years we waste. Look, would it bore you if I told you how I turned on — became gay, I mean? Or what it means to me? C'mon, be straight with me." She raised her eyebrows at the poor pun. "It's probably a bore."

"Go ahead, I'm with you."

She held up a finger. "One last J.W. red for the road, okay? One last wine — or Perrier?"

Miriam smiled. "Wine."

Angela raised herself and took their glasses.

Miriam surveyed the room: the lithe dancers and the suggestive posters . . . the chatter of talk and the drifts of cigarette and grass smoke . . . the stylish women . . . and Connie, back in action, talking with two women while red-cheeked Debra stood at her side, restless, awkward, trying to get her friend's attention.

"Do you mind if I read you something?" Livia, the pigtailed blond, had returned, with a book. "Tell me what you think straight out, huh? From the 'Ninth Talk,' this goes:

" 'There are two types of relationships. One is fright, fear, hatred. This creates ego. The other is of love, compassion, sympathy. These are the two types of relationships.

" 'Wherever love is, fight ceases, ego drops. This is why you cannot love. It is difficult. Because to love means to drop the ego. To drop yourself. Love means not to be. So look at the strange phenomenon lovers go on fighting. How can lovers fight? If there is love, fight should drop and the ego will disappear. Your whole being thirsts for love; your whole mind thirsts for ego. So you make a compromise — you love and you fight. The lover becomes an intimate enemy.' "

She looked up, blue eyes wide, and asked, "How's it goin' down?"

Miriam paused. "I guess you'd have to know the context . . . judge the whole book." What could she say — a selection of corn?

"Livia, you're making a first-class *pest* of yourself," her mannish friend declared, lifting the book from Livia's hands. "*Leave the lady alone.* Behave, won't you? Or else." She took the young woman's wrist firmly.

"Here, a present." Livia took her book and dumped it into Miriam's hands. "Judge the whole and let me know one day — when old Mother Goose here lets me free!"

Livia was pulled off, protesting feebly, and Miriam looked at the book, a paperback called Bogwan's *Eleven Talks,* with a picture of a bearded Indian on the cover. She spotted a large rubber plant nearby and tucked the book in there. Might it take root?

On a wooden table she caught sight of two entwined female figures carved in dark wood. Elegant, she thought, reaching for it. This whole strange world possessed its share of taste, intelligence, and style, despite the clichés and stereotypes. She held the wooden figures in her hand, admiring them.

"Like it?"

Miriam nodded to Angela, who handed her her drink and smiled.

"Very much. Whose? Oh, I see . . . stupid of me. It's *lovely*, congratulations."

"Thanks. Glad you noticed it. Most don't." She held up her drink. "Still ready for my story?"

"Shoot."

She shot, but the tale was neither enlightening nor very interesting. A bisexual wife of a Smith professor had introduced her to the pleasures of the gay life one afternoon, and since then it had been only women. "Well, with one exception, when I made a point of trying a man again." She smiled and shook her head slowly. "No comparison. When it comes to loving a woman and making love to a woman, a male's out of the running. There's just an instinctive knowledge, a *knowingness* about how and when to proceed, that a male hasn't the foggiest about. In fact, having a penis is probably his greatest drawback, because he tends to rely on it so much and forget all the rest." She took a healthy sip of her drink and drew on her cigarette. "I'm really glad you like that piece; it's among my favorite works."

Miriam had held onto the wooden figures all through the narrative, and couldn't help contrasting the work with its creator. With its semiabstract nuances, its Giacometti delicacies, the sculpture was subtle and admirable; but Angela had turned into a crude missionary, out to convert the pagan primitives called heterosexuals. The woman who had made these figures seemed to be an accomplished artist; the woman telling this tale was a simple proselytizer. Okay, Miriam, what do you do now, nod with understanding and say "how interesting"?

Angela suddenly said, "Christ, I'm sorry. You don't need all this. Besides, they're just words. And words are a bore, a royal bore. Besides being *lies* mostly. Look." She glanced at her large, black-faced wristwatch. "It's pretty late for me. I'm gonna split. Can I drop you?"

Miriam sipped wine, saw how late it was, realized she didn't much want to return in the same car with Connie, Mary Lou, and puppy Debra, and said okay — knowing in her gut that a ride home with Angela could involve a very awkward moment or two. She found the address of Connie's apartment, remembered where

the key had been left, and on the way out informed Mary Lou
that she'd see her later. Mary Lou gave her a most interested look,
but asked no questions.

Pure white snow surprised her; a four-inch blanket covered the
streets and houses. The wind had died down. Angela's vehicle was
a high blue pickup truck with cab parked on a nearby street.

"Watch your footing," Angela said, unlocking the doors. She
was wearing a peaked cap and an aviator leather jacket with a fur
collar.

Miriam brushed soft snow away from the door and her eyes.
"My friend Harry should see this; he'd be green with envy."

Inside the cab Angela turned the ignition and smoked while the
engine warmed up. "Yeah, it's a good rig. I can get anywhere with
it, and carry all my stuff too. I just dump a few sandbags in back
for the winter months."

"What is it?"

"Toyota, four-wheel drive." She tipped her cap. "Where to,
Ma'am?"

Miriam gave her the address, and Angela took off.

The snow continued to fall in big, thick, slow flakes, and the
streets were empty and white. For Miriam, all this pure white
nuzzling seemed simple and factual, while humans created the most
Byzantine lives. Oh well.

"Whose pad?"

"Connie Ruhle's."

Angela glanced at her. "*Your* friend?"

"My friend's friend."

Angela smiled, pleased.

They drove through the white streets, the traction sure and the
view rather heady. "I like it way up here," Miriam acknowledged,
and Angela retorted, "We think alike. The height's the first thing
that appealed to me too."

Miriam tried not to think, and was aided by the surplus of wine
she had drunk. She watched the black rubber arms flapping back
and forth on the windshield, cleaning it well, and she sensed that
something was coming.

In a few minutes Angela pulled up alongside an isolated curb
on a darkened street, and Miriam wondered if she was home yet.

"We're not at your address," Angela said, looking at her meaningfully. The attractive woman took Miriam's hand, held it firmly, and said, "Look, I really dig you, flat out and simple. Stay with me tonight. For whatever — you want only bed and breakfast, that's cool. Just hang with me for twenty-four hours, and let's see and feel what's happening between us. I *would* like to get to know you." The cat's inscrutable eyes, the fair face ruddy from scotch and cold, the bomber jacket, plus the appeal couched in unfamiliar terms, all mystified Miriam, and froze her in uncertainty.

The flakes fell white on the windshield, and the black rubber blades flapped back and forth, back and forth.

Sometime during the long, tangled silence Angela leaned over — once again, a slow-motion leap over a vast boundary — and sought Miriam's mouth with her lips. Miriam turned her face away. Angela's strong hands cupped her chin, however, and held it fast, while she moved her face closer, whispering, "Give yourself a chance to *know* yourself . . . You're mature enough to try something new . . . And you do like me well enough, you know that . . ."

Did she? Miriam heard the low, raspy voice and listened to the wipers, saw the hard, attractive face and concentrated on the big flakes falling, felt the firm hands and gripped the vinyl seat, and finally, after what seemed like an hour, she reached up, took hold of those hands, and urged them down. And shook her head slowly at the woman.

Immediately Angela admonished her. "Why let fear overrule your emotion?" Then, in a swift gesture, she zipped open her jacket, lifted her sweater, revealed a naked left breast; taking Miriam's hand, she placed it upon the soft flesh and squeezed softly. She half grinned. "Pleasing?"

Stunned. For a fantastic blur of a moment Miriam allowed herself to hold the breast. It was a strange and not unexciting feeling, and she saw how easy it would be — with the wine, especially — to let the event proceed.

She released her hold, saying, "We'd better go now," and reached over to light a cigarette, shattering the mood.

She sensed Angela's sharp look of resentment but smoked, looking straight ahead. She put on the radio.

"I honestly didn't think you'd come on like this," Angela observed, throwing the truck into gear with an edge of imperiousness.

Clever, that. "Oh? What did you think?" Miriam was breathing easier, curious.

"Well, that you were interested in full liberation, that you'd had enough of timidity and inhibition, that you had tried the straight life and now were ready for some serious change." She pronounced "straight life" like a prison sentence. "But maybe you're not yet ready . . ."

Condemnation had gone far enough, Miriam reasoned. A pass was rejected and the tide of resentment mounted; Angela's ego was not very different from the ego of the male of the species.

She offered Angela a cigarette and said, "You don't really think 'full liberation' is measured by whether I go to bed with you or not? Or even that full liberation is so readily available."

Angela turned off the radio. "*What I know, you don't. And what I can pass on to you,* you won't let me. Because *you can't let go.* So what's the use of rapping? But let me set you straight about one matter: you don't have the slightest idea of where real independence is nowadays. It's with us, with free women only, and until you realize that and its full implications, you're going to remain outdated, a fossil, a hostage to a patriarchal age. A toy for men. Sorry to put it so bluntly, but you'd better hear it straight, and now."

Did free women have to be lesbian women? Miriam saw that there was little point in dialogue here. An axiom from Dad ran through her mind: "The best deals are the ones you don't make." Branch Rickey? She focused on the reflections on the snowy streets and bounced along, imagining she was in a convoy truck during a war, nervous to get safely to her destination.

In a minute Angela pulled up abruptly at the curb in front of the familiar apartment building. "Tell me," she persisted, "is it the sexual or the emotional thing that blocks you?"

Miriam, appreciating "thing," said, "The whole package."

About to say something, Angela got the reference. "Here's your stop."

"Thanks."

"I think it's the sexual thing, to tell you the truth," Angela opined. "Women are afraid of their bodies, and hence afraid of loving those bodies with their own hands. I know what I'm talking about, and I can see body-fear in your eyes."

Oh? Maybe yes. "See you around." Miriam sought the door handle.

"Here," said Angela, reaching across to the glove compartment and removing a small package. Handing Miriam a printed card, she smiled a different smile and offered, "In case you choose to be *bold* sometime. Or just want to say hello."

Miriam walked toward the building, but when she heard the truck take off, she kept on ambling along the empty sidewalk. One third high, one third angry, one third lucid, she felt the snow falling upon her face and hair like some well-timed anointment. Her heart slowed as her pace picked up.

A "decisive moment," in Cartier-Bresson's words. But could you ever photograph it? Hardly. It was one of those packed, potent moments that if detonated, could fragment your life this way and that, with all sorts of violent consequences. And you didn't know how it all started!

One- and two-family clapboard houses, a vacant lot, sloping banks of a frozen river. The dull, real, ordinary world appealed anew. Nice here, this hamlet blanketed in all this feathery white. She took a handful of fresh snow and smelled it; was transported to the smells of Rosie and Yani in their infant months. Scalps of bliss and tummies of baby-smell, faces glowing in new wonder. Memories of purity, inspired by all this fresh white.

By a broad tree whose boughs were laden with white cumulous shapes, she lingered, brushing snow from the trunk and considering the foolish pressures that had just been delivered. She thought: "As if boundaries crossed were easily effaced, or steps retraced. As if life weren't complicated enough — with men, work, feelings, with self-deceptions and truth — and I needed yet another tidal wave of complication. The naiveté and presumptuousness. As if certain boundaries and limits didn't really, finally, test one's degree of independence and liberation. As though a person could fulfill her emotions and desires the way you downed your J.W. red. Body-fear? Sure, absolutely — body was the easy part of the equation. We all wanted to sleep with practically everyone, so what? Do I need a female fuck or an affair with a woman to make me think of myself as adventurous? Are only gays bold? Oh Angela, I have enough richness and confusion, thank you. And if I want more, all I have to do is wake up tomorrow morning and start the day." She patted the pin oak — good listener — and turned around, feeling lighter.

Yet, as she walked back to the apartment building, she felt satisfied too, maybe grateful even, for this Angela. She had inserted some realism into the realm of the hallucinatory. A pass was a pass, rejected or accepted. Fair enough.

And later, in her bed, she was buzzing near sleep when she heard the raised voices of Connie and Debra, the latter screaming obscenities and slamming a door . . . Presently, new voices — Mary Lou and Connie? Not really wanting to know, she got up, feeling foolish, and made sure her own door was latched. Tried to sleep, couldn't, got up, and sat by the smallish window. Peered out into the street, where two ribbons of black cut neatly through the white snow in the mercury-lit darkness . . . She felt so strange here — an outsider among these women, like a traveler shipwrecked on a foreign island. Is that what the added sexuality was supposed to do, separate women from one another? She felt more at home with the wintry streets, the snowy trees, the old-fashioned looped lampposts.

She sat by the narrow window, curtains pulled aside, and stared out at the slowly falling snow. Alert and clear-headed, for hours on end she sat and brooded, while her friends played their bedroom games in the thin-walled apartment. Gradually the street receded into feathery white emptiness and the night wound down like a slow train. Slowly too, in her solitude, Miriam found her spirit rebounding, finding itself, straightening out, and she stretched her arms wide. What a peculiar way to recover, she thought, closing the curtain and pulling the shade at last, when the apartment had quieted. Oh, what should she make of all this? Of herself? Stick-in-the-mud rationalist? Old-fashioned skeptic? Or simply less adventurous than she had imagined? Oh, your rigidities are showing! Your homophobic prejudices! Are you a slave after all, or a free woman? Maybe a little of both. For now, she'd try for sleep before deciding, before morning.

The next day, driving home, Mary Lou asked how she had found the weekend.

"Oh, fine. An education. Northampton is different, that's for sure. A town you'd expect to find in California, maybe, not Massachusetts. I feel . . . enlightened."

Mary Lou laughed her hearty teenaged laugh at that ambiguous answer. "Well, for me it's a *total* recharging of my batteries, which'll last for a few months!"

Miriam heard her friend's passion, or zeal, in the stale image, and felt a mixture of distance and sympathy. She patted Mary Lou's arm affectionately and said, "Music?"

"Sure."

"Pop or classical?"

"Either."

"How about C and W? I like the accents."

"I didn't know you knew about such things." And Mary Lou glanced merrily at Miriam.

Miriam turned the dial until she found a country station. "I'm a sucker for native corn," she said, nestling back and listening to the female twang.

6

EX-HUSBANDS, like old cars, become objects of affection and nostalgia once they have been discarded. She decided this while sitting in the familiar Blue Parrot Café on Mt. Auburn Street, waiting for Stan. All the enormous strain and trouble they made while they were yours, objects of possession and responsibility, later on receded into the far distance. Even the trouble spots — the weak heater, unreliable starter, torn upholstery — you regarded after a while with curiosity and even sentiment. Now you took an interest in those items that, if he were still yours, would drive you batty, make you short-tempered and bored. How was the old jalopy doing now? So, how was Stanley, her husband of thirteen years? What had happened to his passion for science? His poor judgments of people? His foolish punning and superb homilies and wild, manic drive? His strained inability to handle his frustrations? And even, perhaps, how well was he performing in bed with his new wife, Röchel? (Did an Orthodox Jewess turn him on? Miriam wondered perversely.)

She had intentionally arrived early and seated herself. She wanted the discussion to focus on Jon and his recent problems, not on her. She liked this old place with its collegiate movie posters on the walls, low ceilings, small slate tables, and narrow spaces; the Parrot retained the flavor of the old Cambridge, when it had been a kind of Left Bank for Boston.

When Stan did enter, Virgo-punctual as usual, and she spotted his formal attire, he looked handsomer than ever. His thick dark hair, still parted, was now streaked gray with respectability. His button-down oxford shirt and thin necktie, comic perhaps on others, were appropriate for Stan, and preferable to current fashions. (She was glad that she had at the last moment changed into her own outfit of respectability: a blazer and skirt taken from the mothballs. Dressed to the nines for the PTA.) And the new lines of anxiety on his face added character to his prominent features. Forty-six now — or was it forty-seven? — he could easily be taken for a righteous senator or IBM official. Indeed, shouldn't he have become one or the other, once he had abandoned his early roles of Prince Myshkin and J. Robert Oppenheimer? Wouldn't he have been more moral and idealistic, certainly more full of rage, than the normal captains of industry and leaders of government? Perhaps not quite as practical, true.

He greeted her most civilly, sat down beneath a Bogart poster, opened a menu, and spent several minutes assessing the teas as though he were studying the racing charts before betting.

She finished her cappuccino, ordered another, and asked him how he was. She was delighted to discover that her stomach was not fluttering at this meeting.

"Well, thank you; *very* well," he said, not really boasting. Sitting a few feet away, he gazed at her from a kind of distance. The broiling emotion of years past now seemed gone, evaporated.

She was glad, and yet . . . She wouldn't think of it.

"I wanted to talk to you about Jonathan," she began, faltering slightly as she observed his clean-shaven face, expressive brown eyes. Faltering, perhaps, out of a sense of her own faltering with her son? "He's having some troubles, at home as well as school, and I wondered, have you noticed anything . . . happening recently? Anything troublesome, I mean?"

He shook his head, thanked the waitress for the tea, smiled at her brightly, checked his pot. With all in order, he pronounced, "No, no trouble at our place with him, that I can see. What sort of problems?"

She explained about some recent school disturbances and her visit to a teacher, and then discussed her recent discovery that he was smoking grass. It had been grass, not alcohol, that he was high on one night, she had found out. She tried to soften the blow with the word *marijuana*.

The news hit Stan hard. He looked up, the old Stan flaring suddenly, and asked, "Have you been smoking it, too?"

She was on the verge of answering harshly. But why act the same old exhausting roles of years ago? Wasn't this a new decade in their relations? Shouldn't the scene be different? So she fibbed a bit. "No, not really. I still prefer a drink."

He too seemed to catch himself. He poured out his tea and calmed down.

Too bad, she thought. "Don't you like it darker?" He made such a nice contrast to Bogart, this crazy Jewish boy. He would have made a perfect antagonist for Bogart's make-believe detective.

He smiled a wonderful, appeasing smile; his teeth were still quite lovely. "Yes, you're quite right," he said and poured it back to steep a while longer. Whenever she had mothered him, he'd purred like a stroked cat. Things hadn't changed much.

"Well, I'm glad to hear that Jon's been fine with you. Then it's perhaps more my problem." Ah, this adjudication of responsibility for one's children — like trying to distinguish the circuits on a microchip.

"And Rosie?"

"Oh, she's doing fine, dandy. It's just Jon that concerns me." She went on to tell him in detail about her conversations with his teacher, all the time looking at the old movie posters and remembering the movies they had seen together at Ann Arbor, Berkeley, Paris.

"Have you tried talking to him?"

"Yes, as a matter of fact. But before this last incident came up. I thought I'd, uh, consult you first." She wanted to ask him whether he remembered seeing *Fire on the Plains* with her at the old Surf Theater in San Francisco, or *Casque d'Or* at the Paris Cinemateque. She didn't dare just now. Admitted that she, Miriam, was probably being paid back for her past absences.

Stan poured the tea again, and this time it was stronger. He twisted a lemon slice into it and emphatically stirred it with a spoon, savoring her deferential honesty like a British Mandate colonel hearing the confession of a young Jewish terrorist. A female one, to boot.

And Miriam, sensing this, didn't mind so much. She wanted to hear him out, see what he thought, how he judged, no matter what the roles or rules.

Enjoying the tea and looking about, he inquired, "Do you come here, or to . . . these places often nowadays?"

Oh, how lovely! She could have kissed him for that, for making the Blue Parrot into a small iniquitous Cochin. No, she never came, actually. "On and off," she said, allowing him his condescension.

"It has a certain aura, I will admit," he said, like a boy discovering the other side of the tracks, or home turf, again. Especially since he had moved to Newton Center two years ago.

Holding his teacup aloft, he counseled sympathetically, "Why don't we wait and see how he does by the end of the term?" He extended his pinky. "And meanwhile, I'll have a talk with him, about school first, and possibly about the other matter."

"You'll let me know what happens — what he says?"

"Of course!" he said, showing surprise.

Here, in reasonableness, she missed the old Stan. Unreasonable of her, of course, but she couldn't help herself. He had actually become, or was on the way to becoming, *reasonable*. Tamed this way, he was less attractive, she thought, for with this taming of his emotions had come the shaving of his ambition and the neutralizing of his instinct. She felt it and was sorry, even elegiac. He had experienced not an operation or lobotomy but a slow, sure anesthetizing — so much more awful than the few reefers taken by Jonathan. But it was his life, wasn't it?

She asked then, out of the politeness that he always appreciated and looked for and honored, about Röchel and his work. He described his recent successes in the company he was attached to now and two industrial grant proposals in the works. Röchel was fine, doing well in her social work.

"And Rafi, how is he? I liked him very much on the one occasion when we met," he offered, the colonel bathing in magnanimity. He had been most interested in meeting her lover.

"He's well, thank you."

"Back in Israel?"

"Yes."

"We hope to go for Pesach, did I tell you?"

Miriam didn't want to hear about it. Stan as an American tourist, going for a holiday; it was too cruel. Oh, he would have made a first-rate *halutz,* a pioneer, some wild Russian kibbutznick of the second *aliyah.*

"I'm also thinking of becoming observant," he declared, and she said, "Oh, how interesting," thinking just the opposite.

He leaned forward just the slightest bit and whispered some wisdom: "I know you probably think I've grown rather staid, straight-laced, perhaps even boring, but" — and he held up a fore-finger — "watch out that it's not maturity you're really against. Maturity and responsibility."

Considering that, she grew observant, too, sighting Peter Lorre in another poster, smoking a cigarette at a bar and gazing out furtively at the crowd. That beady-eyed monster, who'd sell his sister for the right price.

"And you," he asked, "how are you?"

She longed to be able to tell him something like "I'm going to be moving in with my new lover soon, and her name is Angela," or "I've done some new portraits of male nudes for an upcoming show," to see his reaction. The old wonderful wild reaction; per-haps he would grab her, yes, right there in the little restaurant, his face going chaotic, his accusations flowing — "Up to your old tricks, aren't you? You whore, you slut!" — and maybe even, working on that same powerful juice, wanting to make love to her? Was he right; was she against maturity after all?

"I didn't mean to ask you such a difficult question." He smiled affably.

She smiled back. "Oh, the difficulties are elsewhere. I'm fine, really, thank you. Same old grind, you know — teaching, photo-graphing now and then, not doing too much."

"And what are you photographing these days, if I may ask?"

"Why not?" She smiled, feeling guilty for her adolescent fantasy of a moment ago and yearning now to please him. "Actually, I'm doing some Jewish things. People. Cemeteries. Old objects."

"How marvelous! *That* I'd like very much to see. May I?"

She laughed. "Of course. They're not sacred, you know. My pictures, I mean."

"Now don't sell yourself short. In my opinion, you're developing very seriously indeed."

The language was not his fault; even his silly superiority wasn't. Genes, upbringing, mother.

She began to say something flippant, then caught sight of something out of the corner of her eye. She checked again, looked more closely, to make sure.

"What is it?"

"Uh, nothing. I, uh, thought I saw a friend passing." She had to think fast, recover her balance. Yes, it was him. *Him.* "Sorry. Of course you can see the pictures," she continued, her heart pumping. "Any time. Once I've developed them, that is." She had forgotten to smile and now tried.

Fortunately, Stan began to talk about choosing a new camera for himself, and she was able to sneak more glances and keep *him* in her vision. She didn't want to lose sight of him for some reason, though it terrified her. No, he hadn't changed much: the same angular length, the same menacing handsomeness, the same pale chocolate skin. Sitting at a table hustling a blond girl. Where was his bad-man hat? she wondered. Oh God, she felt helpless and confused and strangely fascinated.

"I asked, what do you think, should I buy the totally automatic Olympus or not?"

The best thing, of course, would be to tell Stan. Yes, that would do it perfectly. "Stan, dearest, the young man who raped me some eight years ago — I think he's sitting right here now, a few tables away. The lovely brown fellow over there, Stanley." Oh yes, oh yes, and there was Stan, leaving his British role and turning into a Russian hero, telling her to stay put, adjusting her collar, and walking directly over to the young man's table. Oh yes.

"Miriam, are you really all right?"

"Uh, yes, of course. Oh, the OM-two is fine."

Annoyed, he said, "But it's the *ten,* the OM-ten, I'm asking you about."

"Uh . . . yes, of course. That's right, the ten." She lit up a cigarette, feeling pressure in her chest, breathing hard, trying to concentrate. Briefly she recalled the Stan of eight years ago, a few days after the rape, when he had barely been able to control himself in his fury. A fury that was not entirely directed at the rapist, but at her, his ex-wife, who had somehow deserved it (her projection?).

"I thought you said you've been fine," he said to her now. "Perhaps Jon is sensing this distractedness in you. Have you" — he adjusted his words — "checked in with a doctor about this?"

She drew in smoke, caught her tongue between her teeth, tried again for a smile. But keeping sight of the young "dude" while appearing to look out the window every now and then, she kept in sight her old acquaintance. What could, should, she do?

"No, I'm okay, really. I just have . . . something on my mind."

He gazed at her, loosened his tie a bit in a gesture of sympathy, and said, with a smile of generosity, "So tell me, what are some sights to see in the Holy Land?"

A reckless laugh broke the lock of her reverie.

"Oh, the sights!" She inhaled, seeing *him* move suddenly; was he getting up? God, no! "Well, look . . . I have an idea. Why don't I lay out a small list of things on paper? That would be the easiest and best, don't you think?" No, he was just getting something from the girl's jacket. But it was clear that Miriam had to get out of here and be ready, outside somewhere, when he did leave. But why, why?

"Yes, that would be very nice of you, indeed," Stanley concurred, finishing up his last cup of tea. "And of course, if there's anything I can do for you over there, you must tell me." His left eyebrow arched. "Or here, of course. Is there something?"

Oh yes, yes, Stan, how good of you to ask, my darling. Stay with me right now for the next half hour or so and let's watch this fellow together. Be my detective, my bodyguard!

She reached over and stroked his cheek. "That's very sweet of you, Stanley. Thanks. If I should need something, I'll ask, rest assured."

Stroked, Stan purred. "Good, Miry. You know, you have an awful lot of potential, and you mustn't let small obstacles stand in the way. You understand?"

Having no idea what in the world he was babbling about, she nodded gravely and said, "Oh course." She paused, looked at him with sincerity, checked her target, and said, "Maybe we should go now; it's getting a bit late. You will speak to Jon, though, won't you?"

"Absolutely. And if you want me to go to Commonwealth next time, just say so."

She thanked him, took her pocketbook, and edged up, turning sideways to *him*. Could he have been the telephone caller too? No, it didn't make sense.

At the cash register she sought to take money out to pay, but Stan insisted on treating, and she let him. Facing the register, she kept her back to the room.

Outside, it was an uncertain day, with sporadic periods of light rain or drizzle. Fortunately, she had worn her raincoat, and now put up her hood.

"Can I drop you somewhere?"

"Ah, thanks, Stan, I'm going to do a bit of shopping in the Square."

Accepting that, he put out his hand, and she took it. His chivalry was kindly, ludicrous.

"Take care of yourself," she said.

"I will; you too."

"And I won't forget that list."

"We'll appreciate it."

Bowing slightly, he turned like a colonel and marched off toward his car. Leaving her alone. She took a few steps to the post office on Mt. Auburn, went in one door and out the other. By then Stan was gone from the street, and she walked back past the café, noting that *he* was still there, and crossed over toward the old Cronin's restaurant. There she huddled in a doorway, shielded from the drizzle, and stood watch.

Why? And what would she do if . . . ?

Should she call the police now? Could they check anything this old? Would her testimony hold water now, eight years later? Absurd. She leaned against the wall, saying that word over and over again. She had little idea of what she was doing, or would do when he emerged. She had her camera with her, but what good was that? Would a revolver have been better? Oh, Angela, maybe I should have taken up your offer of adventure and stayed in Northampton.

She huddled to herself in the light drizzle, her face getting moist and cold.

It seemed like hours, though by her watch it was only twenty minutes, before he did in fact come out, accompanying the blond girl. The sight of him stiffened her with alertness, and she got ready to move.

He wore a beret now, not a cowboy hat, and a smart leather (or vinyl) jacket, beige flare slacks, and low, buckled boots. Also an earring in one ear. What the hell did this dandy do, play pirate with the coeds of Cambridge?

They headed for the Square, and she followed at a distance. The grayness of the day helped, for they were fixed on getting to where they were going quickly. Not that she, Miriam, would have been recognizable as a tail. She hardly looked the part.

When they turned at Eliot Street and headed for the parking lot at the neglected MBTA station tracks, she had a strong suspicion that he was aiming for a car. Panicky, she looked about. C'mon, cab, where are you when I need you?

There.

She hailed it and told the driver she wanted to follow someone. The driver was not a Russian this time, but an ebony man with a West Indian accent, who smiled broadly. "Everyone is playing cops and robbers up here."

"Right there, that's them. Okay?"

"It's your money."

"Keep a distance, though."

The driver laughed, having a grand time while the taxi idled in a separate lane.

Her old acquaintance, somewhere in his thirties, opened the door of a sharp two-toned coupe and escorted the young woman inside, then went around and lowered himself into the driver's seat. The automobile eased out onto the street, its medium, like a big cranberry-colored shark slipping away from its coral reef. The taxi waited, then pulled out and followed slowly, with care.

"What is that car?"

"You mean the make? Cutlass. Cool, isn't it?"

"Be careful he doesn't spot you. Who's Cutlass?"

The cabbie shot her a look. "Where you been? Oldsmobile."

The car in front glided through the side streets and then fled up

Concord to Garden, heading for Fresh Pond. Miriam's taxi took it very easy, and she was full of admiration for her driver. "You're good," she said.

"I've seen it many times on television, you know." He laughed, showing an uneven row of gold caps.

At Linnaean Street the Cutlass turned, and the taxi followed to the first corner, where it halted and peeked around. Miriam saw the car stop by the Radcliffe dorms, where the girl got out, waved good-bye, and shut the door. Miriam barely made out the license plate number and jotted it down — XL 1225. The young woman — a student? — strolled into the dorm area and the car slid away, at which point the cabbie followed, allowing a sports car to pull ahead of the taxi as cover.

For the next ten minutes they pursued the sleek automobile down Mass. Avenue, back through the Square, and around to Memorial Drive, where it turned and headed for Boston. Here it was easy to keep a reasonable distance behind, and also to check on the license. Yes, she had it right.

Suddenly the car veered into the left lane, swerved left off the drive, and went up Western Avenue about fifty yards and into the parking lot of an expensive new apartment complex set on Memorial Drive, overlooking the river. Number 888: she knew. The taxi pulled over on the other side of Western Avenue.

"Wanna go in there?"

Christ. "Sure."

On the red light the taxi cut sharply away from the curb, across the street, and into the parking lot, which, fortunately, was spacious enough to park in anonymously.

"Now what?" the cabbie asked, a wide smile revealing how much fun he was having, watching the natives.

She was frightened but in control, thinking coolly. *He* was already locking his car and heading inside. Think fast! she told herself.

"Look, you go in there, would you, and if you can find out his name or apartment number, there's an extra sawbuck in it for you." Her father's old word. He stared at her, puzzled. "Ten bucks."

He laughed lazily. "You kiddin' me?"

She couldn't tell whether this island man was amused or angry, serious or casual.

She took out a $10 bill and gave it to him. When he hesitated, she said, "Get something, and I'll give you another ten when you return."

The driver turned off the engine and scooted out of the taxi with surprising alacrity. A stocky fellow, he adjusted his vinyl cap while walking.

Miriam sat back, heart thumping loudly, and smoked. She was scared. Resolute. Grateful it was daylight. You finally had to take things into your own hands, didn't you? Somewhere along the line. As crazy as they seemed. She locked all the doors, just in case, and sank down in the back seat. Suddenly the sliding glass partition that separated driver from passenger reminded her of another such partition, years ago. *Where was her baseball cap? What were those policemen's names?*

If this didn't work, she'd have to come back here another time. And if it did, what then? Although this was unreal, this was also real. On another plane, though.

The five or six minutes that passed on her watch seemed like fifty before her driver was tapping at the window. He shook his head, getting in. "You know what? I was myself a little jumpy in there!" He laughed.

"Any luck?"

"DuPres, R., Apartment Ten D. That's your man." Long *a* in *man*. "At least, that's the apartment he entered, and that's what the name of the bell read downstairs."

She handed him another $10 and told him to take her home. But as they drove off, she decided that home might be dangerous for some reason — blackmail? — and said to drop her in Central Square.

Riding, she felt calmer, and allowed herself to feel satisfaction. Slow, enormous waves of satisfaction. Mr. R. DuPres was a target now, her target, and visible. She leaned back, and as she did, she realized just how much strain she had been under. Her body was taut as a drum. Slowly the muscles of her back and neck let go, and those in her legs eased up. God. So the pretty-boy bastard was living right here in her hometown all the time, and even hustled the college girls. Using what disguise — revolutionary, ghetto boy, cowboy loner? She almost laughed aloud as she perceived that real life could, after all, imitate Jon's television shows. Somehow. Where to go from here, however? Where?

She got out at Central Square, paid the driver $14.70 without a tip, and bid him good-bye.

"Lady, you sure are an American woman!" he said, laughing jovially and driving off.

The cold drizzle was fainter, and the air bluish gray. Central Square bustled with people shopping, leaving and entering the subway, hanging around storefronts. The activity pleased her and began to clear her head. At a doughnut shop by the subway station she stopped, waited in a short line, and purchased a sweet Portuguese bread along with two custard éclairs for the kids. From here she could walk over to Harry's, but she didn't feel like talking, really. So she wandered back along Mass. Avenue, stopping in the new Hit or Miss shop that had replaced half of a huge East Indian store. There she tried on two flowery skirts for spring, a pair of off-white balloon trousers, a corduroy blazer. While dressing and undressing in the tiny telephone booth of a changing room, she tried to figure out what to do with her new knowledge. Feed the data to a smart computer and see what it came up with? Feed them to Rafi, due in a few weeks? Check in with Dr. Beaumont for local advice? Or hire a detective for two days and find out more about the fellow? Why not? Maybe he was still raping regularly — and was not just a pretty boy? Shouldn't he be stopped, in one way or another? She settled for a loose knit sweater for $9, and carefully laid her dilemma out on the back burner to simmer. What to do about one's ex-rapist, now that one's ex-husband is taken care of?

At home afterward, while preparing a dinner of hamburgers and mashed potatoes for the kids, she thought that maybe she would, after all, do the dirty work herself, and follow her dangerous dandy around for a few days and see what she could come up with. Save a few hundred bucks, too. To play detective for a day would be interesting; maybe she could even grab a few choice photographs. (Oh, if only she could!) As she served the children, Jon mimicked Rosie: "Ketchup, Mom, ketchup, puh-leeeze!"

Whereupon Rosie smacked him, and Miriam had to break it up, which ended her daydreaming. She brought the ketchup and watched them smother her egg-filled hamburgers with the awful stuff. "Look, Mom, she's bleeding *bad!*" screeched Hollywood Jon, pointing to his sister's red wrists, and Rosie screamed back in protest. The mock gore had a surprisingly salutary effect on Miriam; she told Jon to wipe it from his sister's hands and restored order, but it cut through her detective fantasy and warned her of the real fire she was playing with. The children had instructed her just in time, perhaps.

Not Bogart but T. Arthur Purcell she got: a plump Englishman in his fifties with a ruddy complexion, cleft chin, and somewhat effete manners. "Yes, I see what you mean," he uttered after hearing what she wanted — to have a man tailed for a day or two, to see what he did for a living and who he really was. "Shouldn't be too difficult," he mumbled, shuffling a cup of coffee toward her.

Miriam, sitting in the pebble-glass-walled office of this T. Arthur Purcell, accepted the paper cup. She could hardly believe that she was there. There were two dull landscapes on the wall, a framed diploma of some sort, a few straight-backed chairs and a large oak desk, plus this seedy Englishman. According to Vera, he was reasonably priced and reasonably effective. To Miriam, he sounded and looked — in his tattersall shirt and skinny woolen tie and khaki wool cardigan — like a clerk in the civil service.

"How long have you been doing this, if I may ask, in America?"

His thin smile showed yellowish teeth, and he wiped a long strand of hair back onto his head. "Eleven years, in a fortnight."

"And before that, if I may ask again?"

He smiled less broadly at this question, but acquiesced. "Scotland Yard, actually. Now, we ought to get on with the present matter — that is, if you wish me to go ahead. I should let you know of my charges just now, shouldn't I?"

My God, *he* sounded mysterious! Had he been relieved of his duty in England — a spy scandal, perhaps? Did she need a detective to trail her detective?

He explained that he received $150 per day; she said she couldn't afford that. He leaned back in his tilting chair and lit a Benson and Hedges, put a fey wrist to his pink chin, and asked her what she did for a living.

"Some teaching, some photography," she answered.

"I'll tell you what, then, we'll make it a flat fee of two hundred dollars, and if I need some photographs, I'll hire you."

She smiled, nodded okay, and wondered what she was getting into.

"Of course, it'll be a few days, since for a flat fee I'll fit in the hours that suit me best. Is that agreeable?"

"Sure."

"Good."

She kept wondering when and if he would ask *why* she wanted the information, but the question never came. Politely she asked, "Shall I write you a check?"

"That would be very nice, thank you. Half now, and half when the task is done."

A task. A tisket a tasket — children's terms for children's games. She wrote out the check and handed it over to his pudgy hand. Accepting it, he stood up and escorted her to the door.

"Thank you, Mr. Purcell."

"I hope I can be of service, Miss Scheinman."

When she left the tall, nondescript building in Brookline, she turned and stared at the brick and mortar, to check out its reality. Had she imagined the scene? Entered into something that she'd be sorry for, deeply sorry for? If she was indeed going to trust that fellow, perhaps he could best advise her of what to do with the information, if he got it . . . Oh God, she hoped Vera's judgment was correct!

And for the next few days she was anxious and jumpy, as if T. Arthur Purcell were trailing *her* and not DuPres. How incongruous, to place herself into such a web of insane intrigue! And for such a bizarre assignment! With a British clerk, no less, not a hard-boiled native son. She felt so damned foolish. So involved with melodrama when what she wanted was adult drama; yet how different this stuff looked and felt from the inside.

The week passed and nothing happened; a blank on the calendar. After the weekend, however, Mr. Purcell called her up and asked if she would drop in on Tuesday following; he had some news for her.

On Tuesday, after her MIT class, she drove over to Brookline and found herself once again in that curious office. From high to low life.

"Do these walls really have wire mesh in them to protect against bullets?" she asked.

He looked up at the glass, as if seeing it for the first time, and parceled out a little laugh. "I think so, actually. No one has shot at me yet, so I can't verify it."

She sat down in a straight wooden chair on one side of the enormous desk, while Mr. Purcell sat on the other, opening a manila folder.

"I believe that your Mr. R. DuPres of 888 Memorial Drive in Cambridge is what may be called a procurer. A rather high-class procurer, operating out of the better hotels in the region. The Hyatt Regency, Copley Plaza, and so on."

Just to be sure of the language, she said, "A pimp?"

"As you wish."

"Yes. Thank you."

"Hold on, there is a bit more. Mr. DuPres lives in or possesses several apartments at least — the one in Cambridge, another on Longwood Terrace, a third on the wharf. Either he or his lady friends live at these addresses." He handed her a five-by-eight index card. "He's a rich young man by now, I venture to say."

She suddenly felt weak. "Thank you" was all she could think of to say.

"Is there something, uh, wrong?"

She shook her head, holding back tears.

"Now," he went on, looking at another card, "he also goes under several names, to go along with the apartments. There is R. DuPres and R. Robinson and R. Carter. The R. stands for Reggie, Reggie DuPres, Jr., and he receives mail from someone named DuPres in Baton Rouge, Louisiana. I assume that his true Christian name is Reginald and that the surnames are aliases. Does this help you at all?"

Did it help her? To do what?

She looked up at the ruddy, polite face and explained briefly what had occurred eight years ago. She paused and asked, "Is there anything I can do, legally, now?"

"I *see*," he said, opening a button on his khaki cardigan. "Are you quite sure, after all this time, that it *is* him, the same chap?"

She nodded twice, slowly.

"I see. Well. You can press charges, of course. But I don't think that any positive results would ensue, to be quite frank."

She nodded again. "I understand."

"This *is* a difficult situation, isn't it? Forgive me for asking, but you had no, uh, relationship whatsoever — he and you, I mean — before the incident? You just met him in the park and he accosted you, as a perfect stranger?"

"No relationship, no love affair or meeting. Just rape."

"I *see*." He bent over, asked if she minded cigar smoke, and took a thin cigar from a drawer. "An odd situation, isn't it?"

Exhausted from all the oddness, as if *she* had done the trailing of the past few days, she nodded.

Purcell exhaled smoke to the side, pleasurelessly, she thought, and scratched the middle of his forehead with his index fingernail. Was he homosexual, and had he been fired from the Yard because of a scandal? A rush of sympathy swelled in her.

"It is a pity, isn't it?" he said.

"Yes," she agreed, referring to his past as she had constructed it.

"Look, let me think on it a bit, and if I come up with anything, I'll let you know."

"That's awfully nice of you."

"Please don't expect anything brilliant; I'm not that sort. And furthermore, I don't see what can be done, short of catching him in the act again. For now, at least, he seems free of that . . . preoccupation."

"I understand." She got ready to go, then realized she had not yet paid him. She wrote out a check and handed it over.

"Yes, well, thank you." He accepted it, standing, somewhat embarrassed.

At the door he said, "We do have to live through most peculiar experiences, don't we? What was it Carlyle said?" He caught himself and laughed a small, derisive laugh. "Always the English schoolboy, aren't I?" His smoky gray eyes, usually half hidden beneath their pinkish lids, revealed themselves now like two small animals emerging from their burrow. "Good day, Miss Scheinman."

She nodded good-bye and departed. Down the long, uncarpeted corridor she walked, thinking how she wished he had gone on and quoted Carlyle. But the visit had been comforting; R. DuPres was less of a mysterious element now.

At the front entrance to the building, she turned, retraced her steps, and knocked on Purcell's door.

Once admitted, she asked, "What did Carlyle say?"

The eyes widened ever so slightly in surprise. "Oh. Yes. 'Experience is the best of schoolmasters, only the school fees are heavy.' " Barely, he smiled. "Perhaps not worth returning for."

But it was; not the wisdom but the intonation. It seemed a line of self-explanation as much as anything. "I shall remember that," she said, and left again. School fees.

Afterward, driving.

From a British Mandate colonel to an American psychopath and back to a British civil servant; she had almost circled the bases, she figured.

So now she had on her hands a Hollywood script in potential, a real-life criminal, a peculiar dilemma. Why in the world did you pursue the fellow? she asked herself. Secret attraction? Mischief-making from your thirties? Stupid folly? A danger gene? Miss Miriam Scheinman, where are *you* in all of this chaos, this mixture of the real and the fantastic? What exactly are you pursuing? Do you have a secret plot up your sleeve, lady?

If you are still a woman in the making, I, your patient alter ego, am growing a bit tired. Fatigued. When will you be finished, in one fashion or another?

Answers: none.

One other thing: that little scene a few nights ago, thinking about the return of your Israeli hero and his special aromas and pleasing yourself by means of yourself. You can mention that, you know; allow the play to surface; nothing to be ashamed of. We're big girls around here, have you forgotten?

Blushing, here, alone on the road?

7

RAFI arrived in the first week of March for his two to three months, bringing with him a ten-inch snowstorm. Carrying his B-4 bag and haloed in snow, he showed up at the door looking like some springtime Santa Claus. She felt familiar in his arms, snuggling her face in his neck, feeling his wet face and snowy hair like a benefaction. Her Israeli safety net, after her days of anxiety and uncertainty.

"I thought you promised me spring," he said, shivering in his sports jacket and pullover.

"Never trust me, or New England," she said.

With suitcase and shoulder bag, he was here like a returning soldier, home from the wars. Rosie observed him from the edge of the living room, one arm on the door, face half averted in theatrical shyness; at eleven, she was a studied actress. When he greeted her, she tried out a quick "Shalom" and took a step inside. Rafi didn't push it, however, only wondered whether he might have a drink of whisky to warm up some. But by the time Miriam had reentered with his scotch, Rosie was busy unwrapping her present. Miriam chided, "You couldn't wait, eh?" Rafi answered, "Why should she?" With rapt attention Rosie held up a large doll, dressed in a velvet and cotton Yemenite dress, for her already extensive collection — one fit more for a collector than for a young girl. "You're encouraging her in the wrong direction," Miriam half protested, but Rosie looked at her sharply, then raced to Rafi's chair and gave him a rare kiss. A seductress as well as an actress, Miriam thought, envious.

Miriam too, in her way, couldn't wait to open her own surprise, to see whether her situation with the doctor would enter into her Rafi-feelings. But immediately after Rafi arrived her affection and ardor for him rose up, and stayed that way through the night. The doctor was in a different world from this man, she knew, gazing at Rafi's trim waistline and modest size, curly brown hair and green-blue eyes, fresh white shirt and pressed slacks. He had the look of a colt or a fawn, not a rider. Yet when he said to her, after his snack of minced tomato, cucumber, and cottage cheese, "So have you cleared the closets of his shoes, trousers?" she felt the irony cut. She gave him his tea, helped him unwind with gossip and chat, and escorted him to bed after his sixteen-hour trek (in Rome, naturally, a delay). Hanging up his trousers and shirt as he would have, she stayed and watched him sleep, feeling herself happy, guilty, unsure.

Later Jon came in, and he immediately wanted to rush to Rafi and tell him all about his progress in soccer, at school, and about the Celtics. She told him to cool it and let Rafi sleep, though she was secretly glad to see his enthusiasm. Far too often in the past he had acted out his hostility toward Rafi, directly and indirectly. And when he protested now — "Cheesus, Mom, by the time he wakes I'll be in school, and he'll think I couldn't care less!" — she said she'd explain; he could see Rafi tomorrow. Then she sent him off by asking about his history project, due in a month. Colonial Cambridge, his topic, always sent him scurrying. She checked out Rosie for the night, got undressed, and took her book to bed. Nestling alongside her man, she tried to read, listening to his low breathing and remembering Stan's snore.

Safety. Security. Familiarity. Components of affection (if not love). How long would it take to settle in with him this time? We live like barnacles, hanging on desperately to another's peculiar habits, which become small rites. His way of brushing his teeth in small circles; his care in hanging up his clothes for the night; his odd parceling-out of food (not meals), with a spread of bread and chocolate at 4:30! The frequent cupping of my tush ("making the big leagues," he says, fondly practicing his new idioms). The Israeli way of showering, with water splashing everywhere — desert rats coming to drink. How *curious* to have this man, this torso, this smell, alongside of me again, after months of solitariness! Should he help in the sorting out of my dark ghost? Or the problem of my Montana knight? No, leave him be. He's come for relaxation, easy times, pleasures; let him have those. My burdens are my burdens. Why load my dear sabra?

In the next weeks she gave him his pleasures, while attending to the alternating waves of feeling assaulting her — waves of confusion, fear, and sadness, which formed a steady undercurrent, a private seditiousness, to the ongoing successes and joys. And this was all right with her, in its way; it was a sort of price to be paid for the jaunts of her spirit, the tours of her body. The dark ghost and the white knight moved her in different ways, which she didn't fully understand. Did she need to?

In passion too she wasn't sure how much she was for real, how much for drama (her own). Oh yes, she put her body through the acts, and did well enough; enjoyed her dear lover again, from his tender neck and muscled thighs to his fine prick, and enjoyed herself too. But she knew by now that the self-deceptions of adulthood in the field of play were legion and subtle. And that the body was an actor in pursuit of its own ends, using its own familiar lines and plot. So while she convinced her most important audience, Rafi, of her sincere labors, she remained somewhat skeptical of herself. Yes, it would have been clearer if she had worn some sort of costume or dress, like the black outfit she had worn with Andrei (and remembered too vividly); but on stage with only her nakedness, how could she be anything but *there*, but *honest?* So that when Rafi looked at her directly and said, "Oh I do miss you, even though I don't announce it too much," she could only kiss his cheek and hold him to her, while holding her doubts within.

Still, ardor was ardor, and this fact was not lost on her — not on one who had spent thirteen years in a conjugal bed that had been increasingly passionless. Oh, she remembered those years with a fondness bordering on vengeance. Imprinted on her brain, her nervous system, was the message Thou Shalt Not Go Empty, Unwanted, Unwanting. And she adhered to the principle, though the bed was not conjugal. Never again would she accept unlove, unpassion; the years of bodily deprivation signified years of spiritual drought. The one connected up with the other. True, much of that deprivation had to do with her will to deny pleasure during those lean years of ego alone. No more. She was Miriam of some weight now, of some dominion; trying to be whole, trying to love another, though it was easier said than done. And if ardor didn't necessarily signify that the project of loving had been fulfilled, it at least told her that a line of friendship was being strengthened. (Again, if she was not totally acting.) And friends now, in the middle years, seemed more important than ever.

So secret agent, actress, skeptic that she was, she resorted to pleasure in the return to small routines. Several mornings a week, when Rafi was not going over to the American School for Oriental Research on Inman Street, he hiked a few blocks to pick up croissants or bagels, and they lingered over breakfast and newspapers. He cooked dinner twice a week at least, and instead of eating her thrown-together leftovers, they actually dined — a leg of lamb, fancy pork chops fried with bananas, chicken breasts sautéed with lemon and wine. Once a week they ate the mandatory Chinese meal at one of the new Szechuan restaurants springing up around town like Dutch tulips in spring. "In the kibbutz we've not yet attained Hunan ham," he remarked, when she inquired if she had made him a Szechuan freak. Saturdays or Sundays, depending on the weather, they went bicycling or walking, and if Jon tagged along, they got in some soccer. ("I'm gonna be a goalie, I think — it's easier," Jon quipped one day, after a session of practicing headers and winding up with a bloody nose.) Occasionally, Rafi took Rosie somewhere: a science exhibit, a magic show, *The Pirates of Penzance* at the Peabody School. For themselves, they preferred movies to theater, and mostly went to reruns at the local cinemas. For a few bucks each they saw Hitchcock and Thin Man mysteries in Central Square, Kurosawa and Bergman and Fellini at the Brattle, plus one of Miriam's favorites, the little-known Pietro Germi film *Seduced and Abandoned*.

"Oh no, I won't see it for a third time," Rafi protested one evening, "no matter how much I love Sondra Stefanelli."

"You mean you love your Nabateans more," Miriam said, and she left him to his monograph and proceeded alone to Harvard

Square to see the complex film yet again. And there, in that dark womb of a theater, her dark dilemma returned, riding her consciousness like an incubus. For a moment she was in the peculiar position of playing the hunter who did not know what to do with her prey. To catch him or not? Oh to be this Sondra Stefanelli, up there on the flickering screen, caught in the traditional traps of courtship and illicit pregnancy in a small Sicilian town, rather than Miriam Scheinman, haunted by a live ghost in her New England academic town. For what was this light-skinned pretty-boy pimp but a figure from some Hollywood screen, who by chance had leaped out into real life and settled, like some alien from outer space, into this innocent town? Why not this Italian actor instead, she wondered, feeling the ripped seat, remembering that fateful night on the Common . . .

The rundown moviehouse contrasted with the palatial theater in Northampton. Should she hire Connie, Angela, Livia to form some women's posse, and hunt down the prettyboy outlaw for a citizen's arrest? Slowly the plot up there took hold, the comic-tragic tones infiltrated, and she was able to retreat into Sicily, a woman's honor, black and white dignity. Like Germi, Rafi took her mind elsewhere too, and she still had no desire to involve him in her sullied doings or scrambled puzzle. So what if she'd never be "prudent," was Sondra? She'd protect Rafi, keep him clean.

Three weeks after Rafi's return she lunched with Scotty Beaumont, meeting her doctor in an anonymous place on Charles Street where the French bread was fresh and the clientele neighborhood-stale. It was a difficult meeting for her. They shared opening hugs and greetings, and then she asked some aimless questions about his work, to hear him again. Ages, these weeks, it seemed. He was like some Lipizzaner stallion asked to sit still for lunch: long, pale face, mournful eyes, splendid waving silvery mane, wide spaces in the face that reminded her of Montana. Oh, she had missed him, and longed to reach out and touch his long upper body! Instead she gazed out the window at the busy pedestrians and the narrow street. "Have you been listening?" he asked, and when she lied that she could repeat every word, he shook his head. "It was boring enough the first time." So they ate their mushroom omelettes and

salad and his voice ran through her and finally she told him that
it was impossible for her to see him for a while, and he nodded,
accepting it, keeping his feelings in. She new that, appreciated it,
felt saddened by it. He knew, of course, that her Israeli had come
to town; she had cautioned him beforehand, and he acted now
with stoical understanding. The discrepancy between his gentlemanly politeness and his frayed, frantic passion moved and excited
her. And when he said, as they were having their last coffee, "You
know, you mean a lot to me," she took his hand — the one with
the wedding band — and replied, "You mean a lot to me, too."
She wanted to hear more about his life and how he was, but he
didn't want to get into it at all. It didn't matter just now did it?

When they parted, he grabbed her to him tightly, by surprise,
on a side street, and she felt the force of him again, his exciting
strength and erotic height — where were his Dr. J. leaps? — and
she kissed him quickly once and said she had better go. She walked
away and took the long way home, past the flower garden and
through the Common, with the March wind blowing against her
face and legs, against her desire, her soul, soothing — or fan-
ning? — her feeling for this Scotty Beaumont. She tried her best
to block out his face, his voice, his need, as she finally made her
way to the Park Street subway stop, having passed Frisbee games
and parading citizens and new birds in town and having noticed
nothing.

She couldn't help thinking about timing in life; where had he
been five or six years ago (before Rafi), when he could have filled
the emptiness in her life so powerfully? Why *now?* She sat in the
bumpy subway train, thinking how it was not because of principle
but because of feeling that she couldn't see him now. By feeling,
not logic or ideology, she'd rise or fall, she knew. And now she
had room for Rafi only, as much as she *wanted* Dr. Beaumont
suddenly, now that she had seen him. But the *sudden wanting*
suddenly wasn't enough justification for fulfilling it, now in her
life. She was hurting, as if she had been shot in the woods and
left wounded; the train passed over the Longfellow Bridge and the
blue-black water of the Charles River broke and foamed white
from the high wind. She half wished that the water would rise up
and wash over her and carry her out somewhere, away . . .

Back home, she spent the rest of the day and evening washing the doctor clean from the beach of her consciousness and pushing him back out to deeper seas. Once again she sojourned to a movie alone, to protect herself and Rafi. Though she knew it was a sign of living, this pain, this dilemma, it hurt — it hurt! Better to concentrate for a few hours on the easy glamour up there on the big screen, where the happy ending was in the bag, than on her own life.

She didn't know how she got sick, or rather, how the small cold developed into something bigger and more mystifying. It started out as a head cold, which then traveled to her throat and chest. Tea with lemon and gallons of juice and water, plus aspirins, she tried first. But after a week she found herself with a fever that, oddly enough, came late every afternoon and stayed through the night, and by the morning had vanished. She was so weak by the end of the second week that she had to cancel classes, for the first time since she had begun teaching. The doctor she finally went to see, a tall, lugubrious Dr. Gottfried in Mt. Auburn Hospital, gave her a variety of tests and sent her home to bed. Three days later he called to say that the tests had proved negative, and that whatever it was would probably disappear shortly. Did she still have a fever? Then stay in bed, rest up. Indeed, when she did try to rise, she felt so weak in her knees and foggy in the head that she had to lie down again.

"Dearest, do you think this is a reaction to you?" she asked Rafi one day at the end of the second week. "And to pleasure?"

"I'm sure it must be," he replied, bringing her her one-hundred-and-fortieth cup of tea with a biscuit. "Social tea, for being excellent today."

"I guess I'm just doomed to be punished for having a good time," she said, allowing him to prop her pillow and add another. "You really are a good nurse, though. It's lovely to be cared for by you."

He laughed, his green eyes mirthful. He smelled like oleander and tobacco, and she caressed his neck.

"This is why I came," he rejoined, "precisely to take care of you."

By the beginning of the third week it looked as though the siege had ended and she was headed for recovery. Her head was clear; the periodic nausea was gone; the fever hadn't flared for two days. So she got up, and though she was weak, she decided to teach again and conduct a seminormal life. For the first few hours all went well — getting dressed, traveling to MIT, and giving the early class; then, smack in the middle of photo lab, she nearly passed out. Two students had to hold her, give her water, finally drive her home. And then she felt worse than ever — here she was, back to square zero. When Rafi arrived home from the library, she was in bed, crying with depression. "It's not working," she complained to Rafi, who sat on the bed. "I'm not getting better. What is it?"

"Look, we'll take you to a specialist, especially if the fever returns." He paused and wiped her brow with his hand. "You might have gone back too soon — relapse, you understand."

"But it's been three weeks!"

"Would you like some tea?"

She shook her head in pain.

"Juice?"

She shook her head.

"Ginger ale?"

She opened her eyes at the thought. "Yes."

He went out, and she heard the refrigerator door opening and then the front door closing — Rosie? — and she felt more and more helpless. What would she do if Rafi weren't here now? Or when he left? Oh God, now I see why people stay married — fear, fear!

In the next few days she tried to consider the possible psychosomatic causes of the illness. Was the tension caused by having two men injuring her more than she knew? Was there more guilt involved than she could admit? Did her free-and-easy pleasures go under another name, such as high-cost duplicity? Or was she on the wrong track altogether? She pondered the question, lying in bed and holding a fashion magazine aimlessly. Had she fallen down now in order to test out her relationship to Rafi? To see how he acted when he saw her at her down-and-out worst, not a strong, supporting, adventurous woman but a woman over forty, over the hill physiologically, in decline? Yes, very possibly. Another thing:

did she want Rafi to handle Jonathan just now? And maybe, too, to handle the case of R. DuPres — was her prey preying upon her? Were the queries coagulating, turning into thick gray matter, an indissoluable substance, which she didn't want — couldn't — handle? Where was her sphinx, Dr. Levanda, who had *promised* her all the support she needed, whenever she needed it? From her grave she whispered, only memory.

The fourth week of the illness found Miriam at her lowest point, rock bottom. The late-afternoon fevers had returned, and Dr. Gottfried had asked her to come in for more tests the next day. Jonathan came into her room and complained bitterly that Rafi had promised to play soccer with him that Saturday and was now backing out because of her sickness. "Cheesus, Mom, you've been sick now for a whole month. When is it gonna end? Why should *I* lose out because . . . because . . . well, cheesus! Maybe he's bored with spending time with me, ya know, but can't admit it. What're you goin' to do about it, huh?" She started crying from the wayward assault, and he uttered an expletive and crashed out. The thought hit her that he, too, was beginning to blame her for the illness and her time away from the family, and that pushed her down even farther into the hole.

This setback led to a deeper dejection, a vivid memory of her breakdown year. The same feelings of implacable depression — of not having the will to stir from bed in the morning, of not being able to sleep at night, of constantly being tempted by a small, devilish voice that taunted her with, "Come on now, take some pills, be brave, show your gutsiness and end it all; why go on with this boring self-torment?" — returned now, years later, like a vengeful dream. The present mysterious illness worked as an insidious reminder of the frailty of her stability; once you had been blown up, smashed, the marks stayed like shrapnel scars. And when you weren't looking, when you were swimming casually, the undertow suddenly caught you and swept you out and under, into its cavernous swirls of darkness and chaos, its inlets of injury, and there was little hope, little help from those swimming above. You were alone, unheard.

Ineluctably, it seemed, she receded deeper into gloom, into muck; privately she cried and cried. Never in front of Rafi, who could take anything but an open psychic wound. Not in front of the children, of course. But then who was there to cry in front of — who? And a new sly, persistent voice said, with shrewd timing, "Don't be a fool, no one understands what this is, what you're going through, what you have to face. You're alone, utterly and entirely *alone,* so why not come with me into the bathroom where there are those little white pills, if you don't want the razor blade — yes, the same razor you shave your legs with? Come, things will be easier then, I assure you. A slow fog, some gentle clouding up, and the end of bewildered struggling and the end of losing. Come."

A phone call helped to save her. Paradoxically, the phone call brought news of illness, but this was all right. "Yes, this time the results are positive," Dr. Gottfried said. "It's a viral pneumonia, I'm afraid, which is what it's been all along. The reason why it didn't show up previously . . ." and though he thought he was a bearer of bad news, he was just the opposite. "Yes, yes, sure I understand," she asserted, and when the doctor responded with, "Are you sure you understand me? You sound almost *happy.* This will take another two, maybe three, weeks to work its way completely through your system, and it will mean no teaching or work, but rest and plenty of it." She masked her pleasure and switched to appropriate concern; even self-chastisement. "Oh yes, Doctor, I understand perfectly." That was the way they wanted you to feel, chastised and grateful. And she, feeling happy, acceded to his wishes and played out the emotions. But later, when Rafi arrived, she called to him and said, "We've done it, we've broken through! I'm *really* ill — it's pneumonia!"

Her delight puzzled him. "Then why the celebration?"

Coughing, she said, "Because I wasn't making it up, don't you see? I'm *really* sick. There is a real germ alive in me! I'm really sick, do you see?"

"Have you thought otherwise all this time?" he wondered seriously.

She couldn't admit the entire truth. Even those closest to you didn't — couldn't — understand your depths of depression and fear. "Not all the time, no."

He shook his head and smiled. "I warned you against self-pity, didn't I?"

She nodded, and drew him to her. "Oh yes, you did warn me, and I didn't listen. Oh, I was bad, wasn't I!" Now the little-girl-grateful. And here she began to cough, that rough cough of the past week, and she couldn't finish her sentence, but it didn't matter, for she was ill. She believed it now, and in two or three weeks it would be gone. And it was not imaginary, and not self-punishment. And oh, it was just lovely to have a real illness, a real virus, which you could fight off with T-cells (?) and chemicals, not therapists! Lovely! She held Rafi tightly and wouldn't let him go.

And indeed, the next few weeks saw her funneling serenely upward, taking gorgeous time for reading and listening to music and slowly coming up for air. Rafi did everything from cooking and cleaning and caring for the kids to reading to her at night, from Hardy again. "This is better than Hans Castorp ever had it," she told him one evening. "Who?" "A friend from adolescence who spent some time in a German sanitarium." He stared at her, and when she explained the reference, he said, "I tried at least twice to read Mann, and never succeeded." "Too slow?" He nodded, and added, "I prefer Agnon, who is just as difficult." Those weeks were slow too, a beautiful slowing down of time, which she was able to appreciate now because she knew that she'd be better soon, was better already, save for the piercing cough and the phlegm. Indeed, when the cough woke her at night and drove her into the kitchen for tea and honey (on no account would she permit Rafi to get up for these nightly ordeals), she was able to tolerate the god-awful pain and choking by remembering her recent bout with depression and realizing how petty this passing physical trial was. So she'd cough her head off for fifteen or twenty minutes, stay up half an hour or so, reading and forgetting, and finally climb back into bed and tell herself how lucky she was, how lucky, and kiss her Rafi's arm for more good luck.

As Castorp of Cambridge, she prospered in these weeks. Sat in the small local park on a wooden bench while the April sun slanted through the flowering trees, and read a book or magazine. Took slow strolls to the Cambridge Public Library to see its new brick and glass addition and observe the local residents who read newspapers or studied or just idled. Took Rosie to a children's play, a story about a mouse thrown onto an island during a storm, sep-

arated from his wife and his comfortable New York apartment;
a lyrical adaptation by an American director living in Jerusalem,
with beautiful music and dancing, and even Rosie, a tough critic,
delighted in it. Became an envious spectator at a Cambridge Common softball game, watching the pop flies and line drives with
yearning and memories of her own days at second base, where
she had never dropped a force-out toss or a pop-up, though she
had been less able when it came to hard grounders. How she had
longed to be the first female major leaguer! She admitted, sitting on the grass, that spring in Cambridge was splendid when
you were a patient on the way to recovery, and your best friend
was in town to care for you and your children. In these strolls
and resting stops, she perceived fully the physical slope of middle
aging, down, down. Easy does it body, she accepted, sliding
serenely.

R. DuPres pursued her twice during this period, once in a dream
and another time while she was walking. Near the library one day
she thought she spotted him, only it turned out to be someone
else. She breathed easier when the bad-looking dude moved aside
politely on the narrow path, and she realized as she walked on
that she might never again see her rapist. What to do about him,
about her dangerous knowledge, remained a question mark. But
the case was not finished, not by any means. She had yet another
fantasy of hiring a Northampton group — like Lawrence's story,
"Tickets, Please" — to capture and hold him prisoner and find a
way of "reeducating him," feminist style. (She even found Angela
Jacques's calling card, and had new respect for such a support
network.) The injury to her had been clear-cut, but the punishment
remained a puzzle.

Her dream was a pacific one: DuPres was sitting in the office
of Detective Purcell when Miriam walked in, and she greeted him
with surprise and good will. They had a brief conversation in which
the word *reparations* was used, and she coolly informed DuPres
that he'd have to discuss the figure with her lawyer. Then she
departed, into the waiting arms of Dr. Beaumont, dressed in his
pale green surgeon's outfit; he asked if all had gone well. And
Harry waved to her from his pickup truck, giving her more support. When she awakened, there was Rafi, with fresh orange juice,

asking how she had slept. Could anyone have dreamed better, she thought, or awakened to a lovelier morning?

She didn't use her camera at all during these six weeks or so, and the abstinence was wonderful. To be able to walk out into the world without the compulsion to select, focus, and click was like being released from a mandatory sentence. Suddenly to look, see, sense, capture naturally, with her own eyes, without guilt — this presented a visual holiday. She made a private plan for a show, not for the world but for herself. Nudes and vegetables, limestone formations and Jewish artifacts, self-portraits and color studies; she had enough material for three shows. The plan stirred her. A show for herself, for close friends maybe. Not Miriam at Thirty-four but Miriam in the Middle. Or adventures in the Middle Years. Something like that. She took out her folders of contact sheets, which had been hidden for a few months, and painstakingly went through them with the magnifying glass. Slowly she looked at one shot after another, marking off this scramble of avocados, that limestone spur, the old kibbutz face. And her secret file of private nudes, which struck her now as shockingly fine. Bodies she knew by touch, by memory, were suddenly clipped from time, transformed into cool, curving forms, beautiful male proportions, aesthetic objects. Rafi, Dr. B., Harry cheered her here, her harem of miniature odalisques.

With April as unpredictable as ever, alternating two days of virile winds with two of sun and spring rain, she slowly came up from her depths and recovered. Though the dark descent stuck with her, a shadow life beneath the surface. Still, she had survived those depths of depression, that sister self, and she'd survive the memory too. Almost imperceptibly, strength rallied, routine pleasures returned. No, it was not so much the rich who lived differently from the poor, but the healthy who lived differently from the sick. Simple surfaces began to please again — Rafi's caring, his sturdy body and steadfast commitment, his habits and needs. (Not to mention Jon's bony beauty, Rosie's spiritedness and large brown eyes, and their one thousand and one special ways.) She enjoyed all over the peculiar Israeli tastes: yogurt and cucumbers and tomatoes for breakfast, fresh avocados and eggplants and artichokes whenever, schnitzel, fish, nuts and berries of all sorts. Was it Rafi's penchant for sunflower seeds and pistachios that contributed to clarity? Artichokes and fresh lettuce that sustained passion? An herbivorous palate that fostered high irony?

"You know, your eating habits are nearly Neanderthal," she commented one day as she shelled walnuts for dessert.

Cracking one walnut against the other in his palm — her father's old trick — he responded, "Have you forgotten my origins? Tel Aviv Man is a certain primitive type — nuts for breakfast, roots for lunch, enemies for dinner." He tapped the shells and removed the bits of walnut meticulously, like he arranged his pipe, pouch, research notes, trips.

In the same meticulous manner he had cared for her. And until someone had cared for you, she judged, watched over you when you lay helpless and forlorn and ill, a certain distance remained unbridged. Did you need a different man for each different role — father, friend, confessor, lover? Well, Rafi had passed one test handsomely! (Would he have, she inquired, if he had known about her unfaithfulness? Unfair!) Closer to him now, she edged. And sitting here in the living room, while he sat on the floor studying his 1/100th regional map amid his *Biblical Archeologist* and *Israel Exploration Journal* and books by Glueck and Kenyon, she felt content, deeply content. Saved. Body healed, soul salved. He was real, and she, who had seemed to herself at various stages made up of Polaroid and others' opinions, Kodachrome and daydreams and the projections of others — she felt real and substantial too, with him.

But then why didn't she tell him about rediscovering her old acquaintance and following him? Was she afraid because she looked so foolish, acted so dangerously (possibly)? To which she replied to herself, "Do you have to tell *all* to your friends? Every single detail of fear and folly and momentary imprudence? When the time is ripe, if ever, I'll talk. Explain. Narrate. But for now, let me enjoy my recovery, dear Inquisitor."

To both Rafi and recovery, she toasted now with her cognac. Which reminded her that it had been ages since she had worn the satiny green nightgown that always turned him on. I'll wear it tonight, she decided, thinking about such matters for the first time in a long time and realizing how limited were our mortal means

of gratitude, and yet how rich because of that. Oh, when you were
down and out, passion seemed a long way off, like some piece of
land where once long ago, you traveled.

"Why that look?" Rafi inquired, penciling in a note.

"Oh, no reason," she said, embarrassed at being caught by that
sly fellow and wondering at how deeply.

8

HOW did you handle the real after a week's spin in the unreal? A common Americana puzzle which she was slowly learning about. Meaning that she had just returned from sunny Sonora Desert of Arizona, where — through the good luck and smart management of Kelley M. and her boyfriend — Miriam had been given the cushy job of photographing a gaggle of male models for a fashion spread for a ritzy magazine, under the auspices of a tough British lady director. For six days of shooting the gorgeous young men in their imitation military outfits, detective's raincoats, designer polo shirts, and cowboy hats, she was paid a cool three grand, more than double a month's teaching salary. Plus she had gotten an inside peek at the male model industry, an expensive aquarium where the boys swam about indolently, teasing and adoring each other in narcissistic play. "Better for Jon to grow into an ordinary counterfeiter or gambler than a glamorous model," she told Rafi over the telephone.

The first few days home from the assignment were like returning from a foreign country, stranger perhaps because it all had the same customs and language. But ordinary Cambridge living, teaching and house-caring and shopping and bill-worrying beneath the low gray skies, was a planet apart from photographing hedonistic Adonises in the dazzling Southwest for all that dizzying loot.

"Cities like Tucson or L.A. need a Colette to treat them right," she told Rafi, "with just the right proportion of tender mockery and teasing approval."

"How did Miriam treat them?"

"Like a novice. And a worker. Boringly, I'm afraid."

She surprised the family with gifts. She was rich not merely with anecdotes and details but also with the green stuff. For Jon, she brought a new baseball glove the size of a butterfly net; though the cowhide smelled the same, as her old $10.95 Al Rosen mitt, the $65 price tag was a bit higher. For Rosie, a ten-speed bicycle, a low green and white Raleigh with tool-kit pouch, which excited the cool little cucumber. For her man, an authentic Western shirt with a string tie, and new briar pipe ("What, no holsters or six-shooters?"). And of course they had a Chinese celebration at Changsho on Mass. Ave.

Later that night she began to catch up on her lost week. First she checked in with the MIT colleague who had taught her classes; then, while Rafi read, she looked through mail and her notes on the trip and the pictures. At 10 P.M. they had their familiar tea and talk, which calmed her mind, still buzzing with high-fashion hijinks. After a trek in the American wilderness, this dull coziness was just what the doctor ordered. (Oh, which doctor?) The money still flabbergasted her. "Can you imagine earning all that for doing so little?" She asked Rafi. "Plus expenses? If this is how our society works, then Citizen Warhol knows more about it than de Tocqueville."

"Hmm," he muttered, puffing and tasting the new pipe. "This draws very nicely and goes with my bo-lo tie, don't you think?"

And when he held her in his arms on the sofa, while she replayed some of the week's scenes and scenery (including Nell Wilson, the director, "a Cockney transplant to L.A. not known by Dickens"), she felt cared for again; felt as if she had ventured forth daringly and was now being rewarded. Oh, the feeling was childish, but she couldn't help it. Not only had she earned real money, but she had gone out and played commercial, no small feat for old blue-stocking. Regardless, the reason for satisfaction now being less important than the fact itself, she basked in the fact, here associating virtue with activity, not denial.

On the first Tuesday home, she received a message at her MIT office that Dr. Beaumont had called. She called back, surprised but pleased; when he said quietly that he "had to see her," it surprised her even more. Not in character, that. She wanted to see him, to be sure, but also she didn't. Rafi was the focus of her attention now, and she didn't feel like switching from lake-water back to ocean-feeling. But she couldn't turn him down, and they arranged a meeting on the next afternoon.

It was an overcast April day, punctuated by light drizzle, and they decided to walk along the Charles River Basin, on the Cambridge side. He wore an old raincoat with wide lapels, and he looked . . . worn, anguished?

After some politeness, he began to stumble about. "Look, I, uh . . . don't know quite how to say this . . . I guess I'm not used to it . . ."

Her heart dropped, and she stared at the fog-gray light of the day. Fear and mystery; that light, his hesitation. And yet why, she thought, since all good things had to come to an end? Still, she was on the verge of crying. To lose him suddenly!

"I've discovered that . . . I'm deeply attached to you. And I don't know what to do about it . . . I can't stop myself, or control it, or . . . If I have a spare moment, you're right there." He stopped momentarily and let his full blue-eyed gaze fix upon her face. "Anyway, I wanted you to know this."

He was taking large strides, hands in pockets, and she had to take two for one to keep up with him. She had little idea of the full sense of his words, except that it made her heart beat faster.

"You've become something . . . I can't conceive of giving you up. Along with work . . . you've become that important."

She took his hand, in a daze too. The concrete buildings and steel girders looked less formidable, more dissolvable than usual.

"I think I'm going to move out. Of my home."

She didn't answer, but felt a small new fear growing inside. Fine drops of rain purged her face, and in her body she felt the fine run of his voice, like a cello.

"It's not you, so don't worry. What I mean is, I don't have any illusions that you'll come to live with me or anything so startling. But it's difficult to be with my wife and to be thinking of you. Without trying. You mustn't feel yourself . . . responsible at all. Do you understand?"

She laughed at that, a small ambiguous laugh.

And wanted to touch him now, not to listen to him. But where, how? No matter why.

He went on, speaking awkwardly, and she eyed his stooped shoulders and soaring height. It was like walking beside some great hawk, up there high and alert, whose wings could protect you. She squeezed his hand, and they took a narrow path by the edge of the rolling river.

She could have offered words of discouragement, of course; but after she had formed them, they disappeared. At his age he was entitled to his feelings and to voicing them, wasn't he? No matter what he unearthed, proposed, imagined. The rights of age, like *droit du seigneur*.

She asserted, "I have a life of my own. A full life."

"I know."

"And I . . . want it to continue."

He nodded.

Stupid, crude bluntness! Out of her own fears and jitters, she had hurt him needlessly. Lightly she tapped his arm in affection, and smiled with cheer. "No need for me to have said that," she acknowledged. "Silly."

They walked toward the far bridge spanning the river beside the Science Museum. But once there, instead of walking up and across it, she tugged his arm and they took the path below, toward the long arch of concrete, like some darkened, sonorous seashell. Why?

A curious emotion flooded her: a certain pleasure in this emotion of his, a kind of pleasure in conquering this large bird, a pleasure in her sudden sure dominion over him. She felt the emotion and knew in a moment or two she would censor it, chase it away. Before that, however, she considered. This tall, handsome, married man, this prominent physician who at certain moments reminded her of her father, this towering figure of calmness and authority was now suddenly, *shamelessly* in love with her. And was willing to sacrifice so much for that obsession! Men were the incurable romantics, not women!

The shadowy arch reminded her of other, older arches, in Jerusalem. The river moved darky and slowly transforming one's stolid ways, and she allowed irresistible waves to pull her, and before she or he knew what was happening, they were embracing, hard, and she felt a strange familiarity tinged with the strangeness of the place; and when she felt him aroused, she opened his fly

and fondled his growing member; oh, lovely, lovely its growing
length, and she was urged again and acted upon it, for this man
who was in mad passion for her and was going to break up his
settled and respectable existence for her, so that she went down
on her knees and slowly, surely, used her mouth upon him. In no
time at all he was coming like a teenage boy, and it was just as
exciting for her too, as she heard the lapping water and the overhead traffic and somewhere in between, his breathtaking moans.
She stayed low and hugged him to her and then rose, and he kissed
her. Then they walked out under the other side of the arch, and
sighted a small motor launch heading their way.

"Good timing," she said.

"You're too . . . whatever it is. Something foolish, like perfect."

"You mean crazy."

He shook his head. "No, or maybe yes. But for me, perfect.
Crazy or spontaneous or whatever."

They walked on and up toward the busy rush of traffic on the
bridge, staying on the narrow footpath.

"It's not exactly the Brooklyn Bridge, is it?"

But he was on another track. "You know, I haven't been in
love, well, since I was twenty-five or so, over thirty years ago. And
I have no idea of how to . . . act it out. The emotion is . . . not
comprehensible. Forgive me."

She laughed, in sympathy, half in love herself. Whatever that
loose term meant. (Did it mean doing what she had just done
under the bridge, at her age, and feeling it was good or right?)

During the lovely drizzly walk, comforted by the camouflage of
passing of cars and trains, she told him a bit about her unreal
week.

At the far end of the bridge, in Boston, he put her into a taxi
and kissed her cheek. Whispered, "Not your responsibility, remember."

She nodded and repeated the formula to herself. The cab took
off and recrossed the bridge, and she wondered if it were possible
to believe what he had said.

She had a problem, didn't she? A sort of serious one.

Or did she?

The taxi left her off in Harvard Square, and she bought a plain vanilla cone at the Belgian Fudge shop, eschewing the oversweet fudge. In ordinary terms, the answer to her query was yes. Even to the younger Miriam, the answer was in the affirmative. But the answer for this Miriam, walking, was more uncertain. She headed for home by way of the public library. Wait and see, she decided. Besides, it was not she who had asked the doctor to do this drastic thing; on the contrary. Why project his situation onto hers, which was already complicated? Immersed in the taste of fresh vanilla, she played with the difference between this licking and that, this childhood delight and that adult play. Juvenile, perverse, neurotic? Oh, such tired categories. She went back to the turn of events and the new situation. Let it play itself out, like a new roll of film, and see what was there and how it affected her. Important to remember: she was not losing a friend, only gaining a complication. After forty, friendships were the serious affairs, romances the lighter stuff. Only, was the complication too rich? But wasn't adulthood in part defined by that sort of addition? From blow job to casuistry — my oh my!

Was the strange work with those Arizona mannequins any stranger than the work of her life?

At fifty-five he was falling in love with her; or in love with sex again? Don't split hairs, she cautioned herself, entering the Cambridge Public Library with its spanking new wing of glass and light, attached to the Victorian stucco elephant. She meandered in the aisles for forty-five minutes, touched by the rows and stacks, the wisdom and worlds tucked away. Finally she checked out *The Blue Nile,* a modern *Photography Annual,* a book on the West, a Polaroid study, and, for Jon, two advanced Dungeons & Dragons books, *Monster Manual* and *Players Handbook.* She was surprised by the range of citizens visiting here — teenage blacks in berets, older, pallid-faced Irish, a couple of Orthodox Jewish boys, an old couple with walking sticks glued to their tissue-thin *Manchester Guardian* and London *Times.* Oh, she admired this dense room; it reminded her of the Cleveland Heights branch library, where she had taken out her Bronc Burnett, Louisa May Alcott, Nancy Drew books. (Plus *Kid from Tompkinsville* by Tunis, don't forget!) Did her own kids use this place enough? Doubtful. Leaving the library and its park, she lamented the poor fate of books, gradually being displaced by disks, flicks, computers. Apple over Gutenberg.

Now, in the springy air, she felt temporarily released from the Doctor's Confession. Friends' emotions were weights, sometimes of support, sometimes of burden. But always forces pulling this way and that. It was easier to walk about carefree, affected only by physical infirmities. The library had picked her up, and she promised herself to return more often.

Dinner was pesto al dente by Rafi, salad by Miriam; for Rosie, spaghetti and meatballs with mounds of Heinz ketchup. Jon had called to say he'd be home later; he was eating at a friend's. She found herself acting oversolicitous with Rafi, a sure sign of residual guilt from the afternoon. Gnawing feeling. To assuage it, she drank an extra glass of wine and prohibited any touching of her man.

At ten-thirty Jonathan was still out, and Miriam grew worried. She called two of his friends, but they knew nothing. Rafi restrained her from telephoning the police.

Just after eleven-thirty he entered, slamming the front door.

Rafi cautioned, "Take it easy; he's home now."

But this was difficult when she saw him swagger in boldly, wave his hand, and pass through to the kitchen without any explanation. He took something from the fridge to his room.

Miriam put down her book, removed her reading glasses, and followed him. Not bothering to knock on his closed door, she went in.

"Hey, what the hell do you think you're doing?"

She wanted to slap him immediately, but held off.

"You know the rules, goddamn it. This is a private room," he said, guzzling milk from the carton. "I don't have to take this kind of shit."

She took two steps and slapped him hard twice, holding him by his hair.

His face colored; his eyes dilated with shock and hurt.

"Don't you ever talk that way to me," she said, releasing her hold.

Tears rolled down his cheeks, which made her want to gather him to her.

"Now sit down and tell me where you've been."

He hesitated, not knowing what to do. "I thought this room was private."

"Under ordinary circumstances, yes. These are not ordinary."

"What's the matter, can't I come in late once in my life?"

She looked at his shirt, hanging outside his dungarees, and his wild hair, and watched him breathe deeply from the impact of the slaps. "Where've you been, and with whom?"

His face hardened. "You had to do *that,* didn't you, *in front of him?*"

"What are you talking about?"

They stood and faced each other, a few feet apart.

"You're always showing me up in front of him. Proving yourself!"

Was he going mad? "What *are* you talking about? That door is closed, isn't it? And when was the last time I showed you up?"

"Always. You're always doing it, once *he's* around. Ask him, go ahead!"

And she saw now that he was half conning her, and half something else. What else? "Who were you with? You're going to tell me if it takes all night."

"Oh yeah?"

She nodded.

His look was defiant.

"And you're going to tell me what you've been taking. Tonight."

That unsettled him, and his face shifted once again. No adult cover-ups here. "How'd you . . . What are you talking about, huh? Cheesus, you can't even come in late around here." He tossed a pillow against the wall.

She didn't know what she felt. She didn't want to be here, however, in this movie role of interrogator of her son. A son being infected by the ordinary culture viruses.

"Besides, what's there to do here at night, with him around? And you, *fawning* all over him."

Was that a fact, or Jon's feeling? The latter, probably.

She stared and waited. Then took his desk chair and sat in it, facing him, cornering him.

"Well, Ma, cheesus!" He swirled down into his bed and rolled over, as if in pain.

She observed him, a poor baby who needed her. But first she needed to know how, just now.

"Come on, where've you been? And with whom? And taking what?"

"Christ." He rubbed his eyes. "So I took a little upper; is that worth so much hassle? Would you rather have me take some candy and ruin my teeth?"

She almost laughed but restrained herself. "How'd you get it?"

"At school," he admitted, relenting. "There's a guy that comes around. I mean, you make it sound like trying to get plutonium or something. Look, Mom, *everyone* tries something once or twice. That's all there is to it. So why all this . . . this . . . hassle?"

"Who'd you take it with?"

He lowered his head and sank back against the wall. "Is that really so necessary?"

"Who?"

He scratched his unruly hair, which made him look more like his father. At fifteen he was already a kind of hero from a nineteenth-century Russian novel.

"Kevin Worthington," he let out. "But that's *private*, see?"

She nodded, accepting that. She knew Kevin and his family.

"Who else?"

"Someone you don't know."

"Who?"

"A guy named Tony."

"Who is he?"

"Oh, he's in school, sort of." He rubbed his eyes and sneezed. "When he's not suspended."

Was he coming down, she wondered, or just sleepy?

"And his last name?"

"Private, though, you swear?"

"Private."

"D'Angelo."

She nodded. "And?"

He took one shoe and sock off. "I'm getting real sleepy, you know."

"Who else?"

"Susan Robertson."

Miriam remembered that girl, spoiled but smart. "How often has it been going on now?"

"Come on, huh? I'm not exactly a junkie because I take a few uppers."

"You're going to stop taking them and stop right now." She paused. "Do you understand?"

He looked at the wall and reached over to set his clock, which never worked.

She got up and grasped his shoulder. "That's the end of taking them, believe me. Are you hearing me?"

He didn't want to face her, but did.

She looked into his dark eyes and saw that the pupils were still slightly dilated.

"After school tomorrow, you come directly home. We're going to talk some more."

"I can't," he explained with triumph. "I've got soccer practice."

"Too bad. You're going to miss it."

He grew furious. "You can't do that to me!"

"Yani, you come home after school, right after. You don't want me to embarrass you, do you?"

He was fighting tears now.

"Mom, look, the coach is deciding now on who's going to be on the first team, and —"

"We're going to have a little talk tomorrow, and you can explain it to him any way you wish. But so long as you're living here, under my roof, we're going to have a clear understanding of what the rules are." She saw his furious but crushed look and knew that it was hitting home, this missing of practice tomorrow. "Goodnight, Yani."

She turned and left the room wincing over her use of Sylvia's good old phrase about the roof.

And later, in bed, she was too preoccupied to be loved by Rafi, and let him drift off. At one point she interrupted her thoughts to cite Jon's charge about showing Jon up in front of him. Did she? "Not that I know, or see," he replied sleepily. "Sorry," she said, and kissed him back to his slumber. She felt so odd, so much between the lines of emotions. Between fears and guilt, between a desire to love Yani and a need to steer him onto the right track. Difficult to do now, for a teenager, in America. She'd have to manage it, somehow. Did he really feel the pressure of Rafi in the apartment? Perhaps. C'mon, let's try *probably*. Even though Jon and Rafi got on well, very well, Rafi still was a man sleeping with

Jon's mother. *Living* with his mother. That, my fair innocent, was pressure, no matter how you cut it. And as for the earlier event that day, the confession from her surgeon, what should she do with that? . . .

She found herself lacking the language to describe her emotions, and lacking emotions to fit the events of the day. What she knew was that she'd have to stay right on top of Jon in the next months, to make sure he knew that he was not going to lose her again, this time to a man, not to an illness. Maybe, if Stan permitted, she should even offer to take him to Israel this summer with her?

The darkness crowded in upon her like it had when she was little and afraid of the dark and had insisted that a light be left on, even a tiny hallway light. And how Sylvia had punished her, deceitfully, when Miriam had defied her in something else, by saying, "You're getting too old to be a baby anymore, and you're just going to have to go to sleep without any light!" And Miry, crying to herself, had kept the covers over her eyes and not slept, in mortal terror! Now that same fear slipped back into her, crawling up her spine, and she nestled against Rafi, who turned instinctively and cradled her head in the crook of his arm, settling her, so that gradually she was able to relax and breathe more naturally. The oncoming shapes of darkness returned to desk lamp and highboy, and she edged into sleep.

Jon came home the next day on time, and they continued their talk. Here, from three-thirty to five o'clock, he was reasonable and penitent and understanding: "Yeah, I know, Mom, you're right; it's just dumb. Honest. It was stupid, just stupid of me. I guess I kinda acted on a silly dare." He sat by his desk, wearing sneakers and an old shirt, his thin body fidgeting constantly with extra energy.

She got through the drug part of the conversation and turned to the subject of Rafi. "Now, be truthful; does it disturb you that he stays here?"

Jon shook his head. "Nah, not at all. I like the guy. He's cool. I mean it. Who else plays soccer with me or shows me some of the old Jewish battles? Those Maccabees could fight! Nah, I was just angry with you, so I said those things. Really!" She nodded. "Don't get me wrong; it took me a little while to get used to the idea, back a few years. But it's neat now. Like having two — well, not really *two* fathers, but like one father and one . . . older brother, maybe. Yeah, like an older brother!" He was proud at finding an apt designation.

She went over to him and brushed the thick brown hair from his eyes and hugged him, receiving a fast, tight hug in return before he bolted.

"And you know what? The coach said it was okay, because I was already picked for a second attacking wing. How's *that* for news!"

The conversation boosted her morale, and she went out and bought fresh salmon for dinner at a sky-high price. It was one of their mutual favorite foods, hers and Rafi's and Jon's, and they ate it with almonds in butter sauce and parsley and lemon. "Is there anything better in this world?" she wondered, feasting. "Yes. Catching it and eating it," Rafi responded. To which Rosie said, "God, you guys are too much, falling all over the place over *fish*. Yuck!"

Afterward Miriam went to pick up some work from her seamstress and drove back along Memorial Drive. With her life put back in order somewhat, she had time to reflect upon the predicament of her Dr. Beaumont, and it hurt her, imagining him. She liked that man very, very much; he shouldn't be breaking up his life this way. It would be so difficult, she knew; the first year especially. But then, there was the whole other matter — her feelings for him. What were they, exactly? That last word offered a clue to the difficulty: there was no exactness in such matters. No permanence either. And she wouldn't fake it. She felt for her Montana and wanted his friendship. Wanted that intimacy, and would have it. (Greedy; she confessed.) Even if that intimacy appeared in this irregular, unmonogamous mode. Was hers to be a life of perpetual contradictions, of jigsaw pieces not quite fitting together? So be it. That a Bohemian of dress at twenty-two became a Bohemian of emotions at forty-two was but a normal progression. Why try to resolve the difficult for the sake of resolution?

The driving and the trashy music on the radio soothed her wonderfully. She'd stick with this odd affection, and shadow-friend, and wait for the right cue, when shadow might become substance.

How fragile were the rules governing relations, she saw; not merely between people, but between yourself and your own preconceptions. And once you released yourself from the bondage of fixed conception, you were freer to take things as they really were — fluid, changing, confusing, unconceptualized. Formed one minute, unformed the next.

You were also freer to fall and smash your life apart, she acknowledged, taking a sharp curve with caution.

The resolve to do nothing spectacular to alter her situation relaxed her in the next days, and she once again enjoyed walking the street, smelling the spring air and flowering trees, watching the afternoons lengthen in daylight. With Rafi she attended a soccer scrimmage of Jon's. "He has — what do you call it?" asked Rafi, moving his hands up and down. "Balance?" she wondered. "Yes, he has very nice balance when he dribbles the ball. This is impossible to teach. He's going to be all right." From an old Tel Aviv soccer kid, this was praise indeed, she knew. On the spur of the moment she shot a roll of pictures of Jon-on-the-field, a roll of impulse and love. And during this week of renewal she began the process of looking at and sifting through the developed pictures and contact sheets for her possible show — a process of judging that was only possible with a return of calm, a frame of order in her life.

The reinterpretation of everyday things in her life (rituals and people), like an inventory; the insertion of new patterns in her emotions, on an orderly, provisional basis; the gradual allowance of free flow into and upon a solid core of life, like the opening of new tributaries to irrigate an arid piece of topography — were these the real adventures of the middle years? Did the adult self have its own dark continent, waiting to be discovered and defined? Now, as she journeyed, she grew high, confident; the journey was the thing wherein we caught the mysterious "felt life," she paraphrased.

About ten days later she went back to the public library, returning two books and deciding to plunge into one of those marathon reads, a Victorian novel. Another Hardy, or a George Eliot triple-decker? Maybe Meredith or Butler? Fiction was upstairs in the older wing, and as she walked the narrow, stuffy aisles, she was transported to those crammed stacks of her Ann Arbor and Berkeley student years, and felt at home. How she had missed libraries, wandering about their dusty stacks, browsing in the forgotten world of hardbacks! Where the tracks were clean of systems analysts and industrial consultants and computer mechanics. In the H's, after mistaking the huge row of Maurice Hewletts for Thomas Hardys, she found her man and searched through the worn green Doubleday editions. Each title recalled a particular scene, time, place. In high school she had first read *Return of the Native* and become Eustacia Vye tormenting Sidney Ruderman, her reddleman from the Shaker Heights border. In Ann Arbor she had discovered *Jude* and took on a relationship with slow-pitch Eddie Murrow, the son of a business school professor who couldn't for the life of him understand what "the Obscure" referred to. For Miry it was a determined education in Pity, as she privately made Eddie over into Jude. Finally, as a senior in Professor Harrison's seminar, she read *Tess* and kept seeing everywhere signs of her own imminent doom — a misplaced letter, darkening "lowing" skies, the sure sign of Immanent Will when a flat tire kept her from a crucial exam! The stages of romantic illusion that Hardy took her through seemed endless, and endlessly Important.

She took down a volume of his poetry and began to browse among the poems. Coming across the familiar "Darkling Thrush," she read through it and moved on then to the unfamiliar "In the Servants' Quarters." Read:

> 'Man, you too, aren't you, one of these rough followers of
> the criminal?
> All hanging hereabout to gather how he's going to bear
> Examination in the hall.' She flung disdainful glances on
> The shabby figure standing at the fire with others there,
> Who warmed them by its flare.
> 'No, indeed, my skipping maiden: I know nothing of the trial
> here,
> Or criminal, if so he be. — I chanced to come this way.'

Someone was pushing up against her, and when she turned, annoyed, she saw his big wide grin and brown face. Him. *Him.*

She tried to move away, but he blocked her path.

"I'll scream."

"No, you won't."

He was still grinning. His dark eyes were smallish and brown, inviting a moment of full recognition, like seeing with disbelief an ancient relative. Momentarily she observed his face, mixture of dusky brown and dry high-yellow color, with black kinky hair peeking out beneath his businesslike fedora. He wore a three-piece charcoal suit with a gold watch fob dangling from the striped vest. Not an outlaw, but a corporate VIP. Except, perhaps, for the lavender shirt with its wide white collar. In the wild expanding moment, she thought madly, he flowered like a sultry gladiola.

She found her voice finally. "I'm going to leave, and you're going to let me. Unless you want a more serious crime on your hands."

He reached up and took hold of her hair and held tight. "So you want to play in the big leagues, huh?"

Oh, he was pretty and dangerous, and she had no idea what the words meant, tinged with their Southern accent. She tried to concentrate on the rows and rows of H fiction. Was this fiction too?

He held her by the hair and turned her face slowly this way and that, like showing a beautiful animal at auction. "Yeah, you were *spirited* then, and you're not quittin' yet. I should've expected you to pull something or otha. Yeah, you're gonna make one special workin' woman, did ya know?"

She felt tears come to her eyes from the pressure of his grip. "You're hurting me."

He nodded, grinning, still hurting her but not increasing the pain. "Did ya know that a veteran filly is sometimes worth as much as a little baby colt? Yeah, they ask if you can pick up a woman of ma-tur-ity — especially for some kinky stuff." He lessened his grip a touch. "You into spankin'? By the time you're through with *mah* boot camp, you're gonna be a mistress of the art."

"You're crazy."

"You bet. Crazy as you."

"Please let me go, let me out of this now." A mistake, such politeness.

"When I'm good and ready, you'll go. Now looka here," he

said, pushing up against her, his face inches away but his grip loose. He smelled sweet, the way he had years ago in that nightmare on the grass in the Common. "You're the crazy one, Miss Miriam, and I'm gonna straighten you out once and for all. Yeah. I'm gonna make an *honest woman* outta you. I'm gonna get ridda those *straight* ideas in your head about how to live and who's the *law*, and put some good clean common sense into ya. By the time it's ovah, you're gonna be grateful, believe me." He leaned down to kiss her on the cheek.

She had an urge to kick him hard in the groin, but decided against it, and let him kiss her. Tried to temper her fear, control her panic.

"There, *that's* my girl," he boasted in a whisper. "We're gonna get along jes fine. You wait and see. You're gonna like ridin' with me, and you're gonna get all those pretty things you been doin' without. First off, get ridda that dinky little rat you call an automobile. And fit you up with a wardrobe, too. Now what d'ya think of *those* plans?" He grinned again and let go, allowing her a few inches of breathing space to digest his strategy, and knowledge.

Someone was coming up the aisle now, a husky white boy of seventeen — maybe an athlete. All right now, Miriam, *act*. The fellow excused himself politely and walked on by as Miriam trembled.

She looked up at Reggie, thinking that she was probably in big trouble again but she was going to fix it this time. Handle it, somehow. "Do you have a cigarette?"

He laughed a little. "Sure." He removed from his jacket a gold cigarette case and opened it for her. He turned it over to reveal the inscription: "To the best Daddy I ever had. Ella." When she took a smoke, he pointed to the No Smoking sign.

Still, she put the unlit cigarette in her mouth, to think better.

"Thas a girl, you mull it ovah some. Oh yeah, one other item. You know those two nice children of yours? You know the one who goes to the Shady-something school, and the other one who arrives at the Commonwealth every morning at 8:00 A.M. and leaves at 2:30 P.M.? Well, if you get any tee-vee ideas in your head about callin' any policemen or officials or any more tinny detectives about this private little arrangement of ours, you're gonna have one crippled child on your hands, mother." For emphasis, he took hold of her hair again. "Do you dig?"

She nodded, holding back the tears.

"Now, I know you got a man hangin' around too, and I'll jus' tell you this: men sometimes get notions in their heads about glory and heroism. *Forget it.* Better don't tell him at all. He'll never know, the way we set up our schedules, and he won't get hurt. And your Johnny-boy won't get hurt either. Like his leg snapped" — he jerked her scalp — "or kidney kicked in." He jerked again. "You don't want those pretty little things to be walkin' around with one kidney, do you?"

The threats brought out the tears.

"I can see you don't. Smart. You'll be hearin' from me in a few days. Now, don't go and change your number or anything else rash and useless. Hear me?"

She was crying and didn't nod.

"Yeah, you're gonna make one fine filly out there on the track. I'm bettin' on you now, so don't disappoint me, *Miss* Miriam." The jest appealed to him. "Yeah, that's jus' what I'll call ya in my public relations brochure — Miss Miriam. I once had a Sunday School teacher name a Miss Judith. She taught me the Old Testament, and I loved every single tall story. She treated me *real* fair and square. Jus' like you will." He grinned. "Undoubtedly."

Another person wandered past this stack, a middle-aged man in a suit. He paused suddenly and boldly said to Miriam, "Everything all right here, Miss?"

Wanting to fall into his arms, she found her head nodding.

The gentleman shook his head in dismay at another interracial boy-girl spat and walked on past.

"Yeah, I genuinely like you," her persecutor confessed, and he suddenly produced a handful of green bills to prove it. He forced them into her hand. "Take this on account and buy yourself some fancy clothes. Been nice runnin' into ya this way, ya hear?" And he started to turn away.

She dropped the money onto the floor.

He looked at her, his eyes widening; then he laughed. He said easily, "Now pick 'em up, or I'll cut your face." Holding up the palm of his big hand, he revealed a small safety-razor blade inside a pack of matches.

She bent down and scooped up the bills at his feet.

"Don't *ever* pull that stunt again," he warned, as if she had cursed his religion. Then he tipped his hat and walked away, swinging his pocket chain and whistling softly.

She almost broke down right there, almost sagged to the floor. She wouldn't, couldn't. Forced herself upright, averting her face from a passing young woman; tried to collect herself. In crisis, stay cool. She blew her nose, dried her eyes, and on rubbery legs walked out from the aisle.

At a nearby library table all was well and unchanged. Still catching her breath, she sat down, annoying two readers, who glanced at her before returning to their books. So, she was still just a common reader.

She had an urge to put her head down and cry, just cry and howl.

She forced a small smile and closed her book and prepared to leave. And as she did, she felt like an animal who, trapped finally in a corner, is ready to fight wildly for its life. She would fight wildly, somehow, for her life.

With disciplined care she returned to the aisle, took down the Hardy poetry volume, and included a copy of *The Mayor of Casterbridge*. With a steadying hand she checked both out at the front desk, nodding to the familiar young black librarian, who flashed her a wonderful smile and advised, "Don't let him depress you, now."

"Who?"

"Hardy."

Outside, the lovely late-April afternoon awaited her, and she noted afresh the rows of yellow, red, and fuschia tulips springing up in the park. Dutch treat, announcing the new season. She daydreamed of Amsterdam, pleased by the outburst. Suddenly she stopped at the wire refuse basket, readying the pimp's money to toss it in. First she decided to look at the stuff: five crisp $100 bills. Christ. Marked somehow by a bank? Fighting for her life might mean using that money, she thought. Use his dirty money for a cleansing purpose? Why not? She put the green into her purse and walked on, crazily heated, quietly, crazily determined. Weaving on the sidewalks, she felt somehow as though she had been put on the Wanted list, and the Gestapo now knew of her whereabouts. Jewish treat.

Could she hide out successfully?

Or come out shooting?

9

EVENTS blew in and out with random force, shaping unforeseen consequences for good and bad, providing resolutions by the oddest means, and making a mockery of intention.

The next few days were winners in New England weather, a folklore unto itself — steady spring days of warm sun and evening breeze. For Miriam, her heart and head pressured from her strange recent experience, they were black days. With Rafi she went through the motions, bicycling, attending a chamber music concert, making love. But in fact she kept to herself. She sought desperately to come up with a solution, an answer, a partial remedy. But her jumpy disposition and two newly bitten fingernails announced her fears; she was as unnerved as in her breakdown days. Too frightened to call the police; it wasn't worth the chance, not just yet. Rafi, of course, she *should* tell; and yet she couldn't. Felt paralyzed. She was afraid that he just might do the wrong thing, confuse his countries and customs. What about Dr. Beaumont . . . ? Harry? They were too respectable, she felt, too much on the up-and-up for this sort of low melodrama. The image of her son being suddenly grabbed from behind, tossed into a car, and beaten up and dumped on some vacant lot terrified her, darkened her hopes of civilized rescue. Of course she telephoned Detective Purcell, and when he immediately stammered, lost his voice, said he'd call her back and then didn't, not that afternoon or the next day, she knew that *he* had been the connection to her. Somehow or other the

young maniac had gotten to that Scotland Yard reject, through
bribe or blackmail. Anyway, it was her own fault, for playing with
fire, and now she was burning with fear and stupidity.

To come so far up to solid ground and then be knocked down,
defeated, by stupidity and dumb chance!

She walked around with the pressure until it became a regular
morning headache and slight nausea, as in her pregnancy days.
Weary, gloomy most of the time, she claimed an allergy and told
Rafi it would pass. Every few hours, meanwhile, doing nothing,
she asked herself what the hell she was doing. At first she told
herself that all this couldn't be happening to her, that it was a bad
dream or memory, or even a bad imitation of soap opera. It seemed
too banal, too cheap. But whenever she attempted to cover herself
with that story, to escape into that illusion, she'd go to her drawer
and take the envelope from beneath her sweaters and count those
crisp five hundreds. Ben Franklin never looked more derisive. And
for the next few hours she'd be leaden with grief and dull fear; it
was horrible, and she knew no way out. Would she have to go to
the police eventually, change her number and move, and then live
in perpetual dread for her children?

Scotty Beaumont called and asked to see her, but she couldn't.
"Forgive me for now, Montana, okay? Not just now." Other
friends called too — Harry, Vera, Mary Lou — and she put them
off too. Didn't know what to do with them.

Rafi sensed something wrong, she knew, but figured it was a
private matter, maybe an artistic dilemma of one sort or another.
Believing in her independence and privacy, he let her be. And she,
who didn't want "to be" but who couldn't muster the strength to
do otherwise, felt trapped. How could she explain the new grip
of fatiguing inertia, on top of the original predicament, to anyone?

Five days of holes, black holes, through which she was slipping — or being pulled — and couldn't quite stop or go through
them. And then *he* called, saying breezily, "Hi, *Miss* Miriam, how
goes it? I thought we might have a little celebration, a welcome
feast, me and you. How's this Saturday go down?"

Too confused, too sad, she asked for a postponement. "Look,
this week is impossible, honest. Can we put it off until next week?"

A pause, a decision. "Sure, I'm easy, you'll see that. But you
wouldn't be buyin' time while you contact anyone official, would

ya? You wouldn't be that foolish again, would ya, sweetheart?"

"No," she replied truthfully, defeated by his recent threats, "I wouldn't."

"Okay, fair enough," he decided. "Hey, did ya use that bread for some partyin' clothes? Buy any pretty little things yet?"

"Uh, no, not yet. But maybe I'll wait until I see you and, uh, shop with you." What the hell was she saying!

"Sure," he said, warming to the thought. "I like that number. Why don't ya wait after all, and I'll accompany you to Bonwit's or Lord and Taylor's; they should know me there by now." He laughed. "That's a foxy idea. I'll be catchin' ya next week at this time. Or another time." Click.

Click — don't stop your routine, she advised herself. On the contrary. So in a half hour she was on her way to her dentist's office in Arlington, a few seedy rooms over a sub shop on the corner of Main. There, sitting in the waiting room with *Cosmo* at hand for protection against the secretary's quips, she felt the pressure mount in her chest. She leafed aimlessly through the slick pages, stopping here to glance at a debate about vaginal deodorant, there at one about the wisdom of extramarital affairs. Where was advice for her to be found? Soon she heard the loud guffawing and South African accents of Dr. Julius Rosenwald, and winced. He had been her dentist for more than a decade, and she couldn't quite break away from him, though she had grown to despise him.

"Miriam, I'll be right with you, dear," he said, touching her shoulder. "Diana, take Miriam into G and get her set up."

Diana, of the large bouffant hairdo and larger bosom, escorted Miriam to G, cranked the chair back, settled Miriam into it, and tied a bib around her neck. She began to chatter about a fan*tas*tic sale at the dress shop down the street.

Miriam was left alone at last, and stared up at the intense light, her mind elsewhere.

"So, how we doing?" Dr. Rosenwald began. He was a broad-chested man in his fifties, with a mustache and glasses. "Have you been a good girl, using your Water Pik, flossing regularly? It doesn't look it, my dear," he sang, with some glee, poking around. "Look, we haven't even started and you're bleeding like you're pregnant! If you'll excuse me."

She wouldn't, of course, but felt powerless here, an infant on her back, as he began to use his steel scaler to scrape the tartar from her gums and start the ordeal.

"If you keep this up, I'm going to have to turn you over to a periodontist, and *then* you'll be sorry — ooh, sorry, dear."

She flinched, saw stars from the pain. Beginning a tale of his daughter's fancy wedding in Lexington, Dr. Rosenwald scraped at her gums with the gusto of eating a meal. How appropriate, that she should be in the sadist's hands now! Should she hook him onto his favorite topic, the world's misunderstanding of South African *schvartaas,* and argue against racism?

He cut her; she bled, periodically jumped from shock, and tried a different tack on her dilemma. Was Reggie a metaphor for risk and adventure in a life dedicated now to steadiness and balance? A kind of witness to living on the edge, emotionally? Why not? Oww! You bastard! . . . Another angle: was he proof of the shadow Miriam pursuing the comfortable (complacent) self? A consequence, say, of that past life of liberation, a verification of —

"Yes, I'm trying to hold steady, Doctor." I mean Butcher.

Look, a stupid irritation turns up in life, and if it's not handled immediatly, and adequately, it turns into a major sore, the wound that does you in. A gum problem that slowly evolves into the big G — gingivitis! Not panic but prudence is needed then. Ouch!

"Sorry, dear, but if I don't dig deeply, I'm wasting your time and money. Here take some water first. By the way . . ." He leaned forward, a sure sign of coming humor. "How many New Yorkers does it take to screw in a light bulb?"

Swishing warm water in her mouth, she shook her head.

His eyes lit up. "Fuck you, who cares!" And he guffawed wildly.

She spit out loose tartar and blood with the water, his laugh grating on her nerves.

Piercing again savagely, he whispered, "If you ask a Jewish American princess what fucking, sucking, and cooking are, what does she say?"

Miriam shook her head.

"Three towns in China." He winked, and laughed, and scraped and whittled, until she was crying lightly, steadily.

Was *he* a punishment for her transgression with Dr. B.? Or just this dentist-savage? Yes, get moralistic, that fits you fine!

After three-quarters of an hour she lifted herself from the chair, her mouth very sore, her spirit sore too, and left the office in a daze, hardly noticing the squeeze the dentist sneaked in. Driving home in the slow Mass. Ave. traffic — at every other corner a rude driver pulled out halfway to make a left-hand turn — she promised herself to look around for another dentist. Maybe another town? Surely there were others?

The next afternoon Jon presented her with further evidence that Reggie DuPres was real, not metaphor. On returning home from school, he said he had found this letter for her on his desk in homeroom. "What the hell's going on, Miriam?" Jon asked, perplexed, miffed.

"It's nothing." She smiled tensely, and took the letter away.

Fortunately, he was in a great rush to get to a practice and couldn't check up on her, it, just then. Racing to his room and then scampering out with his baseball mitt, he shouted that he wanted to know what was in it when he returned.

The note read, in typescript:

> My eyes are everywhere
> my spies are everywhere
> from the poolhalls
> to the school halls
> my Empire knows no boundaries
>
> Cassius II

She folded it back into the envelope and tucked it into the drawer with the crisp bills. She felt weak. Weak!

The word *spies* sounded a chord with her. Why?

That night, lying waiting for sleep, groggy from exhaustion, she had an impulse. Got up from bed and went to the kitchen telephone with her address book. Closed the door, dialed the number, and waited.

"Hello?"

"Sure, who is this?"

"You can't tell my voice anymore, huh?"

"Hey, Miry babe, it's you! Nifty! So fast, what a surprise! Are you coming? I heard from Nell Wilson that you took a bundle of nifty photos and . . ."

"Kelley, listen, I'm in a little trouble. Can you —"

"You name it, and I'll destroy it."

Indomitable Kelley. "You're a friend."

Miriam proceeded to tell the story, briefly, and answered a few questions. Kelley reflected, then said, "What a fucker. You hang cool, and I'll get back to you tomorrow, or the next night. Okay?"

Okay. Trying her best to hide her sense of futility, she hung up.

She smoked a cigarette and drank a cup of tea. Sitting alone in the kitchen, in the middle of the night in the middle of her life, with a hundred-watt bulb and an old refrigerator for companionship. What a foolish, foolish mess! But telling the truth to someone, at long last, eased the pressure in her chest and head. Old Westinghouse pal, you made it to old age; I'll make it too.

In bed, Rafi asked her what was happening. Miriam made up a story about how she had just now remembered to ask Kelley about a possible future magazine assignment, so she had called her. It was still early in California, remember? She nestled into his arms, allowing herself his comfort for the first time in a week. A wounded bird seeking the wing of its mother. When this was over, *if* it was ever over, she would tell him the whole story. She opened one eye and noted the shadows forming in the room. When they started to move in on her, she held on tighter to her dear friend. In his drowsiness, he sensed this and held her firmly, and she felt protected enough for this night, at least. In proximity of bodies there flowed furry comfort. At last she was dozing.

When she awoke the next morning at seven, she resolved to cheer herself up somehow and tried her best to be bright at the breakfast table. Drank juice, ate a roll with her coffee, made a joke about Rafi's soft-boiled egg. "Hey, Mom, don't overdo it now," said Jon, gulping his second bowl of corn flakes. When everyone was gone, she decided to give herself a day off and devote it to herself. She found some money, *her* money, and walked in the fine sunshine to the subway at Central Square where she bought a newspaper and began her improvised journey. Glanced at stories of broken détente and a brutal Dorchester street murder and turned desultorily to sports and cartoons. She changed trains and soon found herself walking upstairs at the Haymarket stop, then made her way to the open street markets and gloried in oranges, green and red apples, stalks of green celery and heads of cabbage, early artichokes and avocados. Flooded with orchard memories and photography desires, she bought two oranges and an apple and headed into the North End.

At first, standing by Paul Revere's house in the cool shade, she thought she would take the Freedom Trail and wind up at Old North Church. But the irony saddened her — a prisoner herself on parole for a day — and she wandered instead around the cobblestoned streets of the Italian district. Buoyed by the Old World courtesy of the local merchants, she bought pink Jordan almonds (Rosie's favorite) for the kids at one small shop, and an Italian lemon ice at another. At a used-book store she found two old maps of New England, and imagined her father's face. She felt the cool air circle up her bare legs, and she was glad she had worn a skirt, and of course her great walking shoes, the Bass sandals with the rubber soles. She could walk to China in these cushioned flats. Should she try it, and rent a studio in Shanghai? Presently she smelled ocean air and emerged at the waterfront, heading for the renovated area. Red brick warehouses were now condominiums; restaurants sported new glass; and by the water's edge, a new promenade and mall had been constructed. Where had she been, provincializing in Cambridge? The redolence of sea and fish refreshed her.

At a large white frame restaurant on the water, she lunched on cherrystone clams and butterflied shrimp and fat French fries, and drank imported beer. From her window seat she watched a freighter approach slowly like a gray dream, two sloops with large white sails drift until they picked up wind, a fishing boat come in, nets up. The sea-green water bobbing up and down near shore stretched and flattened itself out like smooth steel reaching to the far horizon. Periodically a silvery jet appeared in the sky, its nose pointed inland, and sliced down toward the airport. Pacified by seascape and stuffed with seafood, she rose up headily, hearing mermaids singing their melodies on the radio.

Outside again, she continued her journey, halting at the low railing of the new sea path, a few feet from Boston Harbor. Momentarily she imagined a jumping-in, a leave-taking, but the melodrama of the event immediately crashed the fantasy. She would try her best to avoid *that* in her already messy life. Two young business types were looking her over, she discovered, and she was flattered, not offended, by their attention. The dark-haired fellow, attending to her legs, asked if she wanted to join him for lunch. She smiled and said she had just eaten. Another afternoon? he wondered, this swarthy junior executive with the flirting eye.

She strolled on, amid open squares, pretty shops, glassy buildings, landscaped grounds. The wind blew through her hair and up her legs and unfurled flags of Colonial America and the Commonwealth of Massachusetts. When May went good, it sailed glorious. Soon she turned away from the water and went inland, walked far, far, leaving the area of new construction and entering a different neighborhood — old brick tenements and littered sidewalks and sleazy markets, autos swerving and honking and mothers screaming at unwieldy children. From somewhere she heard a low collective roar like a loud wind, and like an animal heeding a herd signal, she moved in its direction. The roars, direction signals, grew louder, and she homed with instinctive purpose toward the mystery. And when finally she came within sight of the source of sound, she smiled to herself at the shrewd Fates, the Miriamesque Will Above guiding her, which had led her back — back to early dreams, back to tomboy hopes, back to magic childhood. She bought a ticket and entered Fenway Park at the grandstand entrance.

Sight of the green field manned by the nine white-flanneled young men cheered her immensely and transported her to old Municipal Stadium three decades ago in Cleveland. This park was a bandbox with a high green wall close up in left field and only one deck in center field, instead of the old two-tiered stadium with the huge center field, but it didn't matter. This Fenway was most fair, intimate in its cozy dimensions and closeness of field and fan. She had entered in the bottom of the third inning — the baseball noun scooping memory — so she bought a scorecard and a small yellow pencil and found a wooden seat in the third-base grandstand. She began to record the at bats, groundouts, hits, strikeouts, fielder's choices the way she had done at age eight, Indian cap on head, pigtails waving freely in the bleacher sun, with Dad at her side opening roasted peanuts. Evans, Yaz, Fisk, Lynn, Burleson were easily transformed into Rosen, Lemon, Avila, Hegan, Doby; and sitting beside her was that sad, gaunt man in a lightweight jacket, who had never fulfilled himself in life but here, at the game with her alone, seemed at last serene.

The boyish figures out there cracking the little white ball and hauling it down in the outfields revived the precise pleasures of this slow game, which at certain moments of epiphany sprang alive with a subtle, sudden tension. She noted the smaller items that Dad had showed her: the positioning of center fielder and shortstop before each batter, the preparation for stealing bases by the fleet Detroit outfielder, the exquisite timing of toss and pivot by the Tigers' boys at second and short. Munching an ice cream sandwich (soggy, of course), she watched and listened and tasted, immersed in memory — manual scoreboards, line drives and long pegs to first interminging with a voice, a wish, a touch, expanding that frame of childhood into a permanent photograph untouched by time, joining then and now seamlessly, Papa and Miry and ballpark in a montage of intimacy. A long peg from shortstop to first brought back sweet Boudreau of '48, and she wondered if she should write him now, somewhere.

In the last of the seventh the home crowd stood to stretch, and Miriam was released, got up, and departed through the lazy crowd. She felt rich with emotion, dazed with memory. Soon she was walking up wide Commonwealth Avenue, and the air was cooling her overheated engines. The roars grew fainter, and asphalt reality was replacing green dreams. At first she wished that Jon was with her, but on second thought, thought no; she wouldn't even tell him about the game. At a shop she saw a safari shirt and without her usual hestitation tried it on and bought it. Simple. At the corner of Mass. Ave. she grew tired at last, dead tired, and caught the blunt-faced bus back to Cambridge. She hadn't had a day like this in a long time — a day of no work, random relaxation, easy indulgence. It was only as the bus bumped over Harvard Bridge and rolled toward MIT that the clouds of her life rose up again, and she fought to keep them away. So she invented for herself new forms of indulgence — an apartment in Jerusalem, a series of perfect photographs, a holiday in Sinai with Rafi. At the end of these escapes, however, lay a horizon of reality, a line of bereavement tinged by elegy. For her circumstances, for herself. So she switched her attention to the overhead ads for legal counseling, psychotherapy, contact lenses. Oh yes, she could use all the help she could get. Law. Therapy. Vision!

By the time she alighted at Trowbridge and was walking home, the afternoon of fantasies had fled, and she felt strengthened to face the actual. Or was that an illusion too, a trick of the self in self-defense, a self that was forever creating Jewish illusions of strength against a Roman army of reality?

But she made dinner, ate, and chatted with renewed spirit, staying away from the baseball game and speaking only of the North End and the waterfront, and producing the Jordan almonds as a surprise. After dinner, Rafi drove Jon to a study session, and she looked through her photography books before turning to Hardy's poetry. The phone rang twice, and each time she was disappointed that it was not Kelley. The third phone call was from *him*, who asked whether she had received "my little greetin' card" the other day, and whether she would like to see him this Saturday evening for dinner. She felt his semidrawl like a fist holding her hair and couldn't see a way of ridding herself of it; she accepted, not for Saturday but for Sunday. When she hung up, she had to keep from falling apart. She would have to do something drastic. She returned to reading and considered a gun. By hook or crook, she'd get a pistol and keep it with her. If she couldn't handle him any other way . . . The courts would understand, wouldn't they? In the kitchen she realized the dimensions of her thinking and poured herself and Rafi, who had returned, some Irish whisky. Why didn't that bloody girl call? . . . How could she, Miriam, have gone from the high times of a few weeks ago to this ridiculous low? How? Who else lived in this incongruous, overwrought way? Not the civilized surely . . . Well then, she was the primitive.

She drank her nightcap and they went to bed, and Miriam, to break her blue mood, to try to release her week's frustrations, played the primitive. She molested her fair friend with an aggressiveness that surprised them both. She pursued his body with her hands and mouth, interfered with orifices, unearthed vulnerable regions in buttocks and thighs, tried a new treat of tongue. She performed out of spite, out of lucklessness, out of vengeance, a vengeance born of despair and impotence; and in the shadows of the room she sought a way of climbing up from trouble, of struggling through the world of the senses to a site of spiritual ease. In the service of the deeper need, she used hand and tongue, breast and cunt, and for nearly an hour she lost herself in aggressive seduction, lost herself and felt released and charged her tender one too. And when she was done, and accepted his caresses and kisses in return and finally held him inside of her, she allowed no urged pleasure to ride up and over any residual sadness, thinking dreaming this would happen. But even here she was naive, once again, for at the moment of his coming she was not with him; she could sense his surprise, and she tried her best to mask her sadness in a counterfeit surge. It was a cheap thing, she knew, to do this to him, but just now she couldn't help it; and when he lay above her and she cried lightly, and mistook the sadness for delight, and she did nothing to enlighten him — it consoled her, in fact, that she could cry with him and explain nothing, just hold him and cry and balance his perfect weight with her own measure of grief.

Afterward, when he moved off and onto his side of the bed, he held her hand, and she stayed awake in the closing darkness, filled with a melancholy that blanketed her spirit like a winding sheet. For hours she stayed awake, twisting and turning in an effort to find rest, a way up, but there was only the dull ache of melancholy. Even the milk she warmed and drank provided no reprieve this time. Sinking.

The next day brought no news — for her, not good news. She returned to her routine — children, teaching, cooking — without enthusiasm, groggy and almost bored with her anxiety. (That near-boredom was a punishment too, yes?) It was now Wednesday, and she had three days to find a way of handling her Sunday date. Here it was May, she thought walking home with groceries at four o'clock, and instead of exulting in the unusual New England spring, she felt that it was ruined. She passed by the new wing of Cambridge Rindge and Latin and the public library where her spring hell had begun. It's what she got for going to libraries as a grownup! On Broadway a squad car was parked, and she had an impulse to walk over and tell everything. ("You see, this fellow raped me some eight years ago, and after accidentally spotting him I began to follow him and . . .") Maybe she would, before Sunday. They could fit her out with a minirecorder on her blouse button, and hear the whole dirty spiel and have the evidence! Dare she? Yes, why not? She repeated to herself the maniac's poem and walked on by with her packages, realizing how unfinished her photographic projects remained. How unfinished she was.

As she opened the downstairs door, someone asked if he could help with her bundles, and she said no before she realized that he was a she. She turned, surprised, saw the bright red hair and robust presence, and wanted to cry from happiness. "How —"

"I came to brush up on my boogying," announced Kelley, doing a small step, "and I hear Boston's a hot town on the eastern circuit. So here I am, thank you. Don't mind if I do join you for dinner, Ma'am; thanks for asking."

The big-boned woman took two packages from Miriam, smiling. She looked like a farm girl come to the city in her proper skirt and white blouse. She carried the packages upstairs, and only after she had set them down did she turn and hug Miriam, who hugged back, dropping tears from exhaustion and surprise.

No long-lost sister ever looked so good to Miry as this Kelley! She told her this, and Kelley, looking like the young Rita Hayworth and smoking, said, "Can't let you ruin your life *again,* you know. Once is plenty. I need you as living proof that a liberated chick can live happy and well outside the movement. And outside of a little mining town . . ."

"You're too young to remember Helen Trent," Miriam observed. "Who's been teaching you?"

"My old man has tons of those old radio cassettes. They're a gas!"

"You mean instant nostalgia?"

"For you, maybe, but for me it's instant fun, instant history. Boy, the corn you guys had to grow up with! I thought only *my* generation had to swill that stuff."

"Corn is an old American tradition."

"Just like rape," retorted Kelley, putting things in the refrigerator. "Rape, blackmail, shoot-outs, and" — she exhaled — "old-fashioned rescues. Just when the landlord is about to seduce the poor renter's daughter." She drew an imaginary mustache over her upper lip and threw on an imaginary cape.

"Yes, it is corny, isn't it?" Miriam smiled. "But here it is, with me the daughter."

Her friend nodded and smiled, pensively, revealing two crooked front teeth. She was a big young woman, all right, and already Miriam felt protected by her presence.

"Hey, you cut the locks!"

"I was wondering when you'd notice. Do I look older, more ma*ture*?" She spun around.

"It looks fine, really fine."

"Yeah, now if I can only keep the weight down."

"Did you really come all this way for . . . for . . ." Miriam couldn't finish it.

"For a last-minute rescue? Nah. I came to see —" She turned her attention suddenly to the door, where Rosie was now standing. "— this little creature! Do you remember me, you little squirt?"

Rosie giggled and did a ballet step, saying, "I'm not a *squirt*."

Kelley went over and lifted her high and swung her around, making her scream with glee. "That's who I really came to see, just to make sure she wanted to be the doctor when she grew up, and not the fucking nurse!"

"I'm no *fucking nurse*," replied Rosie.

For the next half hour or so, while Miriam put up dinner, Kelley checked in with Rosie, investigating any possible male incursions on her consciousness and giving her a Kelley seal of approval: "She's clean; no chauvinist fleas."

"Where's your male half?" she finally asked Miry. "Or is he afraid of confronting the Irish on neutral soil?"

"I didn't know you kept up with current events."

Washing the lettuce, Kelley said, "You mean *history*. Current events is L.A."

"Don't worry, he'll be here soon enough. In time for the news."

"An honest-to-goodness Israeli. Jeez, I'm nervous. Does he sleep with his rat-tat-tat beneath his pillow?"

That wouldn't be a bad idea here, Miriam thought. "They're not all heroes. Some are just plain folk."

"According to my reading, just plain folk heroes."

Miriam smiled. "Lemon and nuts on your sole?"

"What else?"

"Hmm . . . you haven't had a military man yet, have you?"

"You bet your bottom dollar I will before I'm through. Though Tyson was in World War Two, a navigator." She paused to recall her former lover. "Swell dude, really. I just met him when I was too young; otherwise, who knows, I might have settled down and had myself a brood. Mind if I hit the bottle early?"

"Yes," Miriam said, "if you do it without me."

Kelley made herself a gin with a pretense of tonic, and gave Miriam a glass of white wine. They brought their drinks to the living room, where Kelley lounged on the couch and Miriam sat in a chair. Miriam asked about her biography since the old Cambridge-Brookline days. After the older Boston professor, Kelley had "transferred" to a California shrink, "a real hot-shot neo-Freudian freak, mentioned again and again by Kohut, do you know him? Unreadable. Anyway, then I guess I got sort of tired of the old-age crowd, and after a few weird scenes I set up shop with Antony. We have a ball together. He lives and eats movies, so I have plenty of time to do my own thing. Which is now" — she bowed from the couch and upped her voice an octave — "the lost art of tapestry. Boy, is that ever an obstacle course for the impatient. Do you dig the scene — sitting in Malibu with my loom, weaving for hours on end, while the surfers and skaters and crazies roll on by, *whoosh!* It's a total groove, and totally un-Malibuish. I go to UCLA for my classes. Are you familiar with the classical works?"

Miriam restrained her laughter when she saw the seriousness of the query. She found herself feeling wonderfully secure in the company of this dynamo. Were all redheads protective? She listened to tall tales of Persian and Flemish weavers, cited as if they were old football heroes.

What about those movie scripts?

"Oh, *that*. Just a vocation with me. Are you kidding?"

Finally, when it was her turn, Miriam briefed Kelley in a few choice sentences about her own, duller life. Her man, her photographs, the children, MIT, and Israel part-time. The doctor stayed private. "And creeping middle age, don't forget. Colds that stay a week, not a day. Creaking joints, in the neck and knees regularly. Rotting gums — I'm diseased with gingivitis. And a sadist-racist dentist. Downhill all the way — it's called middle-aging."

"Yeah, I'll bet. Listen, I look forward to it. I can't wait to slow down."

Rosie danced in, dressed up suddenly in a new tartan skirt, and demanded dinner *now* while flaunting (for Kelley) her skirt, her drawing, her Yemenite doll. Miriam gave her macaroni and cheese in the dining room, and returned to the living room.

Kelley said, "Look, about *the problem*. I have a name or two, and I think we may be able to do some business. One of the best things about my Antony is his connections, especially around Beantown. He's been *around* for a young dude, and he knows some, uh, professionals in the area of crime and its prevention. I'm going to see a gentleman tonight, after dinner. No use in wasting precious time, right?"

For the first time since the nightmare had begun, Miriam felt lighter. A friend was now in on her case. "I just couldn't tell Rafi. I mean, I didn't know how, and I was afraid he might do the wrong thing." She shook her head. "As for the police, if you hadn't shown up, I probably would have gone to them before too long."

Kelley gave a raucous laugh. "Cops? Forget it. There are no cops anymore. 'Cause there ain't no judges anymore. There's just . . . an eye for a rape and a kick in the balls for a pinch in the ass. Don't worry, we'll bail you out of this, nice and smooth too. A parachute ride down. With no one getting hurt on this side of the fence. Now, tell me all about life. On coke yet? Hitting the bottle? Or what else are you doing for maturity these days?" She smiled warmly, freckles showing on her upper cheeks. "Any married men in the closet?"

On cue, some cue, the door closed downstairs, and Miriam nodded, saying, "My maturity and coke rolled into one."

Footsteps on the stairs; Rafi entered the living room. He was wearing a white shirt open at the neck, slacks, sandals — a fragile-looking fellow, perhaps an official from the Sassoon East India Trading Company.

"Hello," he said amiably.

"Hello," Kelley said, standing up to a height greater than Rafi's. Curiously, she seemed a bit stiff, nervous, almost shy.

Rafi set down his small leather briefcase and asked her about Los Angeles, and as she answered (and later too) Miriam saw a wondrous thing. Despite herself, this tough, experienced, wily young woman was turning on the kitten-charm, becoming a seductive, coy ingenue. Miriam smiled to herself at the little gestures: the leaning forward with rapt attentiveness, the fluttering of the eyelashes, even the inching up of the skirt, the devil! A man was a piece of candy, all men, and dear Kelley had one large sweet tooth.

Dinner was fine, with Kelley narrating some outrageous L.A. tales and Rafi listening quietly, attentively. Did he know that behind the pose of Idaho baked potato and virginal wonder there lay a shrewd, self-protective animal who never allowed herself to fall hard, let alone be cornered? Miriam couldn't tell. But she half envied Kelley's magic tricks of personality; what the hell was it like to handle every trouble as if it were a fastball down the middle? And if you struck out, you moved to first base anyway, through sheer chutzpah and youth.

By the time Kelley left, after dinner, to see her friend, Miriam was already lifted. Kelley performing was Kelley cheering you up. Oh, Miriam would have loved to see this young woman play Nora in *A Doll's House,* especially in the last scene.

"What do you make of her?" she asked Rafi, cleaning up.

"She's a *large* woman," he exclaimed, "and I imagine what you could call a man-eater. Though she was very careful with me."

Later Kelley returned, and informed Miriam privately that they had a date the next night in Boston. Miriam was dumbfounded, having forgotten that Kelley had gone out on business so quickly.

"Don't worry, it's a blind date for me too," Kelley consoled her. Then she inquired if Miry happened to own any Revlon "Deep Red" she could use on her toenails?

Over melon and prosciutto and white wine, Miriam gave a thumbnail sketch of her life: schools, career as a photographer, places lived.

Hearing it all was Nick, a wide-shouldered, pockmarked man of about fifty-five — a hard fifty-five — who wore a blue silk suit and an expensive tie and sported a good-sized pinky diamond. His large nose and prominent features gave his face a hawkish look; the dark tan and expressive brown eyes suggested that he was

Italian or Greek. His graying hair was combed forward, Roman style. A veteran Praetorian, Miriam thought, or a Caesar.

Surrounding them in the darkened, cozy North End restaurant were wall murals of Venice, red-jacketed waiters, a marble-tiled floor. Plus two well-dressed gentlemen at the next table, whom Nick turned to occasionally.

"Where are you from originally? You can't be from Cambridge; nobody is."

When she announced, "Cleveland," he arched his eyebrows and said, "Used to be a nice town. Gone down since the old days, like most of the Eastern towns."

Miriam hadn't thought of Cleveland as Eastern or a town, but it sounded right. When she and Kelley had first arrived, Nick had made some joke about Cambridge and its "highfalutin culture" with an appealing restraint.

One of his two sentries leaned across, whispered something; Nick excused himself for a moment and accepted a telephone at the table. He said a few words, low, and gave the phone back to "Mario."

"They're called princesses, I think," he said, nodding at the phone. "Some name. You can't even hold the thing properly." He shook his head. "They're ruining this world by trying to modernize it. Should've left phones phones, bottletops bottletops. Ever tried to open an aspirin bottle lately? Make sure you bring your hammer."

Miriam smiled and drank her wine. She felt relaxed with this man.

The waiter brought over a huge platter filled with cold cuts and anchovies and sliced tomatoes and olives, arranged decoratively.

"Do you really expect us to eat a main course after this?" Kelley wondered.

Nick drank his second, or third, scotch. "Why not? What are you, hummingbirds? I hear you have kids, Miriam; how old are they?"

"Eleven and fifteen," Miriam replied, trying not to think of them.

Nick smiled, showing a row of uneven teeth, and took out an overstuffed wallet. "Mine are a little older," he said, removing a few photos. One showed children of seven and eight, another the same children at a high school graduation, and two others, weddings. "You can guess who that is," he said, pointing to a rabbi at the young man's wedding and noting his Jewish daughter-in-law. "He was all right, this rabbi. He asked me to make a small contribution to the local synagogue. My check surprised him, I think. Best thing that ever happened to me, these two kids. Could have used two more easily. Wife didn't want it. The boy graduated from Northeastern in engineering, the girl in journalism from Syracuse. Because of them I still attend church on Sundays."

Though Miriam was sitting there, she had little idea of what was happening. The food was superb, the atmosphere cozy, this Caesar warm. She asked no questions and was told nothing. She could barely repeat the facts, say who this man was, if you asked her. Of course, she didn't *know* who he was, didn't know his last name, but she knew somehow that, despite his many businesses, his real business was power of some sort. Mafia? She could hardly believe that she was in the middle of this melodrama, that she was the center attraction of this Grade B thriller. Good honest people were having dinner all around them, discussing local politics, college tuition, fettuccini. Perhaps she had lived so far away from ordinary life that she had figured that this sort of man — and such situations — existed on television only, not in life. Nick was pleasant to be with, courteous, old-fashioned, *himself*. Even intelligent, though unintelligible. As when she heard him saying, as she finished her veal Marsala, "So, I understand you've been having some trouble with the fellow who sold you your car. Wouldn't stand behind his guarantee. Yes, I know the type, I think. A fast talker, but not to be trusted. And unfortunately, to get the law after him costs money, and even then you don't win. The damn thing breaks down immediately, 'cause he's sold you a lemon, and what're you going to do? The best thing," he said, draining a glass of club soda, "is to junk it. Just put it to rest in some nice quiet junkyard and not bother to fix it. Forget it; a bad investment. If you try to bring the law in on it" — he shook his head — "it doesn't work so well. A sleazy salesman is a sleazy salesman, and a used car is a used car. Period. That's my advice," he pronounced in his guttural voice. And that was all, through sherbet and espresso and more pleasant, aimless conversation.

It wasn't until later, outside in the evening air, in the taxi hailed by one of Nick's helpers, that she perceived what he had been saying. Not "perceived," really, for she was high from drink and filled with food, but she had a glimmer, perhaps, of what he had been talking about. Now she heard the words again, in the taxi, and said aloud to Kelley, "What did he mean? It can't be what I think, can it?"

Kelley shook her head. "All it means is that the matter will be taken care of, and you won't be bothered. Nothing too drastic will happen, I know that. We'll just go to dinner on Sunday, you and me, and that's it. Don't look at me that way — I'm your chaperone, kiddo. You need one, just now."

The surprising weather continued, the sunny days and splendid nights. But this uncharacteristic flow of beauty struck Miriam with irony, as a kind of cruel harbinger of danger. This was her interpretation as she tried to avoid thinking of her Sunday rendezvous. Having Kelley around helped matters. Walking the city with that bold half-teenager, half-superadult, gave her a new way of perceiving it. Next to Kelley, Miriam felt more 1950s-ish than ever. "Grab onto that, will ya?" Kelley nudged Miriam one morning, indicating a construction worker relaxing in the sun. "That's *obscene,* showing his equipment off that way!" It took Miriam a minute to discern which tools Kelley was referring to. Or Kelley would stop on a dime, day or evening, and, claiming "weakness," would fall into the nearest bar to wolf down a hamburger bathed in mayonnaise and ketchup and gulp two or three beers "to wash the preservatives down and through."

Besides men and eating, she had a third pastime — cars and driving. She had researched the history of Porsche with Gibbonesque fullness; she described the evolution of Cadillacs with the passion of Darwin and raved about the 1953 Austin Healy as if it were *Swann's Way.* One afternoon she treated Miriam and her banged-up Plymouth to a drive in the country; by the time they hit Lincoln, Miriam had had enough. Shaking, she let out, "You know, you were made for Israel. For their roads and their taxi drivers, at least. How have you stayed in one piece for this long?" Kelley brushed back two fallen strands of hair, squinched her face at this odd woman, and emitted her expletive for hopeless adults: "*Huh?*"

All this freewheeling tooling about had its therapeutic side for Miriam, of course — an attempt at camouflaging her anxiety. On Thursday, when Montana called and said, in an unusually plaintive tone, "I miss seeing you," she almost broke down and cried. Her needs and wounds at the surface, she fought the urge to run to him immediately. "Give me some time, will you? I'm just up to my ears in . . ."

A pause, and she felt his remorse. He said, "I shouldn't be bothering you this way."

"Sure you should. Do. You must. Only . . . not this week, okay?"

He okayed back and hung up.

She held onto the phone, contemplating the incongruities of her life. She didn't know how to fit her doctor and their mutual feelings into her present bizarre situation. How to fit pieces of something real, something serious, into a surrealistic puzzle that could break apart at any moment? And why try? She was at a loss to describe the forces pressing in upon her, pressing upon her chest, her head, choking her heart.

Finally she let go of the telephone and went to fix a bowl of cereal for Rosie, who was complaining. When in trouble with the kids, turn to Cheerios, their all-time pacifier.

Where was Miriam's? Oh, Dr. Levanda, did you have to die and leave me?

Sunday evening loomed like a Liberian freighter coming to take her away from home and family; it didn't help that her period was coming too. And yet when she and Kelley approached *him* in the Cambridge Hyatt Regency dining room, it wasn't like exile at all. The gloomy prospect had now materialized into a noisy, shiny kingdom of glass chandeliers, thronelike chairs, thick carpets, flashing jewelry. As she walked amid the barbarous formality and savage glitter, she thought what a nice gambling room this would make, a Vegas on the Charles. And when Kelley whispered, "What better place to meet your pimp?" Miriam let out a nervous laugh.

Reginald DuPres, Jr., a brown stem with a Panama hat on top, stood and smiled broadly. He held a chair for Miriam and eyed her surprise companion with obvious suspicion and curiosity.

"Haven't met you, I don't believe," he said, and he held out a big paw.

Kelley took his hand and said, coolly, "Kelley." When she took out a cigarette, he lit it for her with a fancy gold lighter. She had dressed purposefully for the occasion: purple harem pants, spike heels, and a chartreuse blouse. Her large bosom bounced freely, without a bra, and she fidgeted absentmindedly with two blouse buttons. Her red hair was styled with bangs and revealed long silver triangles dangling from her ears; she also had put on a wedding band with a diamond. She looked every bit the odd part she was going to play — whatever *that* was. All she had told Miriam, on the way up in the dizzying glass elevator, was to stay cool and let her do the talking.

Alongside her now, Miriam sat like a shy spinster, smallish, reticent, dutiful in beige skirt and blouse and low heels and no makeup. For the second time within a week she began a dinner with little idea of what to expect, little belief in the observable reality. Her heart was beating rapidly, overtaking the approaching menstrual pains.

The young man had taken a corner table by the vast window that overlooked the dark Charles and, across the river, the glittering city of Boston. Even here, in the dim light, in the ostentatious room, in the tawdry situation, Miriam appreciated his beauty: the diffused chocolate color of his skin; the thick, sensual lips and flattened nose; the intricate kinks in the jet-black hair; the thin, long, taut body with the narrow hips and shoulders; the long, lovely neck like a swan's. He wore a satiny burgundy shirt with ruffled sleeves, tight off-white trousers, and a thin golden necklace. On his right hand he wore a large ring of green jade; on the other, what looked like black onyx. He was like some exotic tropical bird that had just flown in from Zanzibar — or some sheik of mixed Arab and Berber blood, a hybrid son of slave and slave trader who now, a hundred years later, was taking his sweet revenge by turning master in his own right. For a moment Miriam fantasized herself lying beneath the young prince, having him cockily put it to her, feeling his strength and smelling his smell. Perverse imagination. Unsmiling, she sipped her vermouth and thought that Othello had nothing on this Louisiana Moor. Could Kelley make him gullible, for one night at least?

They feasted on escargots, filet mignon, and Alaskan crab legs, drank two bottles of wine (for Kelley, a gin, too), and talked, sparred, scouted, kidded, played seriously. Miriam watched as one veteran went to work on the other, two teenagers with street smarts circling in an alleyway. Kelley provided all the answers for Reggie, once it was clear why she had come along. She said she lived in a North Shore suburb and could work one night a week, on occasion two; her last name and address were private. She did no overnights but would make a rare exception, and that exception was worth "five Franklins, minimum." She hustled in classy hotel rooms only, arranged by him. She worked two or three tricks a night, no more, and for that came away with "three to four C-notes, depending." Finishing her first after-dinner brandy, she explained that her speciality was kinkiness, adding in a slow, determined voice, "of all sorts, from water sports to strict English." And for Kelley and Miriam to perform together in "one kinky duet," the sky was the limit, once they got in there with the john. As for the education of her cousin here, "Little Miriam," Kelley would be responsible for that. She, and she alone. For the umpteenth time she touched her cleavage and ran her tongue over her painted lips. Then she ordered a second brandy.

Reggie listened with rising admiration. The dangerous Moor had gotten more than he had bargained for, and had been put into the situation of not quite knowing what to make of it all. What had been a small personal pleasure was turning into a serious business deal, at the least. He had started out skeptical and powerful, but by the end of two hours he was relaxed, flattered, slightly complacent. So that when Kelley put the question, "Can you handle those prices or should I, and Miriam, look elsewhere for the trade?" he flashed a confident smile, having drunk a little too much, and replied, "*I* name the price, not my clients. Y'all deliver the merchandise as well as you rap, and we'll be one happy family." He looked from one woman to the other. "*All* of us."

"After *business*," Kelley remarked, reaching over and running an oversized fingernail down his sleeve, "*family* sounds sweet. Real sweet."

His face grew alert with libidinal hope while he massaged the scratch on his arm.

Looking beyond the princely young pimp, out at the shimmering grid of yellow dots and squares upon the river, Miriam thought how much minor talk, the talk of arrangements and negotiations, mattered in the big world. It was so much more significant than her talk of ideals, principles, theories, emotions. At one point she closed her eyes and envisioned a green orchard of peach and plum trees. She longed now for her kibbutz boredom, for blue-uniformed farmers who mixed horticulture with innocence, for the Negev desert and solitude. Oh, to be jeeping around with Rachel now, giving her these new English idioms to use! (Did Miriam understand half of it?) The cramps punished her now, removing her pleasant daydream.

Half listening to Kelley's pitch, and offering up her best innocent smile, she periodically glanced about, but could find no sign of Nick's spies about the place. She saw instead only glancing middle-class faces, some staring with tight disapproval or embarrassment when she caught their eyes. That respectable foursome right there — what could they be thinking, except the obvious? From the outside it was easy to understand the scene. But here on the inside, inside Miriam's skin, it was more mysterious. "Once in Aleppo" had become "Once in Cambridge."

At one point during the long meal she had to excuse herself and go to the bathroom. And when she emerged, there was Prince DuPres, smiling, arms akimbo. "I thought I'd escort you personally back to the table," he drawled, "and just make sure that when you said lad-ies room, you meant lad-ies room, not telephone or relay team."

Nervous, she allowed her arm to be hooked, which attracted more attention. She defiantly declared, "How do you know I didn't meet my contact inside?"

He shook his head. "I don't. But if you did, sugar, you went for the *wrong* sort of reason. And you know what, I just don't think you're that wrong-headed when it comes to your children's welfare."

Only at the end of the evening, when they were driving in his sleek white sports car and she felt the wind in her hair like a genie, did she pop free. ("What happened to your Olds?" He smiled. "For business only.") Leaving them off in front of the Orson Welles

Cinema on Mass. Ave., at their request, Reggie took a billfold from the glove compartment and handed Kelley a crisp packet of Grant-faced bills. "On *account*." He smiled. "You don't look as if you need too much dressin' up."

To Miriam's surprise, Kelley accepted the money, repeating, "On account. One night's work, say. See you next Sunday, same time, same place, and we can begin" — she ran her finger up and down his smooth brown cheek — "operations."

His vanity stroked, DuPres smiled again. "Don't stand me up now."

"Don't you stand us up," she retorted.

"Not with my loot in your hands, I won't, baby doll," he reminded gently.

Kelley got out first, but before Miriam could move, Reggie took her arm, grinned, and held up his wide palm to reveal that same safety razor. "Keep it straight, now; don't be stupid again." He let her out, winked beneath his Panama, and revved his engine.

On impulse, she asked if she could take a few quick pictures of him by the car, and his face tightened. But he said, "Sure, so long as I see them first." She took out her camera, a small Polaroid with flash attachment, and told him to step out from the white sports car and into the light of the marque. First a shot of him leaning, arms crossed, against the flashy car. Next Kelley holding Reggie's arm, and then Kelley shot the two of them, Miriam and Reggie. Finally Miriam took another single shot of Reggie, half smiling beneath his Panama in the driver's seat. While she was shooting pictures, however, his handsome face and subtle color became engraved in her memory once and for all; she could almost smell his lavender scent now. Right there she developed her pics, beneath the Welles, where a small circle had gathered. ("What's all the action for? Is he a *star*?")

She showed him the pictures when they developed in a few minutes.

"I'm photogenic, what d'ya know." Grinning skeptically, he tore them in pieces and tossed them in the gutter, then winked. "I got some better ones," he said. And he sped off.

When he was gone, Miriam bent and retrieved the photos, torn in twos and threes.

"Can you save them?"

"Doubtful . . . As souvenirs, maybe."

Kelley shrugged, then casually lit up a cigarette. "The man has taste in cars. That's a very hard-to-get Porsche."

Miriam's stomach was still doing flip-flops.

Her friend took her arm and said, "Come on, a nightcap will settle you down."

Miriam stared. "How'd you know . . . ?"

"That you've been jittery? Shit, all evening I was waiting for you to wet your pants. It's over now; stop sweating." But as she tried to edge Miriam into a nearby restaurant, she felt her trembling. "Hey, what's happening? Did the crumb say something to you at the end?"

Miriam, near tears, told her of the razor and the threat.

Kelley hugged her, right there in the street. "It's okay, love, really. He won't be bullying you or anyone else for a long, long time." She folded her within a large embrace, and in a minute Miriam had recovered.

They found a corner table beneath a long hanging plant. Kelley ordered a beer, Miriam an herb tea.

"I'm glad I didn't catch that little episode at the end," Kelley said, "or I might just have used this gadget." She revealed a small black automatic in a purse full of cosmetics. "Don't look so astonished; you don't think I go on such blind dates unaccompanied, do you?"

Miriam sipped her tea. "Where'd you come up with that tale?"

"Still the best chaser around," Kelley said, referring to her near-drained beer. "I have a real sister, remember?"

Miriam tried to remember, to digest it all. "And the money — why'd you take it?"

Finishing the beer and radiating happiness, Kelley replied, "If I really was *who* and *what* I was making myself out to be, I had to take it. Especially if you're planning to show up for work next week." She took hold of the trailing vine and began wrapping it around her neck. "Besides, my return ticket to the coast needs to be paid for."

The waitress appeared. "Would you please release the plant?"

Winding it tighter, like a mink, Kelley emoted, "If you're going to play a role, darling, play it all the way." Then she looked up in wide-eyed surprise at the fuming waitress and asked, "Do you mean *this?*" She handed her the vine and turned to Miriam.

Miriam tried to take in Kelley's conventional wisdom, but the unconventionality of the evening was still churning her insides. She remained muddled and excited and afraid. She couldn't have gone through it alone! In awe, Miriam asked, "How'd you get so fucking smart so *young?*"

"Dumb, you mean," her friend replied, downing her next glass of beer. "To know how these punks and crooks tick, or to know them at all, you have to be dumb. Real dumb. Don't believe otherwise. Besides, we were there only as decoys, while our friend was being scouted and sighted. We just had to make it *look* good. Now, if I had told you all that, you wouldn't have carried it off. Hey," she added, coming up with a new idea, "one for the road?"

Back in her own bed, back with her man, back somewhat with her life, Miriam felt something like she had when she almost drowned in a lake at age twelve, her canoe tipping over and Miry not swimming and suddenly being saved and being out for the long count. Yet even now, when she closed her eyes, she saw that razor in the salmon-colored palm and grew terrified. Instinctively she turned toward Rafi, curling her leg upon him. Taking that as a signal of sorts, he ran his hand along her back, down to her tailbone and across her buttocks. Oh, she felt needy now; oh, she wanted his loving now; oh, she wanted to give her body a chance to win out over her brain and beat down all thoughts. But she felt her pelvic area stiffen with pain, felt the cramps grabbing at her stomach and thighs, and knew she just couldn't go through with it. She kissed his cheek, explained what was happening, and asked for a rain check. "From being distant from you this past week, my precious," she murmured, and got out of bed and went to the bathroom. There she took care of herself, changing tampons and washing herself; and then she went to the kitchen and warmed up milk in a saucepan. Drinking it slowly, sitting on her couch, she felt easier. Quieter. Felt her menstrual period now not as pain or punishment but as something cleansing, something bringing her through. Were physical cycles to be viewed as symbolic forms?

Did this movement of blood, coming tonight, perhaps declare an end to her bizarre ordeal, as well as signal how close to disaster she had edged? Or was she fantasizing again, overinterpreting? Looking for resolution — a resolution where there was only shadow? When Kelley left, would DuPres re-emerge? Oh, Kelley, sweet loyal friend!

"You okay?" Rafi asked, slim in his sky-blue briefs, looking sleepy.

"Sure. Go back to your dreams; no need to bother with me. I'll drink this and be fine."

Nodding, he waved sleepily and returned to their room.

What would she do now in her life without friends and their loyalty? Loyalty, *the* prime resource of the human creature. Ahead of passion, way ahead of irony.

She sipped her milk slowly, remembering her old cat, that Merlin of loyalty.

Had she really come through?

Had the monster been real?

Had she courted disaster and in the end been rescued, escaping by the skin of her teeth? Was that stupid venture to be called adventure? Was it really Little Miriam when it came to the big wide world out there?

She promised herself to learn more about Yani's D & D game, where monsters came and went without leaving permanent scars or marks.

Part Two

10

SHE sat on a narrow wooden bench, sipping the hot chocolate that the police chief had made for her. She smoked and stared at the photographs of the governor of the commonwealth and the president of the United States, smiling down at her and Rafi. The jailhouse was a small brick building of two floors, and it felt like a tidy New England home, except for the rattling of keys and bars in the near distance. Chief Willard was in his fifties, smooth-shaven and round-faced, with spectacles and a slow manner in speech and gesture. Jail had its quaint side in this tiny town in the Berkshires; it was not squalid, like Boston, or rough, like Springfield, say. She was grateful for the chocolate, and for the courtesy shown by the chief and his younger deputy while they prepared the necessary papers to release Jon. All told, it was a respite to be here, after the long, harrowing night, the uncertain waiting, the police at 2:10 A.M., the endless, tense drive on the Mass. Pike. And the private oath not to think, or at least not to judge. Not yet. She took a certain pleasure in observing the clean blue summer uniforms of the police, the orderliness of the office, the lack of threats or lectures.

Eventually she was shown into a small gray room with a bench on either side of a steel conference table — a room for lawyers and clients, not mothers and sons. He was already there, sitting on a chair against the wall, knees tucked up to his chin, chin on hands, mouth scrunched tight.

At first he didn't bother to look up. When he did, he asked, "Rafi come?"

She nodded.

"Really?"

"Yes."

She didn't know where to sit, alongside him or on the bench; didn't know really what to do, either.

"How you feeling?"

"Headache. But I'll survive."

She lit a cigarette and took a seat opposite him. "I may not."

"Huh?"

"Tell me about it."

"Aaah." He scratched his wild hair. (She wanted to ask him when he had washed it last, but held off.) "Do I have to, *now?*"

She shook her head. "I guess not now."

She smoked, and he shifted his position in the chair, keeping his head down, face averted. He was wearing his running shoes, a tie-dyed T-shirt over dungarees, and a light jacket. A baseball cap was at his side; it stirred memories.

She didn't say anything; listened to a fan whirring somewhere.

"Can we get outta here?" he wondered.

Gripped by betrayal and hurt, she tried to say as little as possible, and focused on the solid brick wall. The events of the night had depleted her.

"As soon as the papers are signed."

"How's Moon?"

"He's okay," she said, "just some scratches. Where were you going? Why?"

He shrugged. "Aah, I don't know. Just . . . ridin' around. No special place."

She saw the bones in his cheeks that he had inherited from his father, and her eyes in his green-gray ones with the jagged black irises. She tried to remember, as Rafi had cautioned; to remember herself at fifteen — hadn't she been a rebel too? In trouble herself, like stealing from Woolworth's and the lumberyard, to keep up with the tough Italian kids . . . but never this sort of stuff, involving cars and pills and middle-of-the-night journeys clear across the state to a jailhouse.

"Aaah, I'm sorry, Mom," he mumbled.

She stood up and took two steps to him and kissed his hair, his bristly wild mop that she loved so much. He let her.

"It needs washing," she said.

"Yeah, it's been a while."

She held him. Consoled by the proximity of this head, by the release of affection, she perceived a terrible truth — namely, that this was not an isolated incident and would occur again and again, in one or another form. A knowledge unwanted, as she held him. How much of his damage was attributable to that absent year of hers? When would she ever handle a hard event in his life on its own, objectively, without letting her own guilt enter and cloud the issue?

He held onto her tightly, and she held him back. No tears now, she warned herself, crying.

They held each other for several minutes before there was a light knock on the door and the words, "We're all straight here, whenever you're ready." The voice of normalcy defused the hot, igniting moment.

"We'll be right there." She released Jon, who looked up at her with a face so troubled, so confused, and so eager for articulation that she was forced to say, "Why don't you clean yourself up, okay? There's probably a bathroom nearby."

He was grateful. "Yeah, I know one."

Sleepy, shaky, he walked out. Alone, she sat down on the chair by the wall, facing the gray brick. She had an urge to bang her head against the wall, again and again. Or to crawl into the cracks and vanish into mortar. Why this situation? She hadn't deserved it or planned it this way! Controlling herself, she shifted her gaze to see the first glimmers of dawn sneaking into the room through a narrow window. She turned again to the wall, placing her hot cheeks against the cool bricks. Her limbs sagged in exhaustion.

Another knock, and Rafi was saying, "You all right?"

She turned. "Sure. Just overtired."

On the ride home she stayed with Jon in the back seat while Rafi drove. The boy half lay on the seat, his head cradled in her lap, fast asleep. Mountains loomed on the side of the road, passing in this funereal gray light of morning. She recalled being pregnant with Jon and wondering what he would turn out to be, with romantic hope; saw him as a precocious six-year-old, shining with A's in the first grade, already reading adventure stories; remembered his first baseball game in junior high, batting with a real stance and shagging flies in the outfield easily; replayed his mature delicacy and poise when he visited her several times during her breakdown year ("Oh, Ma, you'll be fine. Wait and see, and everything'll be neat again," he had consoled, at seven, already a protector.) She remembered these fleeting moments of success now, while holding her defeated son, the car speeding in the early morning like a projectile in space zipping nowhere. In the midst of this ordeal, it was a reward to be chauffeured in quiet, alone with her men and thoughts. Holding Jon this way, her heart filled with anxiety as she sensed that this was not merely her son but her destiny, too. For events and character — hers — had conspired to create a casualty here, under her unavoidable responsibility. Yet which was the casualty, Yani or herself? She wished it were she alone, and not they together!

The car sped smoothly in the misty morning, and she was flooded with the memory of sitting in the back of a Cambridge police cruiser nearly a decade ago, half naked, fully mad, violated spiritually and physically. And now? Now she was in control, at least. The policeman had turned into a dear friend, and she was going home, not to a hospital ward. A hostage — to fortune and to herself — lay in her hands, true, but there were deep rewards, too. Feeling the mane of thick hair, she knew now she would manage; was managing now, to be sure. Once you've been to hell and made the return passage, the survival gene is nurtured. (Truth, or a necessary illusion?) Warm air redolent of gasoline sliced in the window. A question arose: did she *feel* her son more intensely because he was a wounded creature in need of special caring? Cruel paradox. He was not merely a son but a limb, an emotion, a part of her anatomy. Could you ever explain sons or daughters to those who didn't have them? Or, for that matter, explain full adulthood, with all its brutally unfair demands and ironic, paradoxical satisfactions? If the limb was sick, you were sick too. And the Intensive Care Unit was so private here, so sacred and inviolate from the outside.

She knew she had to be twice as strong now. For the next several years, maybe as long as a decade, this would be her challenge: to help Jon fight the culture; to help him fight himself; to help him fight her (a necessity) without hurting her too much. Could she really accomplish this? Could anyone be that strong? Oh, you could hire doctors, work like crazy to pay their bills, and get lucky or unlucky; that was the trouble — in the end, it was the luck of the draw. The Winnicotts and Levandas of the medical world were too few and far between. If an error was to be made, let her make it directly, from her love, not via a hired outsider. Wasn't a hired theory worse than a hired gun? (Oops, you're slipping!)

Jon moved, adjusted himself in her lap, and scrunched himself closer to her chest, one arm underneath him, the other around her. He needed her, and she needed him *and* his need. And holding him now, fingering the brown hair, feeling his regular breathing, observing his bony body was compensation enough. God. She was protector as well as battering ram, doctor as much as adversary, and there would be no escaping this dual, mixed role. Unless she sought to escape from herself.

"Want me to relieve you?" she asked Rafi, fatigued from her heavy thoughts.

"Not necessary, unless you want to."

She needed relief, however. "Do you think we can get Lurtsema on the radio yet?"

He tried, and classical music filled the moving chamber.

She forced herself to concentrate on the symmetries of genius — much easier than tracking the noises of the ordinary. After a long minute she contemplated the possibility of the absence of this weight upon her, the disappearance of this necessary corporeality, and she wondered if she could survive that. Her own vanishing, yes, but . . . Immediately she censored her anxiety and returned to horns and strings of harmony. She'd wash his hair for him that day — an event from his childhood, when they had been as one — despite his protests.

And later, when she did wash it that afternoon, after everyone had had some sleep, it was wonderful. He protested not at all, but let her lather and rinse the thick tangle and massage the scalp as she had when he was five and she had set him on a small stool so his head could reach over the basin and dip into the sudsy water. She rinsed that fantastic, unruly hair — like Stan's? — with a vigor that seemed to her a ritual of renewal, drying it thoroughly afterward. (Recalling The Bath administered to her by Dr. B.?)

Presently Jon began to bob and weave in a boxer's stance, hair tied in a towel, imploring her to "put up your dukes" and jabbing at her lightly. He offered his taut stomach for a punching bag: "Go ahead, try me."

Entertained, she clipped him a few times.

Unfazed, he beamed. "Not bad, huh?"

"Not too bad," she concurred.

"Give me five years in the gym, and they'll be calling me Sugar Ray!"

"Robinson, I hope."

Feinting and shadow boxing, he glistened still, and she looked on with temporary glee, within that miniature ring of steam, suds, and separate dreams.

In forty-eight hours routines had returned to normal, Jon resuming his old self and everyday demands running full steam ahead. But a black spot had been uncovered in her heart, and it would stay there, as black and emphatic as a spot in the lungs. No matter how hard she sought to brush it away, by censorship or distraction or euphemism, the spot remained, visible to her understanding alone.

Could you photograph *that*? she mocked herself.

But you could photograph other things, escape to beauty and truth. Where to catch them? First she returned to old standbys: the bare rooms of Walker Evans, the abstract vegetables of Weston, the Parisian compositions of Atget, the personal portraits of Steiglitz. (Oh, she had grown impressed with the changing masks of that evolving photographer, who went down his own path and changed his way of seeing and photographing at least three different times.) Great photographs uplifted her, and she returned to them like one returned to good friends — maybe they were better, for they ripened as you did, and waited patiently, silently, for you to probe beyond their surfaces to their depths, camouflaged artfully. And while she studied the photos in the amber light of June afternoons, the face of her son began to weave in and out, that face of a disturbed teenager, and it struck her that there too, in front of her nose, was a subject.

She received this idea as though it were a sliver of wood breaking the skin, hard and painful. The mother in her immediately recoiled at the thought, at the splinter conjured up by the artist. No, the mother censored, you won't exploit your son. No! she rejected, you won't go that low. No, Mother resisted, over my dead body. With all my might, *no!*

What to do?

Feeling cornered, baffled, Miriam walked the streets, trying for compromise. Harry and his young art-models came to mind. Why couldn't she use similar models? Where, how?

She could ask Harry for advice, for starters. She could be low-down and nitty-gritty — which every artist had to be, she knew, within his (her!) limitations at first, and in maturity beyond those limits — and go to McLean's teenage division, or Mass. Mental, or perhaps some of the halfway houses. Of course, she wouldn't have the time now to begin, but in the fall, yes. For now, she was alert with the idea.

During this period there were preparations to be made for the return to Israel, first by Rafi, and three weeks later by Miriam. On a Wednesday evening of Rafi's last week, she said to him, "I'm thinking of asking Jon if he wants to come along this time. What do you think? Supposing he says yes, how will the kibbutz take it? Or, more important, Jon?"

Rafi fiddled with his pipe, pressing down the tobacco into the bowl with his thumb. "I think it's good to ask him. How he'll do there . . ." He shrugged. "If he is willing to work, I imagine they'll accept him well enough."

She smiled at her friend. "Thanks. It'll be a nice surprise for him, I think."

"Speaking of surprises," he countered, lighting up, "how about getting married?"

Slowly she did a double take. "Say that again?"

"It's been almost three years, and my wife agreed to give me a divorce now, remember? So perhaps you'd like to marry me." He puffed and puffed, blowing smoke nicely.

Like a teenager, she flushed at the proposal, took three steps, and hugged him. "I don't know what to say," she whispered, kissing his cheek. "Let me think on it a bit." Her body tingled.

Thinking on it later, in the long afternoon and slow evenings, during a walk, a movie, a bath, she understood a simple thing: she did not want to marry again. Not now, anyway. She had fought too hard to get free last time, and she had fought hard to make her present liberty a space of interest. No longer did she need the familiar structure of marriage to give coherence to her life; it had its own coherence now, in structures different from those of society's desire. No, she didn't want the tangle of legality flung upon her life again, like a fishnet. She liked the flow of her existence now, a flow created by herself, a flow that included seeing Montana if she wished without feeling legal guilt, for example. Furthermore, she had had her children; was there a point to marrying if you weren't going to have more? Sounding formulaic, she posed: marriage was for the masses, an opiate to drug people and glue them together. No wonder murdering your way out was increasingly popular, along with divorcing your way out. So good-bye to adolescent dreams! Good-bye, legitimacy!

And when Rafi said with a smile, two days later, "I gather you're turning me down," she replied, "Not you, but marriage. Not loving you, just marriage." Unsure of how this was affecting him, she added, "Do you mind?"

"I don't know yet. I haven't thought about *not* marrying you, actually."

But she could see and feel, in the next few days, that his feelings were bruised. What a crazy turnaround. It was *she* who was supposed to crave the ring and license and security, *she* who was supposed to feel bruised by rejection! She was extra careful now to make sure he understood her caring and solicitude. Knowing how his wife had savaged his emotions added to her burden. "It's marriage, not you, that I don't want, just now, anyway," she repeated one evening, and he nodded, feigning understanding and acceptance. But she sensed that beneath, he was hurting, and his pride too was pricked. She firmed her will up, in order to be gentle.

For how long would he be secretly, helplessly hurting?

To Jon at his cubbyhole desk she put the question: "Would you like to come with me this summer, to Rafi's kibbutz?"

His face changed, eyes widened, as he received and digested the news. "Yeah. That would be kinda neat. Yeah!"

"You check with your father first, of course, and see if it's all right with him. It's his summer with you, you know."

"I know he'll agree, I just *know*." He got up and buried his head in her stomach, his private "schnuggling." "That'd really be something to tell the guys about — a summer at an Israeli kibbutz. Yea-ah. I gotta call Moon and Darin about this! And Schlossy! He's been braggin' for years about going, but he never has. Hold on!" And he raced past her with the urgent news.

With his excitement, she felt a surge too. Would it be a new beginning for him over there? Would that hustling society of sabra teenagers work a calming spell upon him? Get him high on communal property instead of bad Colombian? Or would it be a fiasco? Fortunately, Rosie was on her way to a camp with her two best chums, for the best part of the summer, so there would be no problem there.

When she left the room, she heard her son already breaking the news to his friend, gushing forth on the phone about deserts and hikes and a Saturday soccer league, which made her think that he had done more clandestine planning with Rafi than she had known about. Those spies!

The Friday before Rafi's departure they attended a dinner party given by Miriam's oldest friends in town, the Reibmans, Cambridge academicians. Happily, Nathalie was showing her saucy self, Miry saw immediately; she admired that more than Nathalie's censorious Puritan-Jewish side. She also looked good, thriving; the bits of gray in her short black hair were becoming, and her flared velvet slacks and white tunic shirt were smartly fashionable. "Come now, you don't look too dusty either," Nathalie returned, indicating Miry's burgundy blouse and quilted vest.

Arthur, her dark-complected husband, was his usual prince-charming-of-the-university self, quiet, unruffled, incorruptible in his demeanor; a saintly gene inhabited this fellow, and had resisted all environmental intrusions. Okay, his old slow-pitch softball purity had been tempted by big-league success, and he had succumbed *somewhat*. He smoked cigars like a mogul, wore natty suede jackets instead of rumpled old sweaters, and invariably included the names of statesmen in this country and Israel in his anecdotes; furthermore, he was forever flying in from some distant city and lecture. But these were climatic diseases, not internal ones, and he remained clean of pomposity, self-importance, self-righteousness, political power. A fellow of honor.

True, success took up time. For example, during Miriam's crisis year, the Reibmans had been just too busy to learn much about her torment or offer the occasional hour of companionship. Busy. An empty space on the calendar, an ally of friendship, was simply not there for busy academics. Just after the show at the City Hall, in the hours of Miriam's deepest humiliation and injury, Arthur has given a lecture on philosophical and political obligations at UCLA, while Nathalie had been working on the flight of the heroine in Victorian literature. What about the plight of their friend, this minor heroine, on the other side of Cambridge? But the passage of time had eased the bruises, erased them almost entirely, and what remained was the familiarity of eighteen years. A survival rate for friendships which Miriam knew was not to be discounted.

In attendance at the dinner: a robust political scientist from Harvard, buttoned down and striped out (Miriam thought) on this hot June night, and his mousy chain-smoking wife, an old-time New York book reviewer; a hot-shot sociologist from the West Coast, a small, plain lady bristling with Theory about Everything; a lively Brandeis historian, high throughout the evening on pills or marijuana; a wet-behind-the-ears Harvard junior fellow, costumed in a movie fedora and double-breasted jacket, fresh from his latest review in the *New York Review of Books;* and the Matthewses, in from Madison for the summer to soak up Cambridge-Harvard academic air. ("God, don't they know it's dangerous for your health?" Miriam whispered to Rafi, who told her, "Behave!")

While the talk flowed hot and cerebral over drinks and cheese, Miriam wondered why in the world she attended such dinners anymore. But then she realized that she didn't, usually. Once a year for the Reibmans she went; and maybe to show Rafi a certain academic (or Jewish) breed?

"Extremism on the one side breeds extremism on the other, true enough. No doubt Begin — well, hello! How are you? Good to see you. Where was I? Yes, Begin has encouraged these fanatics and bears much of the responsibility," claimed Sid Klein, grabbing up pâté. "But remember, Labor started the settlements. And remember another thing, factionalism is as old as Jewish history. It destroyed the Second Temple as much as anything the Romans did. And it may destroy the state of Israel quicker than the PLO."

"All of which makes me think we're better off in the long run," noted Bill Matthews pleasantly. "As long as Israel doesn't go communist, Reagan will be its ally. It's an unpleasant fact, but a fact nonetheless."

"And I say the real price of the existence of the state," asserted the junior fellow in a whiny New York accent, "is our continual exile in the Diaspora. That's the fundamental fact, sad as it may be." At last he laid aside his fedora. "We have to sit here and *dream* of Jerusalem" — he pronounced *dream* like a merchant reaching into a barrel of brine and producing a half-sour — "which Jews have been doing for thousands of years, even when they've been offered the choice of returning." He stood by the mantel and tasted the wine conspicuously; maybe he brought the wine from his recent stay in Davos, Switzerland, Miriam thought, where he had been entertained by a renowned Jewish leader who lived the high life there.

Over dinner the talk about Jews and Israel continued, and Miriam tried to smile politely and look interested and concentrate on other matters, like how to photograph this group in some revealing way.

"Look, Israeli men are more into the power bag than any other males in the world," offered Marcia Saltzman, adjusting her tortoise-shell glasses, "from what I can make out. And it shows up in their politics, their military, their religion of course, and their concept of a state." She paused to offer Rafi a perfunctory smile, excluding him from this wide categorization, and went on. "Even when they had a woman prime minister, she was more in the male than the female mold. But don't worry, power will change one day there too." She smiled thinly. "As it is here."

As Rose Klein chipped in, shifting back to the lunacy of trying to deal with the PLO and the impossibility of any Palestinian state, Miriam realized which photographer fit this group: August Sandor. These stiff-necked Jews deserved their Sandor, that German master of bourgeois rigidity, certainty, complacency.

The entrée was a wonderful fish dish, with curry sauce and baby peas, and Miriam took her second glass of wine, heading for private escape.

"Their version of terrorism is so unlike that of the Irgun, for example. They don't deserve to be dignified as a political entity. Besides," the muscular Sid Klein added, brandishing his fork, "the real issue is not the Palestinians at all, but the Arabs in general. Are they really willing to accept the Jews and a Jewish state in their midst? I doubt it very much. What they couldn't win by war, they *are* winning by rhetoric. And oil, of course. The war of verbal attrition is now theirs, easily. Slowly and surely they are winning friends everywhere, and persuading the Gentile world of their point of view. Which in turn is demoralizing the Jews inside the state, squeezing them, until the Arabs will finally be strong enough to move in and take them at will. The will to win and sacrifice will have been lost. It's a clever strategy, and who knows, maybe it was initiated by Sadat himself. You can even see this in recent contributions to the UJA and CJP, which are decreasing, especially by the rank and file. Last year, for example . . ."

At some point Jerry Maglich, the historian on a high, entered the conversation, raging about the UJA talk. Miriam took a certain pleasure in this fortyish wild man, unhinged by divorce, loosened by marijuana, flapping like a teenager. Laughing while raging, he tore into the provincial talk, and attacked Marcia's premises about "male power." Body gesturing and smoking crazily, he exclaimed, "Everyone in America knows that male power is a euphemism! Ask any divorced man who has the real power — ask me!" He laughed, glassy-eyed.

Diplomatically, Bill Matthews turned to Rafi and asked his opinion on the Palestinian question.

Rafi finished his bite carefully, and offered, "Oh, I don't think a Palestinian entity, or state, would represent a real danger to Israel, if certain preconditions were established. And even if they weren't —"

Rose Klein interrupted, but was stopped short by her husband.

"Actually," Rafi continued, "I think a Palestinian state would be more of a danger to Jordan, ultimately, than to Israel. After all, over fifty percent of Jordan is already Palestinian, so it would be only natural for a West Bank state to merge with Jordan, with the king's permission or not. This is why Jordan has opposed such a state as much as Israel has — in private, of course. It has more real reason to fear it."

"But what about Russian infiltration of such a state via the PLO?"

"And what about the more radical elements in the PLO — Habash and so forth?"

The attacking questions continued, and Miriam fidgeted in her seat, wanting a parachute but settling for wine, memories. If you didn't have the right line with this crew, you were morally culpable, dangerously naive. Oh well. She smiled politely at Nathalie, hoped that Rafi would fight back somehow (though she knew he wouldn't), and let her eye drift. It moved from a hanging ivy in the alcove to a nice framed print to the curved Seth Thomas clock on the mahogany buffet, and stopped there. She found herself transported to another clock, another room, another year . . .

When he greeted her at the door, Bruce Thorndike was clearly heavier than he had been several years before, but Betty looked, if anything, younger, and hugged Miriam like some long-lost aunt. Miriam had turned them down once or twice before, but now, needing some cash suddenly, she had called Bruce back about his recent offer of a fantastic sum for a night or two of shooting. The clock was a round green quartz one, with big Roman numerals, and it hung ostentatiously in the modern living room, which was filled with loud Rya rugs and striped paintings and swooping chrome lamps. Bruce, bulging in a beige leisure suit, offered Miriam a drink, and she took sherry. They sat in the living room and she was introduced to the third party, Thelma, in her forties. Betty looked as bouncy as ever: hair up, cheeks pink, full figure contained modestly in a pullover dress with graceful dolmen sleeves and a self-sash on an elasticized waist. She had been a cheerleader in high school, as Miry recalled. Thelma sat demurely in white blouse and long skirt; an elementary school teacher from a nearby suburb. While Bruce picked up the discussion about property taxes and the local schools, she said hardly a word, nodding shyly now and then. "Look," he was saying, "I'm not one of those guys that goes for Proposition Two-and-a-half, but Jesus, what the hell's the av-

erage Joe supposed to do? Carry the public schools on his back with his savings account?"

Miriam sipped her wine and listened to the high voice, its Midwestern accent creeping in, mixing with the thicker, lecturing New York voice.

In the bedroom Bruce helped Miriam set up the strobe lights and her tripod, and then, smiling brightly, he said he had better change. It was a large, dimly lit room, dominated by a king-size bed in the center stared at by a giant mirror on the ceiling; some hidden speakers piped in music. Before they entered Miriam felt her stomach filling with butterflies, and she wondered if she could go through with it now, some nine years after her first photographic session with the Thorndikes. She glanced around at the walls and saw her old photos there, framed, spare shots of copulation alongside two congested oils. A satisfying contrast. When the others came into the room, half dressed now, and began to play, everything changed, the script and the actors and Miriam too. Thelma, attired in a satiny camisole, silk stockings, and black garters, immediately became the aggressive leader. With a determination bordering on greed she went after Betty, who was quickly stripped of her underwear (keeping on her negligee) by Thelma and busily attacked. Bruce, in contrast, appeared unsteadier now, as he tried to pursue the two women, already deeply entangled.

The biggest surprise was Miriam herself — to herself. As soon as the action started, one woman fondling the other and in turn being fondled, Miriam felt like a surgeon. No sentiments, no emotions, just hardness. It was something like photographing the tractors and caterpillars on the kibbutz — she was intrigued by the machines but not quite emotional about them. She felt like that here — intrigued by the arms and limbs, the cobra tongues and slithery bodies and simple props (a paddle, a candle, a thick rope), but staying methodical and detached. Even, slowly, she relaxed. Yes, she took her photos with a surprising relaxation, realizing that for Thorndikes and Friend, this was a bridge or mahjong hour. Shooting, she smoked a cigarillo, checked out the decoratons (deep wall-to-wall carpeting, Mediterranean-style furniture), tuned in to Donna Summer singing about getting herself some "Hot Stuff Tonight." Managed to photograph that eye of a mirror too, some *trick shots to catch all the activities. So what had started out as a risky necessity, a fearful dare, was nothing more than a night out with the suburban Babbitts. Concupiscence anesthetized.*

She was even surgical enough to examine the bodies and their activities through her lenses. Thelma was a thin-boned, smallish woman, with still-firm pear-shaped breasts and a darting bird's look, and she performed on Betty with an admirable skill, bringing the younger woman to orgasm again and again. Bruce, with the added tire around his waist and the old Marine crew cut, looked spindly and vulnerable naked, as he followed Thelma's lead, gradually becoming her errand boy. (At one point they proceeded to tie up pretty Betty, for teasing pleasures.) Now Betty naked was a pictorial nude, much lovelier than she was bundled in clothes; a Rubens of robust curves and alabaster-smooth skin, a splendid figure. In passion her face too acquired new beauty, the cheekbones growing more pronounced, the smallish features expanding and mellowing, the hair loosened into animal wildness. For her private collection Miriam took a half-dozen shots of that face, and realized that Betty had an odd double in the wide world, a religious woman in Mea Shearim.

During the course of the two-hour session, Miriam was nudged by the short-haired schoolteacher, who smiled provocatively and edged her pink tongue out; in response Miriam asked the lady to hand her a different lens. "Don't you ever loosen up?" asked Thelma with a smile.

"Why are you being so *quiet*?" asked Nathalie. "Daydreaming? Planning revenge?"

And Miriam, who had felt so hard toward these people, softened now. Let them have their talkathons; it was, after all, more civilized than the Thorndike Saturday sexathons. (It was, wasn't it?) Yet how much of a difference was there between this tough schoolmarm book reviewer here and the quietly determined schoolteacher there? Too glib. Trying now to catch up with the thread of the conversation, she stammered to Nathalie, "Yes, well . . . daydreaming, yes." Why the wayward association?

"Come on, you can do better."

"Oh, not really, not with these steamrollers around."

"Oh, come now. I must confess it was rather tactless of Marcia

to generalize about Israeli males without at least consulting Rafi."
She laughed, raising her eyes at her friend's innocence. "But honestly, you're over there more than the rest of us, so you do have
firsthand experience."

Miriam lit up her first cigarette. "Do you think that makes a
difference here?"

Nathalie made a face. "Now, don't be *sarcastic*. Of course we're
interested, everyone here."

"You know," Miriam retorted, "I doubt that. And I don't mean
it sarcastically. Firsthand experience is just not your bag."

In a singsong voice Nathalie mocked her. *"You're playing self-
righteous."*

"Great dinner; the fish was first-class. And *you* look super. You
get younger as I grow older."

"Ha, no one looks better than you in the past year. You have
a perpetual tan, it seems. Even Hannah talks about it." Nathalie
was referring to her eighteen-year-old whiz-kid daughter.

"How is she getting on, by the way? Where is she again?"

Nathalie made a chiding face. "At Stanford. And doing all right,
I suppose. Learning to play tennis and sail, *and* she has a blond
Mormon boyfriend from Salt Lake, with a yellow MG. Of course
she made the dean's list — but that doesn't really count." Meaning,
a Jewish boyfriend would help.

Miriam thought, what will I be saying about Jon one day? "Oh
yes, he's doing very well; Tech Hi-Fi is thinking of making him
manager of their Framingham Mall branch." Or, "Yes, he's doing
nicely, thank you, they may let him out for regular school next
year. Depends on what the parole board (or McLean's) decides at
its next consultation."

To Nathalie she said, "That's lovely." Remembering the clever
daughter, she added, "Give her my best."

"I will. She always asks about you; she says you're the most
adventurous of my friends by far. How's that?"

Miriam wanted to hear the exact phrasing from Hannah herself.
"I'm flattered, I think."

"Always skeptical. Well, you should be flattered, she's not that
loose with her compliments." She laughed, and changed tone.
"How's Jonathan?"

Did she know about Jon and his most recent troubles? Did the whole town already know? How did you answer this? "Doing better, thanks . . . I think so, anyway," giving it a little smile.

"Uh-huh. Yes. Oh good. I heard that he had some difficulty. It's straightened out, I hope. Look, these are difficult times, believe me — and for boys of fifteen, it's very tough." She was sincere and sympathetic now.

Miriam exhaled and noted the ring of whitish smoke ascend upward in slow tranquillity. Involuntarily her heart beat faster. So first it was Miriam and Her Work that had agitated stolid Cambridge; then it was Miriam and Her Life that sent whispers through the cold, bloodless town; and now maybe it was Jon, Son of Miriam, who was grist for the local mills. She'd leave and go off to some forest, to Haifa, to Christchurch.

She recalled a friend's caution — paranoia can be very inconvenient — and tuned in again to the discussion, or Sid Klein's monologue.

Chewing and lecturing, he went on. "I tell you, the sixties tainted our country for the next two decades at least, and maybe more. The porno-pop culture that it manufactured is still with us." He paused to swallow water. "Still corrupting this nation and our children. It began with the kids on the streets trashing in Chicago, heckling and bullying political speakers, and then led to the dirty books and blue movies. Political violence and drugs, rock music, oral sexuality are all part and parcel of the same thing, a true culmination of modernist intentions. Believe me, they're at work on our moral fiber right today, trying to undermine it. And that's why" — he leaned his bulk forward here, for revelation — "Reagan will be a blessing for this country. What he represents, at least. *No more anarchy, and an end to permissiveness.* Enough of polymorphous perversity. If it takes neoconservatism of an extreme stripe to pull this off, so be it."

A flash from some ten years ago hit Miriam: in the other room she had heard the same sort of litany from this Sidney, and in partial defense had parted her legs and offered Sidney a good view of temptation. Red panties, and the promise beyond, had stopped him in his tracks too, she remembered fondly.

Not in the right position now, or the mood, she resorted to a question for El Sid: "What about our little war in Southeast Asia? You haven't mentioned that. Wasn't that more destructive than what happened in Chicago?"

Sid's face grew animated with fury. "Look, when you put together types like Brown and Marcuse, and throw in a little Foucault, and trot out the foot soldiers like Rap Brown and Abbie Hoffman, you're going to have the destructive element in theory and practice. A regular Molotov cocktail. Remind me to write this down, Rose. Sometimes, you see, *democracy can go a little too far.*" His voice changed tone; he was tutoring the populace. "And I am quite sure that the sixties are a perfect example of that. All sorts of lunatics and lunacies were given free rein by our democracy, and you can see now from that experience that there is a real limit to what society can tolerate before it goes haywire and even turns to some sort of dictator for a leader. History has a way of repeating itself, you know. Freedom is possible only when responsibility is taken on, and the books and movies flaunting masturbation and fellatio as *values* are not exactly living up to their share of the responsibilities of art and literature."

"Which books do you mean, the pulp stuff like —"

"*Portnoy's Complaint. The Story of O.*"

"Are you for censoring those?" She wondered, really.

The word hit a chord, and Sid retorted sternly, "Nobody spoke about censorship per se. Yet it's not a terrible thing, you understand. Partial censorship, *intelligent censorship* —"

"You mean like the Vatican's list, say?"

"Don't be a smart aleck," he answered. "But if the alternative is an unbridled breakdown in morality, as preached in certain mass genres lately, why not? What chances do you think our priests and rabbis and teachers have against *Penthouse, Deep Throat, The Story of O*? Not many, I can tell you. And I for one do not wish to bring up my children in a culture where the moral visions of Hugh Hefner or Philip Roth dominate. In fact" — he tapped his glass with a spoon to announce more news — "I'm afraid that in the very near future, Western postindustrial societies are going to have to make some major decisions regarding old definitions of individual freedom in democracies. Otherwise we're going to have on our hands an upsurge in violence and carnality that makes the current epidemic seem like kid's stuff."

Sandor, Sandor, where are you? Miriam wanted to let the discussion rest, leave the venal non sequiturs alone, but her blood was racing. "Forgive me, but I don't see the connection between violence and carnality. And I don't think you've answered my previous question: who did the real destroying back there in the sixties, the kids who protested the war in Vietnam, or the government that presided over it? Did we lose fifty thousand American boys because the streets of Chicago were trashed?"

"That has little to do with what's happening now," Rose Klein interceded, dousing a cigarette in a saucer. "Look at the current breakdown in our morals, and there's no Vietnam. Look, my dear, I don't wish to get personal in all this, but if you were to examine your own life closely, you'll see what Sid has been saying. Do you think the Vietnam War had anything to do with your own wild life, for example?"

Rafi put his hand on Miriam's arm. "Don't dignify that, Miry."

Miriam, her chest pumping, tried to heed the advice. Easy does it, she warned herself; take more wine. Think of orchards. "I believe we've gotten off the topic somewhat. But really" — she leaned ever so slighly toward the older woman — "what are you referring to? And are you acting as the defender of the public morals or on your own here?"

"All right, folks, time for dessert." Nathalie laughed nervously. "If you'll pass your plates . . . Arthur, could you —"

"Don't play the innocent, Miriam," Rose Klein continued, beginning to wag her finger. "Come on. You're a perfect example of what Sid means — the fallout from the sixties. Playing house for eighty-seven varieties of men. In front of your children, no less. Look, dear, you lead your own life. And I don't mean to attack you in any *personal* way" — she stared at Miriam with feigned objectivity and also disbelief at Miriam's incomprehension — "but as an example, a moral example to family and community and children, do you really think your life holds up well?"

Miriam scratched at her knees through her nylons, like she had scratched at her wool socks when she was thirteen, when Sylvia was taunting her in front of Dad. "Do I understand you to be saying," she said slowly, trying for grown-up control, "that if a citizen is not married and monogamous, he or she is a threat to society? Especially a citizen who decides to lead a modestly free life? A woman who wishes to have the same degree of freedom as many males do, say? Well, I'm afraid I disagree with you, *dear*. I think the value of democracy, as I understand it, consists in trying to act out one's freedom, whether it's political or personal. And another value is *privacy*. Otherwise . . ." She hesitated, but added, "we might as well be living in Moscow or Prague, where Stalinist commissars monitor the private lives of all citizens."

"Are you starting to name-call now? That's going a little too far!" cried Rose. "Pulling your pants down and spreading your legs for every John and Rafi who comes along, and then trying to get out of it by ad hominem attack!"

Nathalie stood. "Let's move to the living room, folks, and —"

"Get out of *what*?" Miriam inquired, stomach and chest churning but voice increasingly calm.

"You know what — whoring around, oral sex for whoever happens by with a penis. *That's* what." Rose glared, with malicious glee.

Excited by these words, confused, disturbed, Miriam murmured, "Yes, Rose, I do still fuck and enjoy it. Does that upset you very much?"

Rose reached across the table and slapped Miriam's face, hard.

A chaos: Rafi grabbing Miriam, friends isolating Rose, and voices careening, admonishing. Plants and mahogany furniture grew rubbery, moved. Her cheek stinging, Miriam felt fine, hot, confused. Felt something had gone too far, yes, but a clarity of sorts had been produced. The curved clock chimed ten, and Miriam sensed a clear signal to depart. To her surprise there were tears in her eyes, but they were easily controlled.

Ten feet away Rose was flapping her arms hysterically, and being consoled by friends, as though she had been the one slapped, attacked.

Miriam said quietly to Rafi, "Let's leave now, please."

He led her downstairs, while Nathalie beseeched her to stay. "Please don't go," Nathalie importuned her at the door. "I really feel responsible. That was uncalled-for behavior, and I'd like to tell her in front of everyone, especially you."

"Another time, Nat," Miriam said, and moved quickly outside to the fine fresh air, which cooled her flushed face. She asked Rafi to drive; she didn't trust herself.

Chauffeured again so soon, she sat back and tried to relax, but had a hard time lighting her cigarette because of her trembling. *A tomboy of twelve after being shoved by a male bully in baseball.* Were Cambridge dinner parties to include discussions of her personal life, and her descent into adolescent defensiveness? Or had she behaved just fine, just adult?

She turned on AM radio. Said, "Smokey Robinson sings this better." Paused, and added, "I made only one mistake. I should have mentioned blow jobs — that way, 'oral sex' could have gone back to Masters and Johnson."

Rafi patted her shoulder. "You shouldn't have entered the argument, *that* was your mistake. Especially when Rose charged in. She's a tiger. Why not dessert in the living room?" He glanced over at her. "Apple crisp, and we missed it."

Poor fellow: his favorite. She squeezed his hand. "I know what, let's go to one of those posh joints in the Square and get a replacement. Okay?"

He looked at her as if she had said they should go to Mars. "Noble of you," he rejoined, knowing her distaste for the new places.

"We can check out the beautiful people, and search for any signs of creeping polymorphous perversity. Under the tables, I mean." Beneath the banter she still burned. "Maybe I just like fighting those types."

At the spiffy Harvest restaurant, behind the old glass Design Research building, they got lucky and found a corner table, which afforded a fine view of the late-night pageant. Rafi settled for pecan pie, along with the usual espresso and brandy. Sipping her coffee, Miriam observed a gleaming couple two tables away, the fellow an exotic Iranian or Arab with a notable Semitic nose and jet-black hair, a canary-yellow cashmere sweater, and a leather jacket draped over his shoulders. His companion was a full-busted blond, ruddy-faced and pretty, with a high voice and inimitable social poise. They laughed easily, as though they were in their private dining room. And their dessert was equally stylish: a flamboyant crepe which the waiter lit with a match by their table, sizzling the saucepan with a sudden flame.

"Crepe suzette, maybe," Miriam said. "I didn't know they made it here."

"Why should you? You never permit us to come."

"I surrender — no more high principles," she acknowledged, smiling, warmed with the fine brandy. "I am thoroughly bigoted and provincial about the nouveau riche, and maybe the rich too. I'm going to make a serious effort to change."

"Impossible."

The change or the effort? she wondered. Gradually the tinkle of glasses, the soft shine of leather and amber of brandy, the small performance of social ease smoothed over her anxieties and resentments like glaze over a pot. Or in her case, she changed the image, was it crazing her heart?

In the car and later in bed, she was plagued by thoughts. Self-appointed judges hounded you everywhere — magazines, colleges, dinner parties. These Kleins . . . pillars of self-righteousness, Chosen Citizens of State. Fuck. More like call girl and commissar, power their whore-master . . . And the way they rewrote history, turning the idealists into the sinners and vice versa! Moscow, here they come. Well, at least they won't send old Miriam to Gulag for her sexual misdemeanors. Only a sentence of dinner once every year or two, a *Commentary* every four years or so. And maybe some gossip kills from the rumor mill. Not so bad . . .

Shadows edged along the ceiling, and she switched onto another track. Rafi's responses. Calm and control, or placidness, flaccid will? He had been so *civil* about her rejection of his marriage offer. It was disturbing. Should it be? Was he any different now from before? Wasn't this what she had wanted all along, someone who would accept her right down the line, all support and no struggle/criticism/conflict? Had she gotten not merely used goods but maybe damaged goods too? Severely damaged by the hard separation and divorce? From Rachel and Menachem she had heard how his wife had worn him down, and now was she seeing that defeat or fatigue in a new light?

A wave of sympathy swept her, and she leaned across and kissed the cheek of her sleeping partner.

But of course, that's why she had gravitated to her Dr. B., right? For a sense of something else. Because our man here, peaceful, good, lovely, perhaps accepted too much too often. He was right for a time in my life, a time of healing. Well, he's your responsibility, kid . . . If he found out about your doctor, how would he take that — pacifically too? Did you want this in a man, now?

She felt a terrific urge to wake him, to provoke him sexually, to see his aggressive side! But she let lie her sleeping beauty, who hardly moved or breathed when he slept.

The lives of those middle-class pillars — bitches and pit bulls — returned, and she shuddered with renewed resentment. Gave in, lit a cigarette, awakened Rafi.

She asked, "Why didn't you tell them off tonight?"

"Huh?"

Ask in the morning, for God's sake. "Sorry. I'll put this thing out in a moment."

Oh yes, she had wanted peace and sanity in her life, in her man, after those chaotic years of scrambling to survive, to know, and she had gotten all of that, and more. Was she ready for the wars again? But which ones?

In the morning she put the question to him over coffee, after the kids had left.

"Yes, maybe I should have," he said, "but I'm . . . not like that, I suppose. It doesn't matter that much to me what they think of Israel or the PLO. Or me," he added, wearing a half-mysterious smile, eyeing her. His sleepy, luminous face was so handsome to look at over breakfast. Her own Jewish Gerard Philippe, of course!

And what about me? she wanted to put. How much does that matter? Suppose you lose me — will you *act* then?

Her wants wanted in different directions.

A different man for each different emotion you want now? Your neurosis is exploding into narcissism, Miry.

Not wanting to face the hard questions, not wanting to hurt him here, in this splendid morning light, she put her hand on his hand instead, avoiding any crucial moment. "Yes, why should you bother? Silly."

11

SHE found the thickest steak at the Cambridge butcher's, picked up fresh corn and sweet potatoes with their autumnal color and super skins, and now fumbled with the keys, trying to figure out which way to turn the two double locks. He had wanted to take her out to dine, as he had last Friday, but she realized he was secretly sick of restaurants, and so she was springing this surprise cookout on the small terrace. At last she entered the apartment, the sun pouring through the large louvered windows in the living room; she looked forward to the hour of being alone before he came from the hospital. In the galley kitchen she set the parcels down on the round white table, envying the spanking cleanness and absence of juvenile clutter. You had to live with children to see their marks everywhere. Maybe it paid to leave your spouse and home in the suburbs and take refuge in clean white rooms and gleaming skyscrapers. From the window she stared out at the low roofs of South Boston and the gothic spires of downtown capitalism, marveling at the Erector Set of a city. Up here, on the thirty-third floor, adult buildings resembled children's toys, edifices of fun. (Was this why she was here?) She removed lettuce and scallions from a bag and began to wash them.

Oddly — she smelled cigarette smoke. Turning about, she confronted a woman in the doorway, a pretty, trim woman with short blondish hair and a cigarette dangling from thin lips. Miriam stared, dumfounded, and the woman stared back. In her middle years, too, she wore a tailored suit and ruffled blouse, and the gaze from her smallish face was of intense interest, hardness, and something else.

"Hi," Miriam offered.

The woman lowered her jaw and ran her tongue around inside that prominent structure. She half nodded.

"May I — "

"Just wanted to look over the merchandise," the woman said with a lilt, almost as if speaking to someone else.

"Who —?"

"Ordinary, at best, I'd say." The voice was low and sandy, the accent local and tinged with preppiness. "You could use a little dressing up, dearie. Those trousers would look better on Chaplin."

Miriam reddened, feeling herself examined like a heifer at market. A heifer in fatigue pants. Sensing who the woman was, she sought to recover her wits fast, hearing the background hum of the air-conditioner.

Miriam asked, "Does Scott know you're here? How'd you get in?"

The pixie lady with the short messy hair exhaled slowly, a two- or three-carat diamond flashing on her finger. She wore a perpetual half-leer — or was it a half-smile? Her skin was tanned and creased, and she stood in the doorway with her arms crossed like a jail warden (Miriam's paranoia?). Again she spoke. "To tell you the truth, I thought you'd be much better. You know, the works — big boobs, great gams, waves of hair. A real knockout. But . . . you're just an ordinary little hausfrau." She took a slow puff. "You must be one hot number in bed, sister."

Miriam fought the urge to walk across the kitchen, stand in front of the woman, and challenge her. She grew tremulous in the chest, weak in the knees. Calmly she said, "Do we really have to go though this?"

The woman's gray eyes narrowed. "You bitch, you low-down bitch. Where'd you get the nerve, the friggin' nerve? But then again, your breed is not short on nerve, is it?"

Breed meant *Jew* meant brain spinning. She'd have to hold on, she warned herself. But *why?* she wondered.

"This sort of scene —" she began.

"Do you usually go around snatching husbands, sister? Or should I use your Biblical name? Is that how you seduced him in the first place, by playing the exotic?"

Miriam now perceived the other ingredient in the face — meanness. This was one mean lady, not merely a vengeful wife.

"You little whore. Where'd you learn your hot tricks — in the Bronx somewhere? Well, you're in Boston now, and you're going to face some good old Yankee music."

Called that name again, after so many years, she wanted to laugh, but her stomach was fluttering terribly. She sought a new tack. Casually, she turned and walked out of the other end of the kitchen into the sun-filled living room. When the woman followed her, Miriam turned quickly, spoke evenly. "If I were you, I'd keep my prejudices from showing, and just stick to the husband-snatching." She paused, observing the tight face grow tighter. "Why don't you save the other stuff for bridge nights, say?" A slip, but so what?

The woman's lower jaw protruded further — a thing getting ready for chewing? Miriam wondered. Was she the prey? Did the lady also know about those photographs of her husband?

The tough pixie eyed Miriam from across the square glass coffee table. Scott had received his furniture now, and Miriam saw the expensive tastes of his suburban house in the matching couch and love seat, the brass lamps and rugs. She preferred the earlier ample emptiness, a white tabula rasa.

"Believe me, you're going to get nothing out of him, that much I can tell you. By the time I'm finished with him, he's going to have nothing to give. If that's what you're really after." She had set her hands on her hips, and again spoke as if to someone else in the room. "From what I hear, you don't have a pot to piss in. I didn't know that Jewish girls your age were so . . . imprudent."

Miriam admired the adjective, at least. Yes, it was true, she was imprudent; whorish too?

"Do you have something against Jewish women, or men?"

A crease of a smile appeared. About to answer, the woman changed her mind and inhaled, then said, "How'd you get him, tell me? I'd be curious to hear. What is it you do in bed, honey, that I won't?"

Miriam thought of certain private acts . . . nothing extraordinary, as far as she knew. She glanced at her watch, wondering if she should leave. Too easy. She tried desperately to disguise her steadily rising anger, excitement. "I think you ought to leave before Scotty comes in."

"Oh, I can imagine a few things. Real down and dirty, as they say. Well, let me tell you, he'll dump you in a few months and take up with one of his nurses, and then you know what'll happen? He'll come back on all fours to you know who, *begging* for me to take him back. Sweetheart, I know my man. Or should I say *boy*."

Miriam felt herself a character in a scene out of Ibsen, perhaps, or Shakespeare; or was it just an ordinary soap opera? Was this woman a force, a Lady Macbeth of Concord? Or was it much smaller than all that — did the natives go through this with every other affair? "You do have a foul way of looking at things. The question is whether it's original." She tried to choose her words carefully. "Now, would you like me to call Scott and have you thrown out?"

She shouldn't have said that, since all it did was to inflame the already sizzling woman. (*But didn't she want that, secretly?*)

The tan face reddened perceptibly, and like a bulldog the woman charged around the table. "You slut, you little sheenie slut!"

Glad for the final epithet, Miriam let her blood pump fast, welcoming the action at last, crazily. "Don't be melodramatic, for God's sake!"

But the blond bulldog already had taken a hank of Miriam's hair and now sank her teeth into Miriam's forearm.

Reacting from her bouts of fighting Jon in play, Miriam used her weight and slammed her fist into the soft midsection of the woman, who groaned and sagged, releasing her hold — unlike Jon, who received such blows with triumph. Shocked, Miriam looked at her arm and found teethmarks!

"Christ almighty." The woman panted, sagging by the couch.

Miriam felt foolish, stupid, in pain.

She went into the kitchen, ran cold water over her arm, filled an empty orange-juice bottle with water, and returned to the living room where she poured water on the woman's face.

"Christ almighty," Mrs. Beaumont repeated, sprawled. In defeat her face had relaxed; she looked fiftyish now, and more tired.

"Now come on, get out of here," Miriam said, lifting her by her arm and escorting her to the door.

The woman was crying, but the hysterical rage seemed to have passed, and she followed Miriam's directions with a surprising passivity. Reaching for her pocketbook by the door, she suddenly shifted tone, "Please don't tell him I was here, or what happened. *Please*. You don't know him like I do. Please!"

Miriam listened with incredulity to this flip of personality. What did this fearful pleading signify? Whose madness did it reflect?

"Go on," she directed, and then, for some reason, she advised, "And don't bite. It's not nice." She closed the door and slid the latch.

She held up her forearm and grew frightened. She hurried to the bathroom, where she washed the teethmarks with hydrogen peroxide. It burned. What the hell was she involved in?

After ten minutes of cooling down on the terrace with a whisky, she left the apartment, still dazed, and took a walk along Boylston Street. It was late afternoon, and the street was busy with shoppers and tourists, who at first soothed Miry. But when she noted a well-dressed woman looking at the windows of Lord & Taylor, Miriam had another thought. Was this woman too, beneath the veneer of respectability, a madwoman? Beneath the cotton suit and silk scarf, did she also like to bite? Maybe enjoy getting beaten up? Or perhaps enjoy dressing up her husband in a maid's uniform for their mutual fun? What weird extramural excrescences did this parade of the successful, like the Thorndikes say, mask? She gazed again at her arm and worried. Could you really develop cancer from human bites? Was a bite on the forearm from an abandoned wife no more than a companion to the husband's tender bites? She walked up the street, thinking of soap opera, Ibsen or Strindberg, insanity, vulgarity. Which was she in the middle of, a sick hoax or a fantasy world?

The shopper noticed her staring, shot her a haughty look, and marched into the store.

And Miriam, standing there with the late-afternoon sun glancing off the windshields of cars, had this revelation: she felt sane, saner than ever; she had come through, survived her mad years and grown steadily saner; but here, now, she was living in the middle of a lunatic asylum. That was the truth revealed in these teethmarks. A lunatic asylum posing as a functioning society. The revelation scared her, and yet also pleased her. In a losing context, she personally was winning. But could you win that way?

A well-dressed stranger in a hat was nodding to her, and she moved on.

What to do? Escape into science fiction? Group therapy? Bridge games and antiques? Poetry readings and PTA activities and Shady Hill auctions? Or just get out?

To see Dr. B. now, or go home, was the immediate question. She walked on up the street, past the many shops filled like gas stations with merchants pumping and citizens guzzling. America's major religion was operating, full steam ahead. She entered a bookshop and was overwhelmed with the supermarket aisles and stereo speakers blaring and posters demanding. Books of all sizes competed for attention — nutrition and diet books warning you to Eat Right; how-to sex texts urging you to Find Pleasure in 69 Easy Positions; environmental books instructing you on the latest Poisons in the Air and Water; biofeedback and psychology volumes advising you How to Heal Yourself and Strike at Your Energy Cores. Everywhere, reminders and remainders of what you were missing in life, what you needed to know, what was going on Out There that was influencing you without your knowing it. For $4.95 you could heal yourself, learn how to love, change your life; for another buck, learn much more. Cookbooks, diet books and sex manuals were piled in high stacks, like flapjacks, blocking off the real books. And the ninnies called clerks would be better off selling perfumes or deodorants than books; they'd get competent or get fired. She asked for a novel by Musil, *Man Without Qualities;* the clerk returned, smiling with triumph, holding *Stan the Man* by Musial. In comic despair, she walked out. The asylum had done a rather thorough job, stocking its bookshelves with idiot books and its corridors with illiterate boobs.

What to do? Standing on the neon street in the early evening, she decided: try the rural life, for sure. Or should she go farther, to another country altogether? . . . Was it saner elsewhere?

More than an hour had passed, and she found herself returning
to the Prudential Center and Montana, not knowing exactly why.
Launching herself up thirty-odd floors in this missile of a skyscra-
per, she envied the simple elegance of engineering, contrasted to
the oafishness of human relations.

When she entered, the doctor came to greet her from the living
room, in his white smock still. "Well, there you are. I was getting
a bit worried you were standing me up." He welcomed her with
his big hands, and she allowed it.

"How come you never played any sport besides hockey with
that grip?"

"What do you mean? I could have been a darned good catcher
if I hadn't kept breaking my thumb."

She smiled, thinking how nice it would be to see him spell
Carlton Fisk now and then.

"Here, I'll fix you a drink, and you can tell me about *your* day."
He smiled good-naturedly, and she told him scotch, not vodka.
"Hey, you were here already; why didn't you tell me?"

When they were settled on the terrace, wispy cirrus clouds floating nearby, she told him what had occurred a few hours before.
As she narrated, his calm face grew agitated especially in the wide
forehead.

He shook his head and apologized, as if *he* had created the
scene, not his wife, Ginny. Examining Miriam's arm, he explained,
"She's . . . she's troubled . . . and very upset. Not doing very well,
I guess. You'll pull through this, however," he joked, unconvinc-
ingly. Scott figured the doorman had been bribed to let her in,
somehow.

Miriam sipped her drink and let the alcohol cloud her thinking,
while below, in the gathering darkness, the city began to light up
like a ringing switchboard.

Over the thick porterhouse, the doctor loosened up, describing
his unhappy marriage; the more he spoke and detailed, the less of
an appetite Miriam had. It was such a sad tale, of a marriage that
had been exhausted years ago, a marriage of increasing manipu-
lations, subtle regressions, obvious frustrations. As the words poured
out, she tried to concentrate on the voice itself, which sounded
like a stringed instrument; but the substance continued to intrude

and disturb her. More and more Scott had been made passive, and finally he had burst into attack, hitting Ginny and hurting her; yet she never really did anything to change things — "In fact, she seemed to egg me on purposely at certain times, enjoying it, almost." Finally, he had stopped being physical and had turned off entirely, and she had begun calling him names, slapping and hitting at him, yes, biting him too. This Barnum & Bailey marriage was accompanied by a sex life of coquettish blackmails and teasing rewards "maybe on both sides" and "a strong streak of New England puritanism." (Huh? Miriam wondered, and she couldn't help noticing that, as Montana unfolded his tale of anguish and pain, he turned aggressive with his food.) Had he ever gone to a shrink? Or to a marriage counselor? No. He was too... embarrassed. And Ginny, with her proper, Back Bay Brahmin background, wouldn't hear of such a thing. So the marriage stumbled — smashed — on for him, in masochistic stops and sadistic starts, in durations of accepted celibacy and dutiful sexuality. Until Miriam came along.

During the hour-and-a-half-long narrative, Miriam felt for this large, good man as he tried to come clean, fidgeting in his tubular chair; she didn't want to hear this, and yet she had precipitated it. She had always wanted to see what made this balanced Scandinavian tick, but now that she did, she was regretful. She preferred the solid, secure, good, reasonable doctor, not this flawed man, and his dangerous high-wire balancing act. And how much of it was fact, how much role-reversal, fantasy or projection, et cetera?

But as he narrated and opened up, there was no abandoning him. And so Miriam-the-patient became Dr. Scheinman-the-healer, asking the questions and providing sympathy, security. With proximity, and stamina. Boy, did you need stamina! Oh, she appreciated her old "Magic-User" Dr. Levanda all the more, sitting here on the thirty-third floor, looking out at the concrete order of the city and the beauty of the evening sky while plugging into human disorder and grossness. She stuck it out, Beaumont's painful story crashing through her light drunken fog, his disturbances sobering her. Irony of ironies.

Afterward, she couldn't sleep with him, though he wanted it

and she needed it. She explained that she was getting her period and her cramps were too bad. He bought the story, and she was relieved, but also disappointed, sad. She had looked forward tremendously to holding and feeling him and having him put his mouth on her, all over her, her belly and nipples — no, no, she wouldn't think of it. No. She would miss the great power and perfect relaxation that fucking with Dr. B. spread though her. No. She'd force her thoughts elsewhere.

So at 9:00 P.M. she went home alone and paid the babysitter for a full evening. (Of late she'd taken to using one for Rosie.) She prowled her rooms like a nervous animal, looking for nothing in particular. At one point she stared in the full-length mirror at her unstylish trousers — yes, the charge was true. C'mon, kid, she played Harry, you're a greenhorn next to those big-time Givenchy and St. Laurent hunters. Fine. But she also knew that that world of plenty, of diamond rings and $65 jeans and new Volvo station wagons, didn't straighten the disorders one bit. In fact, the neurosis was compounded, if anything, by the loot. The stuff gave you room to spread your neurotic act around, to use the world like a playpen, to break things in. And Miriam, genius? Restless, she picked up and put down her contact sheets, pictures. Started to read, couldn't concentrate on Hardy novel or magazine article. Tried to answer some perfunctory mail, pay bills; but no go. If only she had tax shelters to worry about, pressing deadlines to meet, research to complete. She remembered the ironing she had put off and turned to that. She got out the ironing board, her two best blouses, and Rosie's favorite dress, and waited for the iron to heat up. Presently she was ironing, avoiding buttons, and taking pleasure in cuffs, collars, and long smooth sleeves. Sure enough, the minor activity precipitated a purpose, a direction.

At her bedroom desk she took out her yellow legal pad and sat by the light of her old gooseneck lamp, but she wound up composing in her head.

Dear Dr. Levanda,

Long time no see, or hear from. Both ways, I mean. Now tell me, is the hereafter worse or better than it's cracked up to be? Does the body stay put in the box while the soul does its traveling act? Are Plato, Steiner, Bellow right about the transmigration of souls? Or is that all wishful thinking, rich imagining?

Anyway, you live vividly with me, Doc. Your frail body and bunned hair are safe in my memory; your kindly spirit remains haloed; your exacting intelligence is admired still. Do you realize it's not easy to get intelligent conversation in a town? When I return to Israel, rest assured I'll place a few more stones around your grave site.

Now, how about a progress report on your favorite patient? Out there on her own, after all those years under your guidance and careful questioning.

Dear General Levanda, the oddest thing has occurred: the more I see of my native people and land, the more I feel on top of things. The more I feel — in this highly nervous and highly comic atmosphere — sane. A sane atom, say. I am quite sure that this hotly charged atmosphere affects all citizens, especially in the cities, more severely than all the chemical pestilences. And yet here I am, sitting in the middle, feeling myself somehow sitting pretty, sitting sanely. Surprising, maybe, in the light of my past history? But there it is, a blunt, if immodest, fact. I've come through somehow and feel the stronger for it, feel up to surviving in our environment of lunacy. You know, Doctor, cracking up in one's thirties is in its way a boon to one's forties. Odd, but true. One has earned one's social credentials; has established one's private psychic credit; has proved one's worldiness. In short, one is ready at last for the higher stage — wisdom, contemporary-style. So, wisdom, where do you reside?

One answer: before one's nose, in this and every moment, every detail of one's life, if one has the time and inclination to study those.

Another answer: nowhere, anymore. There is no more wisdom, just small solutions, partial remedies. Wisdom was a Greek idea.

I called you "General" before, Doctor, and I hope not idly. For it is a war these days, to stay sane. A war against all of the people and influences that have been recruited into the Army of the Crazy, sponsored by computers, how-to books, bored intellectuals, couples in cities, the boob tube and sleazy flicks, smart machines and dumb leaders, quick-change artists and paranoid Kremlinologists, charlatan writers and sincere ad men. A great doctor is therefore a four-star general in disguise; the battle lines are drawn. Without knowing it, I was recruited to your division. And in the past few years I've been out there on the front lines, struggling for sanity.

As for my bout of curiosity about my former attacker, well . . . please don't hold it against me.

I've tried my best to spread the good word to all parts of the self. To the body, stay in good health; to the brain, stay alert, on the move; to the libido, keep flowing and punching, regardless of abuse; to the heart, stay open. To the Mother, don't assume unnecessary or random guilt; to the Woman, keep caring and keep fucking; to the Photographer, find your own angle. Reject the theories and moralities proposed by the many: Orthodox Judaism, Sufism, the Jesus thing, fancy French pessimism or homespun therapies (co-counseling, astrology), consumerism, patriotism, or, alas, female chauvinism. Be a loner. Have patience with the self; if it commits mistakes, forgive it, absolve it, without major confessions. Pride and prejudice and other personal slaveries are part of the arrangement of growing up; nothing to get alarmed about. Be a true Christian — or Don Quixote — on the self's miscues and abuses.

You always told me that living in America, after Europe in the thirties and forties, was like living in a perpetual Disneyland. This had its dangerous side — an excess of fantasy and play, games and rides. Don't let them/us fool you, Doctor. Innocence can be as dangerous as evil, maybe more so, because of its camouflage. The consequences are frequently the same. Perhaps that's why I've begun to put Israel into my quiver of experience. To put reality back into my state of innocence. (Although Sde Boker is hardly pressure-ridden.)

Now men. Ah, men. Always a problem, right? Whether one has one, none, two. Or more. The trouble is one's own moods and seasons. What seems interesting in one season seems rather flat in another. But doesn't being single permit such indulgence? As you reminded me. So what can I say? I've hurt a dear friend by trying not to hurt him and at the same time trying not to hurt myself, or my desires. For I know only too well the lesson of my youth: you start cheating on those desires and they wither away quietly and die. Nix to that! So, for desire's sake, I'll take my lumps, accept my own espionage and entrapment. Oh, I can still get very con-fused out there in real life; like tonight, when I wanted very much to have my doctor in bed, and then all that went up, puff, because of a bite and a sad narrative. How wildly comic. How sadly frus-trating! (Yes, of course I know what to do, and maybe I will, once I'm finished explaining here.)

Am I promiscuous then? And if so, is this promiscuity an avoid-ance of the real, Doc? I hope not. Maybe, just maybe, it's an enhancement of it, like when I was small and bored with school routines and performed this and that naughtiness in order to make things a little more interesting. Are my couplings and attachments a bit like my photos, an assault on the daily drudgery? guerrilla attacks on the straightforward routines of the world? Am I secretly afraid of sleepwalking through life like the majority of the good citizens? If so, what a curious way to signal to myself, Stay Alert.

I worry about death more now, and read the obituaries. Beyond sentimentality, what does this signify — serious middle age? A morbid personality emerging? Thank God for the children, or I'm afraid I would concentrate even more upon that approaching pros-pect called nothingness. As for the children, they grow more and more into your "little hostages of fortune." But they're hostages of American fortune as much as of cosmic fortune. I need a de-tachment process when they hit the teen years, and I haven't learned it yet. (Does one ever "detach" from one's own?) Maybe with your help, I could, but not alone.

Did I ever tell you my futile attempt to replace you? First it was a respected feminist analyst from New York, new to Cambridge; I was treated to a heavy dose of woman's therapy, but not Miriam's therapy. When ideology enters that sacred room and intrudes upon my personal case, I feel cheated, shortchanged. Too many of my stories in those sessions were pigeonholed into the box of female victimization. I'm a bad guinea pig. The second shrink was an older man, a rotund narcissist and transparent tyrant who, I think, would have destroyed all my fine trust in you. It only cost me $750 to discover that his real concern in life was his portfolio, not therapy. Oh well, I didn't really give him a chance, I suppose. But you know, Dr. L, I was spoiled by you. Once one has been in the *hands of a true healer, no two-bit shaman or ordinary doctor will quite do. There were a couple of other, isolated meetings, with a sweet co-counselor who held my hand for an hour and gazed deeply into my eyes and with a Group dynamo with a runt complex. Neither had a fair chance. So, in my Shrinks Hall of Fame there remains only a select group — Levanda, Freud, Winnicott.*

I'm trying, Doctor; that's my message to you. And I'm succeeding, I think. And on this lonely night I wanted to tell you all this. It makes me somehow less lonely to be able to write you this way and to inform you that thoughts of sanity perfume the Scheinman estate. I feel stronger, doctor dear. Despite the comedies, despite the setbacks, despite the misadventures, I feel on top.

Over and out, with fondness and hugs.

She switched off the lamp, slipped on her nightgown, took a book to bed. Started to read then realized she was wearing the same black lace nightgown that Montana so favored, the one time she took it with her. She half smiled at his childish fetish, then slipped into fantasy. He was underneath her, and she had released one breast from her nightgown and put it into his mouth, and he was sucking on it, and her nipple grew hard in excitement; and as she imagined this, feeling his prick with her imaginary hand and her own vagina, both opening and protuberance, with her real hand, she grew heady. With driving power she played both hands, both scenes, feeling her doctor suck her greedily and feeling herself just as avariciously, the two running on parallel planes to one huge circle of pleasure. Oh, she liked his long, lean prick; oh, she adored his greedy mouth and lips and teeth of lust; oh, she needed him to suck and to fuck her, and she felt herself come to a place of hold; she could go over now and come, but she held right there, changing him around in her mind, his mouth now moving on her lower belly and then cunt, while she felt his prick in her own mouth, and with this change of positions she felt the urge grow stronger and more irresistible, and yet, for the next honeyed minutes, as she turned over onto her side, she began to include Rafi too in the picture, strong taut sweet Rafi who was now taking hold of her ass, and she was transported momentarily to a scene of nearly ten years ago with two dandy undergraduates in Eliot

House, and now, with her two present lovers right here, feeling prick of one and mouth of the other, why she was democratic in passion and aristocratic with variety and no longer could hold back and let herself flow into the wide sweeping curve of dalliance, oh she loved it here where she was no longer a good little girl but a bold free woman coming in a galaxy of pleasure whose stars and planets and whole constellations were known only to herself, and there, in the spreading milky way of orgasm, she felt herself shining and magnified.

Afterward, surrounded with aroma of self and redolence of fantasy, she slept like a baby.

The next day Harry called and asked if she wanted to accompany him to Lexington, where he had to deliver some paintings to a gallery. Sure, she answered, if Rosie could come along for a ride in his pickup. He agreed; Rosie, at age eleven, was already a flame of his. Presently Miriam was arranging Rosie and her friend Jessica into the long bed of the Chevy, where she sat them on old wooden milk crates, with his pictures tied securely and partitioned. The kids sat there in anticipation, holding up their magic play bottles for takeoff. The truck ground away, snorting into second gear, and the feisty girls were blowing bubbles into the wind, squealing with joy. (Just as Miriam had delighted, last night, in her own way? The good Dr. L had given her full license to go solo when deep frustration gripped her; made guiltless, she had discovered the act's merit. She recalled her first year out of marriage when, as a Radcliffe Institute fellow, she had taken solo flights by herself again and again, adding up the times like a chart of vengeance upon a wall of puritanism. Now, however, these masturbations occurred rarely, and for different motives. Were they much different from blowing those bubbles, she considered ingenuously, peering through the narrow cab window at the excited girls?)

In Lexington, Harry carried his paintings into a small gallery off Main Street, and Miriam felt another prompting for a show of her own. In the fall, winter? It had been so many years, so many changes, since "Miriam at Thirty-four." Could she face another show?

Harry and the slick gallery owner began to discuss how to hang his pictures, and Miry arranged to meet Harry later at Lexington

Green. The kids tagged along with her, of course, as she toodled up the main street of the lily-white town, past the smart, clean shops and the tidy pedestrians in summer colors, feeling like she was visiting a town of a century ago. Neat, clean, white, quiet. The girls begged for ice cream, and she bought two cones at seventy-five cents each for a single scoop. She remembered when cones had gone up from a dime! At the end of the street they came upon the oblong green, with the statue of the Minuteman facing forward, holding his musket in valiant pride. A good place for the kids to play, and for Miriam to idle.

The kids were set loose on that billiard table of emerald green, and like little fillies with bubbles they raced about, quickly hooking up with other children. Miriam advised them she'd be at the statue, just in case, and she walked in that direction. Pairs of tourists, their 35mm cameras clicking, were snapping pictures of the Minuteman soldier with his musket. A good staunch fellow, pride of New England; cased in bronze and standing for virtue and courage. What had he really been like, she wondered — a redneck, a wild shot, a coward, or indeed a hero? She ambled around the statue, nodding to two young Japanese; she had an urge to be spiteful, blasphemous, but resisted it. Let the soldier represent New England virtue — why not? "You pose, please?" one young Japanese, with horn-rims, asked. Miriam, surprised, said, "Sure." She stood by the noble creature and tried to look like herself: ambiguous and skeptical. Two or three times she allowed herself to be photographed, and then, at the tourist's request, photographed them, using their fine Nikon. As she snapped the busy, cheerful-looking young men, she thought of Tanizaki and Kawabata and Kurosawa, and wondered what lurked behind their eager, innocent looks.

She rambled on. Around the back of the statue, on the freshly cut green, teenagers were tossing a Frisbee, and off to the side a small group of kids lounged on benches, sprawled on grass. Charming.

"Hey Ma'am, can you spare some change?" A long-haired young man was facing her, half smiling, looking somewhat odd.

She turned away, then back again. "For what?"

He smiled sweetly. Shrugged. "For some eats and smokes." He

was about sixteen and wore blue jeans, crew sneakers, an alligator shirt.

She fumbled in her pockets. "What school do you go to?"

"School?" he pronounced, as though he were pronouncing *Zimbabwe*. "Oh, I been to several." He smiled, adding, "And out of several."

She gave him two quarters, and he looked puzzled.

"Not enough?"

He rubbed his nose and eyes. "It's up to you, Ma'am." He stared at her strangely.

She took out her camera and focused on him, just a few feet away. There, in her frame, she perceived the dilated pupils, the oddly stretched mouth, the pallid skin. She snapped him once, twice, three times. The cross hair revealed the same Botticelli face as Melody's, a friend of Jon's: rapt, vapid, crazed.

A smile broke broadly upon his dazed face. "Hey, you gonna put some extra bread down for these?"

She continued to snap. "What are you smoking these days?"

He laughed slowly, like an older man, but rubbed his nose briskly. "Sniffin' today. Wanna snag some?" He nodded at the kids nearby. "I can arrange some sweet stuff for you — liberty caps, reds or blues, coke or quads, whatever's your pleasure, Ma'am."

Clicking, she asked, "What's your dad do?"

The boy pondered for a long moment. "Oh, Pops. Sure. Hauls ass for old Draper Labs — ever hear of it? Designs nose cones." He flared his nostrils wildly. "Old fart Pops. The original grind."

She took a dozen shots of the dazed adolescent locked into his high, floating loose as a kite on Lexington Green. She wondered, "Your friends, are they all . . . flying today?"

He put out his hand, limp and theatrical. "That's private life, if you don't mind, and it'll cost you, Ma'am."

She didn't know whether he was kidding or not.

Just then a buxom young thing in white painter's overalls and visored cap marched up and took the boy's arm. "C'mon, Reed, let's not get busted again so soon. Sorry, lady, I hope he didn't bother you too awful much."

"No," she said, but she couldn't resist voicing concern. "But why don't you take care of him? Isn't he a bit . . . dangerous, on his own this way? To himself, I mean?"

The girl adjusted her cap in annoyance. "Shit, lady, what d'ya think we do all day 'cept take care of each other? Piss off. C'mon, Reed." And she pulled the young man away.

Miriam surveyed the green scene, where the evolution of the old Revolutionary soldier had caused mutant growths. Cochin come to Lexington? In the place of rich Chinese businessmen retiring for their twilight opium dreams, these were native teenagers out for their midafternoon siesta.

Rosie and Jessica were chasing after a Frisbee which landed near the stoned group, and Miriam's blood raced as if she feared contamination by association. This flock of doped sheep made up another world; where was their shepherd? (Or a Fellini, a Sandor?) The visored girl's look came back to her — a look of accusation that read, "Voyeur!" Yes, she was right. But where were the parent-voyeurs of these children — out designing nose cones or teaching English at the university? And was Jon one of this flock, on another green somewhere? Sure; face it squarely. It was happening, baby; the soil was sprouting another sort of grass, and the sons and daughters were the ones grazing. She observed some tall Dutch elms, almost finished by disease, and felt for these American kids.

"What are you dreaming about?" asked Harry.

She looked with relief at her friend standing there, solid in his denim and irony. "Would you believe that most of them are popping something?"

Harry took her arm. "So what else is new? Where've you been for the past decade? Do you want to change trades and become a social worker? A Florence Nightingale for the heads and freaks?" He smiled his friendly, skeptical smile. "That's what I always loved about you — you were never too old to give up your innocence. This whole fucking country is high, sweetheart; it just depends on what they're imbibing, drugs or news, tranquillizers or commercials, coke and aspirin, or Ronnie and the Moral Majority. You'd have to travel to Lubec, Maine, to be sober. And probably not there anymore. Come on, let's get the kids and blow. I gotta get back." He tapped her jaw with a mock punch.

She heeded his wish and called her flock of two.

That night, she developed the day's film and sensed immediately that her growing gallery of troubled teenagers was a catalogue of unusual interest. She had an exciting idea and spent hours in her darkroom, working with chemicals, enlarger, negatives, paper. All the time thinking, are you kidding, sister? How do you think their parents would take it? How about if *you* arrived to see a photography show and lo and behold, there was *your* son up there on the wall, staring out dazed at you and the public? Could you write that off as Art? Try it out next time your Jonathan hits one of his high moods. Let's see you move in on that challenge, Miss Superiority; use *your* son as a model. (Why, at forty-two, are you still challenging yourself to run On Risk Only?)

The questions taunted her as she looked over the series of three portraits she had taken, and blown up: this boy on the green today, a teenage girl in Brigham's, and a model of Harry's. Oh, it was hot stuff, all right, she was sure of it. Exhausted but high from her work, she looked through the haunting daguerreotypes of Southworth and Hawes and admiringly compared them with her own portraits.

She countered her excitement in the next few days with the more prosaic work of checking several final portfolios that had been handed in late, as usual, by her MIT students. The best of these projects were the most conventional: a series of pictures of old seafarers' houses on the Rockport oceanfront, taken by a youngster from Gloucester; compositions examining the changing light at dawn and at dusk, done at a Lincoln farmsite by a Wellesley junior from Concord; an exquisite set of twelve studies of Kansas wheatfields and silos, conceived and executed by a Lawrence farmboy who had taken the course as a lark and wound up obsessed. (The less conventional projects, of course, were flawed badly — like the attempt at a surrealistic urban study, and an experiment in abstract montage, a disaster.) In the successes she saw again the obvious: how working within the tradition had made it much easier for the students to learn the tools of their craft without having to worry about Originality. Roused by the three triumphs, she even telephoned the Kansas lad, Clinton Bean, to praise the work personally. A physics prodigy, the lanky boy had begun to feel pressure from his science teachers and parents about his new passion, and

Miriam had become his sole supporter. When she informed him on the phone that his photographs were full of sentiment without being sentimental, and that the composing elements were good enough for him to try the pictures in a photography magazine's annual contest, he stammered out his thanks, and she could feel his blush over the telephone. Might he come in and see Miry this week and discuss it further? Excited, he thanked her profusely.

Was she ruining a fine career in physics for such an aberrational career? So what. She thought about Dorothea Lange, who had forsaken her career as a studio photographer and wife for the same artistic aberration. Why shouldn't Clinton give it a shot?

The student triumphs encouraged her in various ways, she thought two nights later, looking over her own work again. She felt her teaching ability confirmed, which was important. She was consoled that there were still youngsters growing up in America who were getting through, making it with their talent and heads intact. And another thing — she felt stronger about her own track of work, though less clear about goal and more uncertain of success than those conventional victories. At her stage in photography, she was interested in roads that were less straight and certain than those she had picked when she was younger. The project itself would determine the method and goal, and even define the criteria of failure and success. And the more radical the project, the more difficult it was to measure such matters. Like photographing your dearest pals for their anatomies; was that a test in aesthetics and courage, or a very foolhardy and vain venture?

An urge propelled her now from photographs and ideas to Jon's bedroom, where she checked in on him — her strongest project. Curled like a question mark, with one hand over his eyes and one leg flung out over the side of the bed, his thin body exposed, he looked every bit the sleeping prince. Hers, at least. Was he to be a private model, as well? If so, she would photograph him for beauty, not confusion or pain, she decided, laying out fresh socks and blue jockey underwear and removing the dirty ones. Carefully she lifted his leg back onto the bed, and almost tripped on his collection of tiny D & D figures on the floor. She gathered them and set them upright on his desk: miniature magic-users with torches, bearded fighters with chain mail and daggers, robed clerics with scrolls. The size of her old Crackerjacks prizes. Probably just as dangerous, too. With the room reasonably neat, her prince asleep — and her princess in the next room — she felt at home, rich. That's what counted, after all — these two little projects here, along with herself.

About to leave, she discovered a stray football and picked that up too, suddenly reminded of that addicted boy on the green. And she found herself clutching the football with both arms, squeezing it to her midsection protectively — a gesture that, paradoxically, brought back a childhood memory of her tomboy pleasure when she had first learned how to hold the oddly shaped ball properly, in order to run with it. From voyeur to mother to tomboy, in dizzying succession. She left the room with mixed emotions, anxiety crossing with satisfaction and memory. This fall, when she returned, she'd have to try some touch football. Could she still run and cut like Dad had taught her? Swivel her hips to run free?

Before running off free now, however, she had to attend to her summer subletters and give them last minute instructions. Through Vera, a group of four young moviemakers called Pequod, who had already made a successful documentary, had taken the apartment. "You should come over to the studio in East Cambridge sometime," said Roddy M., adjusting his horn-rims beneath his auburn hair. "Better yet," put in Lindsay, a chain smoker with a Southern drawl, "come for the rushes of the new film in the fall. Your friend Vera is one of the leads." Oh? What a perfect medium for that gregarious egoist, thought Miriam, who rejoined, "If you keep the place from burning down, and don't ruin my collection of *Camera Arts* over there, I'll gladly accept the invitation." The second girl, Dru, was enthused. "Okay if we browse among the photography books? We don't get that much variety in Nap Town."

Miriam nodded, started to ask something about Indianapolis, when the phone interrupted. It was Doctor B., who in a most poignant appeal asked to say good-bye to her face-to-face. When she hesitated he added that it was "rather important."

And all the way over in the taxi across Mass. Ave. she braced herself for the end of the affair, the end of something lovely in her life, and she wanted to jump out by MIT and run to that big swooping Calder bird of black steel and hide there.

At an outdoor café on Newbury Street, they met over cappuccino. The air was warm, but he was dressed impeccably, a tie with
his short sleeve white shirt and jacket. They spoke of the weather,
the small details of her leaving and returning, briefly about their
last meeting. (He started to apologize, but she said, "No need.")
She listened to his musical voice as he offered to take her to the
airport. Listened to the perfect baritone pitch as he asked her to
write. Listened so closely to his voice and observed so intently the
slate eyes and firm chin and long bony hands that she barely
recorded what he was saying now, something about being married.
So she wondered casually, "What's that?"

"I didn't think a marriage proposal would have to be repeated,"
he said. "I want you to know that I'd like to marry you when I'm
free."

She tried to concentrate on the voice, the eyes, the knitted tie,
the reflections off windshields and store windows. On everything
but that strange wild sentence, which paraded around them now
like a leopard strolling.

"You must have *some* feelings about it," he added, slightly
embarrassed.

Oh, Harry was right; it was all too lunatic. Not merely America,
but the human side.

She told herself she was supposed to be happy, deliriously happy —
two proposals within several weeks from two mature, lovely men!

At last she found her tongue. "Why do you . . . propose *that?*"

He shrugged his wide shoulders, half winced. "I . . . wanted you
to know what you mean to me."

She knew, too, that he was being noble and brave; that he
wouldn't be free that easily from that tiger-wife, if ever; that it
was a romance without a future of freedom. That was the (sad)
fact. "Did you think I didn't know that before . . . without . . . this . . . ?"

He sipped his cappuccino, no pinky curled here, perplexed.
"You seem . . . upset by the proposal. I'm sorry I made it then."

She could see the edge of the flower garden from where they
sat, the little bobbing heads of red and yellow and white flowers.
Late tulips? And before them, the busy citizens paraded, marching
with purposeful strides and straight-ahead gazes, broken only by

an interest in a store window. They knew where they were going now, and in life, too. And she. She?

Her face softened. She took his fine hand. "Thank you. Really. I appreciate it, *lots*. I guess I was just surprised."

He squeezed back. "Will you think about it? After all, I won't be free for quite a while under ordinary circumstances. But I could try to be free much earlier if I knew you wanted that."

What do you want? she asked herself. For him to give up absolutely everything for her? Sweet power, the thought.

She shook her head ever so slightly. "Oh, Montana dearest, I'm very fond of you, but I'm not in the mood for marriage. Or for even entertaining the proposal. I'm . . ." She searched for the correct words for her feelings, knowing she would fall short, always fall short at critical junctures. Knowing that the words would fall short, too. "I'm not up for that anymore. At least not now. I like knowing and liking you just the way it is now, without any formal ties, legal issues. My fondness is right just the way it is; let's keep the state out of our affairs, okay?"

He drained his cup and looked at her like a schoolboy chastised. "I should have known that . . . that what means a great deal to most people doesn't mean that much to you."

Like Maytags and Volvos and well-kept lawns? Oh, she wanted those, too, really she did. In some part of her. Wanted those swell comforts just like any sensible soul . . . Would you ever be a sensible soul, however?

He was fumbling now about her "Israeli friend," saying of course he knew how mad the whole thing was, proposing to her while she was going away to him, and . . .

"I'll tell you what," she countered, tired, admiring his admirable battle — old ways and values versus new emotions. "In the fall, why don't you show me where you grew up? What's the name of it again, Flathead Lake?"

He smiled. "You remembered this time."

"Any family still there?"

"Oh, I could probably dig up an ancient cousin or two. Plus memories."

"Perfect. Show it to me in the fall. September in Montana." She daydreamed. "Sounds just perfect."

He laughed, surprised himself now. "All right, if you really want it."

"Yes, I think I would. Let's see herds of elk and moose and at night hear coyotes and whatever else hangs around those parts. Or is it all strip-mined?"

He shook his head. "No, it's still intact. Though you might have to put up with bison rather than moose."

"Great." She leaned over and kissed his cheek. "Great. To the bison in the fall." And she clinked her cup against his. "And herds of elk, and huge skies!"

Later, looking through familiar photographs of two masters, Atget and Dorothea Lange, she remained dumfounded over those proposals. Why did grown adults, once married, want to do it all over again? Did marriage become like a biological gene? Were her old-fashioned gentlemen — one from the dun colored Negev desert and the second from the wide Montana prairie — romantics at heart who needed legitimacy for their right to pleasure? She followed the empty quays and muted streets of Atget's Paris and thought how, one day, she'd like to pursue one city in long sequence. Marriage for her? No, no. She had had too many uneven pieces in her life, too many jagged spaces, and the fit or solution called marriage was not her desire. Put another way, she was One, with many complications; as Two, she would be reduced too drastically. In the simplest terms, how could she give up pluralistic affections? Her autumn winter summer caprices? Her men moods? Her solitary periods? Her interstices of photography space? Weren't those caprices, moods, affections, solitary hours the very substance of her?

She walked to her bookshelf of favorites and chafed at the thought of having to choose among Siskind, Evans, Brassaï, Cartier-Bresson, Brandt, Steichen, the Westons, Frank, Lange, Atget. She turned to Lange's "Back" and admired the sunlight, the figures, the gestures; then to Brett Weston's "Broken Window, San Francisco" and received the exploding force of the black space; at Stieglitz's cumulative portrait of Georgia O'Keeffe she followed the tortuous evolution of character. All this dense variety was part of her sensibility now, earned by her devotion and study, and it was unthinkable to give up one beauty for another. As in art, so in life, she equated foolishly, not caring. Accepting herself as a maximalist then. So, good-bye schoolgirl dreams of rings and oaths and safe comforts, good-bye domesticity, good-bye, good-bye.

And she smoked, with impunity, hearing Jon's severe chiding in her head.

12

IT was a different kind of summer, with Rafi living half the time in a Jerusalem apartment to be nearer his children and commuting during the week to the Negev and the kibbutz. Miriam likewise became a commuter, and liked this manner of getting to know Jersusalem, which she deemed her Emerald City of Adulthood in honor of Dorothy and her colored glasses.

Early on in the summer Miriam caught a bit of good luck, namely, Jonathan's quick acceptance by his kibbutz peers because of a spectacular goal in soccer. He had entered a game as a substitute in the first week, and lo and behold, the little bugger — not so little by Israeli standards; he was five foot eight at fifteen — had scored the winning goal on a marvelous header with less than three minutes remaining. ("Yeah, I lucked out all right," he explained modestly. "The goalie was screened out and never even saw the shot.") From then on he was *in,* a wanted player and comrade. For Miriam this was an unforeseen blessing, for she was able to leave him alone on the kibbutz without much anxiety; there were no muggings or easy dope at Sde Boker, only fruit orchards, sheep, devoted soccer players, and of course some enticing foreign volunteers, including a Swiss girl named Heidi who was three years older and three decades maturer than Yani. In Jerusalem, in contrast, she had to make do with Rafi's children; but if the situation wasn't one of open warmth, especially with Tamar, it was no longer open warfare. Even Tamar was coming around slowly, hinting at maybe having a photography session with Miriam.

For a good part of every other week, when Miriam was in town, she found herself alone in the apartment, and this suited her well — suited her disposition for solitary space, and her instinct for prowling alone in a city. Days in Jerusalem were hot, but the evenings and late afternoons were frequently cool, at times chilly, from the city's high perch in the hills of the Judean desert. The apartment, rented by the kibbutz, was a large flat in an old Arab house in Abu Tor, on the old 1967 border with Jordan; its high ceilings and two-foot walls kept the rooms cool, wonderfully cool, even on blazing days.

In the first weeks she stayed mostly to herself, taking long walks in the late afternoon or at dusk, watching the light slant amber upon the pink and white native stone and turn the city into a crystal of subtle light. Jerusalem at dusk deserved Vermeer, she decided. She walked through wild Abu Tor with its sharp hills and lunatic ravines; along the narrow streets of the German Colony, alive with eucalyptus and flowering gardens; into Old Katamon and its palatial Turkish and Arab houses; around nineteenth-century Mea Shearim, with its inner courtyards and secret synagogues. A series of distinct neighborhoods and architectures, this city was, with a tiny crossroads as the downtown shopping axis. A small town of winding streets, furtive alleys, pungent aromas. And though she had some friends who lived within walking distance, she held off looking them up, wanting instead to take more time with the tantalizing city — the stones, the air, the flowers, the singular scents, the changing light. Like an Atget with his Paris, Miriam tried to know, and focus on, Jerusalem.

Knowing how easy it was to shoot clips of film and come up with rolls of clichés, she kept her camera idle, in its pouch, and forced herself to immerse herself directly, without the intermediary of lenses. She looked, saw, imbibed, sized up, in order to prime her imagination. Not reproducing a place, but creating it anew was her aim. Simultaneously she was more or less biding her time, taking it easy and being aesthetic on the front burner while letting questions and problems simmer on the back — a show in the fall, Jon this summer, finances, Rafi, too. Dark ghost off somewhere; lost forever? Sipping her rich Nescafé in the morning, paper-thin *Jerusalem Post* in her hands, she planned her afternoon walk, peering out beyond the small park to the brown hills, and beyond that to the sliver of blue in the distance, the Dead Sea. A vision as illusory and dreamy as it was real . . . maybe a little like her life these days, these years?

Curiously, she felt at home and also a stranger here. At home with the easy informality, the democratic bustle, the zigzag lines and zany traffic, the neurotic Israelis, but a stranger amid these pale pastels, the fervent Zionists, the dreamy city, the long, too-intense history. A traveler she'd forever be in this overheated place. Whatever corner she turned, a face from Biblical mythology or actual history emerged. And whatever mortal soul she encountered, a tale that impoverished the imagination followed. If you listened and remembered too intently, in fact, sleep wouldn't come easily at night. At afternoon coffee in open-air Camin or Ben Yehuda cafés, or with Rafi on Friday night visits after dinner, from 9:00 P.M. onward, you met friends and listened to gossip, arguments, ideas, dreams, jokes, family history, rivalries, knowledge, tips, hopes, plans, peculiarities, madness, visions. For the citizens, after an exhausting week spent with Germanic and British Mandate bureaucracy, Levantine slowness and frustration, all-around Israeli incompetence — only the armed forces and kibbutzes really worked here — Friday night was the time to get it all out, let loose, talk. And talk, and talk. Thank God they didn't have a two-day weekend!

Slowly she began to acquaint herself with the rites and customs of the curious cabal called Jerusalem society. Like some ancient piece of Earth crust, this society consisted of layer upon rich layer of inventions and histories, intrigues and intimacies, grande dames and grander peacocks. Jerusalem made Cambridge seem like some small, sleepy town buried in an innocent country (wasn't it?). Miriam began to feel more and more an American lamb, a Jewish Isabel Archer, overseas for the first time and over her head too. Take for example the Ricardos, in Rehavia; Sarah, an entomologist, traced her ancestry back a few thousand years to the Old City of Solomon, from which the family had emigrated to Spain and Portugal, where one had assisted Rashi on his Talmud commentaries, another had written one of the earliest treatises on medicine, and a third had served as Queen Isabella's private physician and written famous poetry. When the lady served Miriam a splendid cake and tea and asked where Miriam "came from," what could she say beyond — and how should she say, utter — "Cleveland"? Or take Sarah's husband, Arie, a stout-chested painter whose Russian pioneer parents had helped clear the Galilee of swamps and start an eminent kibbutz and who had lost one son in the Sinai while he was serving in another front. When Arie patted Miriam's knee and asked her about the painting scene in New York — "Are stripes still in?" — she smiled wearily. The Ricardos fed her European cakes and French brandy and spicy tidbits of their past while tweaking her vast innocence.

At another home the richness was played out differently. Here Shula Fuchs entertained with an eye to utility: of what use was the visitor to her academic career? A pretty, charming, black-haired mathematician, the daughter of a famous dead Yeki (German) philosopher, Shula was a careful user of famous foreigners, shimmying her slim figure up the academic ladder and wondering if by chance Miriam knew Smale of Berkeley? Poor Miriam felt like an abandoned chick in a coop in the presence of this clever fox. She felt much easier with Uri, a passionate Pole of forty-five who had once had a brilliant career in physics; he delivered to her a thirty-minute lecture on gravity, from Newton to Feynman, that was lucidly exciting. Dazzled by one, manipulated by the other, Miriam nibbled her turkey schnitzel and clammed up, feeling stupid and tongue-tied when Shula deigned to ask about her "career." Was it true that these two had a tacit understanding whereby Uri knew about his wife's affairs and even periodically gave his open, verbal blessing to the various celebrity lovers? Jerusalem could be as sophisticated as Paris or New York, Miriam learned.

What was more poignant, and subtly pervasive, was the decline of the passion of Zionism in many of the best souls. What had once been a compelling idealism, a family faith, was now an exhausted emotion, a family loss. She witnessed this in Rafi's disillusionment and in that of new friends. In Jacob, for example, a legendary political figure who had run WW II European immigrants in Liberty ships through the British blockade, who had later settled Jews from Yemen and Tunisia and Morocco in new towns, and who had been a leading member of the ruling Labor Party, only to resign over its Palestinian policy — in this fine small fellow she saw forty years of devotion slowly ebbing away. Handsome Dudu, a leading young fighter pilot and idealistic ex-kibbutznik, preferred now to concentrate on his postdoctoral physiology studies in America rather than cope with bleakly changing Israel. And for Elie, a dark-skinned Iraqi Jew of middle age with a laid-back sophistication and an impeccable English learned at age fifteen reading *The New Yorker* and *Partisan Review* — the only magazines available in the Baghdad bookstores of the fifties — it was the Ashkenazi leaders such as Ben-Gurion and Golda Meir who had created the whole mess by trying to turn a Levantine country into a European nation-state. The Ashkenazi, from Poland, Germany, and Russia, had done their best to discriminate against the poorer, more backward Sephardic Jews, sowing the seeds for the present hostility and mistrust between the two groups.

So it was not merely West Bank friction that was eroding idealism, but the deep inner contradictions of the society. Including the religious fanatics who had a powerful role in government, because of the exigencies of coalition government. "For me they're the worst," claimed Mira, a lively social scientist with a small son born out of wedlock in conservative Jerusalem. "More than anyone, the religious choke our spirits." Indeed, Miriam took a small, perverse pleasure in contrasting the Israelis' hard, realistic attitude toward Zionism with the continual effusive froth of the newcomer Americans, who made *aliyah* and frequently joined the most fanatic right-wing groups. "Look, it's a fucked-up situation that will get worse before it gets better," pronounced Judy, an American who had married an Israeli and had been living here for a decade. "And I can't wait to get out for good. Or at least do it the way you do, arrive for visits only." The Dream Society had settled into a Bleak House.

Miriam traveled between the kibbutz in the south and Jerusalem maybe once every two weeks, either with Rafi in his hippo-backed Volvo or from dusty Beersheva by *sherut,* a Mercedes cab that shuttled between towns. The ride was a rollicking, exhausting affair, especially if one sat in one of those fold-down iron seats like those in the old Checker Cabs, with the radio blaring loud pop tunes and seven passengers sardined together. Yet this anonymous riding allowed her to ruminate, to inquire: how Jewish was she? Was Jon healthier in the company of German and Swiss volunteers and kibbutz kids than of Cambridge teenagers? What sort of show did she want — yet another public one? Meanwhile she took in the changing landscape, from the green fields of Sde Boker to the potash factories of Beersheva, from the stucco Arab houses stuck on the hillsides, with their wonderful terraced farms, to the dramatic Judean hills, rising baldly like the New Hampshire granite mountains, leading up to her Emerald City. She was in retreat here, in this cab and in this society and in her two rooms in the desert, and the stark landscape provided the right emotional perspective. It gave her little comfort, left her on her own.

Being a nomad of sorts pleased her, and when Rafi stayed at his sites, Miriam occasionally took trips of her own. On one she journeyed to the small kibbutz between Tel Aviv and Jerusalem where Dr. Levanda was buried. There, in a small graveyard set on a hillside of olive trees (Dr. L's favorite), Miriam found her headstone, with name and dates (1908–1979) and a small pile of stones for a memorial. Miriam spent several hours sitting and remembering Dr. L: wearing her best pillbox hat and wool suit, marching in silent protest against Kissinger's speaking at Harvard after the bombing of Cambodia; searching for mushrooms in the countryside, as excited over her first pair of blue jeans (Miriam's surprise gift) as over the puffballs she discovered; cocking her head to one side, smoking with a cigarette holder, and skeptically asking Miriam whether she really believed what she was saying about a particular scene in her life. Skeptical, devoted, realistic, loving — that saintly European lady. Miriam laid some flowers on the grave, and found several smooth stones to add to the simple memorial. And for an hour she drifted back to a taboo memory of hers, of her real mother's death when Miriam was ten: the remarkably smooth cheeks, the light brown hair and intelligent brown eyes, the long piano player's fingers, and that last kiss, chilling her now as it had pained her over thirty years ago, when her mother had brought her face close for good-bye . . . dying, she had insisted on being dressed in a white gusseted blouse and a necklace of pearls, and . . . Dear mother! whose face was as alive now as it had been then, dying, so vivid that Miriam would avoid it at all costs. She took two photos of Dr. Levanda's grave and departed.

Another time she revisited Dimona, to search for that Falasha, Amos, she had once met. No luck. Among the tacky pastel houses and chipping tenements, amid white-robed Africans and terracotta Indians, however, she ran into an extended family of blacks from Detroit and Chicago — a man, three women, six children. When they heard her English, they gathered round and beseeched her to help with the authorities, claiming that though they were true descendants of the original Hebrews, the government refused to recognize them as Jews. Their case intrigued Miriam, until she perceived that the women thought of themselves as the man's wives, and she sensed that they had the wrong religion. Politely she extricated herself and meandered away, sorry that she had missed the Ethiopian gentleman.

Soon she was wandering out of the town into a kind of semidesert, where she came upon an arrow and sign: NO ENTRANCE WITHOUT PASS, in English and Hebrew. Aha, so here's where they make their big ones! Under cover of a nuclear reactor. Right here in white-hot, dry, Third World Dimona. She pondered how the Old Testament prophets in the wilderness had been transformed into nukes in the desert. Did these new prophets deliver the same sort of apocalyptic wisdom as the old ones had? One through metaphor, the other through concrete . . . or was *she* getting her religions mixed up? . . . Back in the town, Dimona beckoned: come live here and feel a different darker Israel. Come survive and hideout here, and know thyself in a new way!

Late in August she took a trip up north with Rafi to look over Gamla, an historical site rediscovered and unearthed by a friend. Through low brown hills and patches of green fields they drove, turning above the Sea of Galilee and speeding up through the high flat plateau of the Golan Heights. After another hour of driving in perceptibly cooler air, passing old Syrian bunkers in the former wilderness now cultivated by kibbutzes and dotted with an occasional army camp, they arrived at their location — a spectacular camel-backed mountain named Gamla by the complex historian Josephus. As they began their walk in, first down a sharp ridge and across a narrow bottleneck of land and then up the steep mountain, Rafi narrated its history. Described with splendid accuracy by Josephus in *The Jewish War*, Gamla was a Masada of the north; a few thousand valiant Jews had turned their village into a fort and held out against the best Roman legions of Vespasian and Titus for some thirty days before finally succumbing. Choosing death over life as Roman slaves, they committed mass suicide, the men first throwing their wives and children into the ravine below and then jumping themselves. "When Josephus said the Jews were a stiff-necked people," Rafi noted, helping her across a rocky divide, "he meant it."

On the way to the high peak, Rafi stopped to inspect the various rooms that had been uncovered — schoolroom, synagogue, ritual bath, sleeping rooms — along with potsherds and original stone foundations. The peak of the mountain was two separate humps separated by a narrow neck of land. From there the views were memorable. On one side, down a few thousand feet, was a vigorous waterfall, and on another was a good-sized flowing brook; just below was a ferocious fall into forbidding ravines. The only access was the slender path they had just traversed — an easily defendable route. "The Romans lost thousands of soldiers just trying to negotiate this pass, before Titus finally surprised the Jews by managing to climb up from around back," Rafi explained.

In the shade of a cypress they ate their lunch: goat cheese, fresh tomatoes, pita, olives, apple juice. The air was cool, gray, translucent. Rafi touched her arm at one point and motioned skyward, toward a large, broad-winged bird circling languidly overhead. She took the binoculars, astonished by the size and stillness of the bird. "An eagle," he noted, "just as the man says." He pointed to the tiny print of his brown Penguin edition of Josephus, who had recorded this same site as a favorite haunt of these birds nearly two thousand years ago. "Clever fellow, wasn't he?" Miriam said, and Rafi retorted, "Maybe too clever." And he explained how Josephus had eventually gone over to the Romans rather than over the cliffs, "and written his history there in Rome."

When Rafi climbed down the mountain to the excavation level for a closer study, Miriam stayed above on her perch, contemplating eagles and self-destructive Jews. Was suicide a fate she would have chosen? (Had such a fate, without the principle, actually appealed to her once upon a time?) She savored the tartness of the cheese and olives, and peered through the binocs to follow that big bird as it slowly swooped down, an apparition of blackness eclipsing the blue sky. Aroused by the strange beauty, she wanted to shoot a few pictures, but held off . . . And this people, this tribe here, were they again getting ready for their perennial self-destructive pattern? It could be, could very well be. Poor Jews. Surrounded by enemies, they made enemies of themselves; facing real threats, they began imagining others. So reality and paranoia converged, intermingled, and history came round to repeat itself — a monster of self-fulfilling inevitability. And trying to be perfect, the Jews were maddened by imperfection; either they would be best or they would demand self-sacrifice. They were stiff-necked, all right. And uncertain. Restless. Intense. Argumentative. Always itching for action. The leisureliness of that dark bird was beyond this nervous tribe. What was so wrong with being a slave, she wondered, especially if your Roman praetor allowed you to do your photographing and mothering and to see your local shrink? Was it much worse than being an imprisoned wife? So you had to give up your God. Was He that great? Had He ever been? Oh, you'll never make a good Jew! she admonished herself.

They drove back to Jerusalem via the Bekaa, the valley between green hills bordering the emaciated Jordan River. Beyond the double chain-link fence, where the path was swept daily to check for footprints of terrorists, small Jordanian villages were tucked neatly into the far hills. So close, and yet farther than New York for the Israelis. A busy weekend was coming up; Jon was coming up to town with two friends, and Rafi's kids were probably staying over a night. The first meeting of their offspring had been a touchy standoff, two boxers sparring in the opening rounds, feeling each other out. This would be a better test of compatibility, or incompatibility, more likely. Suddenly she sensed how fast Rafi was driving — 110 kilometers per hour on this curving road — and she touched his arm and asked him to slow down. He gave her a queer look, but acquiesced. This mad driving was in their blood. Even the sane ones, like her man here, couldn't resist speeding, tailgating dangerously. She was glad she wasn't driving down this way by herself, through the Arab villages; if you got a flat or had other car troubles, you were at their mercy. Still, when she opened the glove compartment for cigarettes and found a gun, she was shocked. Rafi laughed at her naiveté.

Near Jericho, that sudden green in the middle of the desert, they picked up a couple of hitchhikers, soldiers who were heading for Jerusalem. The lanky blond boy asked her about the Paul Revere walk from Boston to Concord, and was disappointed to discover she had never tried it. The dark girl, a Yemenite beauty with an Uzi submachine gun on her lap, asked whether New York was as dangerous as Kojak made it out to be. "It's not as bad as the West Bank," Miriam opined, not believing herself.

Climbing up to Jerusalem from the desert in a series of dizzying figure-eight turns, they curved through hills of chalky white and dun sandstone, the aridity broken only by Bedouin camps and scrawny flocks of black sheep. Oh, for some Vermont lake or river around these parts! In the bluish distance she made out the rounded minarets and golden mosques of the Old City and the pencil-thin vertical shapes of the YMCA and the Hilton in the new town, an uneven skyline of black silhouettes forming on the high horizon. Here, from the east, she had a sense of why this place appeared as much imaginary as real; it was a kind of vision to dry eyes and parched bodies. Scary now, in the low dusk. Or was she just feeling some new mood slipping in, while Rafi chatted in Hebrew with the kiddie soldiers? Is that what Yani needed, some Israeli Defense Force discipline to go along with Swiss sweets?

She half drowsed . . . This Jerusalem was a flower begging to be plucked, or the site for the child's game of king-of-the-mountain, where you climbed on a hill and saw how long you could stay there while pushing down your enemies. Not a jewel, perhaps, but a sensual center, disguised as a holy place, a soft sexual destiny camouflaged as a religious site, ripe for perennial rape. No wonder Turks and Christians, Mamelukes and Jews, Arabs and Saracens, among the many infidels — the noun so exotic — had sought to gain access, possession, and dominance. From the male point of view, she saw it clearly: if you were coming from the great wilderness, this was She, a moist/holy/profane presence, the virgin and the sirening whore, and you had to conquer her, plunder her, festoon her, keep her. The drive for gratification, after months and maybe years of parched wandering, needed to be satisfied, no matter what the cost.

He was talking to her, she realized over the drone of engine and her own meditation. "Sorry, I was listening to me. What were you saying, dear?"

Eating an orange (peeled by the soldier?), he repeated, in a low voice, "Why haven't you ever told me about your other . . . *friend?*"

Slowly the words sank in, and began to root and spread. The soldiers in back were chattering away in Hebrew. And within moments all the strange beauty and exotic history of the day fell away like innocent leaves. What was left instead was little explosions of pain inside of her.

Carefully he ate his orange, offering her a slice and saying, "Well, if you want to talk about it sometime, I'm interested in hearing." Calmly he was looking at her, looking, until she grew frightened that he'd drive off the road.

He checked the road and resumed his look.

And she felt impelled to meet his gaze without turning away or offering words of defense, in explanation or apology. She stared at the intelligent eyes and mobile mouth and high lineless forehead and tried to absorb his hurt, her responsibility. So he knew, and had known, and had kept silent, waiting for her to speak first!

Finally he turned back to his driving, and she was able to return her gaze to the mundane world of windshields and low hills and darkening sky, pressing the tears back and down. Pressing hard. She saw the particles of dust accumulating on the windshield, mingling with several dead insects, and felt hit by black flak in her chest, head.

He flipped on his wipers, and she watched transfixed as they flapped back and forth, back and forth. She felt their slapping as though upon her cheeks, and reddened.

Free, huh? She mocked herself, and felt near bursting from her misdeed. She tried to concentrate on the cones of lunar hills, the long shadows crossing the Judean desert, and the guttural sounds from behind her. Going over to the Romans seemed like nothing now, alongside her feckless betrayal. Traitor!

Later, after dinner in the apartment, Rafi was going through sketch plans and site maps for his monograph proofs, and Miriam was reading. She looked up and asked, "Tell me, why didn't you mind more that I had another . . . friend?"

Puzzled, he tried to catch on. "More? What do you mean — more than what?"

And she felt a curious black mood building irresistibly in her. "More than you showed."

He shook his head, shrugged, returned to his papers. "You can't measure my feelings by *show*."

"Well, maybe you didn't, or don't, care that much whether I sleep around or not."

He looked up at her, puzzlement turning to skepticism in his eyes. "You're speaking foolishly."

"Maybe I am, but so what? I mean, maybe you don't care that much about me, so you don't care *how* I behave." She smoked, and for the first time really *experienced* the Klee reproduction on the wall: those bizarre, half-aquatic, half-human creatures standing about in green space. "Supposing I told you that I was sleeping around right here, in your home town."

His lips moved, and the eyes widened a fraction. Then, sighing, Rafi reluctantly began to fold up his work. "Maybe I should leave for the evening?"

Where was she heading, and why? She didn't know. "That's it, huh — when the going gets a little rough, get going." She leaned forward, whispered her words like a flame thrower. "Leave the lady alone when she gets crazy, right?" *But weren't you just proclaiming your sanity?*

"Don't put words in my mouth." He was half up now, on his haunches gathering stuff; inconvenienced, at least.

In his khaki shirt and shorts, visibly upset, he suddenly looked sensual to her.

"Well, shit," she uttered, finding a voice and force from some other Miriam, some other time, "if I found out you were fucking that South African number, I'd be pretty pissed. And would definitely let you know about it!"

"South African? What in the world —?"

"Oh come on, what's the difference whether it's an archaeology groupie or someone else, the big thing is the illicitness. You haven't been a goody-goody boy when you're away from me." She held up her hands. "I don't even want to know about it, or whether you do. But *if* I know, I'm gonna let you know about it, in no uncertain terms."

He shot her a look. "You know, sometimes it's a treat to live with you," he said, and after a moment he went to the sofa for his briefcase.

She stood with arms folded as he gathered his papers, maps, pamphlets, proofs, and proceeded to stuff them into his briefcase. Next he went to get his tobacco, his toiletry kit, and an overnight bag.

Oh Klee, she thought, you're right, all our plights are comic, and aquatic!

When Rafi returned, she walked over to him, grabbed the briefcase, and turned it upside down, dumping all the stuff out onto the floor. She faced him squarely.

His pale face flushed as he restrained himself, fighting an internal battle and (she thought) winning. Too bad.

She observed, "What are you going to do about the crazy lady, huh?"

He turned away; she grabbed his arm, hard; he said, "Cut it out now — enough!"

"Why? So you can run out with your tail between your legs? The idiom means —"

The words hit home somehow, and he slapped her once, twice. Stinging her, pleasing her. Oh, there was more in her man here than even *he* knew about!

She slapped him back, twice too. And for a fine, stunning moment they faced each other, she hurting and he furious — he furious for the first time she had ever witnessed — and this provoked in her a certain perverse gleam.

He shook his head in disbelief, fear, and turned to go off and let it all rest.

"Don't leave now," she suddenly implored, taking his arm gently. "It's getting good now. Honest."

He paused, shocked and bewildered again. "Are you really . . . going nuts?"

"No. But you're with me now, here and now, in the moment, connecting. Don't you see, you're not brushing me aside *casually*."

Oh yes, Paul, I'm in green space too, where it's lighter and better. "If I hurt you ever, don't stand by and *accept* it, with your feelings buried somewhere, suppressed. Step up and be with them, with me. I don't care if you take me down a few notches, or even sting me a little. Just don't turn off, go away, and be *passive*."

He didn't know what to say. His face looked more diaphanous than ever, revealing his boy's soul and goodness.

She ran her hand through his hair. Then she got down onto the floor and began to straighten the papers, books, galley tongues. She asked, "Should I put them back, or leave them out?"

Slowly he got down too and sorted them out alongside her. "Leave them out." He nodded, and confessed, "I guess I was hurting more than I knew — half knowing, half denying. Trying not to face the issue."

She had never heard him speak that way. And she was filled with the urge to tell him about Reggie, and maybe too about other friends; but this was countered by other urges, and she let these fill her and flow through. New emotion filled the spaces, and then she covered his face with kisses, his lips, forehead, neck, eyes, surprising him again. But when he tried to reciprocate, she held him off by setting herself within his arms and holding him. And stayed that way, hugging, for a good ten minutes.

Then she backed off, and began to tell him about her ordeal with Reggie, just like that. He eyed her with growing astonishment as she narrated. "I should have used you, I know, darling," she said, "but I didn't want to involve you. And Kelley did it all superbly. But . . . I should have informed you, dear. That way you could have held me, like now. Mmmm!" And what about her Montana? Her photographs? "Look, Klee has it right, doesn't he? I mean, all our troublesome unease and tragic moments and so on — all comic, right?"

She got him to look over his shoulder and up at the reproduction.

"You know, you're pretty difficult to keep up with," he murmured, "though I'm trying. Give me a few more years?"

The road going down to Hebron was narrow and winding, and Maya drove the small Morris as though it were a Coney Island bumper car. True, she did try to keep her distance from Israeli army or police vehicles, for fear of Arab bottles and bullets, which frequently fell astray and hit the vehicle behind the target. Gradually the road grew thicker with traffic as they descended from Jerusalem and sped through the small hillside villages. Gili, aged seven and a Salingeresque child, already a veteran of these Peace Now protests, calmly studied the flowers in her book.

A few miles this side of Hebron the line of traffic ceased to move altogether, and they were forced to leave the car and walk.

"Police roadblock, it seems," informed Rafi, "until they can straighten out matters with the local Arabs, approving all this."

"Looks like a big crowd this time," noted Gili, who had learned her English in the States where her social scientist mother took her sabbaticals.

"Why not?" asked Maya, holding Gili's hand. "Mrs. Levinger's recent rantings have become more and more provocative."

Dozens of Israeli vehicles, with blue plates, were lined up behind one another ("Just like in Godard" Miriam mused, to no one in particular), while from the opposite direction Arab vehicles were being passed through slowly, their passengers smiling and signaling the peace sign to the Jewish doves.

Clumps of protestors in shorts, sandals, and short-sleeved shirts milled about, chatted with soldiers, lounged, and read. It looked like a large family gathering rather than a protest.

Gili wandered off the road for more wildflowers, and Maya went after her.

In the dusty, dry air, Miriam asked Rafi, "How long will it last, do you figure?"

He shook his head resignedly, and uttered, "Who knows? You didn't leave your — oh, good. The cars are not safe anymore."

Up ahead another hundred feet a small group was being preached to by a bearded man wearing a black hat, standing on a small stone wall, and citing the Bible.

They walked closer, and Rafi listened in. Presently he explained, "He's religious, but on our side. He's reading from one of the prophets and showing how this so-called sacred land of Samaria is not sacred at all and was never given to the Jews by God, according to the Bible. Interesting."

As the preacher continued, he was shouted at by three fellows

wearing white shirts and hats and bearing rifles and Uzi submachine guns on their shoulders.

"What's up?" Miriam asked Rafi.

"Learn Hebrew. It's about time."

"Thanks. Now, what's up?"

"Your friends the Americans. At least, two of them are American. One of them is calling the fellow up there a traitor and a
blasphemer. He's pretty angry, too."

"Are you sure he's American?"

"Well, either American or Southern African. No one else has
accents that bad."

The argument quickly descended to bellowing intensity. Another
group of three men, one carrying a (religious) long-haired girl of
six or seven, entered the area, and they began another argument
with others in the outlying crowd.

"Settlers from Kiryat Arba?" she asked.

He nodded, and moved closer to the two arguing factions. She
moved behind him, sliding her hand upon his shoulder and feeling
the delicate shoulder blade.

One group, which Rafi attended to, was arguing in Hebrew,
and Miriam slid over to the smaller group, arguing heatedly in
English.

"If we follow you people and your stinking Labor," said the
American father, "we'll give *all* of Eretz Israel back to the Arabs,
not merely the pre-1967 territory. First it's the Sinai they want
back, and when they get that, then they can go back to being Jew-
haters publicly. Can you imagine what it would be like to give
back the pre-1967 territory? First the Golan Heights, yes? And
then the West Bank, yes? And then they can shoot their rockets
into Tel Aviv whenever they wish! You are naive and dangerous,
and we are fighting for your lives as much as our own!"

"Do me a favor, mister, don't fight for my life — I can fight for
it myself," retorted a slender fellow.

The American shifted the little girl and rejoined, "Do you know
any Yiddish? Bist du meshuga — all of you!"

"Ich forstei seir gut," said the Israeli fellow. "My parents died
in Auschwitz. But I still believe in peace over territory. Law instead
of lawlessness."

"And I suppose that includes Arab rights as well?" The question was put sardonically.

"Yes, that is right, mister. The law applies to one and all, not merely to those you prefer it to apply to."

In a raised voice the man said, "Your greatest trouble is that you are not Jews, holy Jews. You, all of you" — and he waved his arms — "have lost God. *Im eshkachach Yerushalayim!* You have forgotten your original vows to *Adonai* to keep his covenant! Don't lie — you never attend shul, you never open the Bible, your children grow up like goyim right here in Eretz Israel! A *shande!*"

"Mister, how long have you been in this country, if I may ask?"

The American waved his hand in disgust at the question.

"Excuse me, but I have fought in two wars now. Do I not have a right to believe as I wish? About religion, politics, Arabs? Tell me, do I not?"

"You must be a kibbutznik, I can tell from everything about you! Someone who has sold his soul to communism! Meshugana! Thank God you are losing your power in this country, with the young too! King Begin knows the political tricks you have pulled on the rest of the country, and you're finished! And if you think that —"

Suddenly fury broke out nearby; punches were thrown, bodies were flung down, voices dropped to grunts of force. And there was Rafi, trying to bear-hug a settler in order to keep him out of the battle. Instead he was cracked hard in the face and temple, which made Miriam wince. She tried to get to him, tripped over a leg, and fell forward, just missing a boulder and breaking her fall with her arms. There were tears in her eyes and dust in her mouth, and tiny pebbles before her. Gasping, she looked up and saw that the police had moved in, and soon she was being lifted up by a young soldier, who asked in Hebrew if she was all right. She nodded and uttered, "Thank you," gathering her senses and looking around. She spotted Rafi sitting by a boulder, attended by two others, and she ran to him.

"Oh my!" she exclaimed softly, seeing blood trickling from his brow — the first time she had ever seen him bloodied. Crouching, she saw the gash above his eyebrow, now being washed by a middle-aged man. "Are you okay?"

He smiled wanly. "Look, it's the only way I get to see Shmuelig again," indicating the stout army medic dressing the cut. "We were in Africa together in 'sixty-seven, the same reserve unit, and always threatened to visit each other. So now we have."

The heavy-lidded man looked up at her. "A strange sense of humor he still has, I see. In all the wars you never get a scratch, so it was time for you to get wounded, yes?"

"Of course."

Interrupting their grotesque humor, she asked, "Is he, it, all right?"

"No boxing this week, I'm afraid. Otherwise he'll live and do fine. Superficial cut. The religious have very weak aim, thank God."

Later that day they sat on the terraced hillside of an Arab farm that had been raided by the Gush Emunim settlers the week before, and enjoyed the afternoon festivities. Songs, speeches (by Peace Now Israelis and the Arab farmers), and communal feeling swept the day, as the vineyards were repaired and new plants were laid by the children, Gili included. The day was soft and sultry, the color of the hills California brown, and Miriam was reminded momentarily of the high feelings flown at the old Vietnam protests in Cambridge and Washington. Save for the sight of the new stone settlements a mile or so away, homes of the new zealots, who would be back, no doubt, to wreak their fervent destructiveness.

While the songs, including "We Shall Overcome," flowed, and Rafi was visited like a wounded war veteran, she allowed her thoughts to drift. Fights between Jews and Jews, political and religious battles waged with real blows, shocked her, and filled her with profound dismay. Was what she had seen on the road to be the future: Jews with guns on their arms coming after other Jews because of a difference in political and moral belief? Fanatics of recent immigration who were making up their own laws and were funded by the government? It was like America's giving in to a bunch of loony fundamentalists and helping them secure arms. If it dismayed her, what about her man here, whose butterfly bandage spoke for itself? It was his dream they were ripping apart, his ideals they were mutilating.

A kite was lifted into the azure sky as the crowd cheered, and

Miriam wondered if the whole fucking world was turning into one hot rotation of violence. A contagion was going from state to state. Would her kids grow up into the same sort of adults, in whom violent impulses were just there at the surface, a natural reaction to dilemmas? And were the Israelis at it now, just like the Americans? Oh fuck. What an age!

"Will any of this mean *anything* to the settlers, or to this government?"

Smoking, Rafi answered, "Probably not. It's just a nuisance thing. Until some people — Jews, I mean — are killed, by other Jews, and then maybe something will be . . . understood. *Maybe.*"

"How's the eye?"

"It's felt better. What do you call that black swelling?"

"Huh? A shiner?"

"Yes. I will have one probably."

"Jon might take you for a hero then."

"And not you? My effort's been wasted, you mean?"

Evening: home, peaceful. Thank God. Back to the kibbutz in one piece. A day of morning injury and afternoon festivity.

Eating Rachel's mandelbrot — cookie slices with raisins and nuts — with her tea, she went through the packet of mail that had arrived that day. An electric bill (which was supposed to have been intercepted); a note from Rosie; two postcards from traveling friends, one from Kelley in Bali; and a letter from Angola, Louisiana. Who the hell? She opened it. The handwriting was especially studied, a penmanship of fine loops and upright *t*'s beneath a simple blue border and the words *Louisiana State Penitentiary.*

Hi Miss Miriam,

I may have been out of touch for a while you know but not for always. No sir. Its taken me a while to kind of get my head and thought together to figure out just *who* was the pal that played this *bad* practical joke on me. And you had me fooled, I got to confess. I had in mind several other working girls turned canary before I came round to you all, sugar. Well, after some inquiries I figure now how youre *one shrewd jezebel.* Yeah, youre in my future now once and for all, and I sure promise you that. To your credit I *really* under estimated you, even though I knew you was special like that very first night in the Cambridge park years ago, when we first got it on together. I guess I didn't listen to myself close enough.

Well I also got some hard news for you — it looks like Im going to be transferred back up your way soon now, maybe next spring. One of those Mass State prisons, on another phony charge. Why dont you visit me sometime and we can renew our friendship, maybe even put it on a higher plane? I hear that the Mass minimum securities are a picnic after Angola, which is one bad house. My Legal Head informs me that in another 9 months too Im eligible for parole, and then me and you are going to form a team. What do you think? Since youre really just as cunning as me, why not hang tight, real tight? And you can teach me some proper English writing and reading, huh?

Oh yeah, I never helped or aksessoried no one to rob a bank in my life — but truth dont mean dick in a kangaroo court with bought witnesses. But thats all right, whats past is past. Im cool now.

Your Devoted Friend,
Reginald DuPres, Jr.

A bull's-eye — a missive straight from Louisiana to her doorstep in the southern Negev. Stunning, wasn't it? Her brain scrambled as she poured more hot tea. Here was a delayed payment for her risky folly. She had imagined wrongly and naively again; it had not been a crude beating and a breaking of legs, Hollywood-style, but a legal put-away, nice and clean. No sir, there would be no dirt under the fingernails of the modern tough guys; they were more sophisticated and less melodramatic nowadays. So, what now?

"I asked you, any *news*?" Rafi was looking at her inquiringly.

"Oh, sorry. Sort of. Just something to think on a bit. Nothing immediate." That was true, too; the letter was dated July, and she had almost a whole year in which to worry seriously. Lots could be done, a lifetime lived . . . Should she return to the North End and Gentleman Nick? Try that Scotland Yard cast-off, to find more information (and maybe let him sell her out once again)? Take Reggie's suggestion and visit him regularly in the clink, with a baby Leica? Or even buy a revolver and attend one of the popular new vigilante schools for homeowner protection? Oh well. Why not have Rafi here teach her to shoot straight?

"Don't I get any sympathy for this 'shin*er*'?" he called.

She turned to him and saw that he was in bed now, balancing an ice pack. "You're mastering the idiom," she said, and she put away her letter and went to him. "Here, let me hold the ice on your eye for a while; you lie back and rest. Maybe I can even read to us a little."

"Aaah, now I feel more like an Israeli soldier. When do I get to repay this medical aid?"

"When next *I* get the shin*er*," she rejoined, reaching for Hardy, her mind far away.

13

THE show was in two parts, two places, with two audiences.

In her apartment at the kibbutz, she arranged the chairs in the living room so she and Rafi could have coffee and viewing after breakfast.

"Go on, read your highbrow newspaper," she said, referring to his *Ha'aretz*. "I have my own materials." And she held up her United Farm and Strout catalogues.

"What are those?" Browsing in them, he began to smile coquettishly. "So you're becoming a Thoreau woman at last. Don't get any milking animals, or I won't cooperate."

Munching long rolls with her coffee, she looked through advertisements for country properties in Maine and New Hampshire (cheaper than Vermont). Something with an old barn for a darkroom and workshop, if possible. Most of the prices were high, but here and there a farm in the thirties or low forties turned up. Towns like Limerick and Denmark and Belfast in Maine, or New Hampshire's Wentworth and Strafford and Rumney; center-chimney Capes, rambling farmhouses with ells, Colonials needing restoration; rolling hills, hardwood lots, open meadows, Class 4 roads leading to hilltop seclusion. The names and descriptions relaxed and cheered her.

Rafi had finished his eggs and was ready for a second on coffee when she invited him into the living room. Suspicious, he stood up, and she took his mug.

The small room was alive with light, and the rows of photographs, hung on three walls, looked neat and orderly. Some were in wooden frames; others were simply held by metal clips on white backing. There were rows of pictures on one wall, clusters on another, color photos on a third.

"Have a seat, won't you?" she offered, properly. He took one, but only for a minute. Then he was up and prowling, looking.

She poured more coffee for them and perched herself on her wooden stool. He had always taken her work seriously, and she loved him for that. A contrast to snide Stan. She found herself scratching at her knees, a sure sign of muted excitement. Jesus.

He walked back and forth, stopped here and there, sipped his coffee. Was he pretending to be a Critic? He spoke intermittently. "Never knew avocados could look so different . . . These — Negev rock formations? Where did you find such a little Jewish Stonehenge? . . . Well, well. The kibbutzniks may not be up for so much realism in their portraits." Smiling broadly. "My favorites are these still lifes of eggs and bananas." After fifteen minutes, he summed up: "You know, I've seen these pictures at various times, but all together like this they make an impression. A considerable impression."

She sat on her perch and let his appreciation flow around her, bathing her like the sunlight warming the walls. Let Reggie write all the letters he wished, from behind bars!

Rafi sat back down in the armchair, crossed his legs, and looked on, drinking coffee and lighting his first pipe of the day. The early light was just right; in a few hours the sun would be too blazing.

"Some of these go way back, don't they?" he noted. "I must say, you *hide* your work well. A few pictures on the wall and that's it. One gets no sense of . . . *all* of this." He smiled, shaking his head. "Behind my back you're full of secrets, aren't you?"

She fed on his impressions, his admiration. He was still talking, and she saw no need to tell him of the other pictures, another hundred — more private ones perhaps — awaiting her back in Cambridge. *Accomplishment.* She felt new fondness for the noun and its resonance. In fact, as she rolled it over in her mind she saw that it had become perhaps her favorite word in the language, for it stood for what you yourself put in, from yourself only — without the aid of colleagues, friends, or the official offices of the art world. In the end, despite personality, despite circumstance, despite betrayal and distraction, even despite sons and illnesses and pain, you accomplished or you didn't. And here, in thirty-five selected black-and-whites and a dozen color pictures, were the surest emblems of her effort, her health. Of her making, they were the making of her.

"You didn't hear me, did you?"

She shook her head, touching his arm in apology.

"Would you like me to put some of these in the kibbutz gallery?"

The thought struck her as odd now, strangely enough, and she said she'd think on it. "Maybe after I've left," she offered. "But maybe not."

She was explaining about abstraction through color when a knock at the apartment door interrupted her. The door thrust open before she could get out of the living room.

"Hi, anyone up yet?"

She met Yani in the kitchen. He wore a J. Geils Band T-shirt and shorts and sneakers, and his Swiss friend, Heidi, stood alongside in a painter's cap, khaki shorts, plain eyeglasses. A kibbutznik couple in embryo.

"Hey what're you guys up to?"

No, she didn't want him there just now, interrupting the quiet, secluded show. "Just a quiet Saturday morning," she retorted, blocking the door to the living room casually.

At first he was disconcerted by her stiffness. "Well, what I really wanted to tell ya was that we were gonna go up to Tel Aviv for a softball game, if that's okay. There's a car leaving at nine-thirty. Please, Mom, huh?" This was his first request since he had been grounded after an episode of a few weeks ago, and hence his care.

She turned to the girl. "Do you play too?" She shook her head.

The poised young woman replied, "I once saw baseball at Shea Stadium. I don't mind it, you know."

Oh, Miriam liked her. Cool and worldly and kind, she thought. "Well, sometime you'll have to see a good team play. Have a good time, both of you." Looking at Jon, she added, "See you later, right?"

"Thanks, Mom." Acknowledging her look, he said, "Right, for sure," and pulled Heidi from the room.

When the door closed, she returned to her stool in the living room.

"What'll he do without her when he leaves?" Rafi asked, half in jest.

"Survive, I imagine. And go back to Commonwealth girls."

"Or," he speculated, tapping the bowl of his pipe, "she can join him, I suppose. To see the Red Sox play, of course."

Miriam warned him with her forefinger, playfully. Not yet sixteen, was Jon really ready for Heidi, a veteran of three continents and how many boyfriends? Why not?

Gradually she returned to the quiet room, the private showing. Sipping more coffee, she felt thrilled with the simplicity, the clarity, the production of the photos. The morning light splashed the room with whiteness, and she wrapped herself in the light and the silence like a caterpillar making its cocoon. Birds trilled outside, providing morning music. She felt the show's *purity* this way, just herself and her photographs and her dearest friend. Oh, at some point the sharks and plankton and parasites might have their bites and nibbles, but later on. For now, she would concentrate on what she had been up to out here these past several years. And in fruit and vegetables, mountain faces and Jewish faces, jacaranda and dolmens, she saw again that she had been up to calmness, clarity, and beauty. (She had kept off these walls her pictures of Rafi the nude; too startling for the model as viewer, just now.) She had been putting herself together again, defying all the king's men, and some of the movement's women too, who would have kept her in pieces. And she would be *whole,* somehow.

"Okay, you've had enough," she ordered. "Go back to *Ha'aretz.* I'll sit here a while and join you soon. Go ahead."

He raised his eyebrows, saw she was serious, got up and moved out. But in a minute he returned to surprise her with a coffee fill-up. "They're first-rate photographs. And when you're not sitting guard, I'll look in again."

She kissed his smooth cheek, and when he had gone outside, she grew restless and walked up and back in the smallish room, not a guard but a general inspecting her troops. And these troops, her loyal platoon of photographs, looked strong, self-sufficient, honorable. Yes, her show here, for her audience of two, was a success, and she felt quietly elated. And felt too so different from when she had had those shows in public, where she, Miriam, was on exhibit as much as or more than the work. Oh, she was on exhibit here too, but in terms of angle selected, light measured, negative developed, composition designed, not in categories of which lover she had that year, what opinion she held on a political question, what role she played as a Cambridge children-raiser. These pictures were objects in and of themselves — kites free-floating in the sky, attached to her by private, strong string. She had made a serious error in going along passively with the tradition of showing up in person at her shows. Never again, she counseled herself. Never again.

Ambling about, she considered the photos — the jacaranda in bloom in black and white actually was an improvement on gaudy nature *and* her own gaudy color photos (no, she was not yet up to Meyerowitz) — and then sat back down and went over the pictures carefully, making notes on technical matters as much as aesthetic questions. (Use eight-by-ten negatives, view camera, different paper. More grainy daguerreotype texture? new silver-iron process?) She tried to recall precisely the photos back home, in private and public collections. After another forty-five minutes with her gallery, and her gallery of thoughts, she released herself and joined Rafi out on the back porch.

"So, how should we celebrate?" he asked.

"Hmm . . . how about a quiet day, just you and me — a swim, a walk, bicycle ride, whatever."

"Oh, we can improve on that. I know — dinner at an old restaurant, where I haven't been for years. No protests; I decide. Just sign here."

She accepted his Shaeffer fountain pen, signed his newspaper contract for the day, and had the best show celebration she had ever had. After a lazy time of swimming and reading, they made the long drive to Tel Aviv to dine at his old hangout, a boisterous place run by Yemenites in a rundown section of the city that steamed with Renaissance life — soldiers, whores, police, businessmen and their wives, dark-skinned families. The food was spicy and excellent. And for a special treat they walked the old narrow streets down to the sands of the Mediterranean, where Rafi told her about the old town built on the dunes in the 1920s and its eventual overrun by high-rise hotels and glittering misadventures. "The building contractors and *machers* have turned the labor-socialist dream into a second-class Miami Beach. It used to be a lovely small town, where you could make out with your girlfriend under that boardwalk and never be afraid of thugs. Let's go."

The late-night walk stayed with her while they drove back, the sea and the sands and the memories breaking redolently upon her imagination that night in the desert, and in the next days and nights, her last of the summer in Israel. The carnival of Dizengoff Street and the mysterious night air of the Mediterranean resonated in her senses as she traveled back through the time zones in the sky toward home. Slowly, that adventurous land receded in her consciousness, became almost like an ancient drama, a sun-baked fiction, as her mind was propelled back to Cambridge, back to Gray Fact . . . but the first part of her show stayed with her, re-plenishing her.

Sitting in her apartment again, in the middle of September, she looked back upon that sliver of land and its pressured citizenry as if a dream, a sensuous Jewish fantasy, alongside this easy-going native territory. Irony, paradox? Sure. But she couldn't resist that proposition or intuition, namely, that Israel was fantasy and America was reality, and further, she wanted more of that mix in her life. Drinking her Irish whisky and remembering, she felt she needed that fantasy-stuff now, needed dreams and gossamer memories, palm trees and kindly ghosts, soft night air and safe feelings, here in hardboiled Cambridge. That was all the more reason for con-ducting the second part of the show just the way she had planned. For a few odd days she sat and moped, her baggage unopened; a bereaved stranger in her own town and apartment, seek-ing . . . belonging? Even Jon, an adaptable world traveler now, seemed to miss the place as if he had visited the same dream. He expressed this not in words but in subtle gestures; he was slower with his sarcasm and slang, slower moving about, slower to reach for his containers of milk.

On the third day he confessed, "It's kind of a bummer being home, isn't it?"

What could she say? She called him to her and rubbed his hair and said it needed washing badly.

And when he rejoined, "Huh?" she accepted that as acceptance — as wanting, even — and took him into the bathroom and washed it for him. Running her hands through that thick mop, which would stand up this way and that no matter how he tried to tame it, she soaped and lathered with delicious instinct, her fingers working her way to his scalp and to her vital attachment again. Massaging and kneading, she knew that his wild run away to the Berkshires — and later, for overnight in Israel — was part and parcel of this boy, this knotty relationship. At one point he yelled, "Hey, Mom, watch it, will ya!" and she kissed his neck and told him that that was nothing to what she could *really* do. "Oh yeah? Just you try!" he mumbled, water dripping down his face. And as she labored here, she felt high with her work project over there, seeing the discernible shape of the show clearly, once again getting inspiration during moments of distraction. A "Chee-sus!" recalled her to him, and she squeezed his bony frame and told him to hold still, for God's sake, it would be over in a minute. One whole splendid minute more.

It took three weeks to arrange this part, but by the end of the month she had done it.

A late-summer night — September at its best, the breeze soft and aromatic, the season filled with anticipation. She dressed for the occasion, wearing a necktie, a shirtwaist with Eton collar, a suede vest, and a long skirt with high boots. A Victorian Miriam, ready for a Fabian Society meeting perhaps.

She sat in the studio in the worn armchair, enjoying her bagel, cream cheese and smoked salmon, and sipping chablis. She was alone here at night, with her floods and spots. On the white walls were the rest of her pictures, crowded in clusters and series, fighting for space. Around her she had arranged a horseshoe of chairs for the invited guests, and two bottles of white wine. She had inserted a cassette with a Bach cantata on one side and jazz by Teddy Wilson, Johnny Hodges, Billie Holiday on the other. Her gaze followed the photographs: the ancient, secondhand relics of Judaica, the discarded mezuzah in a wood frame, the broken tombstone from the Truro cemetery, the broken brass menorah, the quizzical face of the refugee shammes Viktor . . . the fey boy-models from Arizona, and the torn photographs of her brown pimp . . . Harry's teenybopper groupies with their roller skates and satin shorts and Walkman earphones, listening to the Eagles and doing their homework — pictures of Irish pug noses and cute little behinds and Cokes with straws . . . then the doped-up or schizy adolescents, the deserted girl in Brigham's, the boy flying high on Lexington Green, Jon's spaced-out friend in the Berkshire jail . . . deserted schoolyards at dusk and deserted cities of the Nabateans, lunar landscapes of yesteryear and concrete dreams of today . . .

In the adjoining room, partitioned off, she had arranged her Private Studies: in one area, the group of photos of herself in disheveled melancholy, in grievous pain . . . cheeks hollowed out, eyes dilated, hair wild like a porcupine — small black-and-whites of human disorder. In the second, those pictures of her men — Harry, Dr. Beaumont, Rafi — that series of clean, well-lighted nudes, men she knew and men she transformed, male intimacy revealed in layers of light and angle. Would this series ever see the light of day, of public display? Hardly. There was no need, anyway. They were fine, very fine, just this way, she assessed. Would Dorothea L. or Weston agree? she wondered.

Now all this imagery flowed in and around her, in the bright artificial light, and she drank her wine and followed the tenor singing the cantata and felt pleased, deeply pleased.

Here, in solitariness, in her old studio, she would have her own private show and her own private audience. In solitariness and silence and willful fantasy, aided by wine only, she'd gain her revenge against the betrayal of nine years ago at the Boston City Hall Museum, where the respectable citizens and critics had ganged up on her photographs and taken all the fun and pleasure out of the night, and her life. Now she'd go it alone, fly solipsistic, with her new work. Art deserved a room of grand folly as much as any grand museum.

Going on to her second glass of wine, she was ready when the guests finally began to arrive in her mind, one at a time, conveniently.

First came Montana, dressed in tan suit and necktie and looking like a long-stemmed rose, gangly and slope-shouldered, and as he came toward her Miriam pointed him in the other direction, toward the photos. He shrugged awkwardly, and she gave him a look that said, "Go ahead, don't be so damned shy. See what you think of them; they won't bite." Heeding her at last, he ambled about, peering at the photographs and moving from wall to wall. Then he walked to her, lit a cigarette, and said, "I don't know really what to say. The ones of the kids are terrifying. And who is that black character, pieced together?" She encouraged him to sit down beside her and stay, even though he wanted to leave; he was restless. "I'm an amateur, remember that, but these strike me as . . . unusual photographs. Maybe something like paintings?"

Avery Brody was short, stocky, balding. Her teacher at MIT once upon a time, he was a cantankerous, hard-to-please aesthete who knew as much about photographs as there was to know. Sometimes he was an exquisite photographer himself. Vain as an actor, he furtively slipped on horn-rims and proceeded to move across the room, looking from near and far, from various angles, and using a magnifying glass at several points — the pedant! Miriam sat fidgeting, nervous as a virgin, seeking refuge in a third glass of wine while her old mentor roamed, examined, and inspected. At last he approached her; his voice was a kind of low growl as he assessed the damage. "The pictures of the kids — excellent composition. The Jewish objects — on the sentimental side, but very nice lighting and exposure. The pretty-boy pimp — the profiles are effective; when you're fronting him, you've got studio portraits. The close-ups of the desert ruins — solid overall technique. Successful shots. As for the dopers — a bit sensational, I fear; you've fallen for them somewhat. There's no need. They take dope; they're dopers, period. They get clap because they're stupid; they come prematurely. Those are the facts; don't fudge them. You border on romanticism in those shots. A different angle and you might have protected your feelings more. Subjectivity is not the same as force of personality; one is indulgence, the other can be art. Now, am I done?"

What could she say?

"Is it . . . ?" She stumbled about. "Are they a success?"

Showing bad teeth as he half smiled, the tough-guy critic ad-

mitted, "You're on the right track. That's the main thing. Keep it up; keep right on going."

She was heartened! "Stay awhile, won't you?"

He protested slightly, took a glass of water, and retired to a corner.

Next entered a curious pair, Kelley and Harry. They had met before and had bumped into each other on the way upstairs, it seemed. Kelley held Harry's arm and bowed with deference to Miry, who laughed. She was dressed in an outrageous Chinese green dress, slit right up to the crotch and barely containing her full bosom. Harry was Harry, wearing a Levi's jacket and jeans and his cowboy boots; he was two inches shorter than his escort.

"Do we have to listen to that Lawrence Welk while we're looking around?" Kelley asked.

Miriam smiled. "Bach is not exactly Welk. Besides, it's about time you developed some musical taste." The hefty girl shook her head in dismay and took Harry away.

Miriam held up her glass, poured some wine, and stared through the pale gold liquid at her volatile red-haired pal, a gaudy figure in green, beginning to waver. Would she soon strip-dance like Rita Hayworth in Gilda? For a moment she thought she saw Reggie DuPres, in his place on the wall, slowly wink at her from beneath his Panama hat.

In a little while Kelley approached her again and said, "Now that's music I can move to," referring to the jazz that was now playing. "Honeychile, you got an eye for this world. You got an instinct for the different. Every time I think I know where you're coming from, bang! you're into something new. And those spaced-out kids — oh, I'm glad you're not out my way, in Venice or Malibu, to catch that action. You'd never stop going, bzzzzzz! And I don't know if you'd live through it. As for those pretty mannequins, they blow my mind. Those little horny cocksuckers, wasting their succulent flesh on men. Filthy. And you know what else I really was sucked up by? That old Jewish guy and those other old Jewish things. Looonely-looking critters, like old cowboys with character." She kissed and hugged Miriam, who almost fell out of her chair from the hug. "At forty, I should be so alive. Hold on, look who I see." She moved off toward someone. "Let me say hello for a min."

Now Harry was sidling up to Miriam. "Okay, a little on the virtuous side, maybe, after the last show. But you did it. You stayed right on, through the muck and abuse and breakdown, and beat the odds. Yeah, don't look so surprised. Jimmy the Greek was laying nine to five you wouldn't make it back. Two to one, even. He saw your condition, as we all did; you were down and out, kid. And not in Paris in the thirties, where it was glamorous, but in Cambridge City and McLean's, where it's hell." He took her by the shoulders and looked at her through his wire-rim eyeglasses. "They're good photos. Real production. How good they are ultimately, who knows? None of us, for sure. But you did it, you produced, you photographed, you fucked 'em all. So that's the ticket. And as for your using your own life here and there, good for you. If you're not entitled to such material, who is?" He tapped her playfully on the chin.

Oh, he made her feel good and warm all over!

Now a strange lady, whom Miriam faintly recognized but couldn't place, appeared, confusing her. The woman was in her forties, dressed in a tailored suit from the 1930s and a simple white blouse with oversize buttons, and smoking. Her profile showed a large nose, sensual lips, smooth skin; the hair was cut short and was combed to one side; a wool beret provided a cozy Bohemian air. She smoked and strolled leisurely, though her eyes were intent on the pictures. Miriam leaned forward involuntarily, trying to pierce the mystery. Who was she? At one point the woman turned toward Miriam and indicated the portraits of the sad teenagers derailed by dope. She nodded slowly in approval before moving on. Miriam saw the thick legs and low heels and then noticed what she took to be an old-fashioned box camera, a four-by-five perhaps, in a bag slung across the woman's shoulders. By now the woman had paused and seemed to be taking notes, writing on a pad. Several people brushed by her, but she took no notice. Finally she walked toward Miriam, smiled, and put an envelope into Miriam's hand; and then somehow she disappeared. Surprised, Miriam opened the note and read in small, clear handwriting several points of critique. The last struck her most: "Don't sacrifice content for form. There is no substitute for truth in photography, as there is none for truth in art. Formal beauty by and for itself is a cruel modern deception. At times you seem to forget this." No name, just the initials "D. L."

Excited, Miriam searched for the woman, one of her first heroes — Dorothea Lange. Where was she? Miriam spotted her chatting with Avery Brody, and she went to the pair and motioned to the partitioned room. Here, apart, she showed them the reserved series of pictures — first the wall of Miriam during her days of psychic deluge: nudes, seminudes, hospital-gown portraits. Even Miriam herself found it hard to look at this wall, as if this were not she up there but some other Miriam, some deeply distressed creature. The hollow stare, the self-punishment in the emaciated torso, the incoherence showing in the wild hair; Miriam turned to fiddle with spare prints while the hero and the teacher looked, studied, assessed.

Dorothea spoke first, in her neutral California tones. "In my time, of course, this sort of portraiture, using the self this way as a model, was rather unusual. For a woman especially. I doubt whether I could do it now even. That they are striking poses and compositions, I have no doubt. Perhaps too striking, once you know the photographer. Yet there is an undeniable honesty here, along with technical discipline and know-how. And without honesty and discipline, pictures don't interest me. Also, strictly from a woman's point of view, this is an arresting series. I have one major criticism, however, and surely it is a sign of the times I grew up in and the values I've always held. I worry whether there isn't a surfeit of self here, to the exclusion of social reality. You see, I still have the Depression in my blood, and the poor and downtrodden remain important to me. Which is all the more reason I'm glad I saw those other photographs first." She took Miriam's arm. "Thank you for inviting me."

Avery Brody walked over and began lecturing on and judging the male nudes. "I actually prefer these. The compositions are more finely detailed, the selection more natural; here the object has indeed found the subject. The sense of presence is firm, and I admire the innocence of the eye; very nicely done. Where you disappoint is in your previsualization discipline. You understand *what I refer to? Good. I rate you highly on your concept of experience, but only fair on essence. But that is always difficult to achieve. You've not quite managed to transform the object fully into subject yet. But most important, perhaps, I feel that the poetic is developing in your work. And this is the triumph of the show. You're reaching out now for the lyric as well as the realistic, and for me this reaching is a serious development."* He nodded abruptly, the report card completed, and disappeared.

In a daze, somewhat overwhelmed by her imagined audience, Miriam walked back into the main room. But her sense of excitement, of elation, was short-lived. The next guest approached. *What the hell was he doing here? How . . .* A gaunt, tall figure with a bushy gray mustache and eyes hiding behind sleepy lids; wearing his ragged suede jacket. *Oh, he was handsome, Dad.* He walked about with his lengthy strides, his anatomy awkward — *God, the resemblances to Montana were embarrassing now! Had Montana preferred suede to formal jackets, corduroy to silk at one point? How the doubles turned up in your life, to replace the originals, and you were attracted instinctively, without knowing it!*

Her father walked about, furtively nipping his bourbon from a flask, his refuge from frustration and wife. Miry cried momentarily, then sat up like a good big girl. She guzzled wine and waited while he moseyed about, his rail-thin frame leaning.

"Hello, Cheery, how are you?" He angled down to her like a large bird, and used that ancient nickname. "You're not doing too badly for an old tomboy, are you? These are good photographs, and you look good too. Has the world taken to treating you okay? It's about time. My favorites, by the way, are those strange mountain formations. They look like nothing I've ever seen. Well, maybe in the Badlands a little. Yeah. Done beautifully, Cheery. Keep it up — a deal?"

The low, gravelly voice, the emerging hazel eyes, the unmistakable look of failure froze her. Then he was gone, leaving a physical absence that was filled with his spirit and her emotions.

Her elegiac reverie was broken by scattered applause, and when she turned about, the guests were clapping for her like a chamber-music audience after a performance.

This lasted for a few minutes only, however; an older lady

*wearing a fur stole burst through the door and started to berate
Miriam. "You shouldn't be wasting your time, young lady. This
so-called work brings in no money. You should be out holding
down a job and taking care of your responsibilities. You have
children to raise and an apartment to keep up. Not to mention
your own needs; when are you going to get some up-to-date,
feminine clothes? Look at the way you're dressed — like a man,
at your own show! And one other thing, which I know you'd
rather not think about." Like a prosecuting attorney cross-
examining a witness, she leaned forward and wagged her finger.
"When are you going to get married again? You really can't expect
to go on this way, alone in life, with no regular father for your
children. It doesn't look good, and it isn't good. Where is your
security? Really, young lady, are these pictures necessary? Especially those . . . dirty ones?" She grabbed her stepdaughter's hair
and yanked, like she had when Miriam was eleven!*

Miriam was stunned and told Sylvia politely to leave the studio.

*"You remember what I said, young lady, just remember. I say
it for your own good."*

*Miry breathed deeply, went to the window and opened it. The
primitive — would she ever escape it? Did one ever escape one's
embattled youth and the imprints of claws? Does that stuff emerge
in fantasy as in dreams, unwanted and uninvited? But here, at her
show? She felt confused, betrayed — by herself!*

*Just then a good-looking, stylish woman entered. She took a
quick turn around the studio and then presented herself in front
of Miry, hands on hips, cigarette dangling, smoke curling up into
Miriam's face. She produced a manila envelope. "I have the real
pictures — the ones showing your ethical side, you know. You
low-down bitch, hiding behind those pretty pictures up there.
Through all that fruit-bullshit. Through those adolescents you exploit. Well, sister, I have all the evidence here, for your friends to
see. They can view another side of you. The less aesthetic side,
say." She removed eight-by-ten blowups from the envelope and
held them up. "C'mon, see the artist at work, not her phony
photos. You cheap hustler! Petending to be Little Miss Muffet
eating her curds and whey. Sister, you're more like Linda Lovelace
eating something else. And" — her blue eyes blazed — "here's the*

*evidence." She called to the group to see the explicit photographs,
but no one bothered. Only Harry and Kelley came over, to escort
the lady out.*

*The display cut Miriam, exposing her guilt in a bewildering
way.*

*She finished off her glass and poured herself yet another, seeing
that the first bottle was gone now and she was starting the second.
Unsteady, she shifted in the armchair . . . Take it easy; so you have
your detractors. You can't please everyone. You're not running
for governor, or Woman of the Year. So cool it . . .*

*Intruding upon that cool, however, was a strange whirring sound,
and a motorized wheelchair rolled into the room. Sitting there at
the controls was her old antagonist, the hunter Reggie. He wore
a buckskin jacket over a burgundy silk shirt, a gold medallion at
the neck, and his old leather bad-man hat that he had worn on
the Cambridge Common. He smiled his menacing white smile
framed by the glistening cinnamon skin; his gaze fixed hers, and
she couldn't turn away. He caressed a baseball bat lying across
his immobile legs. And she sensed that there was no end to her
being pursued, even in victory; that undeserved guilt was as wounding
as bloody defeat; and that for some, it was better to lose than to
win. He motored to her, somehow found the nape of her neck
with his strong grip, and drawled, "Did ya think you'd ever lose
me, Miss Miriam? Shit." He grinned a great grin of triumph, and
she felt his urgent anger. He directed her to go to a wall and
ordered her to bring over four pictures, favorites, of fruit. "Now
looky here, my chickadee," he said, and he smashed the frames
and shredded the pictures. "Now, get onto your knees," he ordered. "Go on!" And she, terrified, did as he said. "Now you just
stay there, waitin', expectin', dig?" He smiled beautifully, then
opened his trousers and released his member, a long, uncircumsized
arrow. "Mess with me will ya? Now watch, watch closely!" and
he proceeded to urinate over the torn photographs. Pools of yellow
formed over her beautiful, ripped work.*

Her head reeled, and she felt weak in her knees, shaky.

*And she must have passed out, for when she awoke Reggie was
gone, though the damage was not. Jesus. What now? she wondered. Jesus. She'd clean it up tomorrow — if it still existed then.*

She raised herself to the chair, stumbled up from that too, and found herself walking out the door, through the hall, up the stairway to the roof. She opened the door and weaved onto the roof, feeling the fresh air press her hot face, dazed head. She heard faraway sounds, took in the air, saw the lights of Boston like a sea of lighted ships. Returned to her studio and fell into her chair, exhausted ...

A rattling of the door. Someone approaching. No help for it now; she was helpless. Let him do what he wants.

Strangely, the door was unlocked. A familiar face. Harry, shaking his head kindly. Reaching down for her and lifting her up gently.

"What in the world?" He looked around, open-mouthed. "Okay, you sit back down, you goose. Let me clear the decks a bit, and we'll escort you home. Wow, look at all this stuff — who'd you hang it for? When's the opening? Why didn't you tell me?"

She sat and watched him wiping the floor, picking up debris, moving bottles in slow motion. Real or imagined or ... ? Feeling protected now, in her helplessness, she asked, "How ... how'd you know I was here? What time is it?"

"Who spilled all this wine? Christ, did you really drink ... ?" He laughed (not scolded, she thought). "I stopped by the apartment for a nightcap — wanted to hear about your summer — and Jon told me you had gone over to the studio. I waited around for an hour, and when you didn't show up, I thought I'd check you out here. Lucky you left me a key for the summer, or I'd have been stuck downstairs." He finished up his cleaning and straightening act; deep down, he always loved pleasing her, she knew. "Now, let's get you back home, kiddo. Come on, it's after midnight, late for early-rising mothers."

She felt herself lifted up, somehow borne downstairs, and then set up high into Harry's truck. Oh, it was like being launched in a dream as they fired off and away. One of her men had come to her rescue again. (Was it the right one? Did that make a difference?) Now, in the drizzling night, she tried to focus, but the windshield mingled with the street. Oh dear! She really had tied one on!

"Didn't know you were a drinker," he observed, and patted her leg in approval. "Good for you. Teetotaling Jewish girls remind me of lewd Baptist ministers, for some reason."

And she considered the fact: herself drunk. It sort of shocked her. But it secretly pleased her too. What never happened was happening. The steady swatting of the wipers beat against the windshield and her head.

Harry at first drove without talking, letting her be. Soon she was feeling high and fine in the truck cab, watching the traffic lights reflecting red and green on pools of water at corners.

"Well," he said eventually, "you did the right thing, having a celebration for yourself. Except you might have invited me."

Didn't he know that she had, and that he had attended?

"After all, you're the main audience to please. Were you?"

She nodded dreamily, not quite able to grab hold of her thought or tongue.

"There is no more culture anyway, just the odds and ends we make. Catch as catch can. But as far as a real audience is concerned, forget it. Such people don't exist anymore, if they ever did. For now, anyway, they're led by the noses by the self-anointed critics. They're sheep, not audiences. So why not be your own audience, as well as artist, and make your own taste?" Lecturing himself, he drove slowly and carefully through the winding back streets of Somerville, on the way to Cambridge.

Make your own taste, your own culture, your own life. Well, she was trying, trying.

A bear heading for hibernation, she felt — almost a perfect ending to the evening. She listened to pop music on Harry's AM radio; looked up and noticed the postcards he had pasted up on the dash — Turner's sun and vapor seascape, a classical nativity by Piero della Francesca, the drawing by Ingres of "Madame Moitessier Seated," a self-portrait by Van Gogh. His own Chevy Sistine Chapel, as he claimed. Between his dancing nymphets and classical painters, he covered the low and high. She stared back at the wild determined stare of Van Gogh. What would he have made of her self-portraits? Or Evans, Kertész, Atget, Siskind — the ones who made art of them? Perhaps later on, in the graveyard, they could get together? . . . Oh, this is first-class, she judged — being chauffeured in a pickup after getting plastered at your own opening. Way to go, Mom, way to go!

Then Harry was helping her undress, saying, "I don't think I ever saw you so pretty. Where'd you dig up these ornate duds?"

Dearest Harry. She fondled his hair and kissed his forehead. (Out of pure fondness, or also arousal?)

He was slipping her into her green nightgown, raising her up to slip it over her hips, and then somehow he was kissing her lightly on the lips, and she was returning it. She felt so cozy and warm with this former lover that she allowed him to take her upper lip in his mouth and bite ever so softly down. And then she was lost — lost to his touches, lost to his needs, lost to the moment. Slowly she permitted herself to fall in with his caresses, caressing back just enough to signal to him that she knew what was happening. Dearest Harry, for all his resentment of culture, for all his anger, was the softest, surest of souls with her.

He proceeded to nuzzle her neck and run his hands along her flanks and to lower one strap of her gown to take her nipple in his mouth. He tongued her breast, and she yielded and was thrilled and wanted more. More. Which he out of old knowledge knew and out of old familiarity did. Took her somewhere with his mouth on her breasts, somewhere heavenly, and then glided lower with his tongue, teeth, and lips. He kissed and nipped at her belly, making her very high and very desirous, and she turned to try to escape and perhaps to throw him off; but he was too sure for that. Slowly he slid down lower and began to feel and kiss her pubic area. Remembering her most sensitive spots, he labored upon them with care and soon was sucking her with a beauty and a need that drove her ferocious. He tongued her and teethed her (carefully) and bit the insides of her upper thighs; and she, oh she gave in to this solution, to this Harry-succulence, feeling a deserving gratification in it tonight, feeling a virtue in it tonight, concentrating on this activity as a proper conclusion. So that when she had come and he then moved up upon her and he was inside of her, she took this intercourse as a cardinal virtue, accepted this fucking as beauty, perceived in her heart that this mingling was the highest good; and as she came again, moving with her friend like a soul discovering its old mate by chance in spinning, honeyed space, she forgave herself, forgave her illicitness and sought to call it wisdom, knowing that rules and commandments learned in adolescence were meant for adolescents and real pleasures were meant for an adult woman; and this grown woman allowed herself love this way, permitted herself pleasure with this man; and only later, when he had tucked her in cozily and said goodnight, did she acknowledge fully, somehow, before sleep, that yes, it had been a fitting close to the pure night, yes, she had worked so hard and accomplished so much by herself that she deserved this sort of sharing, and yes, next to her beloved photographs and precious children, this loving, this crazy business of sudden sensuality with dear friends was the surest, sweetest connection in this wide world. Knowing this, assured of this, pleased by this — oh so pleased now — she slept.

14

So she had had her night of orgy, a working tour of fantasy
and memory and wishing, her private Happening; surely this had
been her most satisfactory opening. But what did it all come to,
or mean, if anything? She pondered this in her Cambridge Think-
Tub, lounging in her Vitabath three days later, after the kids had
gone off to school. During that night of fantasy mingled with
reality, her good-girl Walpurgis Night, she had received as much
criticism as praise, as much hard reminding as pure wishing. But
what did the night say, prove? Well, it confirmed for her in these
next days that in those two separate realms of Doing and Imagining — photographing and projecting — she would spend a good
portion of her future life (especially now that *longing* was a per-
missible force or value). Of the great world called Society she had
seen and experienced enough, in her admittedly limited way, to
grow tired of its redundant entertainments and its noisy perceived
culture without feeling the penalties of criticism. As for that blanket
of ordinariness under which most citizens slept their lives away,
acquiring status, money, and power and suppressing desire, curiosity, and alertness, slipping from useful professionalism into
savage pretentiousness — she had had her fill. Through her years
of marriage she had called the common enemies by friendly names —
repression was responsibility, and boredom was adulthood — and
afterward, inevitably, she had swung the other way and formed
alliances with frenzied promiscuity and obsessive self-concern. She

had moved from timidity to anger, indiscriminate (and unrecognized) anger. Here now, in her forty-fourth year, she was navigating a middle course, she surmised. And she viewed herself on this course, this project, say, of the next decade, as functioning in retreat, in private acts and country rooms; her gyroscope said balance there, in rural repose. A fortress of the self could be created in chosen exile, as it were, as she had created a self in her Bohemian youth, save that now it would be built with the solid, selected materials of the past several years. Endurance proven.

Luxuriating in her invigorating Swedish suds, studying her toes, she formed such inchoate thoughts.

What, then, about items like her men, her children? They were part of the fortress, despite the problems of person or loyalty. And in the part of her life that was Jonathan, of course, the problem would intensify before it diminished or disappeared, she knew; he was like one of those quiet volcanoes that suddenly erupt, just when you think it is permanently dormant. With tenacious care and a modicum of guilt (as little as she could get away with), she'd work on Jon. Just as she'd work on work with as much critical exactitude as she could muster. With her men, she'd play it — them? — by ear; if Rafi's warmth for a few seasons per year made her feel virtuous while Montana's made her feel wicked/daring for another, so be it. (And Harry?) It seemed as if her system of emotions had gone far beyond that of reason, as usual, and had worked out its own complex grid of loyalty, desire, sport, and commitment. To be a woman for all seasons was not her ambition. To be a woman of some small free will, some small real independence, was.

In retreat, away from the cauldron of boredom and distraction called modern culture, she would take up more seriously those pursuits suited to privacy and health: reading, listening, select befriending, country living. Why not fill her middle years with Schubert and Dvořák and late Beethoven (to augment early Armstrong and Holiday and Bessie Smith), or Stendhal, George Eliot, Colette, Proust? For her entertainment, she could raise chickens and run sheep, or watch VCR reruns of Hollywood detective stories and comedies of the pre-Art days, when the Thin Man mattered more than Message Art. For interesting movies, she'd watch Japanese sagas or European films. The present American lightweights she'd leave to her children; Jon had already become a better critic than the newspaper guides. The more she planned this invisible chart, the more excited she grew. The next immediate project was the place in the country somewhere. How, with what money? Ah, the perennial rub.

In the next week, while money-gathering and Jonathan-watching, Miriam received two missives of interest. The first was a package along with a note from an ex-student, Hideo, in Kyoto. It contained two photography books, with Japanese text, and a Japanese novel in translation. The note read:

> Please accept these small presents, in honor of my return home. The photographers are Akiyami, the portrait photographer, and Shiotani, the best of all, who grow up in Honsho, like me. *The Tale of Genji* is my favorite novel, and this is a whole, *unabridged* version.
>
> You will visit Hideo one day, yes?

Oh yes, yes! The presents lifted her spirits. Akiyami seemed to be a kind of Irving Penn, stylish but fashionable. Shiotani was a quiet surprise, a photographer of tinted black-and-white photos of village scenes and still-lifes. An exquisite talent, Miriam thought. This *Tale of Genji* was a vast tome, more than a thousand pages long, and it was inscribed, "From Lady Murasaki through Hideo to Lady Miriam." Kyoto, huh?

The second letter was from Reggie. Coming in mid-October, it was a shift in tone and strategy.

> Miss Miriam,
>
> Let me lay something else on you, since I dont hear nothing from you, just white silence. For sure, I laid some kind of trip on you back in that park at night. I accept my part in that crude affair. But now you try to answer this charge, to this poor niggerboy — who set me up in the first place? And I dont mean here in this time, but way back when I was a little nothing, and even before that? *You,* a whitey, and lets say a *good* whitey, okay, with your systems and your powers and your lilywhite color — you all set me up to perform in ways *contrary* to your laws and regulations. And then you want to prove how *bad* I am, we are; now thats not reasonable is it?

Lets start at the start — do you know what Mama and Daddy did to put cornbread and grits on the table for ten kids? Mama cleaned up dentist and doctor offices for *twenty-five years,* hurt her hip and then got her pension — a few boxes of flowers and $50. No minimum wage, no paid vacations, etc. And Daddy, know what he pulled in life? Worked as a redcap in redneck train and bus stations, for forty mother years, picking up and laying down white folks bags for his nickels and dimes. I used to see him sometimes at work and you know what, it wasn't so *uplifting.* He got some emfazema from his smoking and slowly withered away — no hospital, you know, cause there was no dough to pay for it, no good insurence for poor black porters. And let me say a good word about my sister CoraLee, hooking on the streets at age 14, a mama at 15 with a half white kid and dead of dope at 20. Not pretty is it? Now I wont hit you with granddaddy's days as a sharecropper, great granddaddy's days as a African slave, though its true and right here in my papers for you to inspect. But Ill leave that number for a later date, *if* you want to investigate the truth.

Lets move up to me at 16, being pitched by white chickadees in South Side High, cause Im kind of not bad looking and sort of refined, and all the time Im trying to concentrate hard on my studies and you know what, that white stuff won out. So okay, I admit that too, I was a sucker — and got beat on by the white boys for that too. Nevertheless at 18 I find myself without a diploma working as a delivery boy messenger on those shitassed hot streets, with my future bright as a fulltime Western Union boy at $2.10 an hour. You get the picture. Well I sort of began to make use then of my talents as a sweet talker, see, and those honkey girls made use of me too, so it was only logical to turn the tables a little. Enter hustling days. I broke no bones, threatened no jill or jane, just *serviced* folks, white folks primarily. The girlies came round to me and asked to run in my stable, and thats gods truth. Seems they liked me and wanted to do something for me, and before you know it, why Im successful at the business. Its a business like any other, you hear — I had to learn about lots of whitey details, like banking and keeping accounts, renting apartments and keeping track of bad habits, and of course most crucial, bribing officials and the police. Yes sir, thats one subtle science, that game of graft. Some folks are techy about *how* theyre on the take.

And you know, I would never of come north except a reform mayor headed into New Orleans and he went ahead and tried to clean up things, and so I had to make my move up to Boston, where I had to learn the game all over again, with slightly new rules. The game was the same basically, you still paid the fuzz its weekly dues and they looked the other way. Only there it was a real pleasure to hand mr. whitey cop or vice sqd the little manilla envelope with his weekly take, cause I knew just how much he dispised me when he accepted it. Employee making more than employer thing. But you know, for Boston whitey cops, if his little daughter was hustling too, it was a killerdiller that take. But miss only one payment and you were one sorry dude, your ass in the clink and your stable shut tight for a month. (If you think any of this is a fairytale, go find Marty Callahan at CPD, unless he's made Looie by now and transfered over to BPD. Check out his case for what Im saying.)

Okay, me and you. Here's my offer — if you want a heavy challenge, take me on and reform me. Make me learn to respect white folks for the 1st time ever. Take this little old niggerboy and turn him inside out — make me a clean brown gentleman. You know, go get me an education, get me the right books and right outlook, make me self-respecting in whiteys world, and Ill take it from there. You do all that and Ill *forgive* you for taking 2–3 years out of my life on the basis of a LIE. 2–3 years of warding off butt-f —— and bullying from some really bad dudes. You think about this proposition of mine and youll see that what Im talking about is salvation, for you and for me. Now I know youre Jooish and may not believe in salvation, but here's a tune my Mama used to sing, It takes a rubber ball to bounce, it takes a baseball to roll, but it takes a damn good preacher to send salvation to my soul. You see, massa Miriam, everyone needs to be straitened out from being crooked, you too. Are you willing to help me along?

Reggie DuPres, Jr.

Astonished, Miriam read the letter over a few times, and later in the day she read it several more times. The words were like shots of Novocain from her dentist, numbing her understanding. Was he — or it, like the cornbread and grits? and ten kids — for real? Or was he simply angling for a shorter, surer way to parole? Okay, she assessed, half of each, say. (And the parody?) If the facts were true — and she could check those out — then he was asserting, "Look, *I'm human too,* don't dismiss me simply because I happened to rape you and work at an unholy occupation. Look,

I'm human too, forget the labels, there are pressures that made me do what I did and who I am, and they may be too powerful for anyone to fight against. Now I want to come clean, go straight, be saved; will you give me a break? We're linked somehow, and so I'm asking *you*." Crazy. Could she, would she . . . ?

The letter dizzied her, precisely because she began to take it seriously. She knew if she asked anyone sensible — Rafi or Montana, Harry, Mary Lou, a talk-show host or Ann Landers — they'd tell her to forget it. Reason, logic, history . . . But the main point was, was he being serious in the midst of all this madness, and if so, did it mean that one couldn't really tell a damn thing about *anything?* Was every last thing in human affairs, especially the self and perceived reality, in flux, like the molecules? The strange letter stayed with her for the next few days, turning round and round in its peculiar possibilities; or was she simply playing Miriam again, being foolish and romantic and risky at the proclamation of challenge? Who could she talk with or check out the odds with?

To relieve her mind she retreated to the noisy Cambridge junk yards one morning, searching for faces, characters. She found a tattooed Puerto Rican working a hydraulic steel-masher to his own music, two Orthodox Jewish brothers selling used parts, a huge, toothless black pirate with a shaved head and golden earrings — a human zoo competing with the broken-down autos for the wildest shapes and appearances. She snapped three rolls' worth of the characters competing with the junk, working to gather first impressions rather than caring about subtlety or composition. Later she could decide what to look for, select, print.

At quarter to one she quit and returned to the apartment, put away her rolls of film, grabbed some cottage cheese, yogurt, and wheat germ. Made a few phone calls and left a note for Rosie. She felt excited about the junk photos, and jotted down a few brief notes.

Downstairs she picked up her just-delivered mail, then headed out for an afternoon screening by that kids' group, Pequod. She was delighted to see, when she gazed at the address, that it was over on the other side of the tracks, on the seamy side of lily-white academic Cambridge, in a kind of ghetto populated by poor blacks, poor Irish, poor Puerto Ricans. Drove over, parked, and walked about. Grimy brick buildings, bleak storefronts, ramshackle double-decker houses, gaseous air from the small factories running there in grim seclusion. Perhaps one day Harvard or MIT would buy up the area for a song and make a few quick million while sending everyone packing. Or did they already own it? she mused, walking.

She had come early and was led by a gentleman from the millinery factory in front down a narrow alleyway to a wooden door marked PEQUOD ENTERPRISES, INC. The man asked, "You in the movie business too?" She replied, "No such luck." She entered an office filled with metal bookstands and shelves of tin reels, a steel desk and a splicing machine, nostalgic movie posters on walls. The adjoining room was the viewing area; it contained old armchairs, a worn couch, a cropped row of old theater seats with popping springs. Charming. Now let's see how charming the film is, she cautioned herself while she prowled restlessly, staring at old posters of Ray Milland in *Lost Weekend,* James Mason in *Odd Man Out,* Garfield and Lilli Palmer in *Body and Soul,* Peter Lorre in *M.* They have taste in their old flicks, she thought. Poking about, she couldn't help glancing at the titles on the steel cans. Indeed, she conjured up a poster of herself in a belted World War II raincoat, the star of *Odd Woman Out.* A remembrance of her Arizona shooting session, she smiled, smoked, finally sat down in an armchair. Now, if she had a documentary to make, what would it be? The fate of the Dimona Jews, to expose the white Zionists? The situation of a friend in Jerusalem, living in Jewish exile there? Or of herself, in personal exile here? Maybe the quiet, unspectacular life of an old psychiatrist, someone like Dr. Levanda, helping her patients while seeking (or denying) a life of her own?

A whirring sound came from the cutting machines of the factory. A real sweatshop, next door to this film studio — what perfect bedmates! She opened her mail, finding an overdue Filene's bill, a plea to Save the Whales, a six-week-old postcard from Kelley in Bali, advising Miriam to "check out the dancing here, it's a trip." Cheered by the card, Miriam thought that *there* was the perfect subject for a public movie: the wild and woolly life of that modern American cowgirl! To Kelley, that would be like playing with Play-Doh.

The kid moviemakers arrived, greeted her with little Hollywood hugs and pecks — were they being ironic or straight? she wondered — kidded around, and offered her coffee. She took tea.

"Now don't be too hard on us," gibed Dru

"We're just amateurs," reminded Lindsay.

"Stop jivin' the lady," Joe said. "She's not the moneybags, you know."

For an instant his cheerful smile turned into Reggie's sly grin, the ebony black of his skin turning lighter, more cinnamon in tone. Miriam scratched around her knee.

Lights went out; the projector rolled. On the portable screen, after a countdown from ten to one, the title clapped on: *Vera and Lucinda*. Simple; good. Be on the alert, she warned herself, for any undue surprises. Maybe a few shots of her with Dr. B. — a sporting scene, say, beneath the Science Museum bridge. Or at her private show, in the midst of her grand folly, and afterward with Harry. Or with her son in that brick jailhouse in the Berkshires. Yes. The whirring of the projector mingled with the steady noise of the embroidery machines, and for some reason she recalled Emma Bovary listening to the turning of the lathe, contemplating her adultery. Why now? Nerves, or was she projecting Emma's fate onto her own future?

Resolutely she looked on as the 16mm film, in surprising color, passed slowly through the wide assortment of activities of her friend Vera's life: Dr. Hardie's group therapy, Tai Chi exercise and Sesshin meditation at Fresh Pond, a political protest at Harvard on behalf of Russian dissidents. Oh, Vera looked slender and youthful; frenzied, she looked progressive in her jogging suit, and her nervous hands were photographed from a positive angle always. There were shots of her with her professor husband (a subsidiary, to be sure); with Miriam, walking in the Square; with a young, confused student in a co-counseling session, which Miriam found moving. Half prisoner, half cheerleader, Miriam watched, waiting for real turmoil or irony. But what she got was all sugarcoating, the portrait of a kind of superwoman flying right through life, over and through all obstacles and emotions, explaining periodically how the world amused and charmed her!

Lucinda Dodge Phelps, or Lu, the second woman portrayed,

was a local sculptor and a much less verbal subject than Vera. Small, sturdy, determinedly unfeminine in bulky sweaters and blue jeans and work boots, Lu worked diligently on huge projects, hewing from granite and carving monumental hunks of wood. It was left to her willowy friend Sissy to discuss Lu's "creative energies" with good cheer, and their sexual life with casual exposure. A wealthy woman, Lu spent her weekends at her Cape Cod house, and the camera followed along, capturing the mandatory shots of Lu walking the wind- and gull-swept beaches alone, in fall and winter, or surrounded by cats, Sissy, and the harpsichord she built herself, in the clapboard house. All told, it was a rather merry portrait of an artist's life, replete with the rewards and satisfactions of solitude, art, friendship, the only sins being black coffee and too many cigarettes. Or were those virtues here?

The movie showed two women of contrasting styles, Miriam summarized, one outgoing and with various interests, the other inward and narrow; both lives winning, fertile, rich. A smooth fairy tale of success, conviction, ideology. Ah, movies!

While the kids watched with keen interest, making little noises of approval, her own interest drifted and she ran her private mental reel, revealing a less romantic, more pressed, even confused figure. A woman involved with several men, prey to mischievous impulses and improvised follies and daily defeats; a woman driving on to discover . . . herself? Where, in what moments, could one uncover that elusive figure — in acts of id, judgments of ego, censures of superego? Could one define her through her presence in the Negev with her man, through her devotion to camera and photographs, through her high-voltage affections?

While the camera followed superheroines galloping easily through their lives, Miriam sat quietly, smoking, seeing her life in uncertainty, her maturity in contingency. In the whirring, flickering darkness, her men and the risks she took rolled in her inner microcassette: haunted Andrei and his extreme pleasures; Jonathan in a spurt of rage, mocking her maternal capacity during her year of absence; Reggie stroking her face with his vast chocolate hand and saying she'd make "a *fine* working woman"; rangy Montana complicating her life (or was it the other way around?) by appealing so sensually to her. And work, demanding work, always pushing her, teasing her, saying, "Come with me and let's try *everything,* go *everywhere,* become *everyone,* now don't chicken out on me!" And Miriam, poor slave, followed, not knowing where Master Leica was leading or what the consequences might be . . . real adventure, wild-goose chase, dirty joke? The long ardor and slow ordeal of trying to be original.

"So how is it?" Dru interrupted her thoughts.

"Be frank now, no kid gloves."

"Yeah, lay it on the line," Lindsay said, adding, "so long as it's complimentary!"

They kidded, but they were serious and vulnerable, she knew. What could she say? Wanting to say nothing to hurt them, she put on her most sincere look and uttered her best platitudes: "Really very interesting . . . the contrasts are very telling . . . some of the shots, and the color, are just lovely . . . should do a lot for women's lives, I think . . ."

It was done; it had taken months of planning and effort, there was certainly skill here, so let it be. Compliment it softly; small lies won't hurt (will keep hurt away, actually). When she saw that they were not entirely convinced by her praise, she sought to allay their doubts by adding a criticism here, a suggestion there. Anyway, maybe the film was exactly what they had intended, what their audiences wanted. Maybe where Miriam saw sentimentality, their audiences perceived Statement; where she saw oversimplicity and obvious tendentiousness, the audiences found signs of health, role models, and strong Commitment. Who needed her out-of-date assessments? Her preliberation opinions? And maybe after all she was unconsciously envious of those magic movie-lives up there, brimming over with Victory? (Yet she knew, accepting another herb tea, that with Vera at least there were many more pieces to the puzzle, such as teenage incest with her brother and conjugal sexual unhappiness, than showed on the screen.)

She sat sipping her Sleepytime, listening to the kids tell her about voice-overs and experimental montage and antiliterary imagery. Meanwhile the heroes and heroines of yesteryear held their own up on the walls: Ray Milland on a binge, Peter Lorre haunted and hunted, Fred MacMurray and Barbara Stanwyck hatching their insurance plot . . . What could she say? And maybe her own life was a piece of cake (Jon's phrase), not a slice of chaos?

Hugging and kissing everyone good-bye after a half-hour of

talk, she wished *Vera and Lucinda* luck, said it would probably win some prize, and urged them to keep going, keep after it. "After what?" they asked. She smiled. "Beauty, truth, feeling, of course — what else is there?"

She made her departure, then delighted in the cracked mortar and brick of East Cambridge, appearing in the incoming fog. Here in the nether world of East Cambridge surfaces seemed realer than over yonder in packaged Harvard Square, now so different, she thought again, from the Square in the ancient, lovely sixties, when it had been Fellinized by street theater, street kids, and professors playing at The Revolution. For twenty minutes she walked around, looking at the thirties tenements and cement-block factories, inhaling gases and fumes, watching the black, brown, and Irish faces, passing yarn and food stalls, thinking of Dickens's London and Daddy's Brooklyn. Dear Dad; he was showing up everywhere. She bought a chocolate éclair in his honor and sat in the car and ate half. Yes, this small town in Massachusetts would make a nice photographic study, once you included this side of town.

Driving home on Mem. Drive, she was buoyed in thought by the humped banks and familiar curves and choppy river. She had gone to the viewing somewhat skeptical, perhaps jumpy, but she had sat there bored, slightly depressed: the triumph of celluloid over reality, in the dullest of fashions. The young people imagined that what they got on their special Technicolor was the way it was. Oh well. Maybe Jane Fonda and Vanessa Redgrave could do a fictionalized remake, scripted by some Lillian Hellman, and we'd have another modern fairy tale. Don't worry, you Grimm boys, you're in no danger — this was a fairy tale Hollywood–New York style, with no murderous impulses or scary castles, wicked transformations or violent acts; just some thin narcissism and thick sentimentality. The easy life over the complex and enchanting life.

She flicked the radio on and listened to two and a half minutes of Stevie Wonder singing about his lady. A genius, that fellow; Jon was right. His infectious voice sweetened the air and her mood.

As the Valiant rumbled through Central Square, groaning as if it had pulled a muscle, she promised herself that one day soon she'd give up on this jalopy, as Rafi had proposed, and maybe break down and buy something with pep. That would be a breakthrough, wouldn't it?

Up in the apartment, Rosie was happy to see her, exclaiming, "C'mon now, you promised you'd finish our Monopoly game, remember!"

Miriam, delighted too to see her charmer, said, "Sure, okay, with a forty-five-minute time limit."

"An *hour*." Firmly.

"Okay, an hour."

"Besides, I'll bankrupt you before *that* long, everyone knows that." Deftly Rosie moved out the Monopoly set, careful not to upset the board with its hotels and houses, and folded down onto the floor, while Miriam eased down opposite her in several stages.

"Whose roll?" she asked.

"Mmmm. Yours, I think. Yeah, yours."

Miriam jiggled and rolled, came up eight, and moved her silver top hat eight boxes, to Virginia Avenue.

Rosie lit up. "There ya go! Mmmm . . . rent of one hundred eighty, thank you."

Miry reached to her small bundle of money and handed her daughter three fifties, a green twenty, and a yellow ten. Same play money as in her day, and the same rules; only, the hotels and houses were now plastic.

"Mom, you gonna marry again?"

Miriam, who had picked up a contact sheet, said, "Why do you ask?"

"I dunno." Rosie rolled her dice, said, "Wow, close!" and moved her silver boot. " 'Cause I guess I should know. Just in case, like."

Oh, Mom *liked* that. She leaned over and tugged her daughter's ponytail.

"Hey, why'd you do *that*?"

Miriam rolled, hit a six, and landed in Free Parking. "No, I don't think I'll marry again. At least, not in the near future."

Rosie squinched her face, threw her dice, and ended up on Chance. Slowly she turned over the orange card, raised her fists, and read, "Bank pays me dividend of fifty bucks."

Miriam handed over a fifty from the bank, and Rosie, tucking the bill into her growing pile, observed, "You'll hurt Rafi's feelings if you *never* marry him, won't ya?" Handling her mother easily in the game, she began drawing on the side.

"Well, I hope I don't hurt his feelings."

Rosie said, "Your go. Don't big people, I mean *adults,* kinda get hurt if you *don't* marry them?"

Miriam rolled. A seven. "Sometimes, yes. But not all adults are married, you know." She landed on Vermont, owned by herself.

"But all the ones with children are, right?" Rosie was staring with triumph at her mother. "Hey, you're gonna miss Jail this time around."

Miriam remembered the last time, and smiled. "Some have children and remain by themselves."

"That's *lonely,* I'll bet." She rolled the dice in two hands and threw them, and made it to Water Works. "And kids like to have parents, that's for sure."

Aha, Miriam thought. So little daughter is dropping large hints. No guilt now, she warned herself. How much of this was Stan's doing? Should she change the subject?

"Be careful now," Rosie warned, pointing at her blue properties and returning to her drawing.

"Would it hurt *your* feelings if I didn't marry again, anyone, but just remained friends with Rafi say?"

"Hmmm." She looked up and considered the proposal. "Nah, I'm not too interested. I asked . . . *just in case.*"

Oh, Miriam couldn't resist her at that point, and reached over and hugged her, and kissed her cheeks hard.

"Hey cut it out, will ya!" At first laughing, then getting serious. "C'mon now, we don't have that much time left! C'mon, you go."

"Okay." And Miriam released her fiercely independent prize, and got ready to throw again.

Rosie meanwhile emphatically wiped the kiss from her cheek, chiding her mother with a glance, and asked, "What was *that* for, huh?"

Oh, for charm, for love, my dearest. She wanted to repeat, "Just in case," but didn't dare. "Oh, for luck."

"Hah. Just watch it, will ya? And please *go* already."

Miriam knew she had better behave now, and toss the dice, secretly adoring the stubbornness of her critter, who so reminded her of herself at nearly twelve: the stubbornness, the determination, and the shell of apparent indifference to emotions. Oh, some boy was going to have his hands full in a few years.

"All *right!*" Rosie squealed when her mother hit a ten and landed right smack dab on blue Park Place, loaded up with Rosie's properties. "This may just do it, Mom," she said, licking her lips.

And as the daughter added up the sum owed by the mother, the mother figured how much she really owed the daughter, in gratitude, in solicitude, for the years of closeness. Oh, it was fun to go broke this way!

"Yup, you're finished, Mom." Shaking her head, she reached out and scooped up the bills.

And Mom, who was scooping up her own riches, realized again that this creature was the living proof of her own survival, her victory in sanity. "Now, next time watch out," she warned Rose. "No more kidding around."

Rosie shook her head at the poor joke. "But you know what?" She leaned over a bit, to let Miriam in on a small secret. "I love Monopoly almost as much as Cheerios — at least when I play you." Meaning *beat you,* of course.

"Don't count on me to lose forever, pumpkin."

"Mom, I count on you . . . to play your way, that's all." She was already back to her drawing.

But a few days later Miriam played things differently in her life. Acting on impulse when the old Valiant failed to start on Wednesday, and cursing the gray invalid, she went out and bought herself a new one. Well, not exactly a new one, but a new used one. Through the local *Want Advertiser,* she found, in Belmont, a clean, low-mileage automobile: a floor-shift five-speed big-engine Honda Civic station wagon, low and clean as a whistle, a light blue. After taking a five-minute spin, she bought it on the spot. This was not like her at all, and doing it made her feel absolutely daring. As she wrote out the check for $2900, her heart beat as if she were robbing a bank right then.

For Miriam, who had never bought a house or a new car in the grand department store called America, this was the largest sum she had ever laid out. This accounted perhaps for the mixed exhilaration and fear that swept her all through the day as she zipped about doing errands. Shifting gleefully, feeling Honda's pep, she felt affection for a car for the first time, and decided to take it immediately for a wash and wax at Porter Square. After years of playing nurse to broken-down vehicles, she was now going to play the role of real pilot to this forty-six-thousand-mile-old baby. If only Rafi were here to see her splurge this way!

At the car wash the attendant took her ticket, reminded her to close the windows tightly, and directed her onto the automated track. Gradually the car was grabbed and pulled into the inner sanctum, that chaotic tunnel of spraying water and churning brushes which had always frightened her. Now once again the huge apparatus of Frankenstein-genius went to work, its giant brushes and huge wheels rubbing at the car's sides like undersea monsters, its gargantuan sprays swishing tons of water at the windshield, its labyrinthine wheels of wax rotating discs on its steel. What would happen if something went wrong within this vortex of water and rubber and she couldn't escape? To perish in the car wash! But suddenly, with the water cascading and the brushes scrubbing, she felt differently, like a child moving through an exciting magical tunnel at a carnival. No longer feeling childhood fear now, she experienced projections of will and clarity. Through the thick soapy windshield, she seemed to see beyond to a future of purpose, a still-life photograph of an old house with a few flowering maples and a bit of meadow, and Miriam on her own self-created fellowship for a year. Or a real fellowship, why not? Or something or other. She desperately wanted that country place, and she'd find a way by reasonable hook or by unreasonable crook. Slowly, surely, she was fixing her will on that vision, and feeling herself pulled closer and closer. This Honda was evidence.

The attendant was calling to her, she realized, to turn the key and depart from the track and leave the tunnel, and she obeyed, flustered. Sure enough, the car was done; she couldn't resist coming outside and up from her revery and walking around and around the low, sleek machine, admiring it like a tailor approving his work. "Snazzy, ain't it?" complimented the attendant, and she was flattered. She got back in and drove off, dodging in and out of clogged Cambridge traffic, feeling perky, fashionable, exhibitionistic. How would the kids take it, especially Jon? she wondered, driving up Hancock St.

"*Ours?*" he said, incredulous, when she got home. "Jesus," he gasped, "let's go for a ride before dinner, Mom — what d'ya say, huh?"

"Yeah, let's," concurred Rosie.

Again she couldn't resist. She packed the kids in, lifting the back so Rosie could lounge, and drove out toward Storrow Drive, feeling as if she were about to christen a ship for its maiden voyage. Was this hers?

"Really step on it, Mom, and let's see the pickup!"

Taking his suggestion, she shifted up through the gears, stepping on the accelerator and feeling the peppy power of the little car. In no time at all, it seemed, Honda was speeding at sixty.

"Now that's *driving*, Mom, not what you've been doing for the past hundred years!"

They zipped on and around, she secretly exhilarated. So this was modern life, the fast lane of acceleration. Tall gleaming buildings fled by on their right, and on the other side the Charles River glistened. No wonder kids were transfixed by cars, and grown-up kids were killed by them. The speed was breathtaking, and the illusion of power drew you irresistibly; she sensed this as the speedometer climbed to seventy before she knew it and let up and slowed down. Missiles, warheads, supersonic bombers — an extension of the speed infatuation? Or too much "Starsky & Hutch" watching?

"Not too shabby," applauded Jon, and Miriam couldn't help turning to wink at Rosie.

"Actually," she responded, easing the car back across the Harvard Bridge, "I bought it for its front-wheel drive. Just in case we get stuck on a country road in bad weather."

"Yeah, sure," Rosie said, concerning the country road.

"Hey, how do you know about front-wheel drive?" Jon asked. He proceeded to elaborate on its virtues, and surprised her with his automobile knowledge. Oh yes, she was raising a purebred native all right.

When they had returned home, Jon said confidentially, "Mom, you're gonna be all right after all. *Really* okay. Wait till Rafi finds out. And wait till Anthony Scorbella finds out — he's been braggin' to me since last spring about their new Mazda. Boy, that's a brontosaurus next to this greyhound!" He was as excited as if she had bought the car for him. At long last, old Miriam was getting "A-okay" in his book. Should she watch out then?

After the high leveled off in the next week, she remained pleased with her impulsive decision. The purchase of that skillful machine revealed to her a new urge, a hidden sport perhaps. Good for you, old miser, she applauded herself, for breaking down and spending a few bucks, even if you can barely afford it. Now just don't go and smash up in it. Yours is an age of Bellow, not Fitzgerald; parachutes, not crashes. She admired her purchase and interpreted it as a reward for her work, her private show. Honda revved up the spirit.

On the second Sunday of a rainy October, Mary Lou Watson called to ask whether she could drop by Miriam's studio the next day and have a look at the newest photos. "Before they hit Newbury Street!" she said with her usual flourish.

Miriam looked at the tiny black holes in the receiver, wondering if Mary Lou had heard about her curious show already. "Sure, come about one."

Next day, a sunny Monday, promptly at one o'clock, Mary Lou entered, accompanied by a friend whose face was familiar.

"Hi!" Mary Lou embraced Miriam warmly.

The pretty, short-haired friend put out her hand and said, "Angela, Angela Jacques. Remember?"

Covering her awkward feeling with a polite smile, Miriam invited them in. In Wellington boots, French jeans, and dangling jade earrings, Angela made a sharp contrast to Mary Lou, in a suburban skirt and jacket.

While Miriam arranged to coffee and tea, the women wandered in the long main room, offering a steady stream of compliments.

"You sell these privately, I assume?" Angela asked.

"Some, yes."

Miriam handed Mary Lou a black coffee, but the second cup was declined by Angela, and Miriam went to retrieve her tea. Returning, she saw that they had left the main room and called out, "Off limits, friends!" She hurried to the partitioned room holding her private photos.

"No wonder," said Mary Lou with a laugh, "these are *very heavy*."

Feeling foolish, Miriam sputtered, "I'm not sure that you —"

"You don't mind, I hope?" asked Angela.

She was on the verge of saying yes, she did mind, when she saw that Angela was referring to the small silver flask in her hand, and, thrown off, Miriam shook her head. Shrewd change of tracks; shrewd style. "Why should I?"

"Want some? Just Johnny Walker red. I like to hit a little when I'm into knockout stuff. And this is. These, I mean." She saluted the work with a gulp.

The flattery sailed into Miriam's displeasure like a fresh wind, shifting her mood. Why should she be disquieted by two outsiders viewing her pictures? They might be useful even, these objective viewers, she told herself.

"Hey, what can I say?" asserted Mary Lou, cheeks reddening. "Where the hell did you get the models? I mean, I didn't even know you did the model thing."

"Pickups," she kidded, finding photos to adjust on the wall.

"And these personal shots — who said Sylvia Plath had a lock on self-ordeal?"

"Well, if you are selling any of these, I'll take several," Angela said.

"Oh, I don't think these are for sale, Angela."

"Don't think?" The woman eyed her.

"They're not."

"I see. That's cool."

After a few polite minutes, Miriam escorted the women back into the central studio, where they sat on the sofa and chairs and Miriam accepted more compliments on her work. A discussion of fruits, vegetables, and desert ground ensued, calming Miriam.

At just after two Mary Lou giggled and jumped up, declaring, "If I don't split immediately I'm a dead duck. I've got one kid to pick up at Browne and Nick's and transport to dance class, and another to take to a soccer match. John and I are splitting up the custody weeks now, did I tell you, Mir?" She gave Miriam a quick peck on the cheek, said, "Talk to you soon, maybe we can get a last-minute foliage tour in?" tapped Angela on the arm, and flew out the door. Angela held out her hands, indicating the unpredictable nature of their mutual friend.

Was she unpredictable, or had the situation been predesigned this way? Miriam wondered.

Angela shook her head, her narrow cat's eyes accentuated by light eyeshadow and her turquoise rings and bracelet. "I assure you, I had little idea she was going to leave us alone here, or I would have suggested another day."

"I was wondering just that, actually."

She took another small swallow from her flask, and spoke. "They're pretty stunning — of the males especially. It takes a woman artist to catch a man's anatomy that way. When homosexuals do it — unless they're Michelangelo — they're always too cutesy or mannered, I find. But those shots are right on. Full of . . . character." She fidgeted for something in her vest pocket. "And character is higher than intellect, as the man once said."

Miriam settled back in her upholstered chair and sipped her tea. "Did he? Who?"

"Emerson. I did at one time read the male authors as well, you know."

Miriam laughed, tempted by that scotch and glad she was resisting it.

"Try one?"

Miriam reached over and took a cigarillo from Angela, and looked for a match, disregarding Angela's offer of one.

"Let me ask you something," Angela said. "Have you ever tried the female anatomy? In your photographs, I mean."

She shook her head, saying, "No, I haven't. Not for photos." Once upon a time, as an art student at Berkeley, she had drawn female models in class. In fact Diebenkorn had praised her skill in drawing.

"You don't wear jewelry, do you? Or makeup. Look at me, I'm ten pounds heavier with all my trinkets. I like the stuff. Makes me feel . . . less lonely. These rings and bracelets and earrings — like little friends. And God knows, we need all the friends we can get at our age. In our professions." She inhaled, drank from her flask, and asked, "Why do you think you choose to photograph the male rather than the female?"

Miriam relaxed and smoked, trying to gauge the taste. "Men I know, actually," she said, surprising herself.

"Oh, I see."

"It came sort of . . . naturally." Why the need to explain? she wondered, observing the handsome weathered face and embroidered vest of this woman.

"Can I speak frankly to you — here, on your turf?"

"Sure." Really?

Angela took another shot of her whisky, revealing long, cared-for fingernails, and swished the liquid in her mouth. She spoke at last. "You're talented, very talented. And gutsy, up to a point. But until you make full use of *what* and *who* you are, you're not there yet. A *woman* photographer: to make yourself into that, into a full artist, you need to be a full sister, and you need to come to terms with, and photograph, the female anatomy. Now there's an assignment which you're probably as shy of in your art as in your life, right?"

Miriam listened to the line of reasoning and blew smoke out of her mouth slowly.

"Get onto it, friend, you're not getting younger, and phallocentric prejudices get heavier and heavier. You come on over to Northampton again, this time to my studio, and I'll show you that anatomy." She smiled suddenly. "In art, at least."

"Well, thank you for your frankness, and your offer. I'll certainly consider it."

Angela got up and walked, or marched, back and forth, her boots thudding; she had a *presence,* this lady, Miriam observed, and she admired it, no matter what Angela knew or didn't know.

"Look, I was where you are, not too many years ago," she started again. "Before coming out. It's a whole other ground I'm speaking from now, and experiencing. Both as a sculptor and a woman. And until you come over to where I'm at, you have little idea of *how much of yourself* is slowly atrophying, getting wasted. As a body, as a woman, as an artist. It's like operating an engine on half the cylinders. You've got to give yourself a fair shot, you know — walk the female side of the street. You've been walking the other, male side for so long now that you don't even know there are two sides. And to tell you the simple truth, only a woman can take you across, and out, from where you are now. Just as having a baby brought you over to a new ground that's really inexplicable to those who've never been mothers." She paused to drink; her face reddened from the shot, making her appear just a mite older. "Good lunch. Look, I came over here just to see your pictures, to see how good you really were. I had little idea of putting my sermon out. But when you see someone really talented, it's so frigging rare, you've got to throw away your pride and pitch from your gut. Okay?"

"Okay, sure." Miriam looked up at the "priestess," and realized that the taste of the cigarillo was not nearly as subtle as Doctor B.'s Havana. Unfair comparison!

Angela walked closer to Miriam, who stood up to face her. "You come see my stuff sometime soon, won't you? I've an in-town studio now, right over Thorne's, if you remember where that is. Creatures like ourselves owe that much to one another, at least. Just call a few hours ahead of time, okay? Bet you lost my card; here's another. Oh, one other item — I'm having a show in Boston next month, and I'll send you an invite. Come if you can, see what you think. But that's just the frosting. Come and see the whole cake at my place. A deal?" Her hand went out.

Miriam said, "Well, I'll certainly give it some thought." Casually she shook Angela's hand. "Thanks for coming, though."

"If I hear of some collectors, I'll send them your way. You don't mind the business, do you?"

Miriam smiled. "No, so long as they don't offer their opinions first."

Turning to go, hands in her pants pockets, Angela asked, "Are you afraid of me? Am I so threatening?"

"Oh, I don't think so, Angela."

"The aggressive part of me" — she half shrugged, searching herself — "is a casualty of the Male Wars."

"Or the Relationship Wars."

For the first time the woman laughed easily. "Yes, maybe that's better."

And Miriam escorted her to the door politely. Afterward, back inside, she thought how stylish it was to travel about with one's own silver reservoir.

They had dinner in a small Italian restaurant in the North End, two or three rooms with red-checked tablecloths and candles on the tables, run by a local family. "Where have you been for so long?"asked the hefty older woman, holding Dr. Beaumont's hands. "We thought you had abandoned us! Come in to your old table, please." She nodded at Miriam, then led them to a corner table and left immediately.

"You can look at times like a hospital administrator, can't you?" Miriam said, admiring his dark suit and white shirt and tie.

"Absolutely."

The woman returned with antipasto and white wine.

"I hadn't noticed you had ordered."

"Never do here," he said. "I take whatever the Tommasis have made."

Miriam felt cozy quickly in the presence of her doctor again, after the absence of long months. She tried not to look him over too intently.

They were served prosciutto and melon by a waiter, and Scott asked her about Israel.

"The prosciutto is not quite as good, I can tell you," she remarked, tasting the tart-sweet combination. "But the melons — ah, another matter." She went on to describe her life split between Jerusalem and the kibbutz, and the mood of pessimism and bleakness that had taken hold in the country. It was easier to talk about than that other subject.

"Sounds like the good old Nixon days around here," he noted, holding his wineglass.

She noted that large hand, and said, "Maybe worse, because the idealism there was so recent and so intense." My defenseman! remembering his Crimson hockey days. "Now it's almost Jew against Jew, as much as Jew against Arab. In part because of the present government, in part because of the past Labor regimes."

He asked about the election date and whether in a regular parliamentary system the government could fall.

"I don't really know," she said, bored. She tried to explain as much as she understood — the system was parliamentary and it wasn't — while looking at his high forehead, slate-blue eyes, silvery white pompadour. (Here, in 1980!) Oh, it felt good to see her Montana Prince Charming again! Why hadn't she called him before this — guilt, ghosts?

She reached out and squeezed his hand. "It's good to see you again."

"And you, too." He squeezed back, and lifted his glass.

The spaghetti, or tonerrelli, was *al dente* and superb. "Do they do fresh pasta for everyone, or just special guests?" she inquired, twirling a bite.

"Oh, I think for everyone. That's why I try to keep this place a secret."

"I'll keep it a secret with you, then. The only problem is whether I'll have room to eat the main dish after all this. It's a little like Friday nights in Jerusalem, at Cohen's."

"Well, you'll have to invite me there sometime, to compare. Why don't you leave the rest, so you can eat some of your veal."

She smiled, warmed by the wine, him. She set the pasta aside nearby, and presently, while eating her veal Marsala, asked him about work. Had he had time for any research recently?

Eating carefully — would all her men eat more *delicately* than she? — he talked about the hospital and his new administrative responsibilities, which entailed endless conferences and memos. "I did get to that museum you recommended in The Hague, that Something-house . . ."

She wanted to ask, "Were administrative duties that final revenge of society against individual talent?" There was no need, now. Instead she allowed herself to track his voice, that slightly gravelly tenor that ran up and down and through her, sweetening her senses. God, why hadn't she made a cassette of that voice, to soothe her when there was no Mozart around?

And then that consoling voice said the oddest thing: "I've gone back to her. To my wife. It happened in August." He stopped eating to face her squarely, bravely, and she, flustered, said for him to go on if he wished, to explain it. Of course her heart was dropping; she felt like disappearing; and she was as surprised by her own reaction as by the news itself.

Uncharacteristically, he stuttered, stammered; said something about the pressures, internal and outward, of living as a bachelor, something about how he couldn't get used to it, about how separating was harder on his relationship with his children than he had ever imagined. They — especially his son — blamed him.

Listlessly Miriam put bites into her mouth, though she was no longer tasting the food. She noticed a few gilt-edged reproductions of Italian paintings on the walls — gondolas traveling the canals in Venice, courtiers on horses in the squares of Rome and Florence. She remembered herself at twenty-two, in the Piazza Navona, dining on pasta in the long narrow square and daydreaming of a romantic future while looking out at the Egyptian obelisk and fountains. Now, in the North End, she admitted defeat; admitted that she cared far more than she had known about this man; admitted that once again, what she was feeling was far ahead of what she was thinking.

She half smiled and said, as much to herself as to him, "It's okay, I understand. Why not? It makes sense."

And then that voice sprang another odd statement: "I wish you had said yes to me. You don't know how I wished for that, and how much I miss you. Still. Now. Every day. *And* night. But you see, I guess I . . . *need* to be married. At fifty-six, I'm just too old a dog to learn new tricks."

She was playing with her food like a child, and put it down. "You had a birthday since I saw you last." She kept the wetness back. "Happy birthday." No need just now to tell him of hers.

"I did, didn't I? Back in July."

"Excuse me for a minute." She got up quickly and was crying before she hit the bathroom. Couldn't help herself, still, at her age; she cried hard for three or four or five minutes, in pain, then perhaps in sympathy (with and for herself?). She rinsed her face with cold water, rinsed repeatedly, and dried it hard. Felt tricked. Felt dumb. Felt insubstantial.

When she returned, she wanted to say, "Would you mind if we called it a night? I suddenly feel unsociable." Instead she nibbled at bread, watched him try to make conversation and then give it up for silence, listened to other voices, knives and forks, clatter of dishes. Picked up on a conversation at the next table, about the merits of various boarding schools.

Why punish him for her stupidity? For her inflexibility?

She brought up a different subject, the first thing that came into her head — "my new blue Honda" — and when he tried to change that subject, she cut him off with, "Hey, it is getting kind of late, should we get going?"

"But it's only ten to ten. We haven't even had coffee yet," he pleaded, dumfounded.

"Another night, okay?"

And they were driving back to Cambridge in the dark, through twenty minutes more of punishing silence like driving rain, through tunnels of black steel and grids of grim concrete, along the black water. He had hurt her, she had injured him, and there was no reconciling just now. No softening or balm. At the end of her street she allowed him to kiss her cheek, and then she fled upstairs.

In the apartment she sipped tea and smoked. Cried some. It was crazy, not even his fault; the truculent wife had been right, after all, and Miriam had been wrong, after all. (Was just her ego injured?) Wrong not merely about him and his direction, or wrong about how much he meant it when he had proposed; but wrong too about her own feelings. Wrong in her judgment, wrong in her estimation. But would she have acted differently had she known the full consequences beforehand? *No.* She wouldn't have, couldn't have, married him, regardless. But she might have spoken to him more carefully, taken him — and perhaps herself? — more seriously, if she had known her own deepest stirrings! In a way he had been a kind of toy for her, needed and played with at certain convenient moments. But someone deeper, something more significant? *That* she hadn't really known. Part of the problem was language, words. She had used the nouns and verbs of affection to herself, but they were defenses against her fullest feelings. The lies and deceptions of the educated self!

And now, now Montana was back in the hold of that tangled marriage and life which he had tried to escape; and away from her, too. All that sensual sweetness, missing!

Did loss always have to accompany honesty in her life? She took up a photography journal to gaze at pictures, but she might as well have stared at the white wall, for she saw only her serious folly, felt only her hard loss; and hours later, it was only with a concentrated effort that she was able to raise herself to go to bed. For hours of paralyzing insomnia, and remorse.

* * *

Two days later in her office she received a call from the art gallery at MIT; the director, Joan Walsh, asked about a May or June show.

Miriam was at first bewildered, then flattered, though she had half expected the invitation last spring. An embarrassing moment. "I'll be leaving the MIT faculty after this term, and not of my own accord," she finally said. "If this makes a difference to you."

"God, that cuts no ice with the gallery. It's your photographs that we're interested in. Besides, academics are not famous for appreciating creative types for too long. Not if they're alive and kicking."

Miriam acknowledged the sentiment and made an appointment to visit and measure the space, if she decided to go ahead with it.

Joan went on to say, "Your friend Harry took the liberty of showing me your work last week. I'm terribly impressed. I think it'll be a knockout show."

Fucking Harry! Thoughtful Harry too. Oh dear dear dear. "Well," Miriam managed, wondering what he had shown her, "let's see what happens. I would, uh, have to make a selection process, regardless."

"Just so long as you don't dare touch any of those male nudes — they're only perfect, that's all. The best nude series I've seen in years."

Aha, there was the answer. "We'll see, Mrs. Walsh, and thanks."

"Joan. Call me soon, and we'll have a long lunch and discuss details."

"Sure. Bye now." And she rang off.

Decision time once again, my friend. Could you show those? Are you dreaming again? No way, as Yani would say. You have the photos, they worked out well, that was the important thing. So what if the world doesn't see them for a decade or more? Or even posthumously? Legally, ethically, spiritually, no way. And only Harry was egotistic enough — or was it egoless enough — not to mind having his body used for art. But Rafi, Montana? Forget it.

She stared out her mullioned window at the glistening river, dark blue and choppy from autumnal wind, and wondered why rightness for her always seemed entangled with ambivalent decisions, exacting consequences.

She puzzled things over during the next few days; then a call came through from overseas on a Monday night. "Well, what do you imagine?" Rafi spoke clearly. "I'm getting a month in the States."

"What happened to Paris? Didn't your letter say —"

"How does Texas sound, for the month of January? Do you know Austin?"

"Just Jane," she kidded softly, then went on loudly. "No, I don't. You're the traveler."

"Why don't you and the kids join me? They're providing a furnished apartment with all sorts of Texas perks. The Nabateans seem to be hot stuff."

She smiled. What about the kids and school? And that other problem? "Why not?" she responded, mimicking the Israelis' favorite English phrase, and thinking how nice it would be to be away during a show. "You'll have to learn Texan," she warned, growing excited now at the sudden prospect. "Should I buy you a Stetson? Or a pair of holsters?"

"What's that? I didn't get that."

"Holsters," she half shouted, "for your six-shooters."

"Yes, of course. For my pipes, at least. Look, I'll write a letter in a few days and get the details down. All right?"

"All right." Details, everywhere you turned.

He signed off, she blew him a kiss, they hung up. For the next hour she tried to picture her slight, aging archaeologist in a ten-gallon hat, chaps, lasso, string tie, with meerschaum. *Rafi in Austin,* by Zane Grey. Better than *Rafi in the Nude* at MIT, by Miriam Scheinman.

15

ON a Thursday afternoon in late February she was looking through the autochromes of Lartigue when the telephone rang. Reaching for it, she realized she should have taken it off the hook.

"Good evening, how are you?"

"Who — oh, Stan. Fine. I didn't expect you. What's up?"

"Don't you want to know how I — we — are?"

She shook her head. "Oh, sure. How are you both?"

"Well, thank you. Quite well."

Surprise. "So . . . what is it, Stanley?"

"I think we should see a family counselor, Miriam. In fact, I'm afraid we must. To arrange the visits of the children on a more formal basis."

"Huh?" She stared at an oil-company calendar. "What are you talking about?"

"Well, you realize you're not exactly *regular* in making visiting arrangements with the kids, for us I mean. And we need that sort of regularity now. Take Jon and Israel — we don't really want to learn about it a week or two before he takes off. We have to *plan* these things, and I know how much you are, in principle, against planning."

Was he nuts? Or did he just have another Stanley-bee in his bonnet? "I'm not, in principle, against planning; what are you talking about? We've always worked out the kids' visits smoothly enough, since the last court order. What the —" She suppressed *fuck* so as not to rile him up. "What's the reason for wanting to bring in a third party, a family whatever, on this? And who's going to pay for the character?"

"There you go again, Miriam" — and she could see him touching his tie — "you hear the word *professional* and you run for cover. The counselor happens to be a psychologist who is experienced in arranging these things, a person who can mediate between us smoothly. And we can, uh, split the cost. This is the only way it can work peaceably, Röchel and I have decided."

Oh the prick, the stupid prick. "I'll think about it, Stan."

"Don't get me fired up, Miriam," Stan returned, getting fired up. "I'm not asking for anything unreasonable. In fact, this is a way of *insuring* reasonableness. That's the whole point. Must you resist everything reasonable just because I suggest it?"

Yes, my dear, yes. Useless fighting with him now, here. "Find out how much your counselor gets per hour and how many hours this will take, Stan."

"That's more like it, Miriam." Giving his approval, with restraint. "That's more reasonable behavior. And you'll see that —"

"Gotta go now, Stan, you let me know when."

"Well. Good night now, and I'm glad we can arrange this like two rational adults."

She hung up, furious. Oh fuck fuck fuck! The stuffed shirt! Him and his counselors and their "mediating" — they'd be better off levitating!

Take it easy, Miss Superiority, easy.

She returned to Lartigue, and slowly was soothed by his elegant compositions and muted tones. She took notes in her steno book, concentrating on the "Bibi in Antibes" series, staying with the portrait *Bibi in the Edon Roc Restaurant, 1920*.

The telephone rang again, and she decided she wouldn't talk if it was Stan. It rang again and again. Finally she picked up the receiver, wanting to say, "Is it your time of the month, Stan?"

"Miss Scheinman, Miriam Scheinman, please?"

"Yes, speaking." She was grateful for the neutral voice.

"This is Frank Doyle, ma'am, from the Mass. Correctional Institution parole board. I've been given your name by a Shirley MCI inmate, name of Reginald R. DuPres. He's listed you as a character reference, ma'am. Do you know him?"

A few seconds of silence, while she played with the ringlets of the telephone cord like a child. She swallowed, spoke. "Yes, I do."

"Well, you see, we're in the midst of setting up a preliminary case hearing for his possible parole — he becomes eligible in June — and I wonder if you might be willing to help us out by visiting with us sometime in the next several weeks?"

"Hmm," she emitted, still twirling the cord, gathering her senses.

"You don't have to make up your mind now, Miss, uh, Scheinman. Some folks like to think the matter over some. Please do. Let me give you my number, and if you're interested in discussing the inmate with us, phone me."

"Hold on a sec." She reached over for her envelope marker, and told him to go ahead.

"Four five three, twenty-six sixty-seven. That's in Boston. Just ask for me, Frank Doyle. If I'm not in, my administrative assistant can set up an appointment."

"Thank you, Mr. Doyle. I'll . . . perhaps I'll be in touch. Goodbye."

After she had hung up, she realized there were oodles of questions she might have asked, *should* have asked. Like, what was he really in for? Well, she was inside of it now, wasn't she? That "it" — nightmare, fiction, puzzle? Those letters from him . . . play stuff. Yet maybe she could see to it now that he'd never come out, that he'd serve his full sentence?

She took out her road atlas and looked up Shirley. It was beyond Concord, on Route 2; maybe an hour and a half's drive. What do you do now, honeychile, go back to the North End and check with Nick? Call Los Angeles and fly in Kelley pronto for more relief pitching?

She decided to add scotch to her milk, and while sipping it she recognized the irony: the first time she had spotted Reggie again, after the many years, had also been in connection with Stan. At the Blue Parrot. A friend of Dad's used to drink scotch this way; learned it in old Harlem. Stan and Reggie — why not? Ex-husband and ex-rapist. Should Reggie be their family counselor?

Glibness: a sure sign of her fears.

During the next few days of wandering about, taking care of Cambridge chores, and trying to work, she realized it was no use avoiding the issue or calling in friends. Do it yourself, kid. You made your bed, and now either lie in it or unmake it. What was that *R.* in his name for, anyway? If she found out, maybe she should call back that derelict detective, Mr. Purcell, to finish his file off neatly . . .

MCI SHIRLEY was inscribed on a blue and white shield at the entranceway, and for the next few miles she drove on a macadam road that wound through a serene landscape of white birch and pine. It was more like entering an estate than a state prison facility. This Harvard Road cut through the prison grounds on its way to the small town of Shirley, and she turned left at the next sign for the institution. There, facing her, was a high knoll blanketed in snow, with a large brick administrative building with pillars in front at the top, and a series of old houses around it. It was hard to believe that this bucolic setting held criminals, not cows. She checked in at the visitors' sign-in house on the right, and was then accompanied down the hillside by a quiet young guard in a blue uniform.

"What a pretty house," she couldn't help announcing, upon reaching a long, two-story, red brick building.

"It was one of the original eleven Shaker buildings, ma'am," he informed her.

She looked at him. "I see."

Inside, she signed in again at a tiny office manned by two more guards, and was escorted down the hallway to a large square room with a television set and odds and ends of plain furniture: stuffed chairs, sofas, wooden chairs, the sort of stuff she saw advertised in the Sunday *Parade* magazine — living room sets for $599.

Soon he appeared, walking in his high strut, wearing a laundered royal blue shirt and trousers, carrying a newspaper, and looking taller and handsomer than she remembered. Even though she had dressed modestly, in skirt and blouse and heels, she immediately felt overdressed.

"So ya made it out here after all," he noted, nodding and sitting down. "Too bad you couldn't see me at work today. Wouldn't think of me as the barn type, would ya?"

"What do you mean?"

She took out cigarettes and offered him one, but he shook his head. He leaned over and lit hers, however. "I had to work with them Herefords today. Up the road a piece," he mimicked. "Manuel got sick, so they took me off my regular work-release over at Sears and put me with the manure. Once you get used to the smell, it ain't too bad."

She inhaled, savoring the taste of tobacco, and said, "What are the cattle for?"

He gave an animated account of the beef herd on the place and the warden's idea of using it for profit and education. "He's a canny fella, you should meet him. Superintendent Giancani." That lavender scent still trailed him, the same as years ago.

A black woman and her pretty teenage daughter entered, nodded to Reggie, and took a sofa on the other side of the room.

"So what do you say, huh? Can you line up some sort of legit job for me on the outside, so I can ditch this place nice and legal-like? Or should I get help from one of my old pals?"

She smoked, watching him closely. The eyes were almond-shaped, their pupils syrup-brown, with yellow in the iris; his look was alert and cunning. The kinky black hair seemed to be cut shorter, and glistened. The eyebrows were dark too, but delicate. The face was colored that light-brown coffee shade (high yellow?), though up near the right temple was a darker patch. Some other gene? And he had grown a pencil-thin mustache. Oh, he was handsome all right. Handsome like a young Gable, mixed with weimaraner, say.

"Did you just shower?" she wondered.

He rubbed one lip against the other. "How'd ya know?"

"Smells like it."

He smiled his benign smile, which she had seen in the library stacks. She had seen other smiles too. "That reminds me," he said, "how about doin' a little shoppin' for me before your next visit? You can't get too much fine stuff out here in the sticks."

Cocky as always; sure that she'd come again. "Like what do you mean?"

"Oh, you know, some toiletries 'n' stuff. I'm not too used to the prison thangs the boys here use."

For some reason — nerves? — she took out a small notepad and pencil.

He ran his big hand across his face. "I'll tell ya what I need real bad — some fine skin conditioner. M by Clinique, or whatever's hot this year, get. You gotta take care of the old face, ya know, as well as the body. Maybe more. You can use some for yourself. And then some fine soap — a natural, clear soap, or some English stuff, *not* Yardley's. And some sort of lotion, too — French, and lucra-tive." He leaned forward again, and the playful smile disappeared for a moment. "The little things, they hurt the most. Missin' 'em. Like havin' to share five showers with forty-five other cruds. You know" — he charm-smiled now; oh, it was a dazzler — "these boys have a *very diff-erent* background and manners from me."

She reached into her bag. "Here's an apple," she offered.

He looked at her. "Hey, there ya go," he said, and he shined it on his sleeve shoulder. "I'll bet you're the first Jewish lady that's come to visit in this sort of place in *years*."

"What is this thing you have about my being Jewish?" she asked, setting down her pad and pencil. "Do you not like Jews?"

A gradual smile of revelation. From beneath his shirt he lifted out a golden chain with a Hebrew *chai* on it. "My grandfather on my mother's side was Joo-ish. From Africa. Listen." And he leaned closer, and theatrically whispered, "Yit-gadal V'yit-kadash shme rabah." He winked. "Know it?"

She did, but what was it again?

He shook his head in dismay. "Shit, you don't know gonzo about your own tribe!"

"Recite it again."

He did, slower, with careful enunciation, as though he had been rehearsed.

"Kaddish," she said, relieved. "The prayer for the dead." My God, *she* was being tested!

He patted her knee, brotherly. "That's more like it. You were gettin' to worry me some. So." He sat back. "Did you bring some readin' in that tote?"

"Sure. But don't you want to tell me more about that mysterious grandfather?"

"He's not mysterious. But not today. Hey, how'd ya know I love Granny Smiths?" And he took a loud bite.

"Intuition."

"Kinda thoughtful of you. Though I gotta admit the food's not as foul as at some of the hotels I've eaten in. And some of these Eyetalian boys can cook up a pretty fancy feast at times. Let's check out the readin' materials, see what ya got that beats Steve Roper."

From her canvas tote she took out several books, reading the titles as she handed them over. "*Native Son* and *Black Boy,* by Richard Wright. Ever heard of him? A fine writer. *The Souls of Black Folk,* by Du Bois. An elegant book, it seems, though I never read it. *The Fire Next Time,* by James Baldwin — a superb angry essay."

He handled each one separately, looking at the covers and maybe a page here and there, and she asked him if he'd like some Cleaver, or maybe George Jackson. "His prison letters are supposed to be excellent," she explained.

"Hmm." He pointed to the tote. "What's that last one there?"

Surprise. "Just some reading for me, in case I had to wait."

"Let's see it . . . hmm, how do you pronounce this *Sense and Sensibility*? Yeah. Let's start with that. Who's this Janie Austen?"

Taken aback, she at first tried to pry the book away from him, but he wouldn't release it, browsing through the compact Penguin. "A woman in the eighteenth century in England, who never married and wrote novels. Five all told, I think," she finally explained.

"Fiction or true?"

"Huh? Fiction," she said. "Novels are fiction. Made-up stories."

He gazed sideways at her. "Made-up, eh? Pretty good, that. When's that eighteenth century — like 1850?"

"No, like 1750. During the eighteenth century."

"Either of these ladies on the cover this Miss Austen?"

"No, not those. Here, I think." And she turned to the inside cover, which had a portrait of Austen, a drawing.

"My, my, look at that tight little mouth beneath those curls! Whew. That's *one de-ter-mined* lady. Don't be messin' with her! Hey, John boy!" He waved to the large inmate who had just come in and was heading for the two women. "C'mon over to that corner, and we can create a little more privacy. That print's dog-gone small, isn't it?"

They rose and moved to the corner away from the television, turned to a soap rerun by another inmate.

"When ya look like that," he interpreted, with compassion, looking at the portrait, "ya write books or paint pretty pictures, right?"

She sat in a stuffed chair, and he on a two-seater sofa. "Start," he said, taking another bite from his apple.

Self-conscious, she shook her head.

"Hey." He reached over and tapped her funny-bone. "None of that shyness number. These dodos around here won't know Janie from Georgianna — she's their favorite Preview porno queen."

"All right, I'll read a bit — but then we talk seriously a little. Deal?"

"Seriously, huh? Sure, sure." He smiled broadly. "I like that. Yeah. You're on. Now, let's hear some." He finished his apple and set the core aside, then clasped his hands behind his head and leaned back against the divan.

After glancing at the other inmates and their families, engaged in discussion or the soap opera on television, she began, in a low voice, to read:

The family of Dashwood had been long settled in Sussex. Their estate was large, and their residence was at Norland Park, in the centre of their property, where for many generations they had lived in so respectable a manner as to engage the general good opinion of their surrounding acquaintances. The late owner of this estate was a single man, who lived to a very advanced age, and who for many years of his life had a constant companion and housekeeper in his sister. But her death, which happened ten years before his own, produced a great alteration in his home; for to supply her loss, he invited and received into his house the family of his nephew, Mr. Henry Dashwood, the legal inheritor of the Norland estate, and the person to whom he intended to bequeath it. In the society of his nephew and niece, and their children, the old gentleman's days were comfortably spent. His attachment to them all increased . . .

The old gentleman died; his will was read, and like almost every other will, gave as much disappointment as pleasure. He was neither so unjust, nor so ungrateful, as to leave his estate from his nephew; but he left it to him on such terms as destroyed half the value of the bequest. Mr. Dashwood had wished for it more for the sake of his wife and daughters than for himself or his son; but to his son, and his son's son, a child of four years old, it was secured, in such a way, as to leave to himself no power of providing for those who were most dear to him, and who most needed a provision, by any charge on the estate, or by any sale of its valuable woods. The whole was tied up for the benefit of this child, who, in occasional visits with his father and mother at Norland had so far gained on the affections of his uncle, by such attractions as are by no means unusual in children of two or three years old: an imperfect articulation, an earnest desire of having his own way, many cunning tricks, and a great deal of noise, as to outweigh all the value of all the attention which, for years, he had received from his niece and her daughters. He meant not to be unkind, however, and as a mark of his affection for the three girls, he left them a thousand pounds apiece.

"Hey, wait a minute — how much was a thousand pounds in those days?"

"I don't really know."

"Well now, looky here, that's sort of important, right? Could you buy a blue fox with it? A Jag XJS? Why don't ya figure that out for next time, so *we know* what we're talkin' about." His hand motioned for her to continue.

"Are you sure?"

"Sure I'm sure." He gazed at her skeptically. "I wanna see what this stuff is that *you* read and rap about. After all, we're gonna be sharin' some things, right?"

She relaxed, surprisingly, for a minute, and followed his face, flooded by his dusky beauty. Could that dark spot really have come from Ethiopia say, and the Falashas?

"What you smilin' 'bout?"

"The ways of the world." And she went back to Austen:

Mr. Dashwood's diappointment was at first severe; but his temper was cheerful and sanguine, and he might reasonably hope to live many years, and by living economically, lay by a considerable sum from the produce of an estate already large, and capable of almost immediate improvement. But the fortune, which had been so tardy in coming, was his only one twelvemonth. He survived his uncle no longer; and ten thousand pounds, including the late legacies, was all that remained for his widow and daughters.

His son was sent for, as soon as his danger was known, and to him Mr. Dashwood recommended, with all the strength and urgency which illness could command, the interest of his mother-in-law and sisters.

Mr. John Dashwood had not the strong feelings of the rest of the family; but he was affected by a recommendation of such a nature at such a time, and he promised to do everything in his power to make them comfortable. His father was rendered easy by such an assurance, and Mr. John Dashwood had then leisure to consider how much there might prudently be in his power to do for them.

"What's that, *pru-dent*?"

"Safe. At little risk. The cautious way."

"*Pru*-dent." He pursued his lips and rolled the word, like a man enjoying a fine cigar.

She continued. "Elinor saw, with concern, the excess of her sister's sensibility; but by —"

"Hold on. That other word, from the title — *sensibility*?"

"Yes."

"What is it? Like a disposition?"

"Sort of. It's a person's way of looking at the world, implying sensitivity, receptivity. You'd say someone has a fine sensibility if he appreciates art or books, say."

"Uh-huh. But why contrast it to sense? Don't make sense to me."

She tilted her head, figuring. "Well, maybe you have a point. But if we manage . . ." She let the words drift off, not wishing to suggest commitment.

He cradled his head in his arms again and lay down on the divan. "You have a sister?"

"No."

"Brother?"

"Sort of."

"Boy, you like sort-ofs. What do you mean?"

"I have one, but we were never close, and I have no idea where he is now. Should we finish the chapter?"

He measured her. "Yeah."

She read the last paragraphs.

"*Lots a* names and people to remember, ain't there?" he said when she finished.

"It'll quiet down some."

He smiled. "Oh, I don't mind. So that's how the elite folk live, readin' and listenin'. It ain't bad, you know. Peaceful." He nodded toward a white prisoner who had just entered; he was carrying a flower box filled with small plants, and his arm showed a long blue tattoo. "Different sensibilities around here. Tommy-boy is here for murder two — he's served nine years already for knockin' off a buddy of his over that gal he's with, who he then married. Now he does 'horticulture' for his work program. Could've used that ten years ago, huh? Or readin' aloud." He stood up quickly, and stretched his arms with the pleasure of a large cat. "C'mon, we'll catch some fresh air. 'Hogan's Heroes' damages the brain cells after awhile. That Austen's all right, once ya get through *all them words.*"

He got his lined denim jacket, and permission to exit, and they walked outside. The sun had receded, leaving long shadows falling upon the rolling hills and white flatlands. The air was brisk and fine. They strolled up the road, crunching pebbles here and there.

"It's funny, if you keep walkin', you can walk right into town and freedom. But it's a fool's freedom. Sometimes a fool does it, and winds up back at Concord."

She looked at him, and shook her head.

"Concord? Medium security — locks and walls. Pulls more time."

A car came up slowly behind them; they moved to the shoulder, and it went on by, the passenger waving.

"Friendly folk. The town actually likes us. Well, why not, we're always doin' 'em little favors, like fixin' their potholes and ruts for nothin'. Well, dollar fifty a day." He winked.

Walking amid the rural surroundings, she asked, "You sure this is a jail?"

He looked at her knowingly. "Well, not compared to most, I s'pose. But I'll show you my room before you leave, and you'll know it's not the Ritz. Or even *my* style." He moved ahead of her, strutting on the balls of his feet like a peacock in his jogging shoes.

They approached a very long red brick building set on a small hill. Outside, a dozen or so cows, black and white, moseyed about in a fenced meadow.

"Maybe you're better off here than on the outside," she advised.

"Oh yeah? Maybe you'd like to try it sometime? Hey." He took her forearm playfully. "That was one shrewd move you pulled. I mean, you know what you're doin', don't ya?"

Oh no, oh no, not at all!

"Do I?"

"And you know why I'm takin' it so well, *now* at least? Because after thinkin' 'bout it and lookin' back at the whole ledger between me and you, I've decided I owe you one. I'll give ya that much. Though it was a long, long time ago. But Mama always said, pay your debts and be rid of them. Okay" — he nodded to her — "we're almost even. Though I'll tell ya, you can imagine my surprise when they picked me up and charged me with bein' a bank-robbery accessory. Me, rob a bank, can ya dig that? Shit, I want them fuckers to guard the banks — I got my dough stashed there! Now give a peek, anything prettier?"

A pair of Herefords approached tentatively, eyeing them.

"Bucolic," she said. "Are they inmates too?"

"You bet your foxy bottom. In fact, they're lifers, every one of them. Some are slaughtered for our beef; the rest are sold. In fact, the superintendent plans on opening a whole meat-processin' plant, next year maybe. His idea is to make the place *self-sufficient*. Smart boy, that fella. Shootin' for commissioner, I bet."

"This place sounds like a kibbutz."

He looked at her, curious about her foreign term. "Oh yeah?"

Oh, he was a pretty one all right, this tall, slender, dusky-brown rose. (Turning poetic, all of a sudden?) In some long-ago life he'd have been a slave, work-out boy, sharecropper's son, bootblack. What was he in this life, besides a pretty-boy pimp?

"What you be thinkin' now? What and why I pulled that on you nine years ago? C'mon, we have to head back."

His walk was not a full strut but a kind of half-strut, more sport than macho, say. "Did you play basketball?" she asked.

"Yeah, a little. I did in high school, 'fore I dropped out." He smiled. "Tell you what. Let's put a hold on that serious talk until next weekend, when I can get outa this place and we can get us more *hospitable* surroundings."

"What do you mean?"

"I'm gonna take me a small furlough, and me and you are gonna have us a merry little time. A fancy weekend."

"Oh?" He was nuts, wasn't he?

"Next Friday and Saturday evenings — what do ya think? And we can discuss and evaluate whatever's on your mind. And catch up with Janie of course."

"Do they really give you furloughs around here?"

They approached his building. "Why not, for fellows like me? Do you think I'm that dangerous? Shit, we get fourteen days a year, and I still got all mine intact. Once I'm out there you can push all your tough D.A.-type questions, and I can even push a few of mine. But in comfort, ya know, with all the plush trimmings. You know what?" He stopped her, and looked down from his wonderful height. "I'll bet you never spent an entire weekend in luxury before, did ya?" He shook his head in pity, and for a full minute paused to reflect. With his firm chin pushed forward imperially, his dark face in repose against the white hills, he seemed to her not a criminal or a peacock but some sort of prince, in full regal control, surveying the many possibilities even there on prison grounds. "Some dudes sink with adversity," he said with a bemused smile, "but others go on from it to prosperity." And he nodded to himself, pleased with his thriller wisdom. "C'mon inside, and I'll get ya the *per*tinent details for our holiday." He tenderly tapped her arm with his fist. "And I'll show ya how the other animals live."

Later, driving out, on freer ground, she felt much less in control, nervous, excited, uncertain. She had put one foot in adventure; would she be foolish enough to risk the other? That Hebrew *chai* around his neck floated before her, and she smiled at her own fanciful interpretation, concerning his possible Falasha heritage. Hah! More likely he had gotten the trinket and the kaddish words from one of his Sarahs or Rebeccas, some Jewish working girl from the North Shore. She flipped on the radio and listened to Fleetwood Mac crooning their frog-throated mush. I'm over my head all right, she thought; then she smiled and added to herself, Well, isn't that the only way to live?

The two-room suite in the old part of the hotel afforded a fine view of the Public Garden and, just beyond, of the Common rising to the golden dome of the state house. "A touch of Jerusalem, the Old City," she noted, standing by the thick drapes at their sixth-floor sitting-room window, "except the view is more aerial."

"Huh?" He was busy opening the package of toiletries she had purchased for him at Jordan Marsh. "Oh yeah? I've never been. But it's a thought, ain't it? Do you speak . . . Jewish?"

She blinked. "Hebrew. Not really."

Sorting the tiny sample bottles and vials of conditioners and moisturizers at the lacquered end table like a boy playing with an Erector set, he beamed. "Yeah, these look *jus'* right, *jus'* what the complexion *craves*. You buy some for yourself?"

"No, no." She laughed. "I was too intimidated by the Clinique consultant to buy double and have to explain."

"Well, you get yourself some, ya hear? It'll do you good, for sure." He raised his lengthy torso, trim and tapered in a white T-shirt and tan chinos. "I'm gonna have me the first shower, if you don't mind? It's been a while since I had a *real* shower — and all to myself."

She nodded and sat down in a club chair, but realized she didn't want to miss the late-afternoon view and took her book and a cane side chair to the window. The light was bluish, and the Common rose like a long humpback whale or a desert mirage.

Had she done right — if that was the word — to do this? She didn't know anymore; she had just decided to do, not think; to act, not meditate. And to decide alone, for herself. (Well, not entirely alone; she had lunched with Vera, that woman of the world, and conversed with Harry too.) After all, she had reasoned, walking shabby Somerville streets, she had never in her life been to the Ritz and probably never would be there again, so why not? Wasn't she a free woman, since she had made no bargains or contracts with him about this?

Fingering the cane seat, she smiled sardonically at her prolonged adolescence in the big world. Money meant places you read about in the magazines but would never actually visit; money meant dreams turned real. But the men of her life, now and before, had never had such easy money. Nor had she. Yet this character in the shower, ten years ago her abuser and now her gentlemanly escort, had more money than she or her men friends would ever have in a lifetime. Or so it appeared. Jerusalem, for example, was like the Ritz — a hop, skip, and a lawyer's call away. All she had done was turn up at the Brahmin firm of Palmer and Dodge in downtown Boston and show Mr. James Martin her driver's license, and without a single wisecrack that young, bespectacled lawyer had arranged everything from soup to nuts: hotel suite, dinner reservations and show tickets, car rental. At the accountant's office in Cambridge, in the brick building beside the Orson Welles, she had retrieved the necessary plastic and loose change (a grand in fifties) from a tiny, wizened C.P.A., Louis Bimstein, and his coworker, middle-aged, dark-skinned Dora, both of whom had asked to be remembered to Mr. DuPres. And he was a prisoner! No wonder good citizens went crooked!

Meanwhile her adviser, Vera, had supplied her with ammunition. "If you're going to go through with it, then take this along," Vera had counseled as they left the Pamplona after lunch. She handed Miriam a folded manila envelope, strangely heavy. "It's not for melodrama, it's for caution. An adventurous soul deserves a protective hand." Alone in her car, Miriam opened the envelope and found a silver and pearl-handled revolver, with a handwritten note of instruction, including the cheerful mention that this "Rossi" was a family heirloom from Europe! Sitting on Bow Street, shocked, she was sure she was being watched, and felt as though she had already used the weapon. At first she had vowed not to take it along. But then . . .

If she hadn't come to kill him, why had she taken those lessons at O'Grady's Guard Yourself Agency ("Better Tried by Twelve than Carried by Six") during the week? Three lessons in the fundamentals, given by self-regarding Tom O'Grady himself, a former Brinks security guard: how to load and safety-check the thirty-two caliber; how to hit the target, from close up to seventy-five feet away (she hadn't always hit the bull's-eye, of course); how to hold the gun out in front with two hands for steady aim and kickback protection; how to make sure to call out to your attacker, to warn him properly (yes, she had to go along with that). "Well, you're no Wyatt Earp," Tom told her at the end, "but at least you're aiming in the right direction, and don't seem so terrified." Driving back home on the Jamaicaway, and then serving the kids dinner that Thursday night, she had realized another secret of her native land: you could learn whatever you wanted, how to kill just as easily as how to cook; all you needed was the classified ads and a few hours of free time. And now, sitting here, she felt anything but "poised" (O'Grady's term of satisfaction); the feel of the gun almost made her pee.

"Hey, how's the readin' goin'?" Wearing a white terrycloth robe, he was toweling his hair.

Startled, she murmured, "Oh, fine. Just now I'm taking in the view."

He eased himself down in a stuffed chair, his legs too long for him to sit comfortably, and asked, "How 'bout the job front — any de-velop-ments?"

"Well, sort of."

"There you go again, the Sort-Of Lady! Can't you ever come clean and say something straight out and definite?"

Oh, he had her number all right. She was truly amused. "You mentioned playing basketball, yes? Well, there's a chance for a Cambridge Y athletic job — how's that strike you?" From Harry, that lead had come. Only Harry would have connections in the Y as well as in the galleries in Cambridge.

"Workin' with wise-ass kids, huh?" He paused and produced an emery board. "That'll do, I s'pose, as well as any other." He shifted legs. "Sure. What's the difference?"

She didn't quite get it. "You don't plan on going back to your old line of work, I hope?"

Filing his fingernails, he looked over at her. "Why do you ask?"

"Because that would be rather stupid, that's why."

A satisfied smile spread slowly over his face. "Worried for me, huh? That's cool. No sir, I don't plan on that line of work anymore, you're right."

"Good," she said.

"I uh don't need that gig anymore. I sold my entire stable *and* territory to my man Marcus from Back Bay, and I'm settin' pretty just now. I've got mighty sound investments, ya know. My house is in most respectable order these days. And it's gonna stay that way. I got other things on my mind."

"Like what?"

"Jus' you wait and see. Besides, we got a whole forty-eight hours ahead of us, so cool your jets." He looked at his wristwatch. "Hey, want a little liquid before eatin'?"

"Sure."

The telephone rang.

"Grab it, would ya?" And he returned to the bathroom.

She lifted the receiver. "Yes?"

"Mr. Reginald DuPres, please."

"Yes. Uh, who is it?"

"Tony Menotti, from Mass. Correction."

"Oh. Just a moment."

She called to Reggie, who came out with shaving cream on his cheeks and traded her the razor for the receiver. "Yeah? This is DuPres."

He listened. She held the silver razor, and thought of her own silver instrument.

"Good enough. Well, I'll be here, though we'll be out on the town tomorrow, ya know." Not submissive, just factual. "Yeah. Be talkin' to ya." He hung up, smiled at her, and said, "They don't take your word of honor, ya know. Here, thanks." He took back the razor.

Soon, in the large Tea Room lounge adjacent to the dining room, she ordered a Campari and soda and he a Heineken. Sitting alongside him, she felt prickly-alert, as though she were a high school senior out on a fancy date. They — or he — elicited furtive glances; he looked like some performer or movie star in a double-breasted, green-flecked, gray silk suit with thin white pinstripes, a pink-collared white shirt, handcrafted tie, and brown alligator shoes. She wore her simple beige suit, a high-necked blouse with a burgundy scarf, stockings and heels — her adult outfit.

"This is like going to my senior prom," she said, "the one I never made."

"That makes two of us." He drank slowly. "I never made senior year."

"To high school days," she toasted.

He raised his glass.

"You know somethin'?" He edged slightly closer on the two-seater. "That time away may turn out to be the best thing for me in the long run. I got to thinkin' there, and it's gonna result in some changes." He shook his head and recrossed his long legs. "Hustlin' is for punks. Punks, pushers, dopers, and yeah, pimps too. Shit. It was just the ripe time for me to retire, and now I'm gonna get down to it. And go into somethin' . . . more dignified. Definitely."

The tartness of Miriam's Campari was pleasing. "You're getting mature."

"*Pru*dent," he rejoined.

She smiled. "Going straight can't be that hard to adjust to."

He gave her a wide-eyed, slow smile. "Straight?" He repeated the word, let out a small guffaw, and spoke softly. "Straight, who said straight? No more cheap hustlin' is what I said. Straight? You know who was straight — Mama the maid and Daddy the porter for forty-five years. And maybe your mother and father, and all the rest of the good mamas and papas who works hard for a livin' and comes home to the boob tube and taxes, to dreams of stayin' in a joint like this for one whole weekend — but they never make it, and they wind up with a wristwatch for their pension. *Straight?*" His voice went an octave lower, like low drums. "You mean like the coal miners and schoolteachers and postal people — yeah, they've gone straight all right, straight to the ol' poorhouse with their dreams and 'lusions *intact*. Naaah. I mean, my Miriam" — he laid his basketball player's palm on her narrow knee — "I'm gonna go straight like some cor-por-ate exec, some downtown real-estate mogul, some senior partner at Palmer and Dodge. Not Mr. James Martin; he's small fry. Straight like one of them *respectable* crooks, with their oil and gas or cattle tax shelters — oh yeah, straight and legit like any boss." He sat back, abandoning her knee, letting the sly wisdom sink in. "Oh, we'll figure out somethin' nice and casual-like, somethin' that can be run by my counselors, Martin and Bimstein, while me and you are soakin' up the sun and rompin' in the Seychelles or Haiti, or even holidayin' in your Holy Land. Why not? Maybe somethin' in entertainment. Or terrorism." He hit her leg and winked. "And maybe I'll get in the newspapers for givin' to all them charities, ya know. That straight enough?"

She took in his speech, that mixture of common sense and criminal logic.

Presently, beneath the chandeliers of the vast dining room, he began with baked mussels, and she tried the artichoke hearts.

"A mite better than prison fare," he allowed, and went on to order shrimp scampi, while she opted for the recommended escalope de veau Villeroy.

She felt light and loose from the cocktail and white wine. "Why didn't you want to look at those other books I brought last week?"

He shook his head slowly, before understanding. "You mean the ones by the black dudes? What do I need that stuff for? Don't I know all of their rap pretty well? I mean, I been playing the game for thirty-four years on my own, bein' that color. Besides." He drained his beer, wiped his mouth with the linen napkin. "I been hustled and jived by as many blacks and browns as honkeys. It don't mean dick or shoeshine to me what color the fiddle comes in; I learned that long ago. I bet ya there are as many blacks with honkey hearts as there are honkeys with black souls, and you're a fool if you think you can tell which is which from lookin' at their *outsides*! Shit. Skin is skin, and honor is honor, and no one can tell me the two go together according to color. Hey, there's our grub at last. You know what I mean?"

The waiter exchanged the dishes from the trolley for the used ones, and asked if he might bring anything else.

" 'Nother Heineken," Reggie ordered.

She had half a bottle of Chardonnay left.

They ate, and she listened to the low hum of talk, the tinkle of glasses, the periodic pop of a cork. Her veal was light and tasty, and though she lived just across the river, she felt a long way away from home.

"Ain't no red snapper, that's for sure."

"What's that?"

"Best-tastin' fish alive. But you gotta go to the Gulf Coast to get it nice and fresh. Sometime we'll jump down to Orleans, and we'll have a weekend of the snapper, Cajun chicken, and some music. How's yours?"

"Good."

He chewed loudly, with obvious gusto, and she enjoyed it, suddenly realizing how different the habit was from what went on in her polite circles.

"You eat like a mouse, don't ya?"

"Oh?"

"Take some bread, why don't ya? You could use some fattenin' up, ya know."

Was he taking care of her? Fattening her up for what? Foodloose and gutsy, she put forward, "Look, come clean — what do you have in mind, for you and me, I mean? You just want me to help you get out of the clink, right? And then we're truly . . . *even,* say?" Oh, so innocent! she upbraided herself.

He moved back from the table slightly, eyed her from a tilted position, and sipped his beer. "I'm gonna know you. For real. And I don't mean hustlin' you like before, or . . . any of the bad tricks. We, uh, got a 'situation' between us, let's say, by coincidence or accident, years and years ago when I was still a mere boy, and our paths keep crossin'. Call it fate, maybe. Sure. And now we'll take advantage of that joker played." He took a toothpick from the inside of his jacket and began poking at his teeth. His small brown eyes glimmered and seemed to turn slowly into that yellowing, as if for emphasis.

The language slowly carried her to his meaning, just as a young bellhop arrived, bearing flowers.

"Set 'em right down, friend," Reggie indicated. "Better late than never."

The white messenger set down a vase holding a dozen short-stemmed yellow roses, said "Thank you sir!" for the $10 tip, and departed.

"You're flattering me," she offered.

"What's wrong with that? We could all use some of that medicine."

Later, back in their rooms, she lamented eating chocolate mousse for dessert, and he said, "C'mon, let's walk it off." A pleasant surprise and she took him up on it.

Coming down in the elevator, she couldn't help but notice how easily he carried himself in these surroundings. He wore a tasteful fedora and a long soft brown leather coat, stylish, like some actor or author would wear. Indeed, the other couple in the small box kept glancing over, checking out Reggie in case he was a celebrity, while the white-gloved elevator operator dusted lint from his lapel.

Outside the March wind leapt and blew, and he raised her collar, saying, "Man, y'all could use a new coat *bad*." Then he slipped her arm through his.

Up Arlington Street to Newbury they promenaded, she still slightly stunned by his ease, his presence, his ways. She said, "Maybe you should write your memoirs, for starters."

"Oh yeah?" He took it seriously. "I'll bet they wouldn't be half bad, at that." Pondering the idea, he added, "See, that's just where you come in. Head stuff. I wouldn't've thought of that."

"I was kidding."

"So what? It's the *idea* that's interesting, whether you're puttin' me on or not. I bet with you, I could do it, too. Write one of those. You know what you are? The sensibility of the two of us."

She smiled. "And you?"

"The Sense, o' course."

They passed the fancy shops full of rugs, furniture, paintings, clothing. Well-dressed citizens paraded up and down. The cold air circled wildly. She thought she spotted a familiar figure, a familiar walk, out of the corner of her eye . . . was that her Dr. Beaumont? Christ! "Let's go back that way — it's more interesting, I think."

"Seen a ghost, maybe?"

She laughed. "Yes, sure," she jested.

They backtracked. She felt the chaotic brisk air as bracing; her heart hit faster. Only when they headed up Boylston did she turn slightly in order to check the street out. Nothing. Just strangers.

"You nervous or somethin' about takin' a walk with me?"

"Yes, probably; why not? People may take me for one of your girls."

"Don't worry, I won't sell you *cheap*." He reflected. "Ya know, the night is when I come alive. That's another thing I have 'gainst prison, there's no night life — they put you in bed at nine and get you up at five." He shook his head. "But I'm like a wolf, I have to be out at night and do my howlin'."

She sensed his easy mood, felt herself grow easy and bold again, and said, "Look, why'd you pull that . . . scene on me, ten years ago in Cambridge? Tell me about it."

"Huh?" He gazed at her sideways, recalling or . . . deciding. Walked a bit. "To tell you the truth, I was a fool. One big stupid nigger listenin' to his own braggin' tongue and a white boy's dare. You remember that boy with me, four-eyed Sherman from MIT? Well, he was a client of mine. We had sniffed a few lines of coke and were hangin' loose, struttin' about, and suddenly we were in that itty-bitty park and I was *preachin'* how I could do *anything* I wanted to do, and he said, 'Okay, let's get it on with the next chick we see.' I said sure, and that chick *happened* to be you. Oh, he was a loser, that fella, but I didn't know it then. And I was one stupid black boy. Hey, give a —"

"So it was a one-time thing — just me?" Incredulous. Angry.

"What you think, that I needed that sort of action? Shit." He removed her arm from his, offended. "They be rapin' me more than the other way round. Females, white females. Not straight-out rape, like. More subtle kinds."

In a moment she slipped her arm back through his, and he let her.

"It's turned out all right, ya know. I'm knowin' you now, and that's all right. I mean, you got spunk, savvy, in you, like I told ya that first night. And I was right, too. This last stuff, gettin' me turned in on a hoked-up charge, proves it."

She needed more. "Did you think about it, afterward I mean? Or me — about what you had done?"

A well-dressed middle-aged couple edged carefully out of their way, the man half bowing in fearful courtesy, but Reggie, equally courteous, edged aside too.

"Afterward? I was just like I said — one big stupid stud. 'Cept for one thing — I could do what I wanted to do, jus' like that, without pre-plannin' it, without thinkin' about it. I *liked* that. That's freedom of will, as I see it. I just didn't need the *illegal* part, when it didn't concern my businesses. So I was a fool, a dumb nigger, but . . . I made my point." He looked at her, affording her the kindness of the glance, and a possible response.

What could she say — I half wanted it? I wanted my flesh disturbed just as my spirit had been violated at the show an hour earlier? And that it felt good, rich, true, to step into self-destruction as naturally as I slip behind a lens? No, no, that was not to be spoken, announced loudly. Not even to the self. It was too deeply personal, neurotic. She was angry — at that self almost as much as at him.

"Turn back?" she suggested.

"Yeah. I ain't used to Boston wind anymore. We'll get you a new coat tomorrow 'round here; this ain't Phoenix, ya know." They turned about, and he patted her arm. "Yeah, I felt for you, later on, when I came down. I knew it was a honkey asshole thing to do — no dignity, no class. And I knew it, sure." He faced her squarely, saying it; this was as close as he could come to remorse.

She wanted more, but not here, not now, she figured, the wind cutting her.

Back at the hotel, he said, "Ya know what? Let's leave off the readin' till tomorrow night. I'm kinda bushed. Maybe we could watch a little HBO movie if they get it here, which I kinda doubt. The price you pay for high-class accommodations." He yawned widely and stretched, like Jonathan, suddenly growing sleepy. "I gotta get used to these late hours again, after five A.M. wake-ups."

Removing his suit jacket, he walked into the bedroom, while she sat in the living room, tired, bewildered, scratching at her knees. Amid the soft peach walls and formal cushiony furniture, she abruptly noticed that logs and kindling had been laid for a fire in the fireplace. "Who did —"

"Hey, wanna see class?" he interrupted. "C'mere." His big forefinger curled, drawing her to the bedroom entrance. "Look what they did to your bed — thoughtful, ain't it?"

Peering at the turned-back blanket and sheet, she wondered: *her* bed?

"Yes, thoughtful," she repeated, turning the other phrase over in her mind.

"Better be, for two bucks sixty a night."

She was elsewhere. "What did you mean, *my* bed?"

Unbuttoning his shirt, he moved about, saying, "I ain't hustlin' you, friend. Or tyrranizin' you. I'm not your daddy, or your hubby. From now on, with me, you're a free woman. Otherwise" — he ran his sleek hand along her cheek and jaw — "you'll never trust me, and we'll never make it together. As . . . associates." He turned and walked back into the sitting room, nodding. "A little fire to warm the bones, ass-ociate?"

And she was left alone in the bedroom, which had suddenly been given to her like a surprise birthday present, an adult doll-house. Jesus, oh dear confusing Jewish boy Jesus, she intoned, plopping onto the high four-poster bed. Listening to Reggie moving about, she took out her manila envelope and placed the revolver under the pillow, patting it for good luck. Just in case.

After undressing and hearing him wash up, she went to the bathroom and performed her own ablutions. She was impressed by his entire meticulous collection of toiletries, bottles, brushes, vials, even his own soap. Noticed his monogrammed leather kit, and saw the initial *R.* in the middle. Back in the living room, she asked him what it stood for.

"Huh?" He was turning the pages of *TV Guide*. "Yeah, Roo-sevelt. Parents, ya know."

Soon they sat like a married middle-aged couple on the loveseat wearing pajamas and robes, feet on footstools, and watched the Channel 56 movie, which was about a broken-down detective — shades of Mr. Purcell! When Miriam saw Reggie's head begin to jerk, she half-smiled at his helpless sleepiness. "Let's call it a night," she suggested, and helped him get into his roll-away bed, which had been brought in while they were out. And by the time she pulled the blanket up over him he was already fast asleep, mouth open, oblivious to her goodnight peck. For an extra minute she kneeled by his side, observing the broad flat bridge of his nose and the wide nostrils and especially the dusky pigmentation of her Othello. Indeed, the darker area she had spotted earlier had a parallel below the ear on the opposite side, a kind of sister patch of ebony. With her forefinger she traced the territory, imagining Ethiopia again, and gaunt, somber figures seeking to eke out a living from the eroded soil. Did they have markings on the face or rings in the nose instead of *chai*s around the neck? In the mixed pigments of that face in repose, with the features so prominent, she thought she now saw melancoly beneath the beauty. Melan-choly and history. Yes, some dark ancient strain there, not unlike her own tribe's perhaps. Oh, she'd try Dimona and Amos again next summer! In sleep Reggie moved her, and she silently left the room.

She propped her pillows, took out her novel, and tried to read by the globe of the bedside light, listening to the whispering of traffic. She was eased by the percale sheets and goosedown comforter, and repeated to herself her name, the date, and the location, like a woman hit in an accident testing herself for coherence. She read Austen's well-turned sentences concerning Elinor and Willoughby, but the meaning fell away like snowflakes. Instead, the word *associates* rolled back upon her, along with shots of Reggie in his green-flecked suit, T-shirt and chinos, striped pajamas — man about town, criminal, sleepy boy. A man of parts; one too many, perhaps. And here she lay, wearing her favorite nightgown, curiously alone on the one night she thought she wouldn't be. (*Is this why you came?*) Had she expected a sort of mysterious honeymoon? Or was it too mysterious?

A furniture movement, a creaking sound; was this it? But what? She waited . . . Daddy appeared by the window, wearing his suede jacket, holding out his hands — in puzzlement? Daddy, what are you . . . ? "Well, Miriam," cut in Stanley, smiling sardonically, "you've made your bed and now you are *really* going to lie in it." She turned, twisted, shuddered, pulled up the covers. Silence. But she couldn't go through the night this way, in fear! No, she wouldn't! Not from *him* anymore. Isn't that why you brought along your little pearly toy? she asked herself, and reached under her pillow . . . Water rushed suddenly; a door closed, steps, another creaking from the roll-away . . .

Breathing easier after a few moments, she pulled the lamp chain, drawing a curtain of darkness — and doom? — into the room, and slowly the dimness dissolved and fled into recognizable patches of shadow and light. And she grew alert again, aware that it might be worse than rape this time, it could be assault and battery for this "associate," or even murder — some slow, time-delayed payment for her recent betrayal . . . Will I go down willingly, or fighting?

Remembering the line that Kelley had used — "The best defense is a good offense" — when she had taken Miriam to the North End to meet with that Mafia gentleman, she felt her brain spinning, and her body moved toward a resolution of the night's dilemma.

Quietly she slipped off the bed, got into her robe, and, as though in a dream, eased the revolver into her pocket and moved barefoot on the carpet, firmly, surely, toward the other room. Why not? she taunted herself during the twenty-two steps it took to negotiate the obstacle course of strange furniture and enter. Why not? One pull, maybe two, of the smart trigger, and it was done cleanly, finally. Damn, she had forgotten the muffling pillow; she took one from the nearby couch and proceeded on her lengthy journey. Why not? Wasn't this merely the final installment payment on the debt incurred ten years ago? And wasn't this indeed what she had come for anyway, maybe, deep down? Why take along this crazy instrument otherwise, in spite of her fears, trepidations, common sense? Having rehearsed the act through the years in different ways, she'd feel little remorse or penitence over the actual deed; on the contrary, this final payment would free her at last from domestic, bourgeois inhibitions, male intimidations. (*Watch the formulas, my nervous friend, whispered her shadow self.*) She had a fine excuse, or alibi, too (almost knocking over the vase of roses) — he had forced her here, threatened her children; it was her word against a dead con's.

Stealthily she approached him, traversing tables and chairs like a narrow mountain pass, until she stood over his long sleeping form. Leaned lower. Took several deep, slow breaths. The smell of the roses mingled with memories of lilacs in full Cambridge bloom and his younger body above her, knees pinning her, white grin mocking her; old anger and sad pleasure arose, and drove her too.

Perspiring from fear and excitement, she took a seat on the floor, just beside him, on the cushiony rug. He slept, snoring slightly, mouth open. One hand hung loosely off the roll-away; the other was settled on his broad chest, as though he were saluting the flag. The radiators clanged. His smell, lavenderish, mingled with the warm smell of sleep, and reminded her momentarily of the vanilla smell of Rafi in the kibbutz, and the pine-coney smell of campouts with Daddy in northern Michigan. Why had this smell lingered so long in her sense's memory?

Amid the fluttering shadows from the streetlamps she wondered:

had she come to kill him? First to make love with him, and then
to murder the fucker? To pay him back for her shame and the
abuse of that sizzling night of terror ten years ago? Oh, God, why,
why? . . . Lapis lazuli shone on his pinky; he hadn't worn that ring
back then, just his bad-man hat.

Refresh yourself first, Miry. Then if you wish you can pull the
trigger.

In the bathroom she splashed cold water on her perspiring forehead and her lips and neck, took a long drink, and dried herself
briskly. Facing the mirror, she tried to cool down, take stock.
Crow's-feet edged the eyes, the high forehead was wrinkled by
two major furrows, the curly dark hair seemed wild and unruly,
and the look in the face seemed lost and yet determined. A mask
of anxiety, camouflaging what? As much comedy as madness?
Setting down the washcloth, she noted out of the corner of her
eye two small vials filled with water and a tiny white plastic container with two sides, inscribed L and R. So the rotten bastard
was pushing his coke or heroin right here, in the hotel, at night!
Ingenious devil! She couldn't resist opening the case and scruti-
nizing it closely; she was taken aback to find two tiny, curved,
cuplike transparencies floating in solution, one on either side, like
miniature lifeboats. Stunned, she rummaged about and found, off
in the corner, a green plastic bottle marked Flex-Care. Christ,
contact lenses. Glamour-boy had poor vision, along with poor
vanity. Had he kept the lenses in until after he had fallen asleep,
out of that vanity? How endearing, confusing! She felt suddenly
deflated. Now the revolver on her hip struck her as taffy, the
intention as gravely imprudent, and herself as melodramatic. Ridiculous. Just this side of mad. Oh dear, oh crazy dear! She set
down the plastic case with the lucky talismans, and slipped out,
passing the yellow roses and escaping her fantasy, which had almost triggered a grave fate.

God.

In her bed, safe, with the revolver put to rest for good in her
purse, she eased. The physical tension, released, provoked a flow
of involuntary tears at her dangerous folly. She was confused,
humiliated, sickened. She found a cigarette and inhaled slowly.
Were the strongest moments always played out in secret, like re-

hearsals in dark, empty theaters that surpass the finished performances shown to spectators? Was the line so fine between exquisite moral reasoning and subsequent blunt act, that the most serious acts in one's adult life were no more than leaps in the darkness, wild chancy leaps? Had two lives, his and hers, really been saved by that pair of little lifeboats? Or would she have come to her senses on her own, at the moment of truth?

Each puff proved healing now; what did the surgeon-general know about *her* health? She wondered, would she eventually have been turned into a heroine because of the incident — the *Globe*'s headline reading "Raped Woman Takes Cold 10-Year Revenge in Ritz!" — and been interviewed, celebrated, maybe martyred? Wasn't it the case nowadays, in our fairyland country, that when you did your worst, you often came out best? Courting disaster, she had called it freedom; seeking prudence, she had nearly gotten punishment. Flex-Care, thanks for your practical solution to mysterious impulses and late-night imaginings.

A cigarette later, she read the illuminated clock dial — just after midnight — and lay still for a while, alone, in recovery, listening to the silence of the hotel and the cushioning sound of traffic before finally falling off to sleep.

The telephone ringing at an ungodly hour woke her. Six A.M. From the other room she heard Reggie answering in a monotone. Yet another check-up call, it seemed, from the prison authorities. Now that would have been nice, if Miriam had had to explain to the MCI how their prisoner had become a corpse. She turned over and buried her head beneath the pillow, remembering to call Vera in the afternoon — *her* check-up.

At nine o'clock, over room service, including the morning newspapers and a breakfast of scones, smoked salmon, fresh fruit, croissants, scrambled eggs, Canadian bacon, and a whole pitcher of milk for Reggie, she asked him about those contact lenses. "Did you always wear them? For what?"

Chomping a scone, he eyed her. "Nearsighted, since I was twenty-one." He put aside the *Boston Globe,* drained his tall glass, and poured more milk.

"Can you see without them?" she asked casually, tasting the

Nova Scotia lox and noting again Reggie's resemblance to Jon, in his gulping down the milk. Squeezed between memories of father and images of son, how would she ever proceed to full independence?

"Oh, I can see well enough." He licked his fingers. "Well enough to see you up close just fine last night."

"What do you mean?"

"You know, when you sneaked round and tried to pull that Lady Macbeth number on me, like you was gettin' ready to blow my brains away — 'fore you reconsidered the matter." He fixed her with a smile of sly innocence. "Oh yeah, why'd you only put three bullets in the chamber?"

Blanching, and then choking on her bits of food, she murmured, "You don't mean that you knew all the —"

"What do you think? With the kind of dudes I been runnin' with all my life, do you think I just go to sleep with a stranger round and dream easy, on *honor* alone?" He wiped crumbs from his mouth, and took up the eggs. "Nah, you don't survive that way. I checked you out yesterday, thoroughly."

"When? And why'd you let me have —"

"Hey, put your fork down, there. Let you have your fun, your toy? Why not? You wouldn't've hurt anyone." Making a gun out of the span of his hand, he pulled the imaginary trigger. "Bang, bang, all right, but I took the ammo. So no harm might be done."

She eyed him, shaking her head in dumb amazement. Why had she removed the other bullets?

"You took a shower, remember?" He drank orange juice.

She got up, took three steps to the window, and saw the sun tipping the golden dome of the statehouse. What a silly dunce she was next to this fellow. She wondered aloud, "Do you think I'd have done it?"

He laughed, with good humor. "Shit, I dunno. You don't either. But I don't like the odds with chances. *Prudent*, ya knows."

She returned to her seat and drank some coffee. "You don't seem . . . that upset with me."

The humor receded, allowing further instruction. "Look, you got a right to play games with me, until you can trust me, I figure. I take you to this fancy joint, me with my history against you —

who knows what my motives may be? So you're wary and scared
like a Peter in a cabbage patch. Yeah, I can dig that, 'cause I been
there myself. Who knows? I might've done the same thing. Self-
defense — it's an instinct, not a strategy." He leaned forward.
"You should im-bibe more milk, and less caffeine and nicotine.
That stuff'll kill ya faster than grass or alcohol. Here, want a
glass?"

She shook her head slowly.

"Good for the nerves as well as the bones," he instructed, pouring her a glass anyway. "Trust between us, that's what I'm after.
Like this nickel says, see here — only instead of God, it's In Reggie
We Trust. And Miriam too. Me and you, trustin' in each other, a
special team, see? And I'm gonna show you some more trust, right
now — got a pencil? Go on, write somethin' down now, why don't
ya? Yeah, c'mon, ready? Just write; I'll explain. Here's the name
and the address, which I know by memory: Mister Eric Pierrot,
that's P-i-e-r-r-o-t, twenty-two Chemin Rieu 1208, Geneva, Switzerland. Yeah, C-h-e-m-i-n R-i-e-u that is; got it? Okay. Now looky
here." He scratched his thin mustache with his large pinky, the
lapis lazuli ring prominent. "Any ol' time you need cash, emergency
cash, I mean five or ten big bills quick-like, you get a hold of him
pronto. First you write, then you call — I'll give you the number
later today." He shook his head and smiled broadly. "Even my
counselors hereabouts, that lawyer-man and the accountant, would
be blown away by *this* dude. And my, uh, private numbered accounts." He pulled back from his conspiratorial position, and sat
upright again. "I ain't done none too bad for a country boy, ya
know, up in the sophisticated city. The trick is not makin' it" —
he winked — "but *keepin'* it. That's the hard part."

The light glanced off the window and onto the blue drinking
glasses, refracting subtly, and from there glided to the pewter
pitchers and the polished brass handles on the desks. Vermeer and
his dazzling journeys of interior light came to mind, and she longed
for her camera.

"Why are you telling me all this? Why me?"

"Why do you think? 'Cause if you got enough brains to catch
on to me after eight years' absence, based on a half-hour in a dark
park, and then you got enough clout to get me sent up on a phony

charge when I never been in the clink in my life, why then you
are *one talented* woman. And to me, one talented woman is worth
a fistful of wise-ass dudes, fancy lawyers, and tough dumb broads."

She remained puzzled, half believing. "But why trust me? How
do you know that I won't go back on you now?"

He laughed, a rose color fluttering in his cheeks. "You're like
my kid sister Ida used to be, wantin' to know everything at once.
Ask the next question before you got the first answered. Hold your
horses, huh? Hey, look at the time — let's get a move on. We got
some shopping and sightseein' to do, and we gotta set down with
Lawyer Martin for a touch of business. First to Bonwit's. I still got
my old credit account there, ya know, and I kinda like that old
buildin'. And then that museum you mentioned, right? So let's get
a move on. My furlough's over in a meager twenty-four hours,
and I ain't been out on the town yet. What kind of homecoming's
that?"

He gazed at her straight on. The alert brown eyes were crossed
by a line of yellow in the iris, like worldly disillusionment violated
by a strain of lingering belief. Was it the spotless white T-shirt
and chinos, the peach-fuzzed face and look of cocky innocence
that indeed gave him the aura of a serviceman home on furlough?
Was this the way she should think of this weekend, at least, or of
this fellow and their peculiar attachment — like a sort of high
school romance, the forbidden one in which the boy was off limits
because of color, thuggishness, or just extreme good looks?

Still trying to catch up on the missing pieces, she asked, "What
do you know about Lady Macbeth?"

He nodded in appreciation. "My best schoolin', that play-actin'.
Before I checked out of South Side High, I played the part of her
husband for two weeks."

His answers led only to more questions. "Okay," she said, putting down her emptied cup. Glancing at the glistening fantasy of
pewter, brass, and crystal, she realized that she had never before
been here, not even in her wildest dreams, so why not take it as
real after all? For after all, wasn't she in the profession of dissolving
the real and making it over anew, by means of her own lenses and
imagination?

Arising from the small, elegant table, she said, "Sure, let's start at Bonwit's," posting a new firmness in her tone, and for the first time stretching with languorous ease. Here in Boston, just a few minutes from home, routine, and rectitude, she was on furlough, too; civilians needed time off just as much as criminals or soldiers did. "Sure," she repeated, for no reason, realizing she was anything but sure about this new strange territory.

16

HAD she been mad, or was the weekend a mirage, her Lost Weekend? she wondered in the next few days. The new quilted coat from Bonwit's was tangible evidence, however, of the reality of those two bizarre days, so it must have been her madness that had led her there, right? Except that nothing "mad" had occurred, except perhaps in wish/fantasy; and as for exacting consequences . . . Save perhaps for the understanding, percolating still, that Reggie was coming to town, to her little Cambridge, in a few months; yet while that perception was at first shocking, it also had a consoling air. There was no more terror hovering in the wings.

Was it a surprise that her friends understood her new situation-to-be? Harry opined, "Yeah, it doesn't surprise me too much. If you'll excuse the sexism, you always did have balls, and a sizable pair too. Seeing your local rapist in place of a therapist is typical Miriam; it may make more sense too. Oh, this'll go over big with the feminists — should we send out a press release via Alice James Books? Anyway, the Y will be pleased to employ Mr. DuPres when he's ready for it. Don't forget your annual membership."

"Thanks, friend."

"Remember, I get an introduction. I want to see this Jake; we've probably been hustling the same talent pool. Be sure to get him to model for you — Joan Walsh is high on those nudes of yours, and you've *got* to add him to the collection. No fooling. Hey, let's hurry — the opening of *Strangers on a Train* is the best part.

Besides, you'll see how *tame* our so-called extremes are alongside Hitchcock's ladies and gentlemen. I almost forgot — here's the letter from the Y. Sealed. Let's scram."

And a few days later, when she returned the manila envelope and its pearl-handled loan, she listened to Vera put it this way: "I didn't think you'd have to use it, but I bet it was comforting under the pillow at night. So tell me, how was it? The sex, I mean?"

A difficult question to answer with the right nuance, so Miriam answered candidly: "Couldn't tell. We didn't have any. A chaste weekend."

"I *don't* believe you."

"Honest Injun, cross my heart, and all that sort of thing."

Vera shook her head admiringly, "Your games are beyond me."

A letter arrived from Reggie a week later, on Monday.

Hi, Miry —

Hey, writing and corresponding this way aint too bad — like I aint done this kind of number before, and it has its advantages over the horn.

Well this is just to rap a little. Thanks for the R&R weekend out at the hotel and loose on the Boston streets. And to my surprise I sort of — uh oh its catching — I liked those two Museems. I didn't know that crazy white ladies like Miss Gardner lived up north like they do back home. Also, them Chinese and Jap. paintings are staying in my head. At night just before snoozing I still can see that long scroll with those villages and people, and also the three high pictures of the birds on the branches. That was cool, what you told me about doing the same picture again and again and again, for hundreds of years, with just the smallest of changes. I have my own idea about that. And yeah, I owe you a grandpa history.

Anyway, don't forget my European friend, if you ever need to call him.

What else?

Oh — socks. Can you buy me a dozen pairs of cotton and silk, or silk and wool? The French make them, and Brooksie Brothers sells them. This pollyester stuff rides hard on my footsies, and when you glide with sz $12\frac{1}{2}$, the sweat is mean. Big feet, little brain, thats my story.

You take care now, and when you come on in next week, bring in Sister Austen. I like them sentences alot, they curl up and around like snakes. I'd sure like to learn how to write long sentences myself one day.

Yr buddy,
Reggie

Was the Jewish connection possible? Couldn't be, couldn't . . . Didn't he mind the jailkeepers' knowing about his "European friend"? And there at the end, was he serious or playing? Had she really gotten Jane Austen a most unlikely reader? It was too bad Jane wasn't around to witness him, if it was true. Artists could use their unlikely fans. Was he the education project, or she, Miry? Both?

Surprises popped up elsewhere too, and of different proportions. With Yani, for example. After two years of troubled undercurrents, the tide seemed to have reversed itself. Jonathan now seemed propelled forward into sudden growth and intriguing maturity. And the reason turned out to be a female — not Mother, of course. It happened that Jon had kept up a correspondence with his kibbutz friend Heidi, and lo and behold, in early November, she wrote from home, Zurich, to say she was coming to the States for a visit; might she stay in Cambridge for a brief while? Naturally Miriam assented when Jon asked, hesitantly. (His restrained jubilation afforded an early sense of what was to come, as if he himself sensed the meaning of his new calm.) Well, Heidi came, Heidi stayed, Heidi conquered, not merely the son but the mother too. This rather stolid young woman, with straw-colored bangs and wire-rim glasses, a full bosom and easy poise, arrived for a week (before Thanksgiving), and slept in the living room. A week became two, and she moved onto the spare porch, which she cleaned up with Jon and converted into a bedroom; two weeks became a month, a month lengthened to several. Instead of an *au pair* for young children, Heidi was an *au pair* for her teenage boy, a spiritual and sensual sitter. Gradually a routine was worked out, without any words, whereby she slept on weekdays in her cove and on weekends in Jon's room.

Hence, at sixteen, Yani was cohabiting with an eighteen-year-old girl under his mother's roof. What made the experience more unsettling for Miriam was that it worked such wonders upon Jon. The girl was so attractive and inventive, in a casually competent style; she immediately went out and found a job, teaching French and German at the Boylston Street Language Center, and at night twice a week she attended needlework and weaving classes at the Cambridge Adult Education Center. Her purposefulness was striking. Around the house, too, she took an active role, quietly becoming a big sister to Rose, a guide to Jon, an aide to Miriam. (A financial aid, too; she insisted upon buying food for the house, countering Miriam's reluctance with "Why not? I earn a good salary and pay no rent.")

At first Miriam lay in her bed, smoking and trying to read but contemplating what was happening two rooms away — her son, shacking up with this Swiss stranger, fornicating regularly with this kibbutz milkmaid, seduced prematurely by this heathen! Yet very soon, after the novelty had worn off, Miriam began to sense the deeper truth, namely, that this early, steady sexuality was releasing Jon from much of his teenage ambivalence and unfocused (maybe unresolvable) anger, and was directing his high energy into a fitting channel. Replenished, relaxed, Jon began taking on responsibilities that had been unheard of before — he became a brother to his sister, a handyman around the house, an appointment-maker for his mother. Spectacular, these changes, as if a baby rhino had learned to dine with utensils in three weeks' time. Simultaneously, Jon's selection of friends began to shift too, from cruder Cambridge Rindge types to more interesting Commonwealth kids. And through Heidi he began to understand that an automobile was not merely a television stunt toy made for speed and fantasy; she introduced him to the subtler rhythms of bicycling by buying a pair of used ten-speeds and going out with him regularly until he became a fan. Was all this for real? Miriam would marvel, watching that wild boy slowly tamed and civilized.

So what began as a curious visit and a test turned out to be a boon to the household and to Miriam. She found herself with a couple of grownups in the apartment rather than a single chaotic teenager. She had transported him to Israel to get kibbutz-care, and instead he had gotten the Swiss-cure. At times Miriam debated whether to ask practical advice herself from this Heidi ("What do you think, Heidala, am I going cuckoo again?"). In sum, she viewed

the matter as a streak of luck, augmented of course by circumstance, character, chromosomes. Indeed, the three of them made
a merry trio when they attended a Central Square movie or had
a Chinese dinner. (Heidi treated them to a musical night out at
the Peasant Stock Restaurant, where Jon sat through his first
chamber-music concert.) Amid her amused meditating, she wondered how Jon might react if the roles were reversed somewhat,
and he was lying awake in the next room, contemplating his mother
alongside Convict DuPres?

In her journal, Miriam wrote:

> No doubt national environment plays a role in influencing a
> citizen's perspective. Can anyone in dull, reasonable Switzerland
> imagine what it's like to grow up, mature, break down, recover,
> raise children in this grand ole opry called the U.S.A.? From a
> country of chocolates, cuckoo clocks, secret accounts, and political
> neutrality, could you get the hang of a culture of chaos, theatricality,
> violence, neurosis? To paraphrase Trotsky, of a culture of perma-
> nent revelation?
>
> Maybe the best thing for Jon after all is to slip away to cool
> Zurich for a few years?
>
> Or perhaps for Mr. DuPres to kidnap me and take me to Geneva
> or Montreux for a while? If Nabokov and Chaplin can do it, why
> not Scheinman and DuPres? The celebs may need Switzerland for
> a tax shelter, but *we* need it for a nerve shelter.

Surprisingly, while she felt alternately frightened and excited
about the prospect of Reggie in her life, she grew more relaxed
about the puzzling places of Rafi and Scott Beaumont. No matter
what the difficulties of distance or encumbrance, they were easy
to contemplate now. The heated adventure and ambiguous future
of Reggie made these other conundrums seem minor. Ambiguity
suddenly enclosed her, foolishly, truly, as though she were a prism
of translucent sides collecting different intensities of light. And this
cheered her, strangely, gave her new confidence that riding her
own instinct was the best way to move in her life, no matter where
the ride took her.

Besides, she figured, studying the nudes of Weston and Scheinman one night, everyone had a dark past pursuing her. Wasn't it

a relief that that past had caught up, at last, in person? Look here, her own collection was too lilywhite, after all — why not add a fine black body for contrast, for balance, for true beauty? For a suitable sign too of the power of difference in her life — in men, in ways, in impulses. So to hell with your female prudish-prudent ways, Madame Bovary of Cambridge (or better, the Madwoman of Chaillot?); expose yourself, yet again. Oh well. If Edward Weston could gut it out, in that troubled life, why not you? Consider how light, splendid chameleon light, flattered your nudes: the extra-bright summer light of desert morning turning familiar Rafi into a male odalisque; the sharp winter light of her Somerville studio seizing upon the decisive angles and big bones of long-stemmed Dr. B.; the harsh interior strobes of Harry's loft emphasizing his vulnerable aging anatomy. In varieties of captured light lived her fullest affections for her men, her art. (Were they now seriously interchangeable?) And Reggie now appeared in her mind's lenses too, for sure; but just how?

Okay, MIT (and critics, friends, friendly enemies), I'm ready for you, once more, ten years later. Only now you won't crack me. I'm in one piece for good now.

Two days later, on an overcast Thursday, she was filled with a sunny impulse while staring at the gray streets. So, a somewhat free woman, she took a subway at Central Square, crossed the choppy river, and got off at Charles Street, shivering in her tweed skirt. Walking briskly in the frigid Boston wind, she felt the need for a shot of the Caribbean in her life, a quick fix of warmth, and that was that. Impetuous. Needy. Greedy. So bad? Didn't care what the image seemed like — to herself, her friend, outsiders. Didn't care about pride or principle, schoolgirl wisdom or conventional sense. (Yes, she took a certain wicked pleasure in smashing them all, like upsetting the building blocks of her kindergarten mates, motivated by boredom.) No, no, no. Just acted, on the spur, and freedom, of the moment.

She went in the main entrance of Mass. General Hospital, found a telephone, and asked for her doctor. The high-ceilinged lobby was like a busy hotel, crawling with administrators, doctors, patients, visitors. No bellhops?

Dr. Beaumont was surprised to hear her, and shocked to hear her whereabouts. "In *our* White Lobby? An emergency?"

"Well, sort of," she answered, before calming him down by saying she wanted to see him on his "working turf" (a small lie), for an important private chat. She asked where, adding foolishly, "The cafeteria?"

Rejecting that — thank God! she thought — he fumbled around and at last recommended an unused room in a nearby wing of the hospital. "There'd better be a good reason for this," he closed. Stern, or mock stern?

Well, sure there was, she decided, swinging her tote bag, delighted with her childish impulse and her grown-up blazer, high-necked blouse, skirt, and nylons. She wanted to see him, hear his voice, connect with him in the flesh again.

Through the maze of corridors of Baker and then Phillips House she sashayed, engulfed by white smocks and green scrub uniforms and Wheatena walls — the colors of illness, and maybe of children's games too. When she had completed the trek through the labyrinth of connecting branches, she finally found Bulfinch's narrow foyer, where she inspected some old black-and-white photos, mementos of the wing's illustrious history. (Was she hanging on to details out of sudden nervousness?) She climbed the four flights of polished wooden stairwell, self-supporting and leading to a skylight: Bulfinch at his best. With Stan she had once stayed at a small hotel in Paris on the rue des Beaux Arts, where Oscar Wilde had lived and conducted his illicit romances; that too had had such a wonderful stairwell and skylight. Was all high taste meant for illicit romance? All along the way now eminent doctors of the past decorated the walls: Bigelow, Warren, Townsend, Nathaniel Thayer Kidder, even (at the top) a Jew, Eisenberg, chief of psychiatry — of course. She resisted the urge to draw handlebar mustaches on the respectable faces. Should she sneak in one night and put up portraits of that heroic brood of anonymous women who had also played a significant part in forming this wing? So after all she was a suffragette! A young doctor held the swinging door for her; she nodded, and felt him eye her. Health care did mix with pleasure here, maybe.

She found the Ether Dome, with a small plaque citing the room

as a historic landmark. It seemed to be a smallish, unused amphitheater seating maybe a hundred on its semicircular tiers, and
it recalled to her those poignant pictures of nineteenth-century
medical history, like Charcot in Paris performing the first hypnosis.
Only here had been the first use of ether at an operation. She
remembered her one bout with ether, as a child of six having her
tonsils out; going under and cursing like crazy! ("Where did your
daughter learn those words?" the nurse asked a red-faced Mom
and Dad.) But later she had gotten a sweet revenge, cold chocolate
ice cream to soothe her sore, parched throat.

Alone in the high-domed room she poked around, attracted to
the womblike feel of this cozy theater. It had a blackboard in front;
several more gilt-framed portraits of physicians; a marble Greek
statue. Then, a curious sight: a sarcophagus in a glass case. Odd.
She moved closer and examined the preserved coloring of the
plaster eyes and the exquisite line of Egyptian figures, all in profile.
(The Egyptians had had no foreshortening skill, she recalled from
art history class.) The card read: Male Mummy, 26th Egyptian
Dynasty. And across the way was its partner. She walked to it,
enchanted. Called "Paddy," this fellow was a "gift of the god
Hershef." Generous Hershef. Paddy was a blackened skull and
oxidized face, its teeth yellowing and intact, its cheek deeply eroded.
Nice fellow, Paddy. His body was wrapped in its original burial
shroud, now ripped and faded to pale orange but still there. The
black skull stunned her, while she saluted Paddy's longevity. What
a handsome way to be treated through the centuries, she figured;
if only they'd put Leica in the coffin with me, just in case there's
a chance to use it down the line. You never can tell.

Voices, and two ladies trailing. They chatted their way across
the narrow area, not noticing her, and went past the Greek figure
and over into Bigelow. But they brought her back to today, today's
work.

She climbed up the amphitheater, six tiers high, and took a seat,
an armless L made of wood, and looked down, imagining that she
was a spectator back in 1846 when Dr. Warren had performed
that first ether operation. The seat, poking you, kept you alert,
didn't it? Above her was the high blue glass dome, closed now,
giving the impression of a planetarium. Had it been left uncovered

then? The stuffy air of history and disuse suffused the room, and she liked it. Her mind reconstructed the operating table, with the teaching blackboard behind it, lit by two small chandeliers. And slowly the high womb of a room worked its spell, and she was almost back there, trying out the new potion and keeping her fingers crossed when the first scalpel cut! (And was Paddy looking on for good luck? Or, in her case, Rafi?)

She dimly perceived the tall medical person who had entered below and stopped to inspect the old incubator at one side; he was oblivious to his audience.

"Hello, good afternoon, Doctor," she called down, observing the head jerk in surprise. That wonderful head. "Come up and see the view."

He climbed in lengthy strides; she had missed those, too.

"Have you ever been in here before?" she asked innocently.

His face showed that he had other interests, questions. But he played along, temporarily. "A few times, through the years. They sometimes give talks and slide shows in here. It is hard to believe they operated here; it's rather unhygienic, as you can see."

"I hadn't noticed," she said. "It reminds me of the old planetarium in Cleveland. Come on, sit down. This is nice turf of yours."

"Hardly mine, this," he replied, sitting, his long legs sprawled awkwardly in the narrow space. "Okay, why the visit? I thought we . . . would remain long-distance friends. And I'm due to be on my rounds in a little while."

"Do you mean that sternly, or kindly?"

Okay, he relaxed. "Both, I guess," he admitted, smiling for a moment.

"Tell me about ether, first. You know, another minilecture."

"Not again," he said, referring to one he gave her on blood, his long face filled with Western space and prairie memory, his voice beginning to run in her like wine. He pushed several strands of fine silvery hair from his forehead — she aided him, but he pushed her hand down nervously — and, against his will, began.

She heard words, disjointed phrases. " . . . A dentist named Morton, the anesthetist, and Warren, the surgeon . . . John Warren Manfred, but we called him Dutch, and he had the meanest curve ball . . . wanted to throw only the hard one, a stubborn country boy you know, and so he saved the curve for warming up . . . still hanging around Flat Rock, rather than throwing in the majors. I caught him once in a pick-up game . . ."

As he talked and the curve of his humor reached her, she knew clearly now why she had come, and it was fitting, she thought, to be here, for she was his sweet ether, his slow dose of forgetfulness, once again, without rules or recriminations or boring conventions. Somewhere here now, she wanted him to know this now, to feel it, to forget the past and start anew, because the fate of Paddy was near enough and they lacked time for their intensity. Yes, yes, she had principles, ideals, morals, but she was selfish too, and was hooked on his lengthy angularity, his smooth white neck and bony hands, his Montana poverty and Saskatchewan hockey, his doctor's modesty and his conjugal bind, yes yes she was attracted by that punishing domesticity too.

"Come," she interrupted him, "look at these crazy seats," and she urged him up to the aisle above, to the area behind the seats proper, where, in an arched alcove, ran a row of wooden bicycle seats with stirrups for the feet. She sat on one, playfully posing with her hand on her chin, schoolgirl fashion, prepared to listen more, although she realized he was finished and was staring at her, puzzled, off guard, caught between laughing and scolding. Oh yes, she knew that undecided area well, from long long ago, when she had charmed Daddy that way too. Okay, she had to talk now, but she couldn't really say, "Oh Doc, look, I've come down to seduce you here and now, *just because,* period. We have to get back to where we were, it was so rich and sweet then, and —"

Someone had entered the room, and she took his arm and half jerked him down, and before he knew what he was doing, he was playing the game with her, down on his haunches, hiding in complicity, while the people below wandered across the room and out.

She smiled, shining with pleasure at seeing him down here, foolish and childish, with her in this miniature version of a Paris atelier, between dome and amphitheater, between game and passion.

"I came to tell you the Celtics are playing at home next week," she began, but then she was touching him.

Nervous, embarrassed, shocked, he half shrugged to squirm free.

But she reached his neck, planted a small kiss there and on his ear, took his hand inside her blouse to her breast; it excited him, drew him on, despite himself, his good senses, his reason. He protested their "damn folly," and she sensed his rising anger too, but simultaneously she felt the other side, the long-held desire for her, the resented restraint, his furtive call to rebellion. Yes, deep in the heart of this prairie boy there ran a resentment strong against the adult traps of respectability, from his nutty Brahmin bitch to his respectable, enervating profession and his eminent Eastern hospital, and she appealed to this boy's will instinctively, semiknowingly. That rebellious will surged now in the lifting of his medical coat and shirttails, the unbuckling of his trousers, and the hard clutch around her back; he was hurting her for demanding and eliciting this risky adolescent appetite in him. A passion, a confused and ambivalent passion, had gripped him, and he was loving her, with his hands, his mouth, his member, and she was accepting the passion and returning it, at first by provocation but then as a receptacle, from one rebel to another she felt in her heart, not knowing until just now what his secret attraction was for her but knowing it now, deep and firm and rich, feeling him like a cowboy riding her with rebellious spurs, and she felt deeply, sweetly grateful that she had been such a damned fool, such a hussy, as to have indulged her impulse and come on down, down here; and when, at some crazy whirling point, he turned her over so that she was facing the slatted hardwood floor, flooded by white light, and he took her in a different position and opening, it hurt madly at first, it brought tears and a muffled cry, but gradually it was okay in its way, he was growing warmer, hotter, harder, a flagpole planted deep in uncharted backlands, and shit it was strange, so fucking dark and strange, a hole filled with a stump, taking her breath right away, only slowly she was coming back and moving with him while she followed the narrow joints of the wood, she was beginning to prime him for his force and her pleasure, and he had shifted into an animal wildness (cupping her mouth to stop her unrealized gasping), he was a wildebeest with a single curved horn ramming her, and she tightened to him with a bucking pridelust until she was too too exhausted, and needing him to finish she reached around and stroked those soft sacks of grapes and sure enough he couldn't hold off any longer but came strongly, soundly, determinedly, wholeheartedly, beautifully. Yes, filling her up strangely, and yes, turning her from solid flesh to flowing self. Collapsing upon her, a four-legged creature locked into her, panting, having done its duty, and they were linked, indissolubly it seemed, solid rebellion having liquefied into odiferous freedom, and it was sweet, oh it was immensely sweet.

She felt like the Holy Virgin; and her blue-eyed boy here? Couldn't ask him now, he'd be too embarrassed to speak. No need to ask, either. Dried tears. Salty taste. Stickiness back there — semen, blood? Smells of dust and chemicals. Anything else? Fragments of personality laid out, revealed, here on these lovely dark woods.

His breathing signaled that he was coming back to the here and now, to her, after his flight into fantasy, ecstasy, some foggy bottom of truth that went how far back — childhood somewhere? It was not a question of nouns and names, borders, categories, orifices, but of something more subtle, buried, intertwined. The subtle opium of id. For him; for her too. A mystery, this episode, to be interpreted later, if at all.

"You all right?" he whispered, in a new voice.

She kissed his cheek and nodded, seeing his relief.

Slowly, carefully he got himself untangled, moved delicately from her. More voices . . . A finger to his mouth; quiet until the voices and steps had vanished . . . Arrangement of clothes; his handkerchief to wipe herself; hair fixing and tie adjusting (oh, she loved that!). Then they sneaked down a surprise back stairwell, narrow like a submarine chute, and they escaped quietly into a secret curving corridor labeled MUSEUM.

"No more of these visits, ever," he asserted, and she promised, feeling like a spy. Before they departed through opposite exits, he added, softly, "I never knew I was this insane. Not since I was fourteen and . . ."

Outside again, in the cold wind, she walked with rubbery legs across to the esplanade and took a quick stroll along the Charles, feeling her spirit healed, her body raw but good, her brain a fog of forgetfulness. The sky was a dome of gray, broken by banks of white clouds, drifting. Ah, to be one of them, drifting here and there, carefree. Observing the choppy river, she felt a touch of the

Caribbean inside. An old line returned, about playing events as they came, without a priori censorship, and she suddenly felt like a good woman for being a naughty girl. Playing out a role in yet another children's game — right, Miss Superiority — and getting another big person to join in. Wasn't this more freeing than the other way round, where they locked you into their grown-up game of busy routine and coercive responsibility? Where money, in all its forms (plastic, property, paper), turned magically into End, into Value? For Miriam, however, she explained to herself by the esplanade, would discover and define her own rectitude and value in fun, in serious fun, in ways of her own.

Heidi had departed in March, sending postcards from her travels across the States. Now, a few days later she found this note from her son.

> Dear Mom,
>   I'm splitting for a while. No need to press the issue — you know, with the police or missing persons bureau or whatever. I'm okay, and will be okay. I just need to be out on my own to pull things together. You were young once, you probably pulled the same stunt. Can you make some excuse for me over at the 'Wealth? I don't know what, really. Tell Eric Davis that I've gone off to my own Greek island or something. Maybe the kibbutz? Craps.
>   And don't worry too much, really. I'll get in touch with you at some point soon enough. I just need a little space and time to myself right now. Yeah, I miss Heidi, I guess.
>   Tell Brat I'll write her too.
>
> Hugs,
> Y

She cried a little, drank a glass of warm milk, and walked about the apartment and then outside into the cool, wintry air . . . where to? Wandering up Cambridge Street, she was glad Rose was with Stan for the weekend. Two birds, braving it here in the winter, camped on a telephone wire by Cambridge City. Her son, on the loose in the American wilderness. He had pushed off in a civilized way, though, with a note, a promise of sorts. Don't underestimate that, she judged.

She turned back and walked toward the Square, soon sighting

all the pretty costumes and colors of spring, and ducked into a movie at the Brattle. Curled up in the flickering darkness, watching the larger-than-life images on the screen, she felt abandoned, betrayed, bereaved. The cruel imagery of TV news flashed by momentarily; would he turn up in some trash barrel, dismembered by some commonplace murderer? Or had he gone to meet — or hunt for — his Swiss lady? Had she written to him?

After a dinner at the crammed Bel Canto, she went home and immersed herself in Siskind's abstract photos of the Badlands and Vera Cruz, a stark black and white documentary that reflected her mood. Damned circumstance! And the next morning she was shocked by an early phone call from Dr. Beaumont, reminding her that she "owed" him a Sunday hockey game at the Boston Garden. She agreed, reluctantly.

And on Sunday — his wife's regular night out, and an occasional hockey night for him — they sat in the stands behind the transparent plexiglass, watching the Bruins fly up and back on the glaring ice, their skate blades cutting or stopping sharply. The speed was overwhelming, and she wished Jon could be there. By the end of the first period she couldn't bear it, and told her doctor about her son's leave-taking. He was, as usual, solid and wonderful. He handed her a beer and said, "Jon sounds under control, writing you that note. Give it a week and see if you hear from him — unless you want to stir up the authorities, and you probably won't get anything out of it." The reassuring slate-blue eyes, the cello voice. Oh God, I'm glad I'm here with him! she thought. No, my dear Montana, you won't be exposed to the outside world. You'll remain a private model of mine, just like my other friends. Take it or leave it, Mrs. Walsh. "Okay, I'll stay calm; thanks." She squeezed his hand. He assured her that when kids ran off without leaving notes, it was time to worry seriously. A friend this man, pure and simple. More important than lover, that category.

In the next week she felt like a war mother, sometimes a war widow, waiting for the postman to arrive at 11:45 or noon and announce the news: your son is missing in action, out there in the Badlands. The mail became a major event in the day, and she returned from teaching, photographing, printing, to wait for it. For the first time she got to know her mailman, an Irish man with a Victorian mustache. Meanwhile she took care of the administrative details concerning Jon's absence, informing the bewildered Commonwealth School, angry Stan, even his teacher, Mr. Davis, who actually came over and inquired where Jon was. "On vacation, Eric; he'll be back soon enough," she explained. The discrepancy between the way she was feeling and the way she was dealing with these details was enormous, and disconcerting.

Rosie was brave and hopeful. "Don't worry, Mom, he'll be okay," she said. "He just got lonely for Heidi, that's all." Maybe she was right; pure and not so simple?

The second note, postmarked Denver, arrived on Wednesday of the second week.

> I'm okay, so don't worry. Yeah, it's rough out here, that's for sure. Kids are getting leathered up all over the place — by cops, by dirty old men and pimps, even by parents. You should see it, Mom. But I'm holding my own, honest. No big bruises yet. I've even got a part-time job at a supermarket, loading shelves at night when no one's around — Ghosttown USA. So I got some bread coming in— no pun! — and don't have to beg on corners, like some. How are *you* doing, Mom? Sorry, really, I caused you all this hassle, but sometimes you gotta split — you know what I mean, I bet.
>
> I'm writing Rosie separately.
>
> If Heidi should call — well, I don't suppose she will.
>
> Over and out,
Roger
>
> P.S. This is mailed in Denver, but I've left that excellent town, with its arcades *everywhere!*

She breathed easier. A reasonable note. But *she* didn't feel so reasonable. She *understood,* but she wanted him home, needed him safe. Oh God, how she needed him safe! But the Mom for Miriam pleased.

Later, at dinnertime, on the heels of the letter, came a call.

"Will you accept a collect call from Jonathan?"

Controlling her voice, she said, "Yes, I will."

"Go ahead, please." Oh, the lovely gravity of those routine signals!

"Hi, Mom. Look, I'm doing all right and wanted you to know that. I'm not gonna rap too long, I just wanted you to hear me, and to hear you, you know. I'm up in Seattle, and it's cool. I've just written a letter to Eric at Commonwealth, asking for a leave of absence this term, and I think it'll be okay, see? And look, if you don't mind, I'm thinking of going up to Bristol Bay in Alaska for the salmon harvest in July. There's this guy I met who goes every year and makes incredible money for three or four weeks of work, I mean five to six *thousand,* and he thinks he can get me latched on. The only thing is, you have to pay your own way up, and for a room up there, and so I need a few hundred bucks, do you think you can lend me it?" A pause. "Like *five* hundred?"

Oh my dear dearest, you're not dead, you're not injured, you can have what you want! "Sure, Yani. Just tell me where to send it."

"Oh Mom, you are *one excellent person!* I'll give you the address in Seattle, okay? Care of me, twelve twenty Seventeenth Avenue West, Seattle, nine eight one one nine. A money order would be coolest, I think. Hey, is Brat there, or is she with Dad? Yeah, well, maybe I'll call her, say hello to Dad. Gee, Mom, you're not angry or —"

"You're okay, Yani? Really okay?"

"For sure, Mom. I mean I had a virus a week ago, and food poisoning once from lousy tuna fish, but that's all past. Boy, Mom, wait till you hear some of the things I've been seeing out this way. Outasight. I just wrote a letter to Heidi, telling her about it — she's going back to Sde Boker, did I tell you?"

Throttling her emotions, she said calmly, "No Yani, you haven't told me, or written me."

He understood. "Oh yeah, of course, sure. Look, I'll send you a real letter this weekend. I'm gonna split now, I'm late for my job — at a bookstore. I get twenty percent off on any book, how's *that?* Thanks, Mom, a *lot.* I'll talk to ya again, before I go up to Naknek. You have that address, right? You see, if all goes well, I think I can fly straight from Anchorage to Israel after the fishing and spend a whole *six weeks* at the kibbutz. Not too shabby, huh?"

Defeated, she repeated, "Not too shabby, Yani. *Dearest.*"

"Bye for now — hey, love ya, Mom!" And he clicked off.

Several tears, but she restrained herself, too filled with feeling, afraid of a deluge, and focused on the beige princess phone that had brought the voice, the words, the apparition. Once again, for a different reason, she worked in a daze that evening.

And late that night, still dazed and insomniac, she got out of bed, dressed, and slipped out of the apartment, like a fugitive in the night. Without a destination, she hopped into the Honda and drove along dark Memorial Drive, banking curves easily, drifting in and out of thoughts, and arriving, by inadvertence, at the twenty-four-hour Star Market near Fresh Pond. She parked and entered. But why? she wondered.

Oh, the supermarket was different in these mid-night wee hours, like an empty ball park, a ghost town. The fluorescent lights buzzed lightly, the aisles were bare and quiet; a single cashier was reading *Glamour* and fixing her hair. Miriam put her tote into a shopping cart and ambled along, getting a new perspective now on her town, a little girl wandering among the colorful creations of the land. Without customers cluttering the place, the foods took center stage: the bins and mounds of fruit, the dressy tins, jars, and bottles, the fresh meats and pretty poultry, the stacks of boxes and cartons — oh, it was a theatrical production! She proceeded slowly past fruits: pink grapefruit and Florida Temples and California navels, plus tangelos, tangerines, bananas, lemons, limes. Inundated with citrus, she filled two cellophane pouches full. Next, apples and pears beckoned: Granny Smiths, Cortlands, red Deliciouses, Anjous and Boscs; she took some of each. She couldn't resist several heads of lettuce, long Romaine and tender Boston, and a lonesome cabbage (to go with Rafi's corned beef recipe?). Oh yes, sure, she was dazzled; it was a shame, she saw clearly, to miss out on anything hereabouts — radishes, bunches of scallions, packets of dates and figs, fresh mushrooms, vine-grown tomatoes, and green peppers. Without thinking she took out her camera and began to take color close-ups of all this green, red, yellow plenitude.

A boy stacking something at the far end of the aisle glanced up at her, and then away. A kook? read his look. Was he a runaway too, maybe from Denver or Seattle? Was there an underground railroad that took these boys and girls to and fro, away from security and toward chaos and adventure?

Onward to aisle No. 2: cereals, coffees, teas. Cheerios for Rose;

Quaker 100% Natural for herself and Jon, but it was difficult to find the small yellow box amid the competition, lined up three rows high and running maybe the distance from the pitching mound to home plate. Boxes and boxes and boxes of high fiber bran and shredded wheat and oat flakes and . . . the variety hypnotized her. Alone here, she felt smaller, a Gulliver with Leica among the Brobdingnagian cereals. Why resist, why be choosy? Corn Flakes (giant size) and Total, Special K and Grape-Nuts, Cocoa Krispies and Corn Bran — she snapped her photos and took half a dozen cartons. In teas she sought respite, but was distracted by Earl Grey from England, Lapsang Souchong from China, spicy teas from India and Ceylon, cinnamon and orange pekoe and spearmint from California, and even tinned Russian tea! One from each place of origin was only fair, she figured, following through.

"Loading up, aren't you?"

She gazed at the tall stranger, a bland-faced fellow with a smallish face and brown eyes, who had stopped with his cart to observe her. "Yes, I seem to have missed out on a lot during the day."

"There's a sale on New York sirloin," he advised, showing her his batch of red steaks. Oddly, he was dressed formally, in a herringbone jacket, striped tie, button-down shirt, and gray V-neck pullover. "Have a minute?" he asked, taking down a giant jar of instant coffee and searching for the price.

"Sure," she said, understanding perfectly this clandestine tryst in the empty, well-lighted aisle.

"This is the only time to shop, isn't it?" he declared. "I come down at night regularly now." He shook his head at the new brand of coffee. "This is a buy — look at the price, and it's not even red-tagged!" he exclaimed quietly. He smiled awkwardly, or was it a grimace? "You probably want to know how my wife takes these late-night sprees, don't you? She doesn't. She ran off almost four months ago with a graduate student in theater. Left the kids and me one day, and that was it. No great threats or fights beforehand, you know. And since I don't like bars or television, I've taken to coming down here and shopping. It has its points, you realize. The truth is" — he paused, scrunching up his mouth and making the forceful decision to take two jars of coffee — "you don't really know anyone in this life, do you? No one. Not even someone you've lived with for fifteen years." He lowered his voice to a whisper in the bare aisle. "People are the *great deceivers,* aren't they? No animal would act so . . . carelessly or brutishly." He turned wholly toward her, for the first time, she realized, and his expression shifted; he looked like a prisoner addressing his parole board. "It's all right, I know it's foolish; forgive me for boring you this way. But I can't stand it really — or myself. I stay here for an hour or two and then go back home to Belmont, put away the packages, and fall into bed around three-thirty, and I'm up for work and the children at seven. A life, eh? For six or eight weeks now I've been shopping this way . . . incognito . . . What do you think of this, a good buy?" He showed her a giant can of Medaglia d'Oro, nodded to himself, and moved off before she could answer.

She had an urge to follow the fellow and offer words or gestures of consolation, but she understood there was no use; he didn't want that. Just wanted to utter his paragraph of woe here in the dead center of nowhere.

Pushing on to another aisle, she grew more alert. The long, open, refrigerated counter was packed with pink and red meats, whole chickens and parts, roasts and hams, and yes, fish too. She found the New York sirloins on sale, selected several out of deference to and sympathy for the gentleman and thought how everyone was in trouble, everyone who was alive and not sleeping and coping with the species. Sure. The only way you were spared the trouble was to sleep, to be oblivious, to use routine like a heavy drug; otherwise the world rocked you, personal relations whacked you, your children tormented you, your men disconcerted you, you yourself . . . No, no, that wasn't quite true either, she knew, taking some frozen trout and salmon and wondering whether Naknek was a real place or a thought.

Yes, she'd finish off with ice cream; everyone in the family loved that. The logic was somewhere else, in her own misconceptions. She had wanted peace and order, had thought stability was the goal that would satisfy her, after her bouts of disorder. But that was hogwash. Random forces compelled her now, forces with differing velocities and meanings — and her newly discovered, newly won insights were now so many complacencies. Having made herself over, she was now being unmade again. Häagen-Dazs rum-raisin for Rosie and herself; Breyer's coffee for Rafi; and for Jon, anything with chocolate chip. She had been in there, battling — a "counterpuncher," Harry once called her — and she understood now that she could be crushed by all the new and confusing in her life, or roll with it, accept it, hit back if necessary. Not a theory but a fact, life rushing around the corner and bending all one's straight theories and ideas.

In a few minutes she saw the stranger next to soaps and Kleenex, and thought how lucky she was, not to have lost her Rafi when she was on the verge of bolting; not to have lost Yani, who could have self-destructed; not to have abandoned herself, in so many ways, when it was most tempting. No, she was lucky. Inching forward, she was intrigued by the new varieties of tissue paper: pop-up boxes, slender boxes, designer-fashioned boxes that were turquoise-pink like the Red Sea or iridescent brown-silver like evening in the Arizona desert or scented peach like Jerusalem in the late-afternoon sun — how did you choose? She took four boxes, thinking how crises were signs of health, darts of confusion were sure flickerings of life, and picked-up friends like student Hideo were expressions of true instinct. Hers; an instinct that said, *Let me be, I may confuse and tease you, but at least I am you. Don't reduce me for the sake of the adult rules. Let me be, with all my willfulness and mischief-making, and I'll represent you fairly. Shame, embarrassment, piety, propriety, pride, lackeyness — the shabby defenses of the timid. Let me be, with all my complicated gestures and out-of-the-way wantings, and you'll be ahead of the game, a freer soul, a more honest body.*

In the now-empty aisle, she clicked a half-dozen photos of the twenty-two ingenious ways for blowing your nose, then, cart over-flowing, she headed toward the checkout counter, and once again was in synch with the stranger, who was on his way there too.

She touched his shoulder, and he turned to look, in fear. She wanted to say, "You're not such a coward and you're not so alone. You're alive, not sleeping; no wonder you're out midnight shopping. If that's a consolation."

He eyed her, fidgeting with his tie.

But she could offer nothing beyond her hand in support; she gave it, and let him go. He stood there, befuddled, waiting. Then, silently, he moved back up the aisle, eyeing her again, and lost himself in juices.

She paid, rolled her cart outside and began to pack the car with brown paper parcels. Seventy-four fifty, at almost three A.M. Then she drove back leisurely along the Drive. Suddenly, on a whim, she pulled up alongside the Charles and got out. Took a dozen steps down the grassy bank, and lit a cigarette. Cold. A pristine wintry night, with the stars laid out brilliantly on their black background. Her vision adjusted to night seeing, and she scanned the sky for the constellations she knew. (Professor Smits, from Astronomy 1, had given her a B-plus for her fine astrolabe.) Sighted the long splash of smoky white, a "drift of cigar smoke," Dad had called it, the dreamy Milky Way. Found the glittering Big Dipper, and from that located the polestar. Searched out the W of Cassiopeia, the twin stars of Gemini, the three-starred belt of Orion. She smoked, gazed, marveled, listened to the occasional whisking of passing cars. So orderly up there, so disorderly down here. So be it, then. Take what you had and make do with that.

What would she look like as a configuration up yonder? A photographer in the desert, leaning over her tripod, seeking clear focus? A Cambridge adventurer in the streets, prowling with her camera? Or sitting in her stuffed chair, checking out her contact sheets with a magnifying glass? Mentally she sketched in the dotted lines from silvery point to silvery point, imagining the first-magnitude stars: her Gemini pair, Rafi and Montana; her gleaming Betelgeuse and Bellatrix of Rosie and Yani; her revolving North Star of Dad or Harry; her radiant protector Kelley and her dark pursuer Reggie . . . Yet what was she doing in the center of it all? Running, somehow; yes, running . . . for a pass? for her life? Running toward her fate? Yes, yes. The position attracted her, even though the figure was a work-in-progress, and the imagined luminosity was so vivid it shed warmth within her. It was as though forces of uncertainty and pressures of contingency down here had created, up there, a sparkling permanence, an adventurous essence. (Oh, one needs a Siskind to photograph this abstraction.) Fantasizing herself a Runner there in the distant night, a Miriam of permanence, she surprised herself; fantasy though it was, the constellation beckoned with force, signaled a truth, for it signified that all her aspects and manifestations could be put to good use, could form a memorable sequence of self.

And yet there was something else flashing above, symbolically: the portrait was one of solitariness. No men, no friends, not even children at the center: just herself and her camera. Sitting on the darkened bank by the slow black river, she began to perceive another truth, painful and deeper. Down here she was alone too, by herself in more ways than she had known about or acknowledged in recent years. And she had evolved into this keenly self-absorbed figure not by intention but from the curious circumstances of necessity; the process of making herself over, of reconstituting herself, of fighting for her independence had simultaneously steeled and isolated her. That had been the price. Unknown to herself, by means of her camera, lenses, and photographs she had been creating her own fairy-tale castle, complete with moat, drawbridge, stone wall, and ivory tower for the soul; and there she sat, a queen of amour-propre, looking down from her turret room and watching, bemused, as the body entertained a variety of interesting visitors below. So she had been a runaway too. A fool, a blind fool. Opaque, before the simplest of visions. You thought you were attached to these men, deeply attached, but you were more attached to this vividly imagined constellation, to the importunate self in play, and those men were a means to that self. No wonder they served so well and so easily as models, as nudes! Why, the photography itself was a metaphor for seeing them, seeing reality! A grown-up version of the old catcher's mask!

No wonder, then, that she had accepted the wild, maybe sinister challenge presented by Reggie.

She felt tears in her eyes now, tears of sympathy for the deceived and deceiving self. She had wanted what she thought was the most honorable and simplest thing, to love again, but mainly she had been loving Miriam. And it was not even a first-class love, at that, one at least self-conscious and firm, in full support of the self. No. Just a sort of ragged nacissistic self-concern. Self-approving on the sly, self-regarding always. (With Jon, Rosie?) She felt this accusation as truth, and cried lightly, steadily. With ironic consolation she thought of how she had brought this situation on herself, unlike ten years before, when the world, society, critics, and attackers had wrought havoc upon her; yes, she was the principal agent at work now. And she had to face it squarely, accept full responsibility, no matter how much it hurt. And it did hurt, oh yes yes yes; this revelation stabbed and twisted slowly, its blade cutting with the crafty deceits and punishing demands of the ego thrusting for its survival . . . for approval. She cupped her hands, in pain from ignorance and shame, and shook violently —

"Look here. You all right, lady?"

She shook her head, not wanting to look up, not caring. A hand was laid on her, and she had an urge to fall over immediately into a pair of arms!

It couldn't be, but it was, a policeman. *Again.* He was touching her shoulder benevolently, in order to look at her.

"You okay?"

She nodded.

A lean black face; dark eyes; he was about fifty. "That your car up there?"

She checked and nodded, and he continued on, straightforward. "It's parked illegally, you know. Maybe you better go on up and take it away. Besides," he added, to make clearer his intention, "it's not that healthy to be sitting out this way all alone at this hour."

She nodded dumbly. Had the Cambridge lawmen — and the Fates? — conspired to time this perfectly, as a sort of anniversary commemorating her first emergency? "Thank you, officer."

He took her arm nicely and escorted her up the bank to the Drive, like an old-fashioned policeman helping her cross the street by elementary school. His partner, a burly white fellow sitting in the driver's seat of their patrol car, gave her a long moment of involuntary chill, for no good reason. He leaned over and asked, "Everything all right, Buddy?"

"No sweat, John," the first policeman replied, and he started to lead her to her car.

On a peculiar impulse she implored, "Do you mind if I sit inside the cruiser for a moment? Just to . . . gather my wits?"

The one officer looked to the other in bewilderment.

But she had already opened the door and was sliding into the back seat. To show them she wasn't off her rocker completely, she asked for a light. In turn they asked to see her driver's license and registration.

The middle-aged black gave her a light and nodded kindly.

Grateful, she inhaled and relaxed, sinking into the vinyl and trying to recapture those strange, terrifying moments of the crisis of her thirties, when she had been hustled out of Brigham's at the Square in a squad car. Only that Miriam had been injured, humiliated; was half naked, fully mad. Not now. And not now either was there any protective mesh-and-glass partition between the police and her, separating the sane and orderly from the crazed and criminal. Oh, she was in some trouble now, but with herself, with her own laws, not with those of society. She was going to be her own judge and jury on this case, and she briefed herself: go easy, be patient, take it slowly. The case — the self vs. the self — is rich and complicated, so why shouldn't it take a while, several more — no, many more — years? Your whole life, maybe? And this opening statement to herself calmed her, satisfied her.

The policemen called in her credentials, then returned them to her and began chatting to each other.

After several more deep inhalations, she said, "Thank you so much, gentlemen," opened the door, got out, and walked off firmly to her car.

Inside, her little green man signaled to her to put on her seat belt. She felt relieved, somewhat restored, strangely resolute. It was like taking a walk in sea air immediately after driving for hours from inland; the Charles had cleansed her.

Soon she was driving again, this time unescorted, unencumbered. She had a way to go, she knew, to lift herself up to a whole other level. Curving around the Drive and taking the long way back via Soldiers Field Road, she saw how she'd have to storm her hermetic castle and lay siege to her most stubborn defenses, smash through her most protective armor to get inside. To make room for the other, for the others, in her life. Did you ever stop deceiving yourself, she asked, stop letting the ego or whatever slough off into easy self-approval or subtle worship of its most convenient prejudices? Dammit, you thought you were way over there, letting go, but you were still only here, protecting your flanks.

She drove, feeling afresh the pep of her Honda and sensing that maybe she was being too hard on herself. With Reggie in the wings now, she was on her toes, alert. And with Yani out there hunting on his own for the first time, why, she had a whole new sort of lookout or responsibility to keep her loose and limber. Not to mention the presence of her Montana, and her desert professor. Plus her little Monopoly-playing prophetess. No, there were no complacencies here, she realized, proceeding toward Mt. Auburn Street (the kids' Indiana Avenue). There would be no self-inflicted injuries or park attacks or long illnesses, either. Coming down Trowbridge, she knew she had come through, in her fashion — she had missed Jail this time and was throwing the dice again. Wasn't Go just ahead somewhere? So what if there remained a few obstacles, some risky jumps? Hadn't she been a survivor for some time now? Turning up broad Broadway (Park Place?), she saw the dark, empty street laid out before her, lit softly with mercury, and flickering memory; and feeling fine, feeling almost rich, feeling ready to begin, she headed for home.